ECHOES FROM THE PAST

FIRST BOOK IN THE BRIGANDSHAW CHRONICLES

PETER RIMMER

ABOUT PETER RIMMER

≈

Peter Rimmer was born in London, England, and grew up in the south of the city where he went to school. After the Second World War, aged eighteen, he joined the Royal Air Force, reaching the rank of Pilot Officer before he was nineteen. At the end of his National Service, he sailed for Africa to grow tobacco in what was then Rhodesia, now Zimbabwe.

The years went by and Peter found himself in Johannesburg where he established an insurance brokering company. Over 2% of the companies listed on the Johannesburg Stock Exchange were clients of Rimmer Associates. He opened branches in the United States of America, Australia and Hong Kong and travelled extensively between them.

Having lived a reclusive life on his beloved smallholding in Knysna, South Africa, for over 25 years, Peter passed away in July 2018. He has left an enormous legacy of unpublished work for his family to release over the coming years, and not only they but also his readers from around the world will sorely miss him. Peter Rimmer was 81 years old.

ALSO BY PETER RIMMER

~

First published in Great Britain in January 2015 by

KAMBA PUBLISHING, United Kingdom

10 9 8 7 6

BOOK 1 – IN THE BEGINNING

1

JULY 1887

The pony grazed softly. Small bells clung to the reins and round her neck. Opposite the pony, on the other side of the forest glade, a black stallion of seventeen hands stood aloof, firmly tethered to the bough of a tree. Both animals were free of their saddles.

The great oak spread roots above the ground bigger than the thickest boughs. Between the half-submerged roots green moss had grown and, lying on the moss, one elbow propped comfortably, Emily Manderville watched the small white and grey butterfly that was sucking salt moisture from the brow of Seb Brigandshaw, the butterfly's wings opening and closing in ecstasy. He was fast asleep on his back, his lips fluting gently to the rhythm of his breath. They had been alone for hours and had forgotten the other world as they had done since childhood.

"SHE SAID WHAT?" shouted Captain Brigandshaw to his eldest son.

"Emily said she would marry a Brigandshaw but only Seb," said Arthur.

"She'll do what her father tells her. Why didn't you sweep the girl off her feet? She's sixteen. You're thirty. You should know what to do. Manderville wants you as a son-in-law. You and your inheritance. My money. They'd laugh at a seventeen-year-old who has lived in the clouds all his life. Where is the brat?"

"Why don't we send him on a long voyage? The *Indian Queen* is sailing tomorrow night, Father."

"Where is he?"

"When Seb goes riding, he says nothing. Probably meeting Emily. They have secret places."

"I want him in my study when he comes home. Have Walker pack his bags. Who's captain of the *Indian Queen*?"

"Doyle."

"First port?"

"Las Palmas. She is due in Bombay at the end of April. The return voyage is eighteen months."

"Should be long enough. Write Doyle a letter from me and I'll sign it. I will not have my children gainsaying me. We Brigandshaws are on the way up in the world. Manderville's title goes back to the twelfth century, so I've heard. Women have no right to choose their husbands. They make a mess of it. Marriage is a business."

SEB WOKE to the butterfly's flight and smiled into Emily's green eyes, the eyes with orange flecks he knew so well. He was at peace with his world. Her long black hair had come down on the ride into the woods, her small red hat caught by a branch of a waiting tree. Her white blouse with the long puffed sleeves was made of a soft silk and the black riding skirt was of leather. She rode side-saddle. Brown riding boots covered her legs.

"You want to tell me what you're thinking?" he asked.

"No."

Seb sat up and wrapped his arms around his knees, checking his horse instinctively. The animal looked back at him with large, wet eyes the colour of slate. It winked at him, the velvet lash flashing the long delicate eyebrow. A wood pigeon called from somewhere deep in the trees and was answered far away by its mate.

"My father wishes me to marry Arthur," said Emily quietly.

"*Arthur*! What are you talking about? You and I have been inseparable since childhood."

"Father says I am no longer a child. He wants a safe, rich marriage before I do anything silly."

"Arthur's old enough to be your father."

"He's also the heir to Colonial Shipping."

"I'll get a job with them. Become a ship's captain. Commodore of the Fleet. James is going into the army when he comes down from Cambridge and Nat is already in the Church. Arthur may own Colonial Shipping one day but he won't be able to run it. All the time he tells Father what Father wants to hear. He manipulates. Lies when it suits him. Flatters when he has something to gain."

"I told Father I would only marry one Brigandshaw, and that's you, Seb! We've known that all our lives. Why should growing up change anything?"

"I leave school next term and I'll ask Father for a job. I'll make myself so indispensable he'll have to bequeath me shares. Mother will be on my side."

"She is always on your side."

"And she likes you, Em. I know she thinks we belong together."

"But men always decide. We can't do anything in life without our father's blessing. If only my mother was alive. If only I had some sisters. They wouldn't worry about us. We wouldn't be important to them."

"I'm not important to Father."

"But I'm important to mine. I'm his only child."

"You can't inherit his title so why does he want you to marry Arthur?"

"I don't know. I'm hungry. Let's pick some blackberries."

"I have fresh bread and cheese in my saddlebag. Pickled onions, the best Walker ever made."

"Why didn't you tell me earlier?"

"Because we would have eaten it all by now. We'll take the horses to the brook to drink."

Emily watched him place the blanket over the stallion's back and throw up the heavy saddle. From the rear he was so tall and thin, the ponytail of his hair brushing the nape of his neck. Braces held up his riding breeches that clung to his body. It had all changed. Now she wanted more than a kiss. The shudder began around her lips and finished at the base of her throat. He was strapping underneath the belly of his horse, bending his tight rump to her.

"You got that blanket on your pony? Leave the saddle to me," he said without turning around.

She watched him a moment longer and then did as she was told.

The grotto overlooked the brook. Water trickled down the side of the slate walls, moss clustered in the nooks and crannies. A raised part of the floor was soft with green moss and ferns grew thickly at the entrance, watching the gently running water meandering through the woods. The stallion and the pony were drinking.

They had a world of their own.

Long afterwards, Seb questioned whether the fear of separation had drawn them to their climax, instinct stronger than upbringing. Emily had felt little pain, and afterwards they slept on the thick bed of moss and the late afternoon slipped towards evening and the last low sun, beaming through the trees into their grotto, woke them to reality.

With only happiness they saddled the horses and began the ride through the soft evening, smelling the secret scents of flowers as the bridle path took them out of the trees. At the edge of the wood, they heard the echoes of village cricket bringing them back to the world of men. They parted; Emily for Hastings Court and Seb for the house of his father.

ARTHUR WAS WAITING FOR HIM. Next to the front door two portmanteaus were packed. In the courtyard was the family horse and trap, the junior groom seated on the bench.

"Where the hell have you been?" said Arthur, annoyed by Seb's grin.

"Riding the forest."

"Father wants you in his study."

"Why are my bags packed?"

"Father is waiting."

Seb walked down the passage without seeing the dark pictures on the wall. His mother was in London and he felt alone.

"You have been with Emily again," shouted his father.

"No, sir."

"Don't lie to me."

"Yes, sir."

"She is going to marry Arthur."

"She says she is going to marry me."

"Don't talk such poppycock. You're seventeen. Still at school. She will do as she is told. So will you. The *Indian Queen* sails from London docks on tomorrow evening's tide. You, young man, will be on board. You are to leave now with Arthur who'll make sure you do what you are told."

"What about mother, sir?"

"She will be told of your insolence and the consequence. You are interfering with things you don't understand."

"But I do understand, sir."

"Get out of my sight."

"Yes, sir."

"And don't disobey Captain Doyle or the consequences will be far more painful than they already are."

Seb put out his hand to say goodbye but his father turned his back. When he left his father's study, Arthur was waiting.

"May I go to my room?" asked Seb.

"No. Get in the trap."

"One day, Arthur Brigandshaw, when I am older and stronger it will give me pleasure to thrash your hide."

Arthur hit him hard, backhanded across his mouth.

"I'll remember that one too. You really don't like me do you, brother?"

"No. I don't. Get in the trap with your bags and we will be in London before the moon rises."

"She'll make your life miserable."

"She'll do what she's told like every other wife."

"Why my Emily? Or is it because she is my Emily?"

WHILST SEB WAS SAILING on the evening tide from Prince Albert's Wharf, Captain Brigandshaw was being shown into the grand hall of Hastings Court by an old woman. The ceiling was high above his head, dark in the lofty labyrinth of beams. The flagstone floor echoed with his footfall while the crow shuffled along in her slippers. It was the first time The Captain had been in the grand house on the slopes of the Downs. He was surprised by the pervading smell of damp and decay. There was little furniture in the hall and short pickings in the grand reception room that opened by French doors onto a terrace the length of the south wing of the house. The doors and extra windows had been added long after the original structure. Again, the roof was high above his head, the ceilings frescoed with old art dimmed by the ages to virtual extinction.

A surprisingly young Sir Henry Manderville was standing on the terrace looking out over the fields and woods. The tower of a Norman church was visible some distance behind the woods. A black Labrador dog sat at its master's feet. There was no sign or sound of Emily or anyone else after the old crone had shuffled off whence she came. The Captain coughed to announce himself with little effect on the motionless baronet. The dog looked at Captain Brigandshaw with equal disinterest. The sun was down behind the church tower making the old stone livid with a brief moment of light. When it was gone, Sir Henry turned to greet his invited guest.

"Breathtaking," said Sir Henry. "Utterly breathtaking. That I shall miss. Come and sit with me on the wall, Captain Brigandshaw." He had not offered his hand. "That dog would lick an intruder's backside if you'll excuse my expression, sir. No, Emily is not here. Sadly too many tears, so she rode off on her pony. A fine horsewoman, of course... You sent him packing, I trust?"

"On board the *Indian Queen* and halfway out to sea. My ship sailed on the tide."

"Are you sure he was?"

"Arthur was there to make certain." The baronet turned to look again for the lost sunset. "Now may we talk about your daughter's dowry?"

Sir Henry gave a short laugh and bent to stroke his dog's head. The animal looked back at him with absolute love.

"I bought her for Emily when Em was five. Dogs are far more loyal than people. There won't be any dowry, Captain Brigandshaw. I have a very different proposition. How much do you know about my family?"

"Yours have been the squires about here for centuries. Everyone knows who the Mandervilles are. You came over with William the Conqueror. Why the house is called Hastings, I presume? Ancient lineage from Norman knights. The Mandervilles built the church over there."

"Opportunists rather than chivalrous knights. Rape and pillage were more their lines of business. Nothing wrong with a bit of rape and pillage in this life. Beats hard work. Wherever would the empire be without the gunboats? No more sales of opium into China to blow their river cities into the water. Provoke a fight and blame the enemy for aggression. You see, the mighty are always right. But I digress. Your son; my daughter... The irony is, your shenanigans may well have killed my father, and I used the American word of slang on purpose. You must know, sir, I have checked up on you. Your wealth grew from one sailing ship. Fast I agree, but one ship. That one ship made you your fortune which you have traded for a shipping line that sails the oceans of the world. Free trade, we cry! Mother of the free! All a load of rubbish as it's only free trade if you ship on a British boat and no one is free however much they think they are.

"You came to this southern county from the north, first sailing your ship from Liverpool, the ship that was bought with the blood money you earned as mate on a privateer in the Caribbean. You acquired the *Indian Queen* at the height of the American Civil War and sailed her into Mobile, Alabama, with guns for the Confederacy and brought back cotton for the Lancashire mills. The profits from such dangerous sailing were enormous and sad you were when the North defeated the South. You made a fortune in that war and my father died in that same conflict, leaving me his debts.

"My father always had a good cause in mind except his own. Frankly, I think he was running away. He said he was an abolitionist. Hated slavery. Was more of a Republican than a Monarchist despite his title. Away from this pile of ancient stone with its damp walls and leaking roof he was somebody. The English gentleman fighting a just cause. He knew the passion inspired by words that wanted to fight the good fight, someone else's fight. Throughout history, there have been twisted people passionate about other people's affairs. It is a wonderful thing to fight for a cause, Captain Brigandshaw, but whether the slaves would have done any better back in Africa is a matter of conjecture. Africa, I'm told, is sparsely populated. Lands of milk and honey usually overflow with people. He didn't even die in a full-scale battle but in a skirmish in some woods. What they said, anyway. Probably died of dysentery in some small hole of a hospital. Hopefully, he killed some southern gentleman before he died to prove his point, but still I digress.

"To the point. I am bankrupt. After my father gave his life to free some slave he never met, I found myself master of Hastings Court thinking myself rich, which I most definitely was not. I had married when I was eighteen years old for the love of a lady who gave me Emily but departed this world. Her family were penniless of course but with Hastings Court as my heritage, the thought of marrying for money had never crossed my mind. Maybe if father had not run off on his crusades, he would have had time to explain our poverty and my need to trade our ancient title for money, lots and lots of money, the kind of money represented by Colonial Shipping and its great toiling fleet of ships. You see, Captain Brigandshaw, I have something you want and you have what Emily and I most need. Emily will soon recover from her love and see the larger prospects of life. I love my daughter and even though Sebastian is at seventeen twice the man Arthur is at thirty, I will still strike a trade with you. Your son and heir will have Hastings Court along with my daughter and your heirs will meld into the ancient line of Manderville. Your son will change his name to Manderville-Brigandshaw, a mouthful I know but the generations to come will likely drop the Brigandshaw. Your son's grandchildren will be aristocrats and rich. We will have done something for both our lines. For myself, I require a fund of two hundred thousand pounds jointly controlled by our solicitors who will invest in three per cent Consols. I will live in Italy from the interest. Upon my death, the capital will revert to Arthur if he is still married to my daughter. I was never trained to work for trade. All I have to sell is Emily. If your answer is yes, we can have them married in our church towards the end of September. It is such a lovely month. My mother was married in September. Poor mother. Always frail and always second to father's causes. I think she died of boredom. Don't you agree, Captain Brigandshaw? Boredom is the worst affliction on earth. But again I digress."

"Do you have debts to pay off?"

"No. But the house has not been tended to for thirty years. The furniture is sold and the landholding is down to three hundred acres, not nearly enough to support the house. But the world is changing. Wealth, I fear, is no longer in agriculture but in the new industries to the north. Your ships bring wool from the colonies and cut the price of English wool. There is ten times more profit in a shipload of Australian wool than a flock of five thousand sheep. It is the way of progress, even the price of empire."

"How much will it cost to repair this house?"

"I have no idea."

"You are selling me the house and land for two hundred thousand pounds, the price of twenty new sailing ships or five new steamships they are building on the Clyde?"

"Not really. I may die the day after the wedding and then you get it for nothing. A man never knows how long he will live. I am thirty-five. They say fifty is the average lifespan of an English gentleman but you may be lucky. I have always thought from Italy to visit Africa, that vast dark continent so loved by Livingstone and Speke. Out there animals are ferocious and disease is rife."

"You won't let me pay you an annuity of six thousand pounds a year?"

"No. The capital must be free of temptation and the vagaries of trade. Oh, and if you agree my terms I will recommend you and your eldest son to membership of the Athenaeum Club, your first step into society. Captain Brigandshaw, I can turn you into a gentleman, your ultimate achievement I rather think."

CLOUDS SCURRIED across the full moon, black clouds with white lace skirts. The wind was coming up from the southwest. In forty-eight hours Seb had gone from boy to man and each cut of the sharp bow into the rising waves took him further from home and everything he had ever known. Dreadful sadness was beginning to feel the tinge of rising excitement. The North Star was visible between the pattern of clouds and the wind was high in the square sail. The *Indian Queen* was a two-masted brigantine with the foremast square-rigged. They were running before the wind two miles from the French coast entering the Bay of Biscay, their first port the Canary Islands off the northwest coast of Africa in three days' sailing. The third bell of the first watch told Seb it was one-thirty in the morning but he had no wish to find his hammock next to the crew's quarters. He was neither passenger nor crew but something in between where the captain and crew alike were uncomfortable. Captain Brigandshaw, gunrunner and privateer, was legendary in the British marine force and to his youngest son went some of the awe. There were no words of encouragement on the *Indian Queen* for Sebastian Brigandshaw, only the curiosity of everyone as to why he was on board in the first place, escorted by the eldest brother without so much as a smile. All night Seb stood before the mast and searched the stars, pondering his destiny. Everyone left him alone. He could have been a ghost on one of his father's ships.

THE PIRATE, as Sir Henry thought of Captain Brigandshaw, had left at ten o'clock the previous night, absorbed by the cost of getting what he wanted. Henry smiled to himself as he drank his third cup of tea on the terrace the following morning. The sun was warm, and the birds were singing. It was truly so that every man had his price and ambitious men were rarely satisfied with their achievements. Henry was never able to understand the need for more when a man had enough. He had offered to sell his daughter and birthright for six thousand a year but the alternative was destitution for both of them. An obscure baronet without his manor house was of little interest to even the likes of Brigandshaw.

"He's gone, hasn't he?" said Emily from the threshold of the open French doors.

"Can I pour you some tea?" Cousin Maud had put two cups on the tray.

"Tea. It's extraordinary how Englishmen offer tea as if nothing has happened. Father, I love Seb."

"Well, I'm afraid you won't be seeing him for quite a long time. At the moment he's probably approaching the coast of North Africa on a sailing ship bound for Bombay. Now, come and sit with me in the sun and your father will try to explain why being penniless in a hostile world is not the best way to go through life. Young love, Emily, is a very beautiful thing but I have sometimes wondered if it isn't nature's way of making us procreate without thinking of the consequences. Part of this Darwin's theory of evolution. Nature's driving force to sustain the species at any cost. But then nature in its earlier manifestations had not heard of money or the British class system. Nature, according to Darwin, is rather random, picking up the best of the pieces after the event and discarding the rest. In our world, my daughter, marriage is money which provides the means of looking after our future generations. Maybe even Darwin would be proud of us. It's the ingenuity of furthering the race and the Mandervilles in particular. Emily, you must have realised the family is broke. Unless you marry money we are finished with. What I am trying to do is for your good and the good of your children. I agree Sebastian is a far nicer rogue than Arthur, but Arthur has the money. And anyway, who knows what the Sebastians will grow into when they enter a vicious world, even young Sebastian... Now, will you have that cup of tea?"

THE HOUSE BUILT by Captain Brigandshaw was three storeys high including the servants' attic with the sloping ceiling. There were five separate acres of land in a row with a house on each plot, a half-mile from the Epsom racecourse. Everyone had planted trees in the hope of hiding themselves from their neighbours to create the feeling of exclusivity. The Oaks, the name given to the house by the newly rich ship owner, had a curious drive that took a tortuous course through the five acres of oak trees that were doing their best to grow into an avenue. Unfortunately, no one had explained to the sea captain that oaks were the slowest growing tree in all of England. Only his great-great-grandchildren would reap the reward of a leafy canopy on their way to the modest front door with its prime entrance annexed on either side by box trees having, at last, made it level with the top of the front door and just below the eaves.

The morning after his meeting with Sir Henry, when Emily was crying, the tears flowing gently down her lovely face, The Captain, as he liked to refer to himself, was standing outside his front door. He was looking at his four-foot oak trees with their spindly trunks that somehow reminded him of the maze at Hampton Court when it was first planted by Henry VIII. It must have been a ridiculous sight with everyone seeing the tops of everyone else walking aimlessly in different directions. The Captain hated his oak trees.

With his riding crop rhythmically slapping his right riding boot in the manner of an agitated cat, he walked up a side path flanked by apple and pear trees, past the hothouse that was heated in winter to provide The Oaks with flowers, and then past the hen and duck run. The run was his head gardener's one demand because it provided a liquid mixture which was poured on the hothouse plants. Then he walked to the stables where he mounted his horse, held by the junior groom. The Captain had such a curious seat, his back hollowing to the outside of his bottom which made a straight line to his shoulder blades giving the impression of a bent sack of potatoes. The picture forced the groom to place his mucky hand over his laughing mouth before the sound came out bringing forth The Captain's wrath. When The Captain disappeared briefly behind the double-storey henhouse to reappear from the shoulders up between the avenue of oak trees, the groom prudently ran back into the stables before convulsing with mirth. Oblivious, The Captain continued on his way to have another distant gaze at Hastings Court, his future home if he could stomach the extortionate price. Never once had he ever thought of the imminent transaction as giving Arthur the house. Arthur and his bride would be given a suite of rooms in the far west wing. The rest would be his.

As he rode, his mind played between five new steamships that would make him richer by the day, or Hastings Court and the Athenaeum Club. Again, he shuddered at the repair bill to the house.

He rode away from his property across the Downs in a pensive mood until he, at last, looked up at Hastings Court in its ancient glory with the morning sun giving a warm yellow glow to the old stone with its turrets and battlements. To The Captain gazing at his future, it was really a castle, not a mere country manor house with twenty-seven rooms. The horse was still as he gazed up longingly and then his imagination took control. His ships were bringing carpets from Persia, ancient Ming China from the Middle Kingdom, furniture from Sweden and exotic silks from India.

Surprised from its reverie, the startled horse was kicked into action.

FROM THE TERRACE both Emily and her father watched the galloping horse become a horse and rider and with a sinking heart, she recognised the petulant rider. The miracle had not happened. She was going to be bought.

"Life's never easy," her father said, gently taking her hand.

THE WIND HAD CHANGED to the west and the *Indian Queen* was tacking to keep her course. On the horizon, a black squall was running towards them at sixty knots. Seb watched with fascinated horror as the crew ran down and lashed all the canvas, leaving them bare-masted to the coming wind. Captain Doyle was yelling at him from behind the great wheel that had turned the ship east to run with the squall. None of his words reached Seb who bravely smiled at the coming onslaught, his father's words playing in his ears.

"You may be shot, young Sebastian, run through with a sword, but a valiant death from drowning, never. You were born with a caul over your face. Every ship of mine sails with a caul locked in the captain's cabin. Maybe a mariner's superstition but never a boat of mine foundered in a storm. Fifty pounds I've paid for them cauls to keep us safe. But the luckiest of all is a seaman born with a caul over his face."

Watching fascinated, Seb judged the squall would hit them in less than five minutes. A big rope hung from the sail, coiled at his feet. Quickly and with deft fingers learnt from a sea captain father, Seb lashed himself to the mast and waited for the storm. When he looked up, Captain Doyle was smiling instead of yelling at him and Seb understood, raising his thumb in recognition. Rather than being frightened, he was more exhilarated than any other time in his life. He faced the wind, anticipating the lashing of the rain.

ARTHUR BRIGANDSHAW HAD learnt from an early age that doing exactly what his father wanted was the easy way to go through life and as a result, he had never done a hard day's work in his life. When Father told him to do something, Arthur moved at great speed. His second secret in life was always to look busy when anyone was watching. The third was to agree with everything anyone said. The fourth was to make a complimentary remark about clothes or appearance. But of course, all of these only applied in public or with people who could help him along his easy way. He was a calculating, congenital liar, but it worked. The thought of slapping Sebastian's face and making an enemy but pleasing his father was a calculated risk. He neither liked nor disliked his younger brother any more than he really cared whether Emily was Emily or any other young girl. The only thing that mattered to Arthur was Arthur's pleasures, which were many.

From the age of twenty-one, when his father gave him an independent income as the oldest son, he had spent the majority of his lying calculations in seducing women. Class never entered the equation and love was further away than the moon. His mother, who was the only one in the family to know what she had given birth to, had considered him a spoilt brat from an early age, which mattered nothing to Arthur. Love and affection were never part of his life.

When he returned home from London by train, the horse and trap having made the journey back soon after Sebastian had been bundled on board the *Indian Queen*, he found his father both agitated and hilariously excited.

"You will marry Emily Manderville, my son, and your new house will be Hastings Court. Sir Henry is going abroad. The fact is, I've bought Hastings Court and my grandchildren are going to be aristocrats."

"Anything you say, Father. I'm very pleased for you."

"You will call on Emily tomorrow to propose."

"Does Emily concur, Father?"

"She said, I believe her words were, 'why wait until September?'"

"Did she now?" said Arthur, thinking. After a while, he smiled at his father. "If the lady doesn't wish to wait why should we gainsay her wishes?" Arthur liked to use some of his father's words of which 'gainsay' was a choice favourite. By the time he came to ride his horse to Hastings Court, and after a night of deep thought, Arthur knew he would not be marrying a virgin. The wedding would take place as soon as the banns had been read in the Norman church. Arthur never took chances. They were pointless. He was a man who believed that everyone knew with near certainty the identity of their mother, but their father was another kettle of fish.

"WHY DON'T you marry again, Father?" asked Emily as they walked together through the woods. "You are still comparatively young. You, not me, can marry the money and live happily ever after at Hastings Court. Have a son. Pass on the title instead of Cousin George in Canada. What's a lumberjack going to do with a baronetcy anyway, especially when it comes without money?"

"I won't say it's dying love for your mother. Everything fades, Em, even that strange thing they call love that no one can really describe. I have a feeling it fades in life as well as death. I have never met anyone who stayed in love for very long. That occurs in novels, which I hope you are not reading for the only reason they are plain rubbish. They pander to a young lady's imagination. No, it is one thing to set out to marry money, and another to succeed. Most money is difficult to prise away from its owner and fathers are dubious when they see an old widower with a white elephant like Hastings Court wooing an eligible daughter. Better a rake with money. The Captain Brigandshaws of this world are a rare breed who above all want to be recognised. And though I don't like the man, the wife is rather charming and will help you through the worst of your life with Arthur. She may well be the mother you never had."

They walked through the ancient oaks before he spoke again. "If any man tried to best The Captain in business, I'm certain he would fall short. You and I, you see, have not tested him. We have struck a bargain, and in any bargain there are clauses the parties don't like. You see, if Sebastian was the eldest son with glittering prospects, would he be the man you think you love or a lazy reprobate like Arthur who will likely leave you on your own for most of your life with your children? A good, well-provided home with children can so often be better without their persistent, boorish husband. It is rarely possible to rely on other people in life to make us happy, even to make us content. The peace of life only comes from within ourselves. At sixteen you only see a week, a month, a year at most. I think to myself, now that I can see a lifetime, lifetimes are never a grand passion and anyone who says they are, are believers in fairy stories. They are the worst kind of liars as they hold out a hope that never existed, however much we wish it had. Life is hard and uncompromising and with your faith in God, you can face the truth. People, and that includes husbands, are not all bad or all good. We are all a mixture of good and evil. There will be good in Arthur that you must find as there would have been bad in Sebastian you did not want to know about. If you wish to delay the wedding until September..."

"No, Father. Let me get it over with."

"I have taken precautions. A trust containing two hundred thousand pounds will be set up which will go to Arthur upon my death, provided he is still living with you and married to you. If you should die first, the money will go to your children. That wealth may control his mind better than the love of any woman. Em, it is not the best bargain I can offer you for life, but I think it will work. Then again, there is never any certainty. A fool once said that it is better to be poor and happy than rich and miserable. That fool should have tried poor and miserable, which is always the road to poverty. There are few things worse in this life than to end up without money or the means of earning money. Ask any man or woman who is penniless. Wealth, Em, cushions the blows of life and you should mark my words."

"Father, would you have gone bankrupt?"

"Within six months."

WHILE HENRY MANDERVILLE was trying to convince himself that he was doing the right thing, the *Indian Queen* was under full sail beneath a clear sky. The squall had lasted ten minutes the day before, gone as quickly as it had come. The Portuguese island of Madeira was off the starboard bow. Once Seb thought he smelt the African desert blown by the wind and then it was gone again. The entire crew were cleaning the deck, except for the mate and first officer. The excitement of sail and squall had changed to boredom, Seb's dreaded affliction.

He thought of Emily and what she was being made to do. There had always been Em and Seb, and even far away at boarding school, he had written to her every other day, telling her his deepest thoughts, the words so much easier to write than to say. Everything that happened in their lives happened only as it related to each other. For Seb to win a race at the school sports day was to win for Em, not the clamorous sycophants who patted his back and gushed his praise. Everything he had ever done as far back as he could remember was for her. Left alone by a distant, tyrannical father and a mother bemused by four sons and male domination, his real world had only existed through Em. For years they had literally run away from other people to be alone together and finally, right at what was now the end, as the ship careened down the west coast of Africa, they were lovers, a new, more beautiful love he had never known existed, and there was nothing he could do to change the new course of his life. Sadness became anger and then despair as he watched the green, terraced vinelands of Madeira slip slowly by two miles off the starboard bow; too far to swim, and if he got there, he told his despair, what could he do? Find some work and sail back to his father's wrath? And what work could he do? He could write a good essay, even run a fast race, but all his gentleman's education would be of little value on the rugged island passing by. Seb walked the deck as it plunged further away and there was not one thing he could do to change its course. Soon the island was behind them.

MARTINUS OOSTHUIZEN HAD BEEN WAITING two months for the *Indian Queen* to call at Cape Town harbour. Stored under lock and key in the Colonial Shipping warehouse in Strand Street were the tusks of two hundred elephants, five tonnes of ivory.

From Signal Hill, Martinus watched the small brigantine make her way skilfully into the harbour. Slowly he turned his horse to go down and meet the ship. He was waiting when the gangplank was thrown down, and Captain Doyle came ashore.

FROM THE SHIP'S RAIL, Sebastian Brigandshaw watched the captain shake hands with the bearded giant. Seb had no money so there was no point in going ashore other than to kick his heels. He saw the first officer follow the captain down the gangplank. The harbour was bursting with people and only a black man in rags observed idly from the dock, neither of them with anything to do. Forlornly, Seb stretched back his shoulders and looked up at the mountain covered in a white tablecloth of cloud, spilling down the south side towards a range of ragged-tooth mountains. There was a strong southeast wind cutting across the bay, the mountain shielding the harbour. The midday sun was hot even in the African winter. Then he remembered again. It was his eighteenth birthday, and he was quite alone and tears pricked the back of his eyes and the tips of his fingers hurt. The entire world had rejected him.

· · ·

CAPTAIN DOYLE WAS a head shorter and half the size of the Boer, which was little reflection on the Irishman. Martinus Oosthuizen was a very big man. Surprisingly his handshake was firm but gentle and the blue eyes hidden in the chestnut whorls of hair were amused. The surprise of the man's size was matched by the blue eyes. The chestnut brown hair left room for the eyes, a powerful nose and full red lips. There was no sign of the man's ears and little of his forehead. The full beard dropped to a hairy chest that bushed out of his open shirt. The shirt was the grey colour of being washed too often in the rivers of Africa.

"How long have you been waiting?" asked Captain Doyle.

"Two months, *kerel*, two months. You think it matters?"

"What have you got for me?"

"Four hundred tusks. Big tusks. You have room for five tonnes?"

"When we unload some cargo."

"You trade all along the coast?"

"Yes. Half the profit for me and the crew, and half for the owner. Merchants of the sea."

"You English get rich."

"There is risk and profit. You can wait for me to sell your ivory in India and I will take twenty per cent for shipping and selling, or I buy your tusks today for a price."

Captain Doyle turned back to his ship to check the mate was organising the discharge and saw Seb standing by the rail.

"Did you ever meet The Captain?" he said turning back to Tinus.

"He was the first man to buy my ivory."

"That's his son on deck. The youngest son. Trouble with a girl in England. The Captain sent him away. You mind if we bring him to lunch?" Looking back to his ship he cupped his mouth: "Mr Brigandshaw," he shouted, "come ashore."

THE CAB DRIVER had no front teeth and his skin was the colour of parchment. The horse gave the three passengers a melancholy look and waited for the Cape Malay to give him the road out of the harbour. Seb kept quiet in his corner whilst the driver spoke to the horse in a foreign language. There was a road that ran around the bay close to the sea which the cab took, and the pleasure of being off the ship balanced Seb's shyness. All the captain had told him to do was get in the cab, which he had done. The older man continued their conversation. There had been no introduction to the foreigner and no indication of where they were going. Apart from his two days at Las Palmas, this was the first time Seb had been on a foreign shore. The calls at Accra and Lagos to unload goods from England and take on bags of produce had been watched from the ship and permission had been refused for him to go ashore.

Somewhere Seb had read the words of Sir Francis Drake, 'the fairest Cape in the world'. He took in with awe at the beauty of mountain and sea, the calls of seagulls and strange seabirds, and the sea being whipped up where the strong south-easter was unguarded by the towering mountain.

Soon the harbour was left behind and the track went around the bay away from the houses. A mile later the cabbie swung the horse to the left through two white entrance pillars onto a private driveway that rose up towards a large bungalow set against the mountain. In front were tended rose gardens and lawns with strange tall trees Seb had never seen before growing to either side of the house. The sign across the top of the two white pillars had read Oude Kraal. The perfect blue sky framed the mountains that framed the white house. As the cab drove up the front drive, Seb could smell the roses in the terraced gardens that dropped down to the great rocks and the sea three hundred feet below the slope. Seb was told to get out of the cab. Empty of passengers, the cab turned around and the horse trotted away. Seb followed the two men into the house. The foreigner seemed quite at home but Seb had no idea who the house belonged to. A barefoot, red-fezzed servant offered Seb a glass of wine. The toast to Captain Brigandshaw before they drank surprised him. The foreigner had proposed the toast. Seb kept quiet while plates of lobster were put out on the low tables.

The wine was different to the Spanish sherry he had sometimes been allowed when growing up. The colour was pale yellow, the taste sweet and rich with fruit. To Seb's surprise the lobster, as red as any he had seen from the shores of Britain, were free of claws. Putting down the glass of wine on the table, Seb pulled at the white meat offering itself from the slit belly of the Cape lobster. The taste was even better than an English lobster. Unthinking, he began to eat his way through the plate of food, dipping the sweet white flesh into the sauce dishes with his fingers. No one took any notice, so he started on the second plate of food and tried not to think of Emily on his birthday. Lost in the woods of England, Seb continued to eat, clearing all but the shells. The two men ten paces down the veranda had not even noticed his devastation of the food. The wine they had drunk was making them laugh. There were uneaten plates of food on the table with their bottle of wine. Far over the water, the sun was sinking into the sea, layering the heavens with shades of gold. The wind was still whipping foam out of the sea. If necessary he would sleep in the wicker chair and dream of England.

TINUS OOSTHUIZEN'S cheroots were sweet-smelling and augmented the taste of the wine. Both men were watching the last of the sun, silent with admiration. The seascape sky had gone from gold to orange and red, with a pocket of duck egg blue that showed the way to heaven. For five perfect minutes, they watched the light go out across the sea.

"The beauty of God," Tinus said loudly to himself. "The lad's fast asleep."

"The glory of youth," said Captain Doyle. "Six thousand miles from home. Thrown out of house and hearth by his father. Broken his heart on a girl. And there is youth. A good two plates of crayfish, one good glass of Chenin Blanc and fast asleep without the trace of a snore. They told me to take him away and not bring him back for a year and a half. Just before we sailed, Arthur, the eldest brother, brought him on board. What am I going to do with the lad? I can't make him a sailor 'cause he's The Captain's son and I can't make him an officer as he knows nothing about ships. From here to India he'll go mad with boredom if he doesn't jump over the side... He'll wake eventually from the cold. As you know, once the sun goes down in winter the temperature drops quickly."

"Get the Hottentot to cover him with a blanket. He'll be sleeping in peace by the look of him. Pity to let him wake."

When the servant brought the third bottle of wine, he put a heavy blanket over the sleeping boy. The light had almost gone. The two men took their wine inside where a log fire was burning.

"Can the boy ride a horse?" asked Tinus, standing in front of the fire.

"Why do you ask?"

"Shoot a gun? He wouldn't be bored hunting elephant."

"But he might be dead and then what do I say to The Captain?"

"Ships go down. There was a risk. The boy's company would be good."

"He's only a lad."

"He'll be a man before we cross the Limpopo River."

2

FEBRUARY 1888

*S*ebastian Brigandshaw and Tinus Oosthuizen watched in fascinated horror. The witch doctor had careened at speed from the king's cattle kraal to stand motionless before the line of men. The skin of a spotted hyena hung down her back, the skull without the lower jawbone clutching her head. Jackal tails dangled from her waist and crocodile teeth from her ankles. The king, seated in an armchair presented by one of the white concession seekers, paid the hag no attention. Seb, from seventy yards, caught a repulsive sweet smell that came from the half-crouched hag as she walked down the line of men. Behind Lobengula stood the king's executioner. The hag crabbed her way down the front of the men and then began the search from behind. Darting forward, she smelt a man from his shoulder blades to his feet. The total silence in the king's kraal made Seb more frightened than any uproar. The man being smelt out shivered the length of his body. The witch doctor gave a low cackle and moved on behind the line, stopping at the king's general to smell for evil. The man, the second most powerful man after the king in the land conquered by the Matabele, began to shiver with fear. The hag went round him in a crouch and looked up at his face. Backing away from the man while the king, the only person to move, put a bowl of beer to his mouth and drank, the witch doctor screamed and flung out her hand at the man, pointing a finger, making the hackles rise on the back of Seb's neck. The king's executioner moved with practised speed and hit the king's general just behind his right ear with a knobkerrie made of teak, exploding the man's head and sending the soft inside thirty feet in front of the dead man even before he fell to the floor. Seb turned away to be sick and a strong hand gripped his elbow.

"Don't flinch, lad," whispered Tinus as the hag rushed back to the king's cattle kraal through the gap in the thorn thickets that locked the nation's treasure.

The king waved a flywhisk and called for a new bowl of beer. The standing men dispersed as quickly as their dignity and fear allowed them. The dead man was left where he had dropped and the flies found the leftovers of his brain and crawled inside the big nostrils that were oozing with thick blood.

"Why?" asked Seb as normality returned to the king's kraal.

"In a tribe that lives by war, there can only be one king. The general had been too successful. The smelling out is a charade, a way to keep the people in constant fear. The king had fingered the man long before that show of the witch doctor's power. That hag is the only person in the kingdom feared by the king. Only through her can he kill his most powerful rivals. There will be no audience with the king today for you and me. We shall wait. In Africa, there is always time."

Quietly they backed out away from the space in front of the king's kraal, away from the great jackalberry tree that shaded the king as he filled his vast belly with beer. Seb suspected the springs in the armchair had broken long ago.

Walking through the mopane trees to their wagon, Seb wished he was back in the English countryside where nothing threatened his peace of mind. Above the trees, high in the powder blue sky, tufted clouds hung motionless. The main rains had been due for weeks.

THEY HAD TAKEN the train to Kimberley with Tinus Oosthuizen's horse in the horse wagon at the back of the train. From Kimberley they had ridden unencumbered to the new gold mining town of Johannesburg. The horse bought for Seb was salted and able to go through tsetse fly country without falling sick. They had ridden across the veld, sleeping under trees and eating strips of salted dried beef. Once they shot a springbok and roasted the carcass but Tinus was in a hurry.

The wagon and six oxen were waiting for Tinus on a farm eight miles north of the mining camp, and had been brought back to Johannesburg to stock for the hunting trip to the north. Tinus's horse nuzzled the lead oxen. They were the Boer's only family.

The trek north took them along the banks of the Limpopo River to Bain's

Drift where they crossed into the land of the Bechuana. The main rains had not broken and the river crossing was simple. Without pause, Tinus had headed north for Gu-Bulawayo, across the Maklautsi and Shashe rivers to seek permission to hunt elephant from Lobengula.

They had been in Gu-Bulawayo eleven days before they were granted an audience. It was the day after the general's brains had been knocked out of his head. Tinus pulled out a long box from the back of the wagon. There were leather straps on either side of the box and it was heavy.

"The only currency he understands," said Tinus as they lifted the box together. "Guns. The reason he likes the whites. With guns he can maintain his power forever, and they are worth more than any herd of elephant to the king."

"The British made it illegal to sell guns to the natives."

"The Boer has spent his history trekking from authority. Here Lobengula is the law."

"How many?"

"There are three guns, old guns with powder and shot. Chances are they will kill more Matabele than anything else."

There was no sign of the general's remains when they presented the guns to the king. Tinus showed the king how to load one of the muzzleloaders and killed a vulture that had gorged on the general's body. The bird was too heavy to fly. The king laughed with great excitement and would have hugged Tinus if he had been able to move the great bulk of his body out of the armchair.

Permission was given to hunt in the land of the Shona.

THE NEXT MORNING the six oxen pulled the wagon northeast from Gu-Bulawayo, the horses on a loose rein at the back of the wagon. Tinus Oosthuizen was more excited than a schoolboy given permission to shoot his first rabbit. He was free to roam the bush.

THE RAINS CAME in the second week of their journey into the hinterland. Tinus made camp on the high bank of a dried-up river and extended the side of the wagon with waterproof canvas. The covered wagon was dry inside, the canopy having been carefully patched while they waited for Lobengula. Behind the camp stretched the mopane forest with thorn trees along the bank of the dry river. In the middle of the river sand, a great hole had been dug by elephants for water.

"They dig with their trunks. We wait now and we don't shoot elephant. This is still Matabeleland. Lobengula considers the land of the Shona his hunting ground. His sphere of influence as you British would say. This rain will last for weeks. Make yourself comfortable."

The next morning the river was a raging torrent.

THERE WAS little of Seb that Emily would have recognised. The thin man had developed powerful shoulders from pulling the wooden spokes of the wagon wheels to help the straining oxen through rivers and over *kloofs*. The ponytail had parted and dropped long hair to his shoulders. Where the leather hat given to him by Tinus failed to keep out the sun, the brown hair had bleached to a ragged white. His face, that so few years ago had sprouted his first bumfluff, was a full beard. The most striking change after his shoulders were the muscles on his thighs and calves, pounded week after week by straining at the wheel. For something to do as much as anything else, he now smoked the occasional cheroot.

Listening to the rain drumming on the canvas roof, Seb thought more and more of Emily and his home so far away in England. The torrent of rain, flooding off one side of the canvas where it dipped with the weight of water, was alien. The never-ending mopane forest stretched on either side of the raging river that when first seen had been waterless. There were animal and bird cries in the night, a foreigner snoring next to him, the sense of being lost to everything he had ever understood. The crashing, peeling thunder sent the horses to fear as they whinnied and pulled at the long reins, the rainwater pouring from their backs lit by the lightning. There was fear in him mixed with terminal loudness, the end of life itself.

"You look like a man lost in hell," said Tinus taking pity on the man. He had lit the lamp in the wagon and swung his legs over the bunk. "The horses will be all right. It's inherent in everything to fear a storm; part of our evolution. You can't sleep with the thunder, I suppose?"

"No," said Seb miserably.

"When the sun comes out, you'll feel a lot better. Have a cheroot."

"Thank you."

"You never asked how a Boer speaks such good English."

"Don't they all?" replied Seb, reluctant to be drawn into a conversation.

"My mother was a Scot, a Calvinist. Came out with the Scottish missionaries. You ever heard of Andrew Murray? No. Doesn't matter. He was part of the beginning of our church. The Dutch Reformed Church. I was able to read and write English long before the *Taal*. You are sleeping on a chest. Why not look inside?"

Reluctantly, Seb got off his bed and opened up the top of the long chest. It was filled with books.

"When I hunt alone, they are my family. Sir Walter Scott. Every novel of Scott's is in there. Carlyle's essays. Dickens. Translations of the French and Russians. My mother said all the knowledge of the world was between the covers of books. We lived then in the Karoo. A little town called Graaff-Reinet. She wanted me to be a preacher. The bush is also a great teacher, young Sebastian. It grows on you and, in the end, it takes hold of your life. Maybe in a year you won't wish to go home to England. Freedom. Real freedom is intoxicating. Let's have a drop of brandy and listen to the music of the storm. When you hear the music and feel the dry, warm comfort of the wagon, you will sleep through the worst of storms. Now, while the rain comes down, tell me all about this girl you left behind."

FOR THREE WEEKS the rain came down, leaving them huddled in the wagon fighting mosquitoes. The firewood was drenched, and they ate dried beef and drank the rainwater. Everything became wet including their clothes and bedding. To pass the many hours of night and day they talked.

Seb had imagined Tinus to be an old man, as the sun had weathered the visible patches of skin below the blue eyes, and the long hair that hung past his shoulders was streaked with grey. Even some of the full beard was touched with the same sign of age. Surprisingly, the Boer was the same age as Arthur, Seb's older brother, by a week. In detail, they had explained their lives to each other.

Tinus was born Martinus Jacobus McDonald Oosthuizen, of a family that had spent two hundred years avoiding orders that confined the new civilisation of man to a set of rules and the dogmas of an established Church that wished to control the sole right to interpret the word of God. First, the family had left the Low Countries in Europe for the Cape of Good Hope to follow the doctrine of John Calvin and worship God in freedom. But with Jan van Riebeeck and the Dutch East India Company came another set of rules, and the farmers moved inland from Cape Town. Then the British conquered the Cape and masterminded a new and more powerful set of rules that sent Tinus's grandfather on the Great Trek of the Boers into southern Africa. The land was largely empty except for roaming bands of armed natives that fought the Boers. Tinus had joined the commando when he was fourteen and able to fire a rifle. At sixteen he and a middle brother had ridden north on their first hunt to avoid the discipline of their father and neither had ever returned to Graaff-Reinet, the brother leaving his earthly remains on the banks of the Limpopo River. He had also left Tinus with his first wagonload of ivory. He was seventeen, a year younger than Seb, alone and determined. Months later, he had brought the wagon to Mafeking. From Mafeking the wagon had taken him south and his first and only meeting with The Captain. He had had no money to board the train in Mafeking and no one had wanted his ivory. The journey south had taken two and a half lonely years, stopping at farms on the way to work for provisions.

The sun when it came at the end of March steamed the wetland, and many birds that Seb had never heard sang with joy. They waited another three days for the river to fall and made a crossing where rocks had tumbled against broken trees trapped in the land. For a further day, they climbed up through the mopane forest until the passage was blocked by a great dyke, a giant eruption a million years before that had rumbled up from the molten bowels of the earth.

"We spent two months here my first trip, looking for a way to those mountains," said Tinus. "We rode the horses a hundred miles in both directions but found nothing to pass an ox wagon. You see over here, young Seb, where that clump of trees is different from here, shorter with a spreading canopy. Right there in front of us is the only way for the oxen to reach the ancient Kingdom of Monomotapa, a civilisation now extinct. There are only the pickings of legend among the scattered blacks, the stories passed from father to son of a kingdom that traded ivory and gold with the Portuguese traders on the East Coast, that smelted iron and copper, built great fortifications and developed agriculture. There are still traces of them, still traces of the mines, but very few traces of the people who once ruled the high plateau that stretches for hundreds of miles to a great river. The climate is cool, the land well watered. Tomorrow we will start our climb through the mountain and I will show you the most beautiful country on this earth."

AT THE TOP of the great dyke, before they descended the gentle slope to the plateau, Seb looked out over the forest of trees, three times the height of a man, that spread a canopy of green to the far horizon. Swathed into the trees were vast areas of open savannah with tall brown grass the height of a horse's withers, and over all the open ground were herds of game. Thousands upon thousands of animals dispersed by the rain, now able to feed far from the rivers. Elephants standing high out of the grass next to the herds of impala. Giraffe feeding from the tops of trees. Buffalo so numerous he was unable to count.

"A perfect harmony," said Seb, roving his eyes over the great panorama.

"On the surface, young Seb. You can't see the lion from here. They rest up under the trees in the day, hidden by the elephant grass. You ever see anything more beautiful?"

The puffed white clouds rested above the landscape capped by a clear blue sky, the air clear, washed by the recent rain. There was no wind.

"We camp here for a day to rest the oxen," said Tinus.

"Where are the people?" asked Seb. "There are no villages. Nothing but grass, trees and the thousands upon thousands of animals."

"They killed each other."

"What do you mean?"

"Rape and pillage are more common in these parts. Africa can be cruel."

They stood together looking at the scenery for some time before Seb broke the silence of respect.

"No," he said. "I never saw anything more beautiful. How long are we staying?"

"We want to be back over the dyke before next year's rains. It won't rain now for eight or nine months. By then you'll be able to go home."

"You think I will want to go home?"

"Your Emily will take you home."

"Poor girl. She will wonder where I am."

With new grass pushing through the old, green emerging from last year's fallen brown, the legacy of the soaking rains, they outspanned the oxen and untethered their horses from the rear of the wagon. The animals moved slowly away grazing, trailing their long leads.

SEB THOUGHT the flat area around the camp to be five or six acres with a drop in front of five hundred feet to the plain below. Craggy outcrops of rock pushed out of the grass and some of the trees were growing out of cracks in the rocks. Tinus had gone off with two guns as the red ball of the sun began to slide down below the far horizon to Seb's right, showering the clouds orange and gold with great stabs of fire. The broken wood he had collected from beneath the trees was piled high. The shotgun fired twice behind him and all sound was extinguished at the moment the rim of sun slid from sight. The birds and insects, the frogs and animals, waited for a moment and began the noise again. Down in the plain, a lion roared. Using one precious match, Seb lit the dry twigs he had gathered beneath a rock overhang and the fire took hold that would burn all night. The animals had been tethered to stop them straying in the night and to be close to the protection of the firelight, the loss of horse and oxen the greatest fear of the distant hunter.

The night came swiftly as Seb hung a pot over one side of the fire filled with water from the stream that broke out of an outcrop of rocks to cascade over the escarpment, turning to rain long before the water brushed the lush canopy of trees far below. Tinus came out of the trees into the new firelight carrying two birds Seb judged to be the size of a partridge. Tinus called them Cape Franklin but explained the colouring was different. The guns were strapped on his back and the belt of cartridges hung over his chest. In his right hand, the leather hat that never left his head during the day was filled with a strange, orange fruit a little larger than a gooseberry. The big man put the birds and hat next to Seb before unloading the guns against the rear of the wagon. A second and third lion roared from the darkened plain below as the last light of day faded into darkness, the firelight reaching further and further into the new dark, sparks flying high into the night. Without being asked, Seb began to pluck the warm birds, letting the downy chest feathers be drawn to the flames. The smell was pungent. Tinus had lit his first cheroot and came to stand by the fire. Neither spoke, both listening to the sounds of the African night.

When the birds were plucked and gutted, Seb went to the wagon and ground a handful of coffee beans. Back at the fire, he dropped the ground coffee into the pot of boiling water and the smell mingled with the cheroot and the smell of burning feathers. A hyena laughed hysterically from behind them and one of the horses whickered.

"Smelt your feathers," said Tinus comfortably, watching the firelight dance among the under boughs of the trees.

"What's in the hat?" asked Seb as he pushed the green stick through the body of the second bird and popped it over embers he had drawn away from the fire. The one forked stick that made up half of the crude spit was shorter than the other but it didn't matter. The headless bird would roast looking halfway up to heaven.

"Fruit," answered Tinus.

"Have you eaten them before?"

"Never seen them before."

"They could be poisonous."

"There were two monkeys that fell backwards out of the tree when I fired the gun. Frightened the shit out of them. Under the tree was a mess of half-eaten fruit. We can eat anything a monkey eats."

"How come you've never seen one before?"

"Never frightened a monkey out of the tree before. Try one?"

"You try one first."

REPLETE WITH BIRD and wild fruit, they watched the flames of fire. The oxen had got down on the ground to chew the cud and both of the horses were fast asleep standing up. The empty mug of coffee stood on the earth next to Seb's right foot as he stared into the constantly changing flames. To get a better view of the fire, he lay on his side and shortly he was sound asleep. Tinus got up and loaded the fire and sat back on the ground with his back to a fallen tree. The hyena drew a few feet closer to the fire and Tinus waited with the shotgun across his knees. An hour passed before the animal's courage drew it close enough for Tinus to see the fire reflected in the yellow eyes. Both barrels were loaded with birdshot and the hyena, whose jaws could break a man's leg in half with one bite, was forty yards from the campfire. Gently, Tinus pulled back the right hammer and in one movement took the gun to his shoulder and fired.

"What the hell?" shouted Seb scrambling to his feet.

"Now we can both go to sleep."

They could hear the hyena yelping further and further into the trees.

"Birdshot. More fright than pain. Won't come back tonight and the others will sense his fear. Always works. Now go back to sleep, young Seb. Tomorrow is the first day in the territory where we will hunt."

By the time the sun was burning overhead, the wagon was making a trail through the grassland. The path they had taken down was a gentle slope compared to the precipice from their camp. Seb looked back and not a trace of smoke rose from the dampened fire that he had covered over with dry grass. They both rode on horseback on either side of the wagon with Tinus coaxing the lead ox to plod on deeper into Africa. Since they had crossed the swollen river, they had seen no sign of man. Just game in quantities Seb had never imagined.

For seven days they travelled deep into the virgin land where the trees had never been cut and ploughs had never turned the earth. Not once had they seen the sign of living man, only the remnants of *rongwas*, stone fortifications that Tinus had heard were once part of the Kingdom of Monomotapa. Each night, away from the fires, Tinus checked their direction by reading the stars, checking the exact position of south from the Southern Cross.

At the end of March, they reached a small river where the signs of man were seen in an old fire site with logs drawn on either side to make a seat. A little way from the remnants of old charcoal a hut had stood, the building burnt to the ground. A long piece of rope hung from a fever tree, the thorns on the tree longer than Seb's index finger. The area was well shaded and high on the banks of the river.

"This is where we camp in the dry season," said Tinus.

"Someone's been here before."

"Me. There are few tribesmen in the mountains. None on the plains. The Matabele cleared them out years ago. That's why we needed Lobengula's permission to hunt. In the trees is a kraal I made of thorn bush for the oxen. That river is full of bream. Near the river, we sleep under nets against the mosquitoes. Tomorrow we plant the vegetable seeds and water them from the river. I'll show you my old vegetable garden with its fence to keep out the buck and pigs. The soil in the *vlei* is black and rich. By the time we break camp, there will be enough maize to reap for our journey. Welcome to my home, young Seb, such as it is. Now if you'll excuse me, I wish to thank God for my safe return."

Quietly and without fuss, the big man sank to his knees and began to pray in the *Taal*. Seb watched him for a moment before dropping to his knees and joining the prayer. Behind them, the oxen and horses watched with quiet regard. Over from the opposite side of the river, a fish eagle called the triple call, achingly lonely.

IT FELT to Seb they were the only people left in the world, and when the seeds broke from the black earth, he felt a primal excitement. The old hut had been burnt to the ground by Tinus to prevent black ants, scorpions, geckos and snakes infesting the rough bush thatch. The new rondavels had taken them a week to build, enough protection at night to give them the feeling of safety. An old anthill made the oven and a pulley system drew buckets of water up from the river.

The day Emily gave birth to his son, Seb set out to hunt the elephant, nine months after he had been bundled on board the *Indian Queen* by his brother.

"You all right?" asked Tinus.

"I have a terrible pain in my stomach but I think it's going."

"Wind. Probably wind. You all right to get on your horse?"

"I'll be fine. You sure the oxen won't break out of the kraal?"

"Never have before."

Both men carried heavy-calibre Mausers strapped to their backs. The leather ammunition belts moved on their chests with the rhythm of the horses. By the time they sighted the herd of elephant, Seb had forgotten the pain in his stomach, overwhelmed by the excitement of the hunt. The long grass brushed his knees as they brought their mounts to walk. A herd of impala broke and ran away from them and in the distance upwards of fifty vultures were circling a kill, waiting their turn. The white fluffy clouds had been sucked dry of water and the sun was blazing hot.

Tinus gauged the elephant and signalled Seb to move around the herd. A herd of buffalo watched them aggressively from a leafless thorn thicket as they rode off towards the vultures.

"I killed the old bull in that herd on my last hunt," said Tinus. "We are going to ride up into the foothills of those mountains and camp for the night. I only kill an old elephant with the biggest tusks, the bulls pushed out of the herd, poor old bastards. Nature has no sympathy for the weak or useless. Survival, that's all it thinks about. They usually die of starvation, the old bulls, or loneliness. Better they find Martinus Jacobus McDonald Oosthuizen than dying of thirst too weak to reach the waterhole or too weak to climb out of the mud. We are looking for the spoor of the lone elephant, young Seb. How's your stomach?"

"It's fine now."

"Like the animals, if you get sick out here, you die."

THEY PASSED the vultures an hour before sunset, the birds so graceful in the air now ugly on the ground. The lions had left the kill and gone off to sleep under a tree. Hyena and black-backed jackal snarled at each other over the remains of a wildebeest, the ungainly vultures watching impatiently from the ground and surrounding trees. Seb could hear the flies in the dead animal's gutted stomach and the smell of putrefying flesh was strong. Seb judged the kill was three, possibly four days old.

The light of the sun was turning from white to yellow and throwing long tree shadows over the elephant grass as they took a path up into the hills. As the sun was setting, they found a stream and let the horses loose to graze and drink. Together they gathered the firewood before the light had gone; their vast world had shrunk to the surrounding trees picked out by the firelight.

They drank coffee sitting around the fire with their backs to a tree trunk they had hauled into position, Seb encouraging Tinus to tell him the stories of Africa. The once frightening sounds around them were now familiar and Sebastian Brigandshaw had become one with the bush.

· · ·

THEY WOKE to the sound of gunfire and for a moment Seb thought Tinus had gone off on his own. The night was paling behind their range of mountains from where the sun was rising. Their own camp was in darkness, the fire still burning.

"Hunters," said Seb.

"Lobengula," said Tinus. "Those are muzzleloaders, probably mine. This is Lobengula's hunting ground. We hunt game whereas the Matabele hunt people, the Shona in particular. What's left of the original tribe live in the mountains, hiding from the king's regiments."

"Can't we help?"

"You had better see this so you understand Africa better. Saddle up, young Seb."

The mountain range was covered in trees, the slopes gentle and easy to climb with streams running down to the plain. While waiting for the light to come over the hill, they had drunk the first coffee and eaten cold venison. The gunfire behind them had stopped.

"There's a small valley in the hills," said Tinus. "I found it many years ago."

"Won't the Matabele attack us?"

"Only if we sided with the Shona."

As the sun came up into the valley, the two horsemen reached the rim of the escarpment. Down in the valley, the Matabele impi was loading grain onto a wagon directed by an induna, the man's headgear different to the soldiers. Most of the soldiers were carrying assegais. A small group of young women and children were huddled together under guard. The bodies of dead men and old women were strewn over the ground between the huts. Away from the huts broken stems of maize spread in the open spaces between the trees, reaching far into the valley. It was the recently harvested cobs that were now being loaded onto the wagons. Soldiers were going among the dead, cutting open the stomachs to let out the spirits. There was no animosity in their actions. Behind the loading wagons, the cattle were being brought together. With military efficiency the soldiers fired the huts and empty grain silos and left with the valuables; the grain, cattle, young women and children. Even as Seb and Tinus watched, the valley began to empty of living people. Soon all that was left of the Shona village was the dead bodies and the burning huts. Then the morning doves began to call again.

"Mzilikazi, Lobengula's father, ran away from Shaka with his regiment," explained Tinus. "Over sixty years ago. Shaka was going to kill Mzilikazi. The man cut a swathe through the Transvaal until Hendrik Potgieter chased him over the Limpopo. By then the original Zulus were outnumbered by the remnants of the slaughtered tribes. What you just saw down there. Young women who will do what they are told and young children who will grow up speaking Zulu, the future wives, the future soldiers of the impis. The short stabbing spear of the Zulu is Africa's equivalent of gunpowder. That and Shaka's training made them invincible. It is easier to rape and pillage than working the land. Every year Lobengula throws the spear in a different direction where the industrious Shona will have grown the crops and fattened the cattle. A whole year's work is stolen in a morning. Someday the Matabele, the Zulu, will grow fat and complacent. Then they will be raped and pillaged.

"Military power determines wealth, not hard work. Maybe all through history until one great power maintains law and order like the Romans. The beaten tribes of Africa have looked to the Boers for protection and now they are looking to the British. Rhodes has a charter from your Queen Victoria to protect these people and bring them the word of God. He wants to subdue Lobengula by buying from him the concessions to look for gold. Lobengula fears the white man. Why he gave his permission to hunt. Every dog has his day and the days of Lobengula are short. The British use massacres like that to further their own conquest; the righteous rush to do good. The power of the stabbing spear will give way to the power of the chattering machine gun. Maybe there will be peace for a while. But peace like wealth never seems to last. Someone is always stealing it."

"There is someone coming out of the trees," said Seb.

"Yes. I saw him half an hour ago. He was making sure the soldiers had gone. The remarkable thing about mankind is the survivor. There is always a survivor or otherwise, you and I would not be here. Somewhere back in ancient history, one of our own ancestors came out of the forest to look at the destruction."

"It's a child."

"Probably a young herd boy, sent into the forest to look for a stray animal."

"Won't he starve with the food gone?"

"Maybe. If he's strong, he'll survive."

"Can't we help that one?" asked Seb.

"Maybe."

THE BOY WAS CRYING. A man with his stomach split open lay at his feet. Overhead the vultures were circling while the village smouldered in ruins.

Seb dismounted and walked towards the boy, across the packed, dry earth between the ruins. Even the chickens and dogs had been killed. Seb stopped twenty yards short and waited, the sun burning his back. The child kept staring at his dead father while the tears cut a clean path through the red dust on his face. Three vultures came to earth in a spread and attacked the intestines spilling from one of the bodies. The sound of flies was as loud as swarming bees. A dust devil swirled through the dead village sending new sparks from the smouldering piles that had been huts where people had slept that night. The dust devil moved away from the boy and Seb, running off into the trees, raising old leaves and grass high into the sky.

The boy looked up and saw the apparition with long straight hair the colour of sun-bleached maize, a wide-brimmed hat shielding eyes the colour of the morning sky, carrying a stick that spat death and he waited to die. The apparition took off the hat and swatted at the flies and then put it back on top of the long straight hair. The boy looked further, and another strange man was looking at him from the top of a horse, the man's eyes almost shut against the sun. More of the birds clattered to the ground to feed, and the boy waited. There was nowhere to run and no one to help.

"Leave him alone," called Tinus. "Come, young Seb. We came to hunt. There's nothing you can do. The boy's terrified. Let's get out of here."

Seb looked the boy in the eye and made a gesture to follow before turning around. Walking slowly, he returned to his horse, and when he remounted the boy had left the corpse and was walking towards them.

Tatenda was eleven years old and his grandfather had been chief of the Makori tribe, a branch of the Kalanga people, before it was wiped out by Mzilikazi. He was the sixth child of his father's first wife and the first boy. It was why his mother had called him Tatenda, the Shona word for thank you. His mother had been taken with his two surviving older sisters and the three youngest children. Tatenda's ten-year-old brother was slaughtered with the other men, a boy too old to forget. At the same time as Seb and Tinus, Tatenda had heard the dreadful sound of the muzzleloaders. The remnants of the Makori hidden in their small, mountain valley had been found by an impi of Lobengula, son of Mzilikazi. From his perch halfway up the escarpment on the other side of the valley from where the two horsemen had appeared, Tatenda had watched the slaughter of his father and brother. He had watched with hatred the remnants of the tribe being taken away to Matabeleland.

WHEN HE LOOKED up at the first white man he had ever seen, the prospect of revenge was embedded in his young mind. There had been many stories of these white men on horses with sticks that spat death, and the ones that had most interested his father were the wild stories that these men had defeated Mzilikazi far to the south.

He would have lived in the forest without starving to death. Three of the cows had strayed and two were in milk. There were game and fruit and many small rivers coming down the mountain. Alone he would have survived to find the remnants of another Shona tribe as the Makori were not the only ones hiding in the hills. Wiping the tears from his face for the last time, he followed the white man, the cold, bitter taste of revenge deep in his body. When the younger of the two white men, the one who had called with his hand, held it out again to pull him up onto the horse, he allowed himself to be jerked up behind the rider. He made a prayer to God through his ancestors that these men would show him the way. For a brief moment, he smiled at the rest of his life.

3

DECEMBER 1889

*A*rthur Brigandshaw was having the time of his life. He had once again avoided a tedious weekend at Hastings Court, and the girl he had had in mind had agreed to the theatre and supper at the Café Royal. She was coarse and sexy which was how Arthur liked his women. By the time he had finished flattering the lady, telling her how refined and well bred and beautiful she was, the lady would be back in his Baker Street house, and right in his bed. Flattery and champagne were his chief weapons of conquest.

Six months before, the *Indian Queen* had returned to London from a profitable voyage and without his youngest brother. Captain Doyle had told some story of Seb going off to hunt elephant in darkest Africa. Arthur was quite sure the good captain had taken his words 'keep the brat out of England for at least eighteen months' most literally. He had, of course, emphasised the words 'at least' and as the months had stretched his brother's absence, he was convinced Sebastian was dead.

The boy would be two years old in April, and even though he and Emily knew perfectly well the boy belonged to Seb, The Captain was none the wiser. Ensconced at Hastings Court as Lord of the Manor, he was in his element and it was just a pity the man's accent had not changed with his wealth and new position. Arthur, in fact, had never touched Emily, which amused him. The girl had been bought and paid for along with the house. There was an heir to the great future dynasty of the Brigandshaws. Arthur himself received an excessive salary from Colonial Shipping for very little work, and the poor girl was largely chaperoned by his father who now made the captains of his ships attend him at Hastings Court. The king, thought Arthur, was very much in his counting chamber.

To cap it all, he was going to make his personal fortune. The East India Club was largely for rich merchants and underwriters at Lloyd's, and as titular manager of Colonial Shipping, Arthur had been offered membership on his thirtieth birthday, which at first had seemed a crashing bore, but afterwards the source of fun listening to the old codgers pontificating on their fortune and the fortune of the great British Empire. On three occasions he picked up tips for the Stock Exchange and made a quick profit. His habits as a new, young member were to be demure and eavesdrop. Two of the men he had overheard were Alfred Beit and Cecil John Rhodes, respectively the wealthiest man in Africa and the likely next Prime Minister of the Cape. And if these two did not know what they were talking about, Arthur asked himself, then whoever did? Beit, the financier, was reputed to be as rich as Rhodes. Arthur had overheard the whole thing in his high-backed armchair, away from the fire, in a small alcove that had made him anonymous. He was quite sure neither man knew he was there. Lazy as usual, he had spent the afternoon in the club reading a detective novel rather than going back to the office after his lunch.

What he overheard was going to be bigger than the East India Company that had made Clive a rich man and the Queen Empress of all India. The new royal charter would at first cover southern Africa but Arthur had overheard Rhodes talking about a rail link from the Cape to Cairo that was to be built by his Charter Company. Rhodes had told Beit about the German surveyor, Karl Mauch, who predicted more gold in southern Africa than anywhere else in the world. And Rhodes, Arthur had learnt as he eavesdropped avidly, had bought Lobengula's mining concession from Charles Rudd and was launching a pioneer column the next spring to travel into the interior. The new British South Africa Company, which had some time ago been floated on the London Stock Exchange, was going to make a fortune. New shares were being offered to the public.

Arthur had gone to his bank and mortgaged his existing shares, his house in Baker Street and two years' salary. To Arthur's surprise, buying BSAC shares was the easiest part of the exercise, which made him chuckle. Only Beit, Rhodes and Arthur Brigandshaw knew what was going on. His fifty thousand pound investment was not only going to make him rich but it was also going to make him independent. There would no longer be any need to pretend to his father. At last, he would be his own man. Rhodes and

Africa were going to make him his fortune. He was having the time of his life.

THE FACT that Rhodes had been quite well aware of young Brigandshaw sitting with his back to them in the alcove was the one piece of information of which Arthur was unaware. Beit and Rhodes needed investors, it being better to use other people's money than their own. And young Brigandshaw's father was rich. Rhodes had gone from mining magnate to empire builder. He wanted his name in history and to do it he was going to conquer southern Africa with his private army for his Queen. Beit and Rhodes had no intention of paying a dividend anytime soon.

THE RUMOUR REACHED Sir Henry Manderville, Emily's father, and Arthur's father-in-law, during his sojourn in Florence where he had spent two of the most boring years of his life for somewhere better to go. England, now that he'd sold his house and daughter for a lifelong annuity, was too painful. Emily wrote but never once asked him back to England. News of the birth of Harry reached him three months after the event. Having looked at every conceivable piece of Italian art and with his life in the pit of boredom, he had made friends with a reprobate Englishman who was also disinclined to return to the island of his birth. Sir Henry had just turned thirty-seven and should have been in the prime of life. Rich Italian food, too much wine, very little exercise and a permanent balding head, made him look fifty. He had nothing to live for so it didn't matter and the wine bottle was likely to get him into less trouble than Italian women. He had loved a woman once; that had been enough for him.

Gregory Shaw had been in the army, the Indian Army, and Henry suspected something had gone wrong with his career but had never asked the question. Basically, they were both in the same boat so it didn't matter. They were exiles. Exiles from home, country, family and friends. Neither delved into the other's past, glad enough to drink together and talk English. Drinking alone was the bottom of the pit in Henry's opinion of life, and the two almost middle-aged exiles had made friends, each day meeting in the same hotel bar to get drunk. The local ladies had long given them up for lost and left them alone. The Italian barman kept the drinks coming and also left them alone, and when the rumour reached them, they were sitting at the bar drinking the second glass of wine, the bottle between them in a silver ice bucket next to a large bowl of olives. It usually took them a bottle of wine to become talkative so they drank and ate olives in silence, staring separately into the past of their lives where everything they were existed. The knack at the end of the first bottle of wine was to talk trivia and keep to trivia through the third. After that, it didn't matter.

In mutual silence, both of them listened to two Englishmen talking at the table next to the bar, oblivious to anyone else understanding English. Henry had gone quite dark from strolling in the Italian sun, his only exercise. They looked like locals in clothes they had bought in Italy. When the two men left the table, Henry looked at Gregory. "We'd better go," he said.

"I agree, old boy."

Abandoning half-filled glasses, they left the bar with a rare purpose. The barman picked the bottle out of the ice bucket. It was more than half full. For a moment he wondered what he had done wrong. Then he shrugged his shoulders. He had seen a lot of foreigners come and go to Florence.

"Where are we going so fast, old boy?" asked Gregory out on the pavement.

"The shipping company. We can take a boat through the new canal, and down the east coast of Africa to Cape Town. Cape Town isn't England."

"Or India," said Gregory, quickening his pace. "The right to peg fifteen gold claims and a three thousand acre farm."

"No, it was two farms and ten gold claims."

"Major Johnson."

"Major Frank Johnson."

"You're a baronet and I was a captain."

"What if they don't take us on the column?"

"Then we've wasted a passage to Cape Town but relieved our boredom. I'll stake you a passage for one of your farms. Five thousand acre farms."

"I'm sure it was six, old boy. We better get ourselves fit between here and Cape Town."

"We will."

"Oh, and I'll buy my own ticket."

"You will?"

"Yes I will, old boy."

THE ONE PROBLEM worrying Gregory Shaw, as they walked briskly towards the offices of Lloyd-Triestino, was communication. Was it possible that the major recruiting for Rhodes would know that Captain Gregory Shaw had been drummed out of his regiment? Would the nightmare continue? The colonel's words rang as clearly in his ears as they had the first time.

"We British, Captain Shaw, rule the Indians, we do not live with them. Do I make myself clear? There are twenty thousand Englishmen ruling two hundred million Indians because they respect us. We are aloof. We are their superiors. We do not allow them into the mess any more than we allow them into our bedrooms. May I remind you, Captain Shaw, that your family are one of the most respected in Dorset and I will not have a scandal, sir. No, I most definitely will not have a scandal. I want your word that you will never see the woman in question again. Do I have your word, Captain Shaw?"

"Her grandfather is..."

"I don't care if her grandfather was the Maharaja. She is Indian, sir, and you are an Englishman. Do I make myself clear!"

A cold Florentine wind played across the street. He could see her as clearly as if she were walking with him. They had been discreet, but the love was far stronger than the warnings from her father or Colonel Jones and they were found out.

"You will resign your commission, sir. Immediately, do you hear? I want you out of India and I shall write to your father, though I rather think that will be unnecessary. Your conduct is unbecoming of an officer and a gentleman. Worse, you gave me your word. When an Englishman breaks his word, he breaks the cornerstone of our code of conduct. This time I will not ask for your word. I want your signature. Now. You are no longer welcome in the officers' mess. I have given an instruction that no officer in my regiment will speak to you again. You are a disgrace to this regiment and your country. Good day to you, sir."

They were the last words spoken to him by a fellow officer. He signed the paper, resigning his commission. He had left Chittagong by boat the same day; an Italian boat which had brought him to Italy.

Looking silently at Sir Henry Manderville walking next to him, he wondered what the baronet had done to be 'sent to Coventry', to be cut off from his own people, to be exiled. Maybe this Africa with its thousands of acres would give them the chance to talk about their past. He just hoped the new country they were to occupy for Rhodes had never heard of Captain Gregory Shaw, ex-Indian Army.

WHILST HER FATHER and Gregory Shaw were buying the only two passenger tickets on a boat carrying marble to Cape Town, Emily was watching the snow fall on the stone terrace at Hastings Court. The long sash windows through which she stared were little protection against the winter. Once the heavy curtains were drawn, the room would grow warmer. The falling flakes removed all thought from her mind. Soon the light would go. A sharp wind rattled the windows and without thinking, she tightened the central lock without any effort and ice cold air blew on her chapped hand. The rest was silence throughout the house and outside were the stark, leafless trees in front of the terrace and a leaden sky above the battlements of the old house. Apart from the servants and her son, she had not spoken to a soul all week; The Captain and his wife had made a rare visit to London and Arthur. Finally, putting the heavy curtains together, she turned away from the winter cold. Even her son had become a burden to her misery. She might just as well have been dead. Without her son, she would have killed herself. She was quite sure Sebastian was long dead. Even the fire, when she walked to it, failed to warm her body, let alone her soul.

SOME PEOPLE SAID the Reverend Nathanial Brigandshaw was the nicest member of the family and with better connections, he could become a bishop in the Church of England and take his place in the House of Lords. Arthur was known to be devious. James the military member of the family was aloof and superior. The youngest, Sebastian, had been sent away to sea never to be seen again. No one said it to his face but The Captain, with all his money and mansion, was far too pushy and really rather common. His wife, Mathilda, rumoured to be the daughter of a draper from Chester, wherever that was, agreed with everything everyone ever said to her and had never been heard to hold an opinion of her own. No, they said, Nathanial, the second son who had gone into the church, was the pick of the bunch. He listened, he advised, and he was always available night and day in his squalid parish which included part of the London docks. He had been administering the small, impoverished parish for three and a half years as many potential vicars older than himself preferred to remain curates until something better came along. Career paths in the Church were as clearly defined as career paths in the army. Good regiments and well-to-do parishes were the way to military and ecclesiastical promotion. The chances were that Nathanial, two years younger than Arthur, would end up a saint rather than a bishop. His was the way of all good men.

His wife was so glad. She had found herself a husband, and she put up with the parish, yet Nat gave away to the poor the money he sometimes received from his father.

. . .

BESS HEARD the loud knock on the front door and put down her sewing. Placing the guard in front of the coal fire, she went down the narrow stairs to the small hall that made enough room for a hat and an umbrella stand. The grandfather clock began striking eleven o'clock the same time the brass door knocker was again struck with authority. 'The police again at this time of night,' thought Bess, hurrying down the wooden stairs, sliding her hand down the polished banister to prevent herself going down head first in such a hurry. The peelers often consulted the vicar but never before, to her knowledge, at eleven o'clock at night.

Drawing the top and bottom bolts having first lit the gas lamp in the hall to see what she was doing, Bess opened the front door of what was nicely called the vicarage, there being identical doors up and down the long street of attached houses, all narrow and four storeys high. The lamplight showed her a tall man with broad shoulders wearing a hat made of grey leather of a style Bess had never seen before. The smiling man was wearing a long coat of the same leather which came down to the bottom of his boots and she noticed they were covered in mud. The long hair down to the shoulders and full beard disguised the man's features. The man stood on the top of the steps that led from the road and kept on smiling, the blue eyes watching her with great amusement. With great aplomb, the strange-looking man swept off the wide-brimmed hat and made her an overly ridiculous bow.

"Is this the residence of Reverend Nathanial Brigandshaw?"

"It is, but the vicar is out. Maybe you could call...?"

"I'll wait."

"You can't."

"And why ever not... Bess?"

"You know my name?"

"Of course. Have I changed that much?" He knew perfectly well that he had. "I'm your brother-in-law, Bess."

"You can't be."

"I can be. Now, may I come in?"

With the front door closed, Sebastian threw his heavy coat over the top of the hat stand. A hook on the wall took his hat. Slowly he followed his sister-in-law up the narrow stairs, to the cosy room with the coal fire burning. The girl seemed struck dumb and picked up her sewing. With Seb left standing, they listened to the clocks in the house while they waited for the vicar to return.

Nathanial was tired, very tired when he reached the steps leading up to his front door. He told himself some people were incapable of helping themselves with an attitude of 'woe is me' in their self-induced poverty. It was always somebody else's fault, the reason for their plight. They never thought of blaming themselves. Their greatest happiness was to find themselves reliant on others. The couple he had just left had never tried to do a day's work, and to listen to them, which is what they enjoyed most, the poor were a creation of the rich. Only the poor were right in their misery. He was quite sure the shilling he had just given them would have now been converted into gin. The woman was no more sick than dying. The vicar, if he came, was good for a shilling. Nat sighed to himself. 'God made man in strange ways.'

It had begun to snow again, the flakes quickly turning into a dark sludge. The streetlight behind him spluttered from a surge of gas as he put a foot on the first step up to the door. All he wanted to do was get into bed and go to sleep.

The first thing confronting him when Bess opened the door was a long coat made from grey leather he had never seen before. He stood looking at the coat as his wife closed the door. A pattern of what looked like wrinkles ran the length of the coat. On the hook where he normally placed his own hat was a strange headgear with a wider rim than Nat had ever seen before and made of the same grey leather.

"Your brother is upstairs," was all she said.

There was no room for his own coat so he left it on and followed his wife upstairs. Standing with his back to the fire was an unknown man well over six feet tall who began speaking to him like an old friend.

"Sorry about the late hour, Nat, but I need your help. I sail for Africa again in two days' time and the tide waits for no man... Glory be, have I really changed that much? Now look, as far as I see it Father wanted me out of the way while Arthur married Emily. There was no other motive. Hastings Court was a bonus."

"How do you know all this?"

"Captain Doyle. I'm one of his customers. I also know that Harry is mine and not Arthur's. You all must be aware of that?"

"Seb, be careful. You don't know what you're saying."

"But I can count, which is more than you can. Em and I were lovers."

"What do you want of me?"

"Nat, that's not very friendly for a priest. What I want is the woman who should be my wife and my son."

"She's married to Arthur. You can't break God's words. They were married before God. 'In the name of the Lord, I pronounce you man and wife.' You can't change that, Sebastian."

"Sit down, Nat, you look exhausted."

"I am. Look, I'm sorry. The last person I expected to find in front of my fire tonight was you. I've prayed for you, Seb."

"I'm glad because quite often I needed the help."

"What have you been doing?"

"Hunting elephant. Just the old and discarded. Even old elephants got thrown out by their relatives."

"Yes of course." Nat had no idea what his brother was talking about.

"Bess, ask the maid to bring some tea, please?"

"She's sound asleep. I'll go while you talk. The prodigal son returns," she said over her shoulder.

"Without the fatted calf," finished Seb. "You got any whisky, brother Nat?"

"Yes I have, matter of fact."

"Good. Cancel the tea, Bess. Now, are Mother and Father back home at Hastings Court?"

"No, they return tomorrow afternoon. You want to see them?"

"Not really."

"You're going to abduct Emily?"

"Yes, I am. But first a whisky with my brother. I had to be sure where the parents were tonight. Have you been to Hastings Court?"

"Of course. It's Father's home now. Well, Arthur's really."

"But he doesn't stay there too much? Arthur, I mean."

"You seem to know everything. What's that coat downstairs made out of?" Nat was trying to change the subject.

"Elephant hide."

"How did you come by it?"

"Well, first I shot the elephant."

"You'd better start at the beginning. I rather think it's a long story. Funny, I'm not tired anymore."

SEBASTIAN LEFT at one o'clock in the morning with his brother's blessing. There were things about Arthur that Nat had never heard. Their elder brother was a sadist with a taste for perversion, something first heard of by Seb in Cape Town. Once Seb was making Captain Doyle money, their relationship had gone into reverse. The most profitable high value, low weight cargo for the *Indian Queen* was ivory, and this was known to Doyle and his crew who shared in the profit. From being the disgraced youngest son of The Captain, he, with Tinus, was a source of wealth. Another five-tonne shipment of ivory would see the senior hands going ashore for the rest of their lives with enough money to buy a small business. There were many ships plying the route to India, some with captains equally well known to the Bombay ivory carvers. From Captain Doyle to the second mate, they all wanted to curry favour with the men who brought them the ivory. Their talk in the taverns of Cape Town to Seb was mostly about Arthur. Even the crew knew The Captain's eldest son was a parasite. When he found out the date of Harry's birth, the day The Captain had marked by giving the crews of Colonial Shipping a bonus, he knew he had to go home.

Leaving Tinus and Tatenda in Cape Town to wait for him, he had taken the fastest boat back to England, arriving ten days before the late-night confrontation with Nat. By the time Seb walked quickly to the docks and his waiting coach, any shadow of doubt about his brother's behaviour had vanished. The vicar, his own brother, knew a lot more than he was prepared to say and even as Seb walked fast he knew his brother was going out to warn their mother and father. He doubted if he would go to warn Arthur as he doubted if Arthur could give a damn.

The first call was to borrow an extension ladder from the ostler and then with two fresh horses they began the dash down south to Hastings Court. The ladder was strapped on top of the coach. By the time his mother had fuddled around and got in his father's way, it would be near to dawn.

An hour before dawn Seb was racing across Epsom Downs.

EMILY WOKE to a thud on her bedroom window followed by the sound of breaking glass and the squeaking of the sash window moving on its cords. A draft of bitterly cold air came into the room.

"Emily," called a voice, "have I got the right bedroom? Em, are you in there? It's dark and I can't see. Light the gaslight for heaven's sake before I break my neck. And hurry. Hell, it's cold in this country."

The light flared, and the bedroom came into perspective and Emily screamed. Seb moved across the room quickly.

"Quiet or you will wake the servants. Put on warm clothes and get Harry from the nursery." The girl's face was pressed against his chest while he stroked her hair to calm her down. "We are going back down the ladder before anyone can do anything to stop us. By tomorrow night we'll be out of the country. Em, you do want to come with me?"

THE CAPTAIN, knowing his business, went to the docks first to block his youngest son from leaving the country. There were only three ships bound for Africa within the week and their captains were warned of the consequences of sailing with an abducted wife. The description of a tall, bearded man with a young woman and young son was more than enough. Leaving his hysterical wife in their suite at the Savoy Hotel overlooking the Thames River, The Captain took a fresh horse and rode for Hastings Court. It was still dark when he left the stables at the Savoy. He was in a cold rage.

BACK IN HIS house feeling more like Judas than Nathanial, Nat was unable to sleep. He had never before seen a man totally lose his temper. For a moment in the hotel suite, The Captain was insane and Nat had moved quickly between his mother and father. The cold fury that followed the rage was even more frightening. "I will not have a son of mine gainsay me!"

AT DAWN, Nat's conscience and the remains of the bottle of whisky got the better of him. He walked quickly in the cold light of dawn to the local inn and took a cab to his elder brother's house in Baker Street. Never before had he called at the house. The address had been given to him by his father with the instructions to tell Arthur. Asking the cabbie to wait outside, Nat walked up the steps similar to his own and knocked on his brother's front door. The woman who answered was in a dressing gown that fell open as she shut the door on the cold morning showing the vicar two large naked breasts.

"Well, what can I do for you, luvvy?" said the woman he had first imagined was the maid.

"My brother, Arthur Brigandshaw, is he at home?"

"Art's asleep in bed."

It was obvious the woman was more than a servant to 'Art', a derivative Nat had never before associated with his brother.

"Could you call him down? It's urgent."

"You want me to wake him up? Don't be daft. He only went to bed an hour ago."

"Show me his room."

"Go up them stairs and you'll hear him snoring. Always snores when he's drunk. Rather you than me waking him up still drunk."

"I am his brother."

"So you said but be careful. You want a cup of tea?"

"No thank you."

· · ·

THE LADDER WAS STILL UP against the window when The Captain arrived at the front door. The butler opened it and stood back silently. None of the other servants were to be seen. Silence, empty silence wrapped the old house.

"Where is my grandson?" asked The Captain too quietly. The butler chose to keep his mouth shut. "Did you hear me?" The butler had served in better circumstances and was unable to keep the contempt out of his eyes. With the last of the Mandervilles out of the house, he intended handing in his notice. Good service required good manners in return. "You're fired."

"Thank you, sir," said the butler allowing himself the glimmer of a smile.

"And don't smirk."

"Shall I leave straight away?"

"Get out of my sight."

"Thank you, sir."

"Have they both gone?"

"I believe so, sir."

"Why didn't anyone stop them?"

"They went out through the window rather quickly." This time he allowed a smile to spread over his entire face.

"You're smirking again."

"Thank you, sir."

Frustrated, The Captain turned tail and once in the forecourt he remounted his horse without any idea of which way to ride. Making up his mind he rode the exhausted horse to his own stable and took a fresh horse. In the village, he asked if a coach with his daughter-in-law had passed their way. The villagers gave him dumb looks. They all knew. In deeper fury, the once popular ship's captain realised he was hated, and it was all the fault of his youngest son. Ever since Sebastian had been sent to the colonies, the people had turned their backs. Nothing was ever said. The disapproval was written on their faces.

BY THE TIME The Captain reached his son's townhouse in Baker Street, Arthur Brigandshaw had sobered up and sent the lady home to her mother. It was a Sunday and the office of Colonial Shipping was closed. Subduing the feeling of relief and delight, Arthur was full of righteous indignation and went to the local police station to lay a charge against his brother for abduction. The process was painfully slow and his hangover was screaming for a drink.

The Captain had sent horsemen to all the ports in southern England with letters to the Port Captains. The brat could hide in England but in the end, the police would find them. The Captain's wife was packed off back to Hastings Court. To The Captain, Emily mattered little. It was her son, his grandson, the heir to all his wealth and Hastings Court, with the blood of ancient knights and aristocrats pumping through his veins, the heir that would be recognised for all time as a gentleman, that was what hurt him to the quick. The boy was the reason for everything The Captain had ever done in his life. If they would not let *him* become a gentleman, they would never gainsay his grandson, Harry Manderville-Brigandshaw.

AFTER RECOVERING from the shock of recognising Seb's voice and seeing a stranger coming through her bedroom window, Emily turned up the gaslight, recovered her wits and went straight down the long, old corridor with the Manderville family portraits on the walls to the nursery and her son. The young nurse was asleep in the bed next to the child's cot, and when the gaslight at the door was turned up, the girl awoke.

"I'm going away, Alison, and taking Harry with me. Would you care to come with us?"

"Where are you going?"

"At this moment I have no idea but I won't be back. If you don't come, I'm afraid you won't have a job and Harry is very fond of you. We have to go back to my bedroom as I don't wish to wake the servants."

"How are we getting out of your bedroom, ma'am?"

"Down a ladder to be exact. Pack his warm clothes and some for yourself and we'll be away before anyone else is awake."

Within half an hour of Seb's breaking into Hastings Court, the nurse was the first to go down the ladder carrying a small case. She dropped into the flowerbed and looked up at the second-floor window where the man was coming down with the boy clinging to his back, Harry's arms around the man's throat. Acting on the instinct of the trouble she would be in with the boy disappearing from her care, she thought it better to abscond. The man handed her the child and went back up for the blankets and the second case. It was freezing cold in the grounds and she wanted to stamp her feet to make them warm. She could neither see horse nor coach and when they were all together on the ground, they walked away through the elm trees, across the well-kept lawns. Five minutes later the nurse saw a coach and horses standing next to the unoccupied gatehouse. Behind them, there was no sign of life at Hastings Court, the only light coming from the old house the one they had left on in the bedroom. The young girl could not make up her mind whether she was excited or terrified. The coachman cracked his whip and a journey she had never imagined began. To her surprise when they passed through the village as the day was dawning, they took the Guildford Road to the west rather than the road to London. Harry was asleep again on her lap. Opposite, the bearded stranger and her mistress were in deep conversation.

"We are going out of Bristol, Em. Father would know to block the ships out of London. We sail out of Avonmouth on the evening tide."

"Where are we going?"

"As far away from my father and brother as possible. Africa."

"They'll find us in the colonies."

"Not where we are going. It's over, Em."

"It's never over."

Only then did the nurse understand. The stranger had come to collect his son. Even if The Captain and Arthur Brigandshaw could not count, Cousin Maud was not so stupid. "The boy belongs to young Sebastian. You can count on that," she had told the new housekeeper as she left Hastings Court to live off the annuity settled on her by Sir Henry Manderville. "The girl belonged to Sebastian from when she was five years old, not that dreadful Arthur."

ALISON FORD HAD GONE into service as there was nothing else she could do, her parents dead and her brother gone to sea. Six years older than Emily, she had been to school up to the age of fifteen. When her father died without leaving her mother any money, she had taken a job as a child nurse in a house with eleven children, the three youngest each with a nurse to keep them out of trouble while their parents did more important things than looking after their children. Young Harry was the third child for whom Alison was a surrogate mother. Children were brought up in the nursery whatever Emily tried to change. In the nursery and as far away from the grown-ups as possible. When they were fifteen going on sixteen, the father had a look at the son to see if he had bred anything worthwhile. Some of the fathers took more care of their horses than their children. The mothers fussed around the girls of the same age trying to marry them off as well as possible and as soon as they could. It was the way it was done in the English upper classes and every time she had had to leave the child in her care, it broke Alison's heart. At five, the children were placed under a governess for their training in manners and the nurse was asked to look for a new position.

Through the day, the coach raced through the English countryside changing horses twice on the way. If they missed the tide, the venture would come to an ignominious end and with the young man Alison suspected of being The Captain's younger son sent to prison or forced to leave England alone forever. When Harry woke and found himself in a pounding coach, he was delighted and tried to pull down the window and climb out of the racing coach. A strong male hand pulled the boy back by the scruff of the neck. With the light in the sky well gone, they drove through Bristol and along the River Avon to the Port of Avonmouth. The bearded man knew exactly where he was going and within minutes of finding their ship, they went on board. It was obvious to Alison that the bearded man had bought the captain of the ship before they arrived. They seemed to know each other as friends. Papers and tickets were ignored.

Alison was put in a small cabin on her own with Harry and food sent down to both of them. An hour later she felt the sails crack, and the ship got underway. Trusting in God and Emily Manderville-Brigandshaw, Alison put Harry down to sleep. For a while, lying in her bunk, she felt the movement of the wooden ship increase as they moved out to sea, the bunk tilting to the steady pull of the sails. Then she slept right through the night alongside her ward. Her dreams were full of clear blue skies and fluffy white clouds, none of which she remembered when she woke with a winter's sun shining on her face through the porthole. Outside, there was no sign of land. She answered the knock on her cabin door and Emily came in with a tray of tea and hot milk for Harry.

To Alison's surprise, Emily poured the tea and sat down on Alison's bunk. Harry was still fast asleep from the journey.

"I think I owe you a full explanation," said Emily.

"It's young Sebastian, isn't it?"

"Yes."

"And he's Harry's father, isn't he?"

"Yes. How did you know?"

"Your Cousin Maud told the new housekeeper."

"I see."

"So there's nothing to explain. Where is Mister Sebastian now?"

"Talking to Captain Doyle. If the wind stays fair, Captain Doyle says we will be in Cape Town the week after Christmas. It's summer in Cape Town, which will be nice."

"Won't they look for us there?"

"Maybe. The day we reach Cape Town we start the journey north by train. My husband won't give a damn. Only The Captain. Well, we shall see.

Central southern Africa is large and mostly virgin land. That's where Seb says we are going to get away from them all."

THE *INDIAN QUEEN* was under full sail thirty miles out of the Bristol Channel having originally brought Seb to the Port of London. Then she had sailed with a full cargo a week later and rounded the south of England to wait for Seb at Avonmouth.

"Captain," said Seb, "if my father finds out, you'll lose your job along with the officers and crew. Why did you all help me?"

"Some things are right and some things are wrong," said Captain Doyle standing on his bridge. "Just 'cause The Captain employs us doesn't say he's right in everything. Loyalty I give 'im. Honesty I give 'im. But as captain of this ship I 'ave the right to say what sails on her. Those are The Captain's rules. When he made them he wasn't thinking of you. We've talked, me and the officers. If he takes away our ship, we'll buy our own thanks to your ivory. My guess is The Captain will turn a blind eye to you sailing on this voyage. Funny how people never want to throw away a good profit. It's not the ship what makes the money, it's an honest crew. Money will speak louder than The Captain's temper. I know 'im. Sailed with 'im. If he gets his hands on you, he'd be very rough but he won't harm me and the crew. Money, Mr Brigandshaw. The only thing that matters in the end. The best things in life may be free but the second best is bloody expensive, if you'd pardon my words. The Captain won't piss in 'is own rice bowl, if you'll excuse my words again. You go up north and bring back some more ivory. By then this will all 'ave blown away in the wind. Remember the rice bowl. Nobody ever pisses on their own money unless they are stupid. And The Captain ain't stupid. Not by a long way. One day he'll see the matter more clearly. That's my opinion. Now, if you'll excuse me, Mr Brigandshaw, I have a ship to sail."

BOOK 2 – THE OCCUPATION

1

SEPTEMBER 1890

From the vantage point of the kopje, Trooper Gregory Shaw watched the ceremony down below in the plain as the Union Jack rose slowly to the top of the newly constructed masthead, the officers of the Pioneer Column rigidly saluting the flag. With the dismissal of the flag-raising party, Gregory Shaw and Henry Manderville were free to occupy their reward of land or search for gold.

Rhodes's Pioneer Column had cut a road from British South Africa to the high ground of the interior; six months of work, tension and expected attack that had never materialised. Below the kopje Fort Salisbury was taking shape, a town being laid out by the surveyors with roads wide enough for an ox wagon to turn. British Africa had taken a long stride forward. Looking further than the ceremony now dispersing, Gregory looked for signs of native occupation. The land he searched was fallow, long grass to the height of a man's waist, interspersed with flat-topped trees whose canopies had spread under the weight of the sun. The sky and clouds, fluffy white and powder blue, were close to the earth the further he looked towards the heat-shimmered horizon. There were no huts or villages, nothing but herds of animals. Far away to his left, the vultures circled the kill.

Turning to the hunter Frederick Selous, who had guided the column, Gregory asked the question that had been on his mind all the months they had been cutting the road through the mopane and msasa trees.

"Where are the people? The land is bush, well watered, animals everywhere, but where are the people?"

"Africa," said Selous, "looks easier than it is. The animals have adapted to the droughts better than man. Then there was Mzilikazi and Lobengula, Zulu impis raiding the cattle and grain and killing what they were unable to carry away with them. There are people but they hide. Now they are hiding from us. Africa is cruel, Mr Shaw. I wish you all the best of British luck."

"That kind of luck I'd rather not have wished upon me," said Henry Manderville when the hunter was out of earshot. "But all this has got to be better than the relics of Rome and the Medici. Now we go and buy us a pick and shovel and go and find us that pot of gold. When does it rain in this country? Nothing since we started the road. Nothing."

THAT EVENING, having handed in their uniforms, Henry Manderville and Gregory Shaw left Fort Salisbury as prospectors. Behind each of their horses, on long reins, followed the packhorses. All the animals were salted, immune to the tsetse fly that killed most of the domesticated ones. They were heading northwest through the bush following a course set by the sinking sun. Henry had shot a small buck which hung over the back of Gregory's packhorse. There were pools of water among the rock outcrops that made up part of the riverbed. The river had stopped flowing months before and the heavy sand between the rocks had been trampled by animals. Far behind them, the campfires of Fort Salisbury were no longer visible and for the first time since leaving Italy, they were alone. From the largest pool, a twelve-foot crocodile watched them malevolently, the stone green eyes reflecting the fiery red of the setting sun. Carefully, Henry chose a campsite on high ground, overlooking the pools. They gathered wood for the nightly fire.

With the sky blood-red behind them, Gregory gutted the small buck and skinned it like a rabbit, cutting off the feet and head. With the first coals, they roasted the heart, liver and kidneys as the sun came down and the insects screeched in the long grass. From further downriver and from a larger pool, a hippopotamus grunted with pleasure before climbing out of the pool in search of grazing. The warm night air quickly dried the animal's hide. Then the night belonged to the frogs calling for mates in a diligent cacophony.

Having fed, the two men lit their pipes and smoked for a while in silence. They recognised the animal calls from the night and were content. The fire flickered comfortably in front of them some ten feet from their outstretched legs. The horses were tethered within the firelight. Both men had their army-issue haversacks at their backs. There were no mosquitoes, a blessing to both of them.

Gregory Shaw was the first to break the companionable silence.

"Henry, old boy. Do you think we English are a bit potty?"

"What makes you say that?"

"Well, here we are in the middle of nowhere looking for gold we don't need."

"It's the hunt for the gold that counts, Gregory. Not the gold."

"The excitement, you mean?"

"Of course. We were both bored stiff in Italy. A man has to do something. Probably why we ended up with an empire. That and England's dreadful climate. I might even stay in this country. Stake out the allotted farm. They say the thing to grow is native tobacco and ship it back to England. Even steal a bit of seed from the Americans and give those Virginians a run for their money."

"So you don't think we're potty, old boy?"

"Probably not."

Sir Henry Manderville woke in the middle of the night. It was pitch black, and the frogs were silent. The fire had burnt down and he got up to put on more wood, the crush of the new branches throwing sparks up into the night. Gregory was asleep, curled around his service revolver, the new firelight reflecting from the gunmetal. The night air was pleasantly cool and still free of mosquitoes. He smiled to himself. He was thirty-eight years old and fitter than at any other time in his life.

In Cape Town, it had quickly become clear that Major Johnson wanted troopers to cut his road through the bush, there being officers aplenty. Happily, Gregory had buried his captaincy in the past and Henry had not mentioned his title. They were two fit men looking for a challenge and sufficiently educated to occupy the new territory. Soldiers for six months and pioneers for the rest of their lives. Rhodes wanted strong men to hold the occupation of his new country between the Limpopo and the Zambezi rivers, men who would take up roots in the new, virgin soil that stretched in every direction.

Henry sat still, wide awake, and pondered the absurdity of his situation, all the time strangely content. An owl hooted behind the river and was answered by its mate. For a while, Henry listened to their conversation and then they were silent. The expectancy was palpable all around him. Had his ancestor felt the same when he had helped William the Conqueror to subdue the Saxons and conquer the land of the Britons? Was man ever satisfied in staying put? The question made him smile at the generations of Mandervilles at Hastings Court, the generations to follow. Then he thought of Emily by now content with Brigandshaw, absorbed in her son and probably pregnant again. The old house needed the cry of children. Maybe here he would make his second home and bring up a second family in a new country. Then he chuckled inwardly at the absurdity. What kind of Englishman would live in the middle of the African bush, far from friends and neighbours? Now there was a real problem with both of them, he and Gregory, if they were serious about Africa.

Satisfied with the fire, he lay back against his haversack and was quickly asleep. Soon afterwards the moon rose and showed the clouds in the heavens in shades of black and white, the moonlight pale and colourless. The moon struck the sleeping men through the trees, but neither of them woke and the owls resumed their conversation. A soft wind came up and rustled the last dry leaves and the msasa trees. Just before dawn, the hippo got back into its pool. Slowly a pale light came in the east and the birds began to sing.

Gregory was the first to wake in the new dawn and hung a can of water over the embers of the fire, throwing in a handful of ground coffee. Henry stirred, his dream broken by the smell.

"Hell, it's good to be alive, old boy," said Gregory Shaw, and Henry smiled to himself. On an average day, Gregory said 'old boy' more than thirty times. Henry had counted them. Strangely, he rather liked being an 'old boy'.

"Yes," he replied, "it is rather nice to be alive. Have the ants eaten the rest of our venison?"

"I hung the carcass in a tree."

"I think we're learning."

"I rather think we are... You any idea what gold-bearing rock looks like?"

"No idea at all."

"Then how do we find the stuff, old boy?"

"Find a native who knows what it looks like. This was the kingdom of Monomotapa. They traded gold with the Portuguese."

As the day progressed the clouds built up in the west, a prelude to the rains.

THE LAST PLACE Alison Ford expected to find herself was standing on a rock high on the escarpment overlooking the valley of the Zambezi River in the company of two white hunters, one the size of a mountain, a two-year-old boy, and a woman who had run away from her husband. And she was happier than she had ever been in her life before. Down below, what Tinus had told her was bushfire haze obscured any site of the river that had meandered over the millennia and cut the deep valley now teeming with game. The young black boy who spoke good English had gone off to make contact with the remnants of the local tribes still hiding away from Lobengula.

She had been in Africa seven months and taken the train from Cape Town to Kimberley the day after the *Indian Queen* docked in Cape Town harbour. She had first met Tinus Oosthuizen and the black boy Tatenda on the train. In Kimberley, they had purchased two ox wagons, sixteen oxen, supplies for a year and, without a pause, headed out into the bush and out of reach of reprisal. As the weeks turned into months, they made their way into the interior, calling first at Gu-Bulawayo to ask the king of the Matabele for permission to hunt, and Harry became the child of his parents. By the end of the third month on the trail, Tinus had taught her how to fire a shotgun without bruising her shoulder and she was as brown as a berry, the soft brown hair had been bleached by the sun and her body was taut from the constant exercise. For weeks on end their party was alone in the bush, the men hunting for the old bull elephants among the great herds, the tusks cut from the dead animals and left on the ground overnight for the ants to clean before loading on top of the wagons.

BY THE END OF SEPTEMBER, when Henry Manderville and Gregory Shaw were camped one hundred and twenty-three miles to the southeast, the clouds had built up and Alison heard the first rumblings of thunder. It was then too that Tatenda returned to camp with the news Tinus Oosthuizen had searched for even before Sebastian had joined the hunt. The local tribesmen had seen the spore of the great bull elephant, the elephant tusks so big he was forced to rest them on the ground when his old body made him stop for rest.

TINUS HAD LISTENED to Tatenda's story of the rogue bull elephant, far from its herd. It had ripped through the storage silos, tearing down the rickety bush timber legs that held up the covered platforms from the ground to keep the rats and mice away from the maize. The cobs were scattered among the bent, brown stalks of the old maize stands, cobs trampled in the dust and three of the pole and dagga huts were squashed in its rage. One small girl had been trampled to death, and half the food that would feed the people until the rains grew the next crop had been eaten or destroyed.

"Did he rest his tusks on the ground?"

"The people ran away, baas. Not look. Very frightened. The marks of feet in dust bigger than I see."

"Where did the elephant go?"

"To big river," said Tatenda, pointing down into the valley.

SEBASTIAN ARGUED the heat and mosquitoes in the valley were too dangerous for the women and children once the rains broke.

"Then I will hunt alone," said Tinus. "I have seen him once, from a distance. He is old now and needs my help. You see, Sebastian, a man is brave when he is alone but he can never be brave for his family. To die is to die but to be left alone when you have found your family is worse than death. Our own deaths we don't know about. It is the death of others we feel. Make a camp up here and I will come back from the valley when I have killed him. When the rains break, some of the herds will migrate this way and you can have your picking. Make the best of it. This will be our last hunt."

"Why?"

"Rhodes. He wants everything. The minerals, the land and the elephants. We Boers know you British. With you British, there are always rules and all of them stop a man from being free to do what he wants."

"Then next time we hunt north of the Zambezi."

"Rhodes will go north of the river until he fills the vacuum between the Belgians to the far north and the Portuguese to the east and west."

"ARE the mosquitoes any bigger down there?" Emily asked later. "Won't there be some comfort from the cool water of the river? How am I going to explain to Alison that the apple of her eye is off alone chasing an elephant bigger than a house? Now if we all go down together we can have a nice time and come back all together with the trophy that would excite the whole wide world. Hunting elephant is better in pairs, you have both said a dozen times. Are we women so weak we can't get a little hot and bothered every now and again? I think the best thing is to start our journey down there first thing in the morning before all this evening thunder turns to rain. If we hurry, I am sure we can reach the river and build ourselves little grass huts before the rains break. Now, won't that be nice? Little grass huts on the bank of a very nice river. I'm going to tell Harry. He'll be very excited."

Six thousand miles away at Hastings Court, Mathilda Brigandshaw, mother of Sebastian, was in one of her 'states'. Her husband, The Captain, had built up a cold rage and none of her timid words of protest had had any effect. After seven months of constant badgering, the case against her youngest son had been heard in the Bow Street Magistrates' Court and Sebastian was now a criminal, wanted anywhere in the empire for abducting his brother's wife and kidnapping his brother's son. When found, the penalty was death and there would be nothing the family could do to change the court's decision. After the months of fruitless search, her husband had seen fit to use the courts to bring down his rage on his own son for frustrating his ambition. Mathilda was well aware The Captain did not give a jot about Emily. All he wanted was Harry, the future master of Hastings Court, his grandson dressed up as a Manderville.

When she had first met The Captain, he was a common seaman sailing out of the Port of Liverpool for sixteen shillings a month, coming back a year later after each voyage with less than five pounds in his pocket.

In those early young days they called her Tilda, and many said she was the prettiest girl in Chester, some even went as far as the whole of the Wirral of Cheshire, but all of them said she could have done ten times better than the roving seaman who told strange tales and talked of great wealth that had no reflection in his seaman's clothes. They called him a big mouth but within three voyages he came back to Liverpool as coxswain of the ship, appointed halfway through the voyage when the original coxswain died of yellow fever. It was at the end of that voyage they were married. She had been dominated by her father and was now dominated by her husband. She was to have his children, look after his small house and behave herself while he took the steps to move them out of poverty. Never once had she looked at another man during the long months alone for fear of reprisal. He had learnt the word 'gainsay' at an early age. As the years went by, she forgot who she was and did as he told her, and the big mouth proved his worth and the small house grew to a mansion. The one thing she had never understood was the loyalty of his crews, but then she had never been to sea and seen the bond of men in danger and the need for leadership to survive.

She had tried to help Emily when they came to Hastings Court after the wedding but had failed. The young extrovert who had cantered over the county with Sebastian had withdrawn into her shell, and even when the boy was born Emily had left most of the bringing up to the nurse, brooding alone in her room or walking for hours in the woods. The light had gone out of her eyes. Mathilda never once heard her laugh and Harry had reached out for affection from Alison Ford. Emily's father had left for Italy the day after the wedding in the old church. Some letters came for Emily but after the first, they were left on the silver tray in the hall unopened. First, she put it down to Arthur spending his weeks and more often his weekends in London, but even before Harry was born she recognised a cold indifference. They were pawns in two other people's game of chess, strangers in a marriage of their fathers' convenience. The only person Mathilda could see who was happy with the arrangement was her husband. He was the squire, the real master of Hastings Court, and his heir, young Harry, was the apple of his eye because young Harry was going to be recognised by the county as a gentleman.

"Five hundred pounds," he was raging again. "I'll offer anyone five hundred pounds who finds that boy and brings him back to his ancestral home. Good God, woman, there have been Mandervilles on this estate since the time of the Conqueror. That brat can't take that away."

"If they find Harry they will find Sebastian," she said miserably.

"And bring him to justice."

"Hang him, Captain! You're talking about our youngest son!"

"He kidnapped my grandson, for God's sake. And his mother."

"I rather think she went willingly. They were inseparable since childhood."

"She consented to marry Arthur."

"Maybe. She loved her father. Did what he said. Have you ever looked at the calendar?"

"What do you mean?" snapped The Captain as he stopped pacing the front terrace. The sun was throwing the shadows of the old trees from far away. "What do you mean by that?"

"I think our grandson was born a little too early to have anything to do with Arthur. Anyway, she's not his type. He likes sluts."

"What do you mean, sluts?"

"Whores. The woman he keeps in that house in London. I think that Sebastian kidnapped his own son and that will make a difference in a court of law. Leave well alone."

"What about my grandson?"

"He'll be living his life without your help and maybe his mother is smiling again."

"Five hundred pounds'll bring 'em back. Brass, that's what people understand. Someone must know where they are and this time I have the law on my side. Five hundred pounds is a lot of money. Five hundred pounds will find them."

"Don't you see what you're doing?"

"Of course I do. I want my grandson back in Hastings Court."

THE REVEREND NATHANIAL BRIGANDSHAW saw the reward posted on a billboard in the docks, the youthful face of Sebastian grinning at his fate.

"It is the enemy within us that destroys. A family, a nation is the same, Bess," he told his wife. "We Brigandshaws are destroying ourselves as we are trying to be what we are not. Mother was a scullery maid and father a common seaman, for God's sake. Now look at what we are trying to be. Why did I go to Arthur that morning?"

"Because you thought it was right."

"We are too quick to impose our judgement. Why should I be right? The judge. The arbiter of good. Now mother tells me the boy's more likely Seb's. Why couldn't I mind my own business? If he hangs, I will have helped to cast the rope. If I had not told Arthur Seb was here, it could have been any maniac running off with Emily and the child. Good God, Bess, no one knew Seb was in the country until I told them. And I do it every day. Every day I am telling people what to do because I think, me, Nat Brigandshaw, the holy reverend, that it is good for them. What do I really know about their lives except I would not like to live the same way? I tell all those poor souls what *I* want. What would be good for me. Why do we interfere, Bess?"

"Because we want to help," answered his wife.

"But do we help?"

"I don't know."

ARTHUR BRIGANDSHAW SAW the reward in the *Times* which ruined a generous day. The last thing Arthur wanted was Emily back in Hastings Court. Paying for another man's bastard was not on Arthur's itinerary, and the status quo was much to his satisfaction. When the latest of his live-in housekeepers demanded he make her an honest woman, he could honestly say he would be delighted but the law would have something else to say. He told himself he would happily have his cake and eat it too. It was the kind of situation that appealed to Arthur.

The day before, news of the Jack being raised in southern Africa had sent the shares in the British South Africa Company up twenty-two shillings; more than Arthur's purchase price but, he was not going to sell. Soon the thousands of prospectors who were combing the countryside would strike it rich and the flow of royalties to the BSAC would send the price of their shares to the sky. Why, Arthur told himself, letting greed get the better of him, last week's newspaper had said there was more gold in the country than in the whole of the Transvaal. Everyone knew the gold on the Witwatersrand was more than anything they found in California. If he sold his shares and paid off his debts, he calculated he would have twenty thousand and some pounds in his pocket. But if he waited for the gold to flow out of the earth, he would become a millionaire, a man richer than his father, and without the impediments of his father's birth. Rich, free of his wife and father, unable to marry, the combination for Arthur was idyllic. He could have as many mistresses as he wanted without the slightest chance of a problem.

Ignoring his father's request to return to Hastings Court, Arthur took the train to Dover. Paris in the autumn was as perfect as Paris in the spring. Even with a house and twenty thousand pounds he was a rich man. The banks would not worry him. Their loans were now covered well above the hilt. Mentally he wished his young brother well. The man and small boy were out of the country. It was obvious. If only his father would let the matter rest. He was master of Hastings Court, wasn't that enough? How much did one's vanity require to quench its thirst?

ALISON FORD WAS the first to discard her corset, the stay that strapped in her stomach. The temperature in the valley had risen to a hundred and ten degrees in the shade and the rains refused to break. Each afternoon the clouds built up ominously and twice there were streaks of lightning but not one drop of rain. Four rondavels, pole and mud huts, had been built under a spreading acacia tree that rose a hundred feet above the roughly thatched roofs, the roots of the great thorn tree tapping the living waters of the Zambezi River. Across from their camp, a long island stood out in midstream, rich in tangled, green undergrowth with ilala palms stretching out of the thickets to reach for the sky. On the near shore of the island, crocodiles sunned themselves and when their blood temperature rose too high, they slid into the water and floated with the stream, nose and eyes bulging.

By the time the first big drops of rain splashed the dark surface of the flowing river, Alison had discarded the top stay made from strips of whalebone and elastic a quarter-inch thick, and Emily had followed suit. The temperature had risen another five degrees Fahrenheit and convention had been sacrificed to the heat. The men still wore breeches and shirts with long sleeves, the breeches held up with thick braces that Tinus used to hook his thumbs into when he was standing looking out at the great river and the herds of animals forced near the water by the six-month drought. All the waterholes away from the big river had dried up along with the watercourses. Everything, man and beast, was waiting for the rain and tempers flared as the heat pressed down. Even the girls in print frocks that came to the ground and showed the shape of their bodies underneath in the bright sunlight, were too hot to worry about the breach of decorum. English ladies of good breeding had never before lived in the valley of heat. During the day, it had become too hot to talk or complain, and even Harry sat quietly in the shade of the big acacia tree and envied the crocodiles' cool water. Finally, Tinus had given up his search for the spoor of the Great Elephant and only shot the meat they cooked over the evening fire to the rumbling sounds of distant thunder.

In the middle of November, the rains broke, and they laughed with joy and for the first time amid the clashes of monstrous thunder, using the excuse of her fear, Alison and Tinus became lovers, each returning to their huts before morning. Not one of them thought of the past or the future. Even Tatenda smiled at the white man's happiness.

EARLY IN THE MORNING, at the time Emily was conceiving her second child out of wedlock, the Pool of London was gripped by a black frost. Jeremiah Shank, sitting half-frozen on a discarded wooden railway sleeper, was out of money, out of a job, and out of the smallest prospect of finding one. The Certificate of Character given to him by Captain Doyle, after his discharge from the *Indian Queen*, was tantamount to a blacklisting from any British boat or any boat calling at a British port. The Merchant Navy had ostracised him. Jeremiah Shank was a man of small stature and sharp features, the nose slightly twisted to the left from birth. Unfortunately, he also had one eyelid that permanently drooped but these were not the features that got him into trouble. Unbeknownst to him, and quite outside his control, the combination of the bent, twisted nose and one drooping eyelid gave him the cocky look of a man sneering at the world and particularly his fellow man. Even perfect strangers found their fists involuntarily clenching when they perceived him in the line of sight. When men grew to know the man, they not only clenched their fists but punched him on the crooked nose. Over the years of punishment, the constantly broken nose had tilted more and more to the left. Even dogs ran away from him.

The east wind was cutting through his short seaman's jacket and the scarf that wrapped around his face. Beneath this paltry protection against winter weather, there was nothing left in his stomach to make a noise. At one point during the night, he had thought he was going to die. The Mission to Seamen had told him to go away as they were tired of his fights. Before the dawn and as the temperature continued to fall, he began to pray, and when the dawn showed him where he was, sitting in the lee of Colonial Shipping's Pool of London warehouse, where he had staggered, cold and hungry in the early part of the night, he looked up at the post on the wall and the grinning youthful face of Sebastian Brigandshaw.

"There is a God," he croaked to himself and got up to stamp the circulation back into his feet. With the first glimmer of hope, he began to work his way round to the front of the building. Clutched in his right hand was the poster.

FIVE MEN in winged collars sat at high lecterns in the counting room. The youngest of them was forty years old. None of them looked up. Leading off from the counting room were private offices and behind these, the warehouses stuffed full of the proceeds of empire. Chests of tea from India and Ceylon, demerara sugar from British Guiana, cloves from Zanzibar, raw wool in great bales from Australia, hogsheads of tobacco from America, the first empire, and waiting to go out, cloth from the Lancashire cotton mills, steel from Sheffield and every kind of new-fangled machine known to man. Even in the counting house, Jeremiah Shank could smell the cloves. He waited in the warmth, the coal fire acting as a blood transfusion. For more than an hour, no one took the slightest notice of him sitting on the wooden bench next to the roaring fire. Even the tearing east wind failed to penetrate the building. On the bench sat the notice, Sebastian looking at the ceiling. When he was quite warm and sure he could stand properly, he stood up, lifting his head above the sanctuary of the shipping counter, catching the eye of one of the scribes.

"You!" shouted the man. "What are you doing there? Out! Out! No seamen. Dear oh dear. Get out, I say. The Captain is almost due. Get out, you hear me?"

"I want to see The Captain."

"Don't they all? Now out. What's wrong with your face?"

"I'll wait for The Captain."

"You'll do nothing of the sort. You know who I am! Chief clerk! Chief clerk!"

At the moment the chief clerk, puny as he was, clutched his right hand into a fist, the owner of Colonial Shipping, still in town to pursue his younger son, opened the second door from the outside, the first already shut behind him against the winter wind, and took in Jeremiah and the poster all in one.

"Good morning, Captain, sir," five men said in unison standing to attention.

"I know this man," said Jeremiah; the Lord was still on his side. He was pointing down at the poster still lying face up on the bench.

"Then you'd better follow me into my office," said The Captain, by which time the five men were diligently back to their tasks.

"Close the door," said The Captain. "Now, who is he?"

"Sebastian Brigandshaw, your youngest son."

"Where is he?"

"First the reward, Captain, sir. Then I'll tell. I ain't ate nothin' for four days so I want my money first."

"Don't be stupid. You're probably lying."

"How I know his face? One more night like last night and I'll be dead, and then you'll never know Captain, sir... All right. Give me fifty quid and I'll tell you all about the *Indian Queen*."

"You sailed out with my boy?"

"And back again. Now, can I 'ave my fifty quid?"

The Captain thought for a moment and smiled. "I rather think you can."

OUTSIDE, with his back to the warehouse buildings, Captain Doyle contemplated the bleakness of the London docks. Ships with furled sails were like trees without leaves, struck equally by the bitter cold. One two-master was tacking with the east wind into port and a steamship threw sooty clouds of black and white smoke that smelt of sulphur into the morning air: she would sail on the tide that pulled back and forth from the Thames Estuary and the Royal Navy port of Chatham. In his pocket was his letter of resignation and a list of his officers and men, with their signatures, who wished to leave Colonial Shipping and follow their captain. Only seven members of the crew had not been asked to sign. All those asked were listed on his sheet of paper.

From the corner where he had stood waiting, Doyle had seen The Captain go through the outside door into the building but still his conscience pricked, the loyalty given over so many years he now found difficult to throw away. Before The Captain had stridden across the dockyard, Doyle had seen Shank and known his purpose. The man was a misfit in a world that hated difference. There was no compassion for a misfit out at sea. Friends turned on friends after weeks of close quarters and a Shank was a catalyst for disaster. The first time he had sent him away with a good Certificate of Character, taken him back for pity and finally thrown him off the ship at Cape Town, thinking any white man could make some kind of life for himself in the colony.

The door banged in the wind behind him and Doyle turned to watch a rejuvenated Shank stride away from the building. In a way, Doyle was glad and hoped the man would put the reward to good use.

The *Indian Queen* had sailed home three weeks earlier and every member of the crew knew about the reward and was ashamed of a man pursuing his own son through the law. The deputation had been led by the coxswain and the first officer and the pre-emptive plan had been set. They all knew it was only a matter of time before someone told The Captain but with the days in port, the mood of his crew had changed. The contingency plan they had made called for the purchase of a new ship driven by steam with the crew and officers owning half the shares according to their rank. Not only would they own half the profits but half the ship, when the bank was repaid its loan. The other half would be owned by their backers, Sebastian Brigandshaw and Tinus Oosthuizen, from the proceeds of the last ivory hunt; Tinus's last hunt for the Great Elephant.

Being a man who had always faced his dangers, Captain Doyle turned away from the tall masts and black funnels and walked towards the front door of Colonial Shipping.

As Doyle expected, the last person The Captain expected to see in his office that morning was the master of the *Indian Queen*.

They were both the same size and build; stocky men who had weathered all the oceans of the world. The Captain was fifty-four years old and Doyle, five years younger. They had first sailed together when Doyle was nineteen and the wind and sun had not turned his face into hard leather run through with rivers and ravines. A piece of Doyle's right ear was missing, lost to frostbite on a deadly voyage round the Horn into the waters of the Antarctic. The Captain had a small finger, the pinkie, missing from his left hand, a reminder of the same deadly voyage. Nine Englishmen had died on that voyage round the Horn of South America fighting the Cape Horn current and the west wind drift, taking English machinery on the short route to Chile in a ship of three hundred and four tonnes. Doyle had been The Captain's coxswain. Doyle remembered in those days, before his obsession with the gentry, The Captain had a heart, as all the profit from the owner's and Captain's portion of the profit had been given to the families of the nine dead men, according to their rank. Even in death, there had been an order of seniority. For a moment Doyle thought of letting The Captain verbally vent his feelings and for him to keep the papers closed in his pocket.

"Traitor," screamed The Captain.

"What did you say... Sir?"

"You're a bloody traitor. You stole my grandson from his father."

Doyle, for want of a better way to control his temper, held his breath telling himself it would be safer to say nothing than telling the truth. There were too many lives at stake.

"I'll have you charged with conspiracy to kidnap. Accessory to the fact."

"Did you give Shank the five hundred pounds?"

"I gave him fifty quid."

"You promised five hundred."

"Shut your bloody mouth."

"Where's the gentleman's word in that one?" sneered Doyle. They glared at each other while Doyle gained control of his temper.

Coming to attention, he pulled his letter of resignation from his right pocket.

"Captain Brigandshaw, I regretfully resign my command."

"You'll never get another one. I'll bloody well see to that even if I can't put you in jail."

"And here is the list and signatures of officers and crew who will be leaving your employ on completion of their contracts."

"They're all fired. Never sail again. Not a bloody one of 'em. I will not be gainsaid."

"As you wish, Captain Brigandshaw."

"Get out."

"Yes, Captain, sir. You will find the *Indian Queen* shipshape at her berth. By this evening she'll be empty of officers and crew."

"What are you going to do, Doyle?"

"That is for me to know and you to find out, Captain, sir." Even with the best of discipline, there was a faint smile on his face.

"You bastard!"

"Don't forget Shank's four hundred and fifty pounds. A gentleman's word is his bond, I think they say. Shall I have them call for his full reward, or will you send it for him to the Mission to Seamen?" Doyle reached the door to

The Captain's office and had it open before turning back to the man still seated behind his desk. "He's a good boy... Fact is, he's the best of your litter."

They glared back at each other, thinking of Sebastian.

When the door to his office had closed quietly and the sound of Doyle's boots had receded from the building, The Captain got up from his desk and looked out the side window. Doyle was walking briskly away into the cold morning. 'He's probably right,' he said to himself and suddenly the smell of cloves was no longer to his taste... "But I will not be gainsaid," he said out loud when Doyle was long gone out of sight.

At three o'clock that afternoon a crew member of the *Indian Queen* found Jeremiah Shank drinking gin. Miraculously he was surrounded by friends. All of them were drunk but only Shank had been buying the gin.

"If you go to the Mission to Seamen ye'll find't rest of ye thirty pieces of silver, Judas," said the crewman from the *Indian Queen*.

"Who are you callin' Judas?" asked a big man standing up from his bench. He had been the first to sense a free drink soon after Shank had entered the tavern.

"Enjoy the free drink, mister," said the seaman, "cause there's plenty more. Best thing you can do, Jeremiah Shank, is get out of the country. And stay out."

Surrounded by his sycophants Shank leered back at the seamen. At five hundred pounds to his credit, he could leer back at anyone. He was the richest ordinary seaman in the British Merchant Navy, to hell with his Certificate of Character. Shouting louder than the last time, he ordered everyone a drink. For the first time in his life, he liked his fellow man.

2

APRIL 1891

*A*fter seven months in the bush, Henry Manderville and Gregory Shaw had nothing to show for it but the smiles of men content with themselves and the world around them. The last night's camp had been within sight of Fort Salisbury that had changed from tents and men in uniform to brick buildings, shiny tin roofs and civilians everywhere. Gregory counted eight Union Jacks snapping in the wind. Everywhere were wagons and people, the road they had cut from South Africa bringing a tidal wave of experts and artisans, prospectors and spectators and with them, the rule of law. The Standard Bank that had opened for business in a tent was housed in a one-roomed building with a stoep in front to shade the customers where Henry presented his letter of credit to his London bank.

The police station further down the wide road rutted by ox wagons was immaculate, the stones demarcating the building painted twice a day with whitewash to fight the fine red dust spread by the wheels and hooves. The rains had been over a month. The roads were straight and the front of the buildings in a perfect line. Water pipes were being laid from the new pump station on the Makabuzi River. A sewage engineer had arrived from Liverpool and railwaymen were discussing with the British South Africa Company, in terms of its charter from Queen Victoria, the best route to link up with the British rail from Cape Town. A few black men had come out of hiding away from Lobengula and were working on the roads, bewildered men in a world they had never imagined. Further down the wide road, as Henry and Gregory edged their horses through the traffic and noise, another building blazoned the *Rhodesia Herald*, the new press providing a weekly broadsheet having named itself after Cecil Rhodes. The British Empire had arrived and nothing would ever be the same. A life that had gone on little changed from the advent of man had come to an abrupt halt in less than a year.

Having tethered their horses to a newly erected hitching rail and with the firm belief that British law would protect them from theft, they began a walk back down the main road they had ridden. They looked more like tramps than English gentlemen and if they were honest with themselves they stank. Their open shirts and tattered breeches were the same well-washed dirty grey, the soap having run out months earlier. Their beards were thick and matted, their hair chopped irregularly with blunt scissors.

"You think we could find a beer, old boy?" asked Gregory.

"We'll ask at the police station."

As they approached the newly whitewashed line of stones, a man was standing in the shade of the front stoep of the police station looking at the noticeboard. He had a nasty sharp face, and the nose was slanted to the left. The man's right eyelid drooped. He was smirking at a poster on the board and both approaching men found their right fist clenching with a wish to punch the man in the face for no reason whatsoever. Neither Gregory nor Henry had set eyes on the man who then caught sight of them. The nasty look turned to one of mild disgust. Henry caught the man's shifty eye and laughed.

"Sorry, old chap. Probably pong. Been in the old bush too long."

"You know where we can get a beer, old boy?" asked Gregory.

"Not like that," said the man cutting them dead as he turned away from the noticeboard. The man's accent was forced and strange but the suit he was wearing had probably been tailored in Savile Row.

"I say, how rude," said Gregory as they both began to laugh.

In mid-laugh, Henry stopped and stared at the poster. "I know that face," he said. "Looks like young Seb."

Gregory walked closer and read the caption.

"Sebastian Brigandshaw," he read, "wanted in England for kidnapping. The notice is quite old. Do you know the young man?"

"He was my daughter's sweetheart. They were friends from childhood."

"How strange! What's he doing wanted out here, old boy?"

THE POLICEMAN WAS IMMACULATELY DRESSED in the uniform of the newly constituted British South Africa Company Police, the starched brown of his sleeveless shirt as stiff as a board. The black peaked cap was on the desk to his right and Gregory smiled at the polished shine of his knee-high boots planted under the drawer-less table. The man was more a boy and probably eighteen years old, one of the new arrivals that had come up north once the Pioneer Column had opened the road.

"Do you have a file on Sebastian Brigandshaw?" asked Henry.

"Man before you asked the same question, sir."

"You know of a hotel with a bath?" interrupted Gregory.

"Believe it or not, a bloke called Meikle opened one last week. But he only takes cash. Won't give credit to prospectors."

"Wise man," said Henry. "Now about Brigandshaw?"

"Some story he's a white hunter. We've looked for months. No sign of him. Kidnapped his brother's wife and son."

"No word of him?"

"Not a word, sir."

"Where is this hotel?"

"Halfway down Pioneer Street on the left. Find any gold?"

"Not a glimmer."

"Same as the rest. A few are digging into old Shona workings. Not much there either. Pity. Company shares have dropped in half so they say. Lucky I couldn't afford to buy any shares... Have a nice bath, sir."

To Henry and Gregory, the first bottle of Cape red wine tasted like nectar from the gods and the second was tasting even better. They had found an English barber doing his trade under a msasa tree waiting for his shop to be built, the shaving-water boiling in a bathtub over an open fire just fifty yards behind the new hotel. The hot bath in their room had come from a similar heating system while the steam boilers were being shipped from England. Each had bought a new shirt and a pair of trousers smelling of mothballs stronger than soap. The roast beef on their plates was not a fallen ox after all and both decided that even if the peas and potatoes came out of tin cans, who were they to complain? After eating game for six months with the pioneer column and seven months fruitlessly searching for their pot of gold, the roast beef of old England was much to their taste. Both of them sent their plates back for a second helping and after the canned peaches were eaten, they settled on a bottle of old Cape brandy and a large cigar, content with life.

"You want to talk about them?" asked Gregory.

"No, not really. Nothing I can do. The boy's Sebastian's. Even I can count.

My own fault. Damn stupid. All about money and pride and vanity. Poor Emily. I hope she is safe... You ever do something damn stupid in your life?"

Gregory Shaw thought for a while. "I think I pieced the story together. We've been together alone for a long time... But what I want now is a woman. You ever think of women, Henry?"

"My wife most of the time. My daughter some of the time. My own selfish stupidity all the time. If they are out here, we need a farm big enough for all of us. They haven't any money. Brigandshaw, the Pirate, will have cut off the boy. That policeman was damn helpful letting me see the file. Vanity, Gregory. It's all vanity once you have a roof over your head and enough to eat. Let's forget gold and buy any of the land concessions the pioneers want to sell. Many will have had enough by now and want to go home. I can deal with the Pirate. Or I think I can. One thing none of us can do permanently is go back to England, you as well. A big farm and lots of cows. There's so much empty land out here you could build yourself a private empire. I like the idea of being far away from all the avarice and greed in this world."

Above them, the punkahs were turning but having little effect on the heat. Even in April, it was stifling hot with all the bodies in the dining room generating heat as they ate and talked.

ON THE OTHER side of the room at a table set for one, Jeremiah Shank had put down his knife and fork to better eavesdrop the conversation at the table next to him. He had seen Gregory and Henry across the dining room but had failed to connect them with the two prospectors at the police station. After receiving the letter from Captain Brigandshaw at the Mission to Seaman, he had called again as requested at Colonial Shipping, received the balance of his five hundred pounds, and struck a deal. For the chance of another five hundred pounds, he had set out to Africa to find the errant boy, report him to the police and have him shipped back to England for trial. Even Jeremiah had been surprised at The Captain's hatred of his youngest son. As a passenger this time, he had taken ship on the first Colonial Shipping vessel sailing for the Cape, lording his status over the crew. By then he had dressed properly and spent five shillings of his new money on elocution lessons.

He had arrived in Cape Town and taken the train to Kimberley, recently annexed by the British from the Boers as the place was an underground mountain of diamonds. From Kimberley he had made his way to the new mining camp at Johannesburg, where he had been told the main rains had flooded the rivers and cut the road to the interior. Along with the avalanche of suppliers, he had arrived in Fort Salisbury three weeks earlier when the drifts across the Shushi, the Bubye, Nuanetsi and Lundi had become impassable. Until the moment he put down his knife and fork there had not been a trace of his quarry. The word Brigandshaw, spoken by the big man with a beard down to his chest, rang the bell for Jeremiah that silenced every other thought in his mind.

"You think Oosthuizen has found the Great Elephant?" asked Frederick Selous at the next table.

"Never will. Hunted him for years myself," said Henry Hartley, the man's companion.

"They haven't come in?"

"Camped on the Zambezi I'll bet. They won't come through here if they have any sense. Rhodes thinks he owns every elephant south of the Zambezi."

When Henry Hartley looked up from his place, a short man with a crooked nose was standing at his elbow. The old hunter felt an immediate flash of dislike.

"Do you know the whereabouts of Sebastian Brigandshaw?" asked the stranger.

"What's it to you?" said Hartley, annoyed at the interruption. He had spoken louder than intended and the conversation in the dining room came to an abrupt halt, the silence broken by the swish and creak of the punkah.

"He's wanted by the police," said Shank into the quiet. "In England," he added. "He's kidnapped his brother's wife and son."

"Has he now? Maybe the brother was a tad careless."

The gale of laughter made Shank's right eyelid droop further, and the pulverised cartilage in his twisted nose began to hurt.

"It's a capital offence," he said, trying to maintain his authority.

"No, mister whoever you are, never heard of Sebastian Brigandshaw."

"But I distinctly overheard you mention his name."

"Then you shouldn't listen to private conversations," replied Hartley standing up. Selous, who had been chief scout for the Pioneer Column, also got to his feet. They were the most famous hunters in Africa.

"I'll report you to the police," said Shank, standing his ground in his new suit.

The two hunters laughed with the rest of the dining room and sat down again, picking up their knives and forks and leaving Shank standing. Everyone in the room went back to their food except Henry Manderville on the other side of the room.

Shank sat down well pleased with himself. His quarry was camped on the banks of the Zambezi River. The man was still in the country. All he had to do was wait and listen. Jeremiah Shank knew that Oosthuizen was Brigandshaw's partner. He sat back comfortably in his chair and watched Hartley turn and glare at him. He smiled back. With another five hundred pounds he would buy himself half a dozen of the farms they were talking about and turn himself into a gentleman.

JEREMIAH SHANK WAS ALREADY in the office of the BSA Company when Gregory Shaw arrived the next morning to register his claim for the farmland he would receive as payment for being a member of the Pioneer Column. Next to Shank was a disgruntled young man who had sold his farm-right for twenty pounds. The man had been interested in quick gold, not the hard work of farming.

"If you don't occupy the land within twelve months, you will forfeit the title," said the company man to Shank. "Beacons will be completed next month when you may choose your farm, all of which are within fifteen miles of Salisbury. Now, if you wish to renounce your right to Mr J Shank, sign here," he said to the disgruntled young man... "Now, good day to you... Mr Shank, twelve months remember." The BSA Company wanted Englishmen, any Englishmen occupying the land to deter any aggression from Lobengula when he realised Rhodes had taken the land that he valued and not just the minerals that were worthless to the Matabele.

Ten minutes later, having chosen neighbouring farms from a surveyor's map, Gregory took up their right to six thousand acres north of Fort Salisbury.

"Sir Henry Manderville will sign for his three thousand acres this afternoon."

"The company store will sell you implements and seed."

"I'm sure it will."

Smiling to himself, he left the office to join Henry who was selling the pack horses and prospecting equipment. 'Whatever it is, wherever it is,' he said to himself, 'there's always a racket.'

At first light the following morning, Henry and Gregory began the ride south that would take them back to England. They had exactly twelve months to complete their business and return.

Even as they rode back close to Matabele territory, there was no sign of Lobengula's impis. Wisely they travelled with a group of Englishmen going the same way. They were all armed with the new Martini-Henry repeating rifles. Largely the English had conquered the country by force of arms, the

Rudd concessions with its prospecting rights merely providing an excuse to pacify the British government and convince the Queen this particular imperialism was legal. The Shona, coming out of their hiding in ever-increasing numbers, had never once been consulted about what was happening to their ancestral home. They were bewildered and hungry and many of them took jobs working for the Englishmen. All the Shona had managed to do was change masters. Instead of losing their lives, they had lost their land to British protection.

EMILY KNEW in her heart that the last seven months would be the best part of her life but their provisions were exhausted, the trail through the bush was dry and it was time to return to the world. For the seven months, they had not even seen the footprint of another man and nothing had disturbed their harmony. Not only had Tatenda learnt to speak good English but Harry, just three years old, was the first Englishman to speak Shona without an accent. He moved from English to Shona as if they were all the same language.

Tinus had made the decision for them.

"You, young lady, will need a doctor in three months' time, and Alison and I need a priest. Break camp. We must move."

The largest wagon was used to store the ivory from the hunt, stacked high and roped to the bed of the wagon with a canvas pulled tight over the top. The vegetable garden was left to go to seed and feed the buck and at the end of April, the journey back to civilisation began. Not one of them wanted to go.

"Life is made of memories," explained Tinus as he in-spanned the sixteen oxen into two teams. "At the end of it, you look back and remember the good memories. The rest are forgotten. The mosaic of life. You cannot hold the good moments forever. We never reach eternal happiness in this life and maybe not in the next. What we have found on the banks of this great river is joy for weeks on end. Remember them and thank God, for such weeks are rare. They are the reason for coming into this world. Now, put my chest of books in the wagon, young Seb, and we will go. We can never stand still, more's the pity... Friends, my speech is over. May God bless our journey. Tatenda, you will ride with me and Harry in the big wagon. Yes, indeed, we must go."

Tinus led the way slowly across the Zambezi Valley, followed by Seb driving the second wagon and the two saddleless horses on long reins behind. The sky was puffed by small white clouds, motionless below the perfect blue. The sun was white-light on the dust and long grass that brushed against the chests of the lead oxen. A fish eagle's triple call from the river floated out to them. Ahead, the escarpment was another day's journey.

DAY AFTER DAY followed as they slowly journeyed through a country empty of people, villages and cattle, the country south of the Zambezi stripped bare by first Mzilikazi and then his son Lobengula. It had taken the Zulu impi fifty years to decimate the tribes of the Shona. All the hunters saw was game; herds of elephant which they left alone; stampedes of buffalo; prides of lions; cheetahs running down the buck: impala, waterbuck, springbok, kudu. Even the great eland was prey to the predators. Among the buffalo, herds of the gnu. Among the elephant, at respectful distances, prehistoric rhinoceros. In the rivers, crocodile and hippopotamus. High in the sky, eagles and falcons, hawks and buzzards, calling their lonely cries. And always behind them the long line of crushed grass to prove their passage and mark their trail for weeks to come.

The nights were the best for Alison. Camped in the wilderness, with the upward heat of the fire curling sparks high into the heavens, the bulk of her man next to her, Harry asleep, the last of their coffee simmering over a small, secondary fire mingling pungent sweetness with the smell of woodsmoke. Away, close to the smaller wagon, Sebastian and Emily holding hands.

Above them, the great vault of heaven, layer upon layer of crystal stars fixed in their paradise, the wagons the centre of the dome, the Milky Way splashed like cloud among the heavenly stars. And then the moon rising from the wilderness... Stacking the fire and falling asleep in each other's arms.

BY THE MIDDLE OF MAY, Jeremiah Shank had given up on his second five hundred pounds and was turning his mind to the estate he was going to carve out of the African bush. He had studied the map in the company office that showed the Zambezi River cutting them off from the north, hundreds of miles of one of Africa's greatest rivers. Somewhere along that river, in territory previously controlled by Lobengula, his quarry had camped for the duration of the rains. The consensus, drawn from prospectors back from their fruitless hunt for gold, elicited after buying round after round of drinks in the new hotel, was that any sane hunter would bring his ivory out on a line that to the west would keep his wagons far away from Gu-Bulawayo, Lobengula's military kraal, and far east of Fort Salisbury in case Rhodes levied a tax on the ivory. Somewhere there in the middle for weeks, Jeremiah had ridden across this line, climbing kopjes that stuck out of the flat grassland with his telescope looking for the trail of his quarry. All he ever saw were the vast herds of game which he found permanently irritating. To Jeremiah, there was only beauty in gold or pound notes.

His horse was going lame, and he reasoned there was no reason for Brigandshaw to travel at all. Hartley, he heard in the hotel, had spent years in the wilderness without the need of his fellow man. Jeremiah made camp for the last time on his journey. Even before he had made his supper, the hyenas were laugh-whooping at him from the darkness of the bush, and then the first lion roared and sent a shiver down his spine. Owls were calling to each other from the clumps of trees. A leopard coughed and Jeremiah clutched his rifle in fear and loathing. Even as exhaustion made him sleep to the dancing light of his fire, he dreamed of horrors through the night.

THE DAWN CAME SLOWLY with the song of birds and the fire was still burning high. Jeremiah was glad to be going. The BSA Company would have placed their beacons to demarcate his farm and he would find some blacks to work for him. There were whites without money who would build him a house and oxen to clear patches of his land that would grow the food for the fools looking for the gold that wasn't there. He would buy cattle from the company and very soon he would be a man of property. He began to walk his horse the thirty miles back to Fort Salisbury.

Around midday, with the sun a ball of fire above his head, he crossed the trail he had been seeking for four weeks. Even his inexperienced eye showed the trail was less than two days old. The wagons, two of them he read from the tracks, had travelled much closer to the British camp than he had expected and the one wagon drove a rut far deeper than the other. Jeremiah threw his hat in the air and whooped. The only load in the wilderness going south would be ivory, the only hunter not accounted for, Sebastian Brigandshaw. For the first five minutes, he actually ran towards Fort Salisbury. With a wagon that heavy, the police would catch up with them easily.

THE POLICE WERE NOT INTERESTED.

"Mr Shank, you saw a wagon trail in the bush and want me to ride out and arrest the wagon master for kidnapping somebody's wife in England. Please, Mr Shank. Anyone capable of hunting elephant in the bush for months on end is not, I would think, the kind of person to drag someone else's wife off to Africa and stick her in an ox wagon at the far extremity of our empire. Having said all that, you did not see this Brigandshaw but a rut in the ground miles from nowhere."

"But he is the type," insisted Jeremiah Shank patiently. He had learnt years ago that losing his temper with authority was a worthless extravagance. "The man's face is on the poster outside and if you capture him, you will have your name in every newspaper in England." For a moment the look in the policeman's eyes changed from *how do I get rid of this man without losing my temper*, to one of personal interest. For a moment the man regarded Jeremiah and then his expression became one of resignation.

"I'm stuck behind this desk. Anyway, Major Johnson would never authorise the expenditure of sending two men down a cold trail without proof that Brigandshaw was at the end of it. Fact is, Mr Shank, the company is tight with money now they find there isn't any gold."

"Who owns the ivory on that wagon?" said Jeremiah Shank, seeing his opportunity.

"Well, the company, of course. Anyone hunting for ivory in company territory needs a licence and has to sell any to the company."

"And if the hunter does not have a licence?"

"The ivory would be confiscated."

"Thank you, Constable, you have been of extreme help."

Puzzled, the policeman watched the man abruptly leave the charge office. He thought for a moment the man was being sarcastic and then he wasn't so sure. Through the open door, he saw the man he had been trying to get rid of for the last half an hour running down Pioneer Street as if a full Matabele impi had swept into Fort Salisbury.

WHEN JEREMIAH ENTERED the office of the BSA Company, the same company in which Arthur Brigandshaw had invested all his money, the ex-seaman was out of breath.

"I wish to see the man who issues hunting licences."

"You may fill in this form... Is there something wrong?"

"There's a man without a licence not fifteen miles from here with a full wagonload of ivory going south, and if you don't move very quickly, your company will lose a great deal of money."

"A full load of ivory? My word, the company will be very angry if that slips through our fingers. Mr Rhodes said every penny counts. How much ivory, do you think?"

"Well over five tonnes."

"Goodness gracious me... Can you show us where it is?"

"Will there be a reward?" asked Jeremiah, thinking on his feet.

"I rather think so."

"I'll need that in writing before we go. But hurry up. Every minute the ivory is getting further away. We'll need a company policeman to make the arrest."

"Yes, I rather think we do. Now, what is your name and I will report all of this to my superior?"

TINUS OOSTHUIZEN WAS in no hurry. It was the middle of May, the best time of the year. There had been no rain for well over a month and the days were cooler, the nights mildly cold. The long elephant grass was brown and beginning to bend, and the tsetse flies no longer attacked them at dusk and dawn. Most of the small rivers were still pooled with water and the game dispersed far and wide across the grasslands of the highveld. The oxen plodded slowly across the veld and had not felt the whip since climbing the escarpment out of the Zambezi Valley.

On the second wagon, Harry sat between his mother and father, Tatenda taking the shade sitting on the tailgate behind. They all watched the face of a giraffe which topped a clump of trees ten yards from the wagon. The animal had stopped chewing at the last leaves on top of the tree and seemed to smile at their passing. Harry looked back, and the animal had begun to chew a leaf stuck in his mouth still watching the wagon. Harry smiled back at the giraffe.

From the back of the almost empty wagon, Tatenda spoke to him in Shona. Someone was coming. Someone was coming down their trail. A cloud of dust was back on their trail. There were horses and men, the first he had seen for so many months.

"Tatenda says we are being followed," he told his father.

In front the heavily loaded wagon pushed on into the long grass, moving around a red anthill that rose out of the head-high grass.

"We've cut a new trail, Harry."

JACK SLATER, the company man, believed in rules, particularly the rules of the British Empire as without the rules, man would return to primitive anarchy. He was a product, as had been his father and grandfather, of a minor public school in the south of England. He had been sent to the preparatory section of the school as a boy of seven and put in a dormitory with twenty more young boys who had been taken from their parents and given to a housemaster who would teach them how to become English gentlemen, how to comply with the rules. The family had been solicitors for three generations and before that, minor squires. The Slater graves in the church at Tonbridge went back to the time of Cromwell. The family had had something to do with the Great Protector and somehow held onto their land when King Charles the Second was restored to the throne of England. The junior and senior school had so indoctrinated Jack Slater that he believed in his heart that the British Empire was the only source of stability in the world, but any nation or people that were lucky enough to become part of the empire would live in peace, that individuals who complied with the rules would be protected from the vagaries and rapacious nature of his fellow man. Under the flag of England, a man could walk the streets without fear for his life or property. All he had to do was comply with the rules and all would be well for him for the rest of his life.

After Jack's two elder brothers joined the family firm of solicitors, it was left to Jack and his younger brothers to use their training to help govern the empire. He was twenty-four years old when the office of the Colonial Secretary seconded him to the British South Africa Company to make certain they complied with the rules set down in the Royal Charter. It was a splendid way of making the men of business pay for the administration of the empire. Clive had gone about expanding the empire in India, Brooke in Sarawak and now Rhodes in Africa. And the rules said the Charter Company, as it was now being called, had the right of protection over the indigenous people, provided the company enabled the missionaries to do their work and convert the heathens to Christianity. Their rights included the land and what was below and above the land, which included the animals. When the young man at the front desk had brought the horrible little man into his office, who had proceeded to sneak on someone taking ivory out of the new country, his instinct had been to throw Jeremiah Shank straight out again.

His upbringing overcame his dislike for the man with the crooked nose and drooping eyelid. If one rule could be broken, then so could the rest. A blind eye turned to a breach of the rules was the equivalent of taking a bribe, and for the British civil servant that was the worst crime that could be perpetrated against the empire. Honesty was the first rule of them all.

Half an hour later, accompanied by the young policeman who had first spoken to Jeremiah, he rode out of Fort Salisbury to arrest the wagonload of ivory. They were the rules. The owner of the ivory would be given a fair hearing as to why he was not in possession of the permit, a fact that Jack Slater was certain of because no one had yet been given the right to hunt. Everyone had been more interested in finding the gold in King Solomon's mines.

Unaware of anything untoward, Tinus Oosthuizen in the lead wagon, with his left hand resting comfortably on Alison Ford's knee, was enjoying the pungent smell of wild sage and the sight of a herd of buffalo whose heads, and sometimes part of their backs, was visible as they moved through the long grass looking for choice grazing. The idea of a farm and family was foremost in his mind, with a tug of war between land in this new country, or a farm with his fellow Boers in the Transvaal Republic or the Republic of the Orange Free State. Even though his mother had been from Scotland and a major influence on his life, his reading of English books and his command of the English language, never once had he considered himself anything other than a Boer of Dutch descent. He was an African Oosthuizen as his family had been for seven generations, for over two hundred years. One of the first tasks on the new farm, wherever it was to be, was to teach Alison how to speak the *Taal*, the Dutch van Riebeeck had brought to the Cape in the seventeenth century. Tinus let his thoughts meander and realised he was happier than he had been for all of his years.

The buffalo were the first to spook and Tinus took his hand away from Alison's knee to have them both on the reins. The grass was so tall the predator lions could be anywhere, and Tinus searched the bush with a practised eye for the head of a lioness. Back in the cool shade of a tree the lion would be waiting. The buffalo were properly spooked and were running through the long grass, pushing a cloud of dust up into the sky. Puzzled, Tinus looked again but there were no lionesses leaping through the grass in pursuit of their quarry. The crash of hundreds of hooves pounding the dry earth was so loud they obliterated the sound of the crickets singing in the grass. Tinus brought the oxen to a halt and watched the spectacle.

"You own this ivory, sir?" said a young man on horseback who had ridden up on his right, away from Alison. Tinus turned slowly to look at the Englishman and told him to mind his own business in the *Taal*.

"Sorry, old chap. Don't speak that lingo. Do you speak English by any chance? Name's Jack Slater from the Charter Company. I believe, sir, you don't have a licence to shoot our elephant."

Tinus cracked the rawhide whip over the lead oxen and the wagon lumbered forward again. He pressed Alison's knee telling her to keep quiet.

An emptiness had found its way into the pit of his stomach: the English again; why his people had made the Great Trek out of the Cape to be free of British rule. The young man on his right was joined by a second young rider, this one in uniform. Then a third horseman came up and Tinus looked into the sneering eyes of the man with a crooked face. One of the man's eyes drooped half shut and the hollow in Tinus's stomach became a certainty: this was no accident.

The young policeman rode to the front of the team of eight oxen and, with a quiet expertise, took hold of the onside leading ox by jumping off his horse onto its back. He then tried to bring the animal to a halt with little success. For Tinus, the target was too great a temptation and before he could control his temper, the long thong of his whip curled out and cut a hole in the man's starched uniform making him scream with pain. In the commotion, Sebastian caught up with the lead wagon.

"I say, do you speak English?" asked Jack Slater, appalled at the unprovoked attack on the policeman.

"Of course. Why did your man try to stop this wagon?"

"Carrying ivory without a permit."

Instead of becoming more annoyed, Sebastian smiled to himself. Now he understood. There was a new law in the land and the laws had to be complied with. The men were doing their job as they thought best.

"Tinus, bring the wagon to a halt."

"So he does speak English?" said Jack Slater.

"Of course he does. His mother was a Scot." Sebastian climbed down from the box in front of his wagon and walked across to the policeman slumped over the lead oxen, blood staining the back of his uniform. The buffalo were far away in the distance, still in full stampede.

"You all right, old chap?" asked Sebastian. "My partner was a bit hasty."

"That hurt."

"He's a bit of an expert, so to speak. Can I help you down? My wife has some iodine. It will sting but stop any trouble. Now, what's all this about? You see, we have a permit. A very valid and at the time a very important permit from Lobengula. We left to hunt long before you chaps invaded the country. You can't arrest a chap for a crime he hasn't done, now can you? And if you don't believe we wasted three weeks at Gu-Bulawayo, you can ask Lobengula yourself, but that probably would not be wise. He still thinks this country belongs to him. All you have is the right to prospect for minerals. So you see we are complying with the law. Lobengula's law. But if you go and ask him he might just bash your head in with a knobkerrie. Saw him do that to his top general. Nasty mess. Whole head split open. Dead before the poor chap hit the ground. So be a good fellow, can you, and put in a proper report after my wife has looked at your back? Sorry about that, I really am."

The policeman, still in pain, slid off the back of the ox and Seb helped him to the ground.

Jack Slater had also heard the conversation and was duly relieved. Now he had an excuse. The rules had not been broken. These people had come into the country before the Pioneer Column had crossed the Shashe River.

"Well, that clears it up," he said thankfully. "Apology accepted. How bad is that back, old chap? Oh, that's a nasty gash. 'Fraid you'll have a scar but all in the line of duty. I'll put that in my report to the company. So, there we are. No permit required. You will, of course, apply for one when you come back again. You may find it easier, old chap, instead of lugging all that stuff down to Cape Town. The rules are, we give you a permit to hunt provided you sell the ivory to the company. Saves you all the trouble. You shoot the poor old elephants and we find a market for the ivory. That way everyone is happy. Better than having your brains knocked out by a savage, I'd say."

Seb had quickly noticed the man with the crooked face had not said a word but every time Seb looked in his direction, the half-hooded eye was watching him, the expression malicious. By the look of the small man he was neither a policeman nor did he seem, like a man who had spent his life indoors. The more Seb's glance returned to the man the more Seb was sure he was a seaman. The face away from the bent nose and drooping eyelid had been seared by sun and wind. He had the same dried-up-looking skin as Seb's own father, and when his horse moved its head down to eat the new green shoots at the stem of the dry grass, the man stretched out his left hand, forcing his sleeve to ride up to his elbow and show an anchor tattooed on his arm. For Seb, the coincidence was too great. This man staring at him with such malicious intent had been sent by his father, the man who always said he would never be gainsaid. With a sharp surge of adrenaline running through his brain, Seb was certain the ivory was not the problem but the way by which the seaman had convinced the company man to bring a policeman out in pursuit of him. It was also obvious to Seb that the seaman was not of the other two men's class.

"Look, while my wife's looking after your man, why don't we make camp here and boil some coffee? We have all been in the bush for a long time and you can tell us what has been happening. I gather Rhodes has come into the country, that much is clear, but what is the news from England? What do you think of my son... Mister?"

"Jack Slater."

"Sebastian Brigandshaw. Harry here is probably the only white man in your new country who speaks the local lingo."

"He speaks Zulu?" said Jack Slater surprised, falling into the ploy.

"No, Shona, the language of the tribes hereabouts. Over the decades the Zulus of Mzilikazi and Lobengula only raided these people. Stole their grain and cattle. We saved that young lad over there from the assegais. The Matabele killed the rest of his family and he's been with us ever since. He looks after my son and taught him Shona... You'd better take that shirt right off and have my wife wash your wound. Tinus, come and meet some new friends of ours. We are all going to have some coffee and a bit of a chat. Mr Jack Slater, meet my very best friend, Tinus Oosthuizen, and the shy lady who is still up on the box is his wife, Alison. Please forgive how we look but there aren't exactly barbers on the banks of the Zambezi River. And this is my wife Emily, who will now make Florence Nightingale look like a lady who had never nursed anyone in her life. Healing hands, has my darling Emily. Soon, my friend, you will wish you had more than one cut, the pleasure of being looked after by Mrs Brigandshaw will be so great."

"That's the man," interrupted Jeremiah Shank, pointing at Seb and taking the policeman by the right elbow. "He'd be Sebastian Brigandshaw wanted for kidnapping. You 'ave 'is picture on your wall, Constable. Now arrest him." The five shillings' worth of elocution lessons had left him in his excitement. Even if he had lost his reward for the ivory, five hundred pounds from Captain Brigandshaw was definitely his; the journey to Africa had been well worth his while.

Seb gave the man a look up and down and then down and up and put on his best air of indignation.

"Why don't you trot off back to Fort Salisbury?" said Jack Slater to Jeremiah Shank. "Come here, lad. Is this your father?"

"Daddy, what's the man saying?"

"He wants to know if you're my son."

Shyly, Harry put his thumb in his mouth and buried his head against Seb's thigh.

"Mr Shank," said Jack Slater. "Please leave this company. One wild-goose chase is enough for one day. How can this man have possibly kidnapped his own son?"

"Excuse me, madam, but are you Mrs Brigandshaw?" persisted Jeremiah.

"Yes," replied Emily in all truthfulness.

"Please Mr Shank, please trot along," said Jack Slater losing his patience. "You've been rather a bore. This man is obviously a gentleman."

The slight chuckle from Tinus changed to a cough. Five minutes later the coffee was boiling over the small wood fire. The policeman had had his wound attended to and the smell of iodine mingled with the coffee and the woodsmoke.

With the men sitting around the fire, Alison and Emily went off behind the big wagon where they held each other to suppress their giggles of relief.

An hour later the posse left them to continue the journey south in the morning.

That night the new moon smiled down on the wagons. The smell of wild sage was stronger at night and fireflies were flitting through the grass looking for their mates, and Emily felt the new baby stirring in her belly.

3

JUNE 1891

What struck Henry Manderville most was all the people. They had caught a steamship from Cape Town to England and in their hurry to catch the first boat leaving for home, they boarded a large cargo vessel that proceeded to stop at every available port. In St Helena alone, they spent three days kicking their heels. Finally, at Waterloo station, there were the London crowds: hordes of people going in every direction possible, all with a purpose and a destination. The noise and bustle after months in the African bush were continuous: train whistles, steam engines huff-huffing and billowing sulphurous smoke, the shouts of guards echoing under the great roof of the railway station at the heart of the greatest empire on earth.

Gregory Shaw would have stayed at the Naval and Military Club if they had not blackballed him for his love affair in India, and Henry Manderville, poor until he had sold his daughter, had never had the money for a London club. Gregory's family lived in Nottingham and neither of them had relatives in the capital.

"Why don't we rent a flat in Mayfair, old boy?" said Gregory as they stood in the station concourse with their luggage and nowhere to go. "I think we may be here for months and I have some plans of my own. Somewhere close to the Cape Royal. All that tramping around in Africa not spending money. Same for you, old boy. We can spend in three months what we would have spent in a year."

"Are you going up to Nottingham?"

"Probably not. My parents are rather ashamed of me. Father said he would never mention my name. Fact is, were it not for Grandfather's will, yours truly would be poor as a church mouse. Father would have loved to have cut me off. So there we are. Lots of lovely lolly in London waiting for the charm of Gregory Shaw."

"You mean the ladies of London."

"It has been a long time. Fact is, I have a mind to find a wife. That farm on our own will be lovely, old boy. I'm thirty-seven and fancy creating a dynasty. The Shaws of Africa. Such a nice ring."

"Who on earth would go and live in the bush?"

"I've no idea but I'm going to find out. Wouldn't do you any harm yourself."

"Don't be ridiculous. I'm nearly forty."

"Had a friend in the Indian Army. Said there was always old cheese for old cheese. Now if Methuselah could bend down and pick up his luggage, we could find a cab. We don't even have enough baggage for a porter. We should have some lunch and a bottle of wine and then I will think more clearly. I'm going to have six children. The Pirate can wait one more day for his comeuppance."

ARTHUR BRIGANDSHAW WISHED he had never heard of Cecil John Rhodes. For a week he had not been to the office and had holed up in the Baker Street house that no longer belonged to him. In late October of the previous year, when the Charter Company shares had peaked, he had gone again to his bank manager and, with a smirk, laid his Charter Company share certificate on the table and borrowed ninety per cent of its stock market value to buy more Charter shares. On the Tuesday with the new shares, he did the same thing. And with greed propelling his certainty of great wealth, he followed the same procedure on the Wednesday and Thursday. On the following Monday, the shares began to go the other way when the first gold rush in the new country they were calling Rhodesia proved fruitless. The telegraph had by then reached Fort Salisbury, so the rumours reached London soon after the first Pioneers said they were wasting their time prospecting for gold. By Wednesday, Arthur was broke and by Friday, as the Charter shares went into free fall with everyone including Rhodes and Beit dumping shares, he owed the bank manager eighty thousand pounds he did not have. By the time Henry arrived at Waterloo station, Arthur was about to be declared a bankrupt. For eight months he and the bank manager had hoped the shares would go up again, that someone would strike gold in the land of Ophir, the legendary land of King Solomon's mines, that someone would quickly find the gold reefs that were going to make the new Witwatersrand look poor. Then the bank manager was fired and the new man tried to force The Captain to bail out his eldest son and failed.

"The lad got himself in muck. Lad can get himself out of muck. Teach him a lesson. That lad's been nothing but trouble these last couple of years. Put him in jail for all I care but you ain't getting a brass farthing from me. I made my money. Worked for it. You should do the same, Mr Bank Manager, without bothering me. Lad's of age. Nought to do with me."

"He's your son."

"And it's your money he's lost not mine. You and your bank are just as stupid as he is. Lending the lad money to gamble. Oh, I know, you thought his father would stand guarantee. Bloody likely. Now go and do your work. Now is the time to buy Charter shares when they're worth near nothing. Rhodes won't let a country with his name on it go down the drain. Mark my words. Fact is, you've given me a good idea. Maybe you haven't wasted my time after all."

AT THE AGE OF FIFTY-ONE, Tilda Brigandshaw, the mother of the four boys, looked like a little old lady. She lived mostly in her memories. The Captain had not touched her for fifteen years. Arthur never visited Hastings Court, not even when Emily was having the child. Nathanial was too busy doing good in the slums of London and preparing to go out to Africa as a missionary. Captain James Brigandshaw, her third and snooty son, would cut his mother dead in the street if she found him with his army friends, and Sebastian, her favourite, had been sent out of England and was now being hounded by his father and the police. Tilda had tried with Emily but she was so in awe of the daughter of a baronet that she found it difficult to communicate.

The once prettiest girl in Chester was so lonely she felt the pain every minute of the day. Even the servants, who were her own class, rebuffed any conversation that did not relate to the running of the house for fear of dismissal. The Captain had made it quite plain, his wife was to be treated as mistress of the house in the same way the Manderville women in the portraits on the walls had been treated by their servants. There were only the dogs and cats to be talked to and they never answered back.

Moving from The Oaks with its half-grown trees had severed the memories of her children when they needed their mother and came to her with their pains, the cuts and bumps of childhood. At first The Oaks had seemed the answer to her dreams, the perfect setting for the prettiest girl in Chester, but she was far from home, far from her mother, brothers, sisters and people who spoke the same way with the accent of the north, the accent of honest folk who worked for a living and made their own beds. She had lost her world and the one she found rejected her. The children at private schools found their way into the homes of the gentry but never their mother. She cried for the days when her husband was a rough-and-ready seaman and cursed his ambition to become a gentleman, something she knew he would never be, however much wealth and power he accumulated. She knew with the certainty of her native stock, ancestors with hands raw from hard work, that a man or woman had to remain in their class to be happy.

A carpenter was comfortable with a carpenter, they had something in common, there was no poison to despise or greed to envy. The Oaks had been the separation from her life and Hastings Court a living death, far worse than the grave, the nightmare of hell her sanctimonious parson son had railed about. But what had she done, she asked herself? A faithful wife even with an unfaithful husband. Children she had tried to love despite the shame they showed their mother, their mother who had once been in service. All ashamed of her except Sebastian, and he had lived his own life more with Emily than his family. And she had tried with Emily, tried ever so hard. If the sin was not so mortal, the terror of eternal fire so vivid in her mind, she would have killed herself.

They had begun so well, Tilda Brennan as she was then, and the young, ordinary seaman, Archibald. She even thought they were both in love and had looked forward to a family like her own. Ordinary, hard-working people who laughed a lot and loved each other. Father loving mother without any fooling or sad surprise, older siblings helping the younger, the boys admiring the pretty girls that were their sisters, the sisters admiring the boys for being liked by everyone and all of them telling each other the truth. Granny Brennan and her stories of Grandpa Brennan who had fought Napoleon. Granny Jones, the one from Wales, who told her stories of hills and vales, and all together in the one same street, all supporting each other. And Archibald, who now made her call him The Captain, with his dreams she also dreamed along.

The first two voyages, one to America and one to India. Waiting for him, knowing he saved every penny of his wages for their life together. Waiting for months on end, never sure if he was safe on the great wide ocean of the world. Then they had married and only after his third voyage, when he came back as coxswain, did she hear them call him 'big mouth' and should have known. A few months of happiness and then it was gone. Slowly, imperceptibly, her life grew into pain. And then the American Civil War and Archibald running guns to the Confederacy and bringing shiploads of cotton back to Liverpool and they were rich. All that had been good in her simple life of family fell to dust. By '66 they had moved south, away from people who knew who he was.

She had miscarried the girls and Sebastian had been born at The Oaks, but there was no family like there had been in Chester. The boys were sent to boarding schools, and Chester was a million miles away and no one visited, neither her family from the north, who were snubbed by Archibald, nor the gentry around Epsom Downs, who called them *nouveau riche*, people in trade, common. Even the children kept their schoolfriends away from The Oaks for fear of them hearing their mother's accent, for fear of what she might say, for fear of being ridiculed at school as different from the rest. The whole family was in fear of someone finding out, not even realising that everyone had found out a long time before. Emily had come to The Oaks. Emily had not cared... And Tilda Brigandshaw had tried so hard with Emily and failed.

The splendour and history of Hastings Court were lost on her. The sweeping lawns and tall box hedges cut in a perfect trim, green peacocks growing from the top looking blindly at the ornamental carp swimming round and round the lily ponds, each as useless as the other. The old house roofed and renovated, tall-ceilinged and cold as charity. Servants everywhere. Nowhere for privacy. Eating at a table so long it was ridiculous and mostly alone, the cold clatter of porcelain banged too often by her cutlery bringing a look of disgust from the butler. And when The Captain entertained his clients, she felt a stranger in a house that would never be her own. And she had once been the prettiest girl in Chester.

The bower beside the ornamental lake was her secret spot. The June afternoon was hot and languid, the birds quiet in the heat. Dragonflies were busy over the water, flashing brightly coloured wings. Bees searched for food among the honeysuckle that wrapped the arbour. Somewhere far behind her two of the new gardeners were arguing with each other. Why was it people so often argued, she asked herself? She left their words alone as background to the summer's day. She would have wished to fling off her clothes and rush into the lake up to her neck and let the cool water calm the aches of mind and body. All alone she giggled at the thought, a scandal to beat all scandals. Once, somewhere back in history, there had been no rules or inhibitions and people had been part of nature, able to run naked through the woods and into the water to swim with the frogs. Tilda sighed at the thought of so much happiness lost.

For a few brief, sweet moments she slept and dreamt of swimming in the lake. She woke to the clatter of horse and carriage and the inevitable intrusion. There was never any peace at Hastings Court. With dread, she heard her husband shout for the servants and wondered how long she could stay by the lake. The noise grew from behind her, from the direction of the house, and a cock pheasant rushed out of the bushes and ran along the shore. Even the bird disliked the noise of man. By the time the pheasant reached a more distant sanctuary, there was a real commotion coming from the house. To Tilda by the lake, it sounded like a second carriage in a hurry. Men were shouting at each other.

Henry Manderville was out of the carriage before it stopped properly. There was a carriage already in the driveway and Henry recognised his quarry.

"I want a word with you," he shouted to The Captain, who was arguing with a young man red in the face.

"What do you want?" answered The Captain without turning around, the arrogance of ownership making him rude.

"You know damn well what I want. How can you have your own son arrested for a capital offence?"

The Captain slowly turned and recognised the previous owner of Hastings Court. A sweet smile of success turned his annoyance to pleasure. "What did you say?"

"The arrest of Sebastian is bloody outrageous," said Henry.

"You mean they've caught him? Where?"

"In Cape Town. Some man you sent out followed him down from Rhodesia and when he reached the jurisdiction of the Cape Colony, he had Sebastian arrested."

"Well, I'll be blowed. Shank was worth his money after all... They are sending my grandson back to England? Good. We'll have a new nurse ready for him... Arthur, you go into the house and I'll deal with you later."

"The boy is with his mother," said Henry.

"I don't care who he is with as long as he comes back to Hastings Court. I've made him my sole heir if he comes back here with or without his mother. Now, where is Harry, seeing you know so much?"

"In Cape Town with his mother."

"Then the police will bring him back to his father."

"You don't care about Emily do you?"

"Not particularly."

"Or Sebastian?"

"He gainsaid me and the law is the law. We can't go having people running off kidnapping. Can we, Sir Henry? The law. There always have to be rules and the rules say a son and wife shall live with their father. And that's how it will be. The law, Sir Henry, is on my side. Now, seeing that we Brigandshaws own this house I suggest you get back whence you came. I bought you, remember? A man who sells his daughter and then interferes with a man protecting his family makes me laugh frankly. Why don't you get off your high horse?"

HALF AN HOUR LATER, when it was quiet, Tilda left the sanctuary of her bower and walked back to the house, collecting on the way a basket of flowers to arrange in the dining room. They gave her pleasure though none of the men appreciated her work. The June flowers were rich and plentiful in the borders that lined the old garden paths and she picked them with care. At each intersection of the paths, a sundial, old and difficult to read, centred the cross paths. Below the high terrace a groom was removing the evidence of one of the horses and from inside the house, deep inside, came a muffled shout and a banged door and Arthur, her eldest son, rushed into view and told the groom to drive him to Epsom railway station. He ignored his mother standing quietly with a basket of flowers. Sadly she remembered the pain he had given her at birth and wondered when it would stop. Having done her job so long ago she was irrelevant to all of them.

"Where are you going, Arthur?" she called, but he walked on following the groom.

"They found Harry and arrested Sebastian," her husband's voice said from the high terrace behind as she watched her son turn the corner to the stables without looking back in her direction. There was great satisfaction in the voice of her husband. She turned and only his head and shoulders were visible to her from the end of the garden path. She hated them. Slowly she turned and walked back down the path.

"Where are you going?" shouted The Captain.

This time it was Tilda's turn to do all the ignoring.

QUITE PROBABLY THE man had forgotten Gregory Shaw had been drummed out of the Indian Army. He had not been at Chittagong and possibly had never served under Colonel Jones. Whatever the reason, he seemed very pleased to see a fellow officer so far from where they had served together.

"Captain Gregory Shaw. Well, I'll be damned. What brings you here?"

For no other reason than needing a meal and company, Gregory had left the empty flat he shared with Henry Manderville and gone to the Cafe Royal. Before supper he sat at the bar and ordered a chata-peg, and maybe the name of the drink which the barman had failed to understand had focused the mind of the man seated at the bar to Gregory's left.

"Johnny White. Good Lord, old boy, what are you doing here?... Make it a pink gin," he said to the barman with the blank face.

"On leave. You on leave, old chap?"

"In a way, I suppose. The army found out about Sing and told me to give her up or leave the army. So I left. Can I buy you that drink, old boy?"

"Don't mind if I do." For a long moment there was silence while the man decided to be polite and leave enquiries to another place and another time. Johnny White was alone in London, Gregory decided, and smiled to himself as he reordered the second drink. For a moment he wondered how she was and put that thought out of his mind: it was the one path he always stopped himself from travelling, the path back to the last time when he had been happy.

"Are you staying at the In and Out?" asked Johnny White, referring to the Naval and Military Club.

"No. With an old friend. Sir Henry Manderville." White was impressed by the title as he was meant to be. "We've just come back from Africa."

"Shoot any tigers?"

"They don't have tigers in Africa. Only lions and leopards. Nothing as big as a Bengal tiger, I'm afraid. No, nothing that size. Cheers, old boy. Good to see you."

"Do you miss the army?"

"Yes, I rather think I do. All parts of it." He was again thinking of Sing. He had wined and dined a string of young ladies while Henry made his plans against his daughter's father-in-law, and none of them had sparked his interest. Pale London versions were just not his type. He wondered if Sing was still a virgin or married with children, and he put that out of his mind as it came.

"Pity that company of Rhodes is falling apart," said White.

"Only the share price. Not the company. The Charter Company is alive and well and I can vouch for that. Taken up a farm myself and intend to go back to Rhodesia."

"Met a chap two nights ago at the East India Club who had lost all his money. Bought shares, mortgaged them at the top and bought more shares using the bank's money, poor chap, and now the bank wants the money back and he doesn't have it. Fearfully in debt. Said he was going down to Epsom to plead with his father to bail him out. Poor chap could go to jail as he told the bank when he borrowed the money that his house was worth more than anyone will pay. Mortgaged his house as well, you see. Now that's fraud. Nasty business."

"His name wasn't Brigandshaw by any luck?" said Gregory, turning his full attention to Johnny White. "Arthur Brigandshaw?"

"How did you know? Bad news does travel fast. I say, old chap, would you care to dine with me?"

"An absolute pleasure."

By the end of the evening, Johnny White had learnt nothing more about Sing but as the wine and conversation flowed, Gregory Shaw extracted every detail of the man's meeting in the East India Club and stored the facts carefully where he could bring them out again. The only figure which Gregory was unable to pull from the conversation was the amount Arthur Brigandshaw owed the bank. But he had the name of the bank and the branch.

THE BANK MANAGER came out of a small office wringing his hands with dutiful subservience. Somewhere in the right hand among the wringing was the visiting card of Sir Henry Manderville. Henry had presented it at the front desk when he asked for an appointment on the following Monday morning expecting to call back later in the week. Henry found the man's behaviour ridiculous, but it served its purpose.

"Sir Henry, what a pleasure," said the bank manager, ingratiating himself further while trying to give his staff the impression they had known each other for years, bank manager to the favoured client. Henry wondered once again what it was about a title that made people grovel in the dirt. He put out a calloused hand, calloused from months of cutting trees from Tuli in Bechuanaland to Fort Salisbury, and saw the puzzled expression on the bank manager's face as he took the pressure in a pudgy hand that had never felt work in its life. The card miraculously had transferred to the man's left hand.

"How can I help you? Please come into my office. Would you care for a cup of tea, Sir Henry?"

"That would be kind of you. Now, let me explain. My son-in-law is Arthur Brigandshaw." By the reaction of the man who was still not quite behind his desk, banging his knee on the corner, Henry knew he had the right bank.

"You wish to honour the debt?"

"Of course. Why else would I be here? All I need to know is the amount."

"It is a great deal of money."

"Well, we Mandervilles have been around a long time making money. I am sure it will be a mere bagatelle."

"Is eighty thousand three hundred and twelve pounds seven shillings and sixpence, a mere bagatelle?" said the bank manager, nervously having forgotten all about the tea.

"A mere bagatelle," said Sir Henry not showing the least sign of a wince. "Write it down on a piece of paper and I'll have it here for you within a week."

As the bank manager sat down in his chair and wrote the figure, he was unable to speak. The man who had so rashly lent the money in the first place was his brother-in-law.

Sir Henry reached the open door and turned back waving the piece of paper. "Thank you for the tea."

HENRY'S own solicitor had drawn up the agreement that settled two hundred thousand pounds in three per cent Consols with the capital going to Arthur Brigandshaw on Henry's death, provided Arthur was still married to Emily: the clause had been worded to safeguard Emily and her children should she have any. From The Captain's point of view, it ensured his money did not leave his family. All he would have paid for Hastings Court, and the even more valuable family connection, was six thousand pounds a year for as long as Sir Henry lived. A small price to pay to make his eldest son Lord of the Manor, a subsidiary title that went with the house. The Captain had thought himself very smart at the time and hoped the Baronet would die as soon as possible: most men with too much time on their hands and too much money, drank themselves to death as there was nothing else to do to pass the time.

"You want to release this eighty-three thousand pounds to your son-in-law to pay his debt?" asked the solicitor.

"Yes. In exchange for Arthur withdrawing all complaints against Sebastian and to acknowledge that Harry is Seb's son and that he had never consummated his marriage with Emily, allowing the marriage to be dissolved by the Church and the law. Will the police then withdraw the charges against Sebastian?"

"I rather think they will."

"I should never have let them marry in the first place."

"I rather think I said that at the time, Sir Henry. Arranged marriages into the lower classes are usually unfortunate, despite their money."

"I wanted to protect Emily from poverty."

"Hindsight is an exact science, Sir Henry. Now the question is, will this reprobate Arthur accept your offer?"

"Why ever not?"

"Because he knows you control two hundred thousand pounds."

"Legally, can I give him part of the money without The Captain's consent?"

"One of the tasks of a family solicitor is to protect the family's interest. The sub-clauses in the agreement were brushed over by Captain Brigandshaw as he was only concerned with you walking off with the capital. What I had in mind was Arthur's premature death and your wish to give Emily's children part of the capital. The clause in question says you are entitled to give all or part of the money to Arthur or his offspring in the event of his death, or prior to his death at your discretion, otherwise the money could have stayed in limbo. We solicitors have to think of every legal eventuality. Do you wish me to negotiate with Arthur?"

"I'll do it myself."

"Unwise, I would say. And please don't hit the young man. I have no wish to defend you in a nasty case of assault."

THE WEDDING in Cape Town was a black affair. While Jeremiah Shank was receiving his pieces of silver at the offices of Colonial Shipping, Tinus Oosthuizen took Alison Ford to be his lawfully wedded wife. Two strangers they had found at the Mount Nelson Hotel signed the marriage certificate and left soon afterwards. Alison's dress, run up quickly in the Malay quarter by a seamstress, billowed from the bodice down to hide her pregnancy from the dominie and was the colour of dark sand. Tinus wore a suit for the first time in his life, a well-barbered Tinus with a clipped beard and well-cut hair that hung to his shoulders. The tailor said he had never made a larger suit. Tatenda, forlorn and frightened by so large a building, sat at the back. Emily was at the police station.

Outside the Dutch Reformed Church at the top of Strand Street, the clock tower stared up at Signal Hill and to the right, far out and down the hill, a squall lashed across Table Bay tearing at the anchored ships. A pair of black-backed gulls had drifted up from the bay and cried their lonely cry, cutting and dropping, lifting in the wind. A weak and wintry sunlight crept towards the door of the church as Tinus thanked the dominie in the *Taal* and helped his wife into the hired coach. The dominie watched them sadly.

Tatenda was already on the coach. As soon as the pair of horses began the cobbled road down the hill, following the strangers in their own coach back to the hotel, the squall hit the face of the clock in the tower and the big hands quivered in the grasp of the wind. The dominie had closed the door of his church and gone about his business. Despite the howling wind, the long arm clunked to half-past eleven in the morning and the gulls, wings pinned back in mocking authority over the squall, veered down and away from the clanging sound of man. It was the only sound of wedding bells.

THE WIND WAS HOWLING outside the small high window with the thick bars and Seb felt more dejected than at any other time in his life. He was sick to the very pit of his stomach and the terrible hurt drained through all his feelings.

They had ridden the wagons to Johannesburg, the mining camp in Paul Kruger's Transvaal Republic, to load the ivory on the train and travel with the great tusks to Cape Town. Leaving the two locked railway wagons with the ivory in the Cape Town goods siding they had hired a cab to drive them to the Mount Nelson Hotel. Harry was tired and irritable, Emily and Alison were pregnant. Most of what they wanted was a good meal and a good night's sleep, and they would worry about the ivory in the morning. There was nothing to suggest the closed wagons held anything more than machinery going north to the gold mines. Not even the stationmaster was told the contents, and the wagons stood alone and uninteresting.

Harry was asleep in his dirty clothes and they left him on the bed with Tatenda fast asleep, as they thought, on the couch. So much had happened to Tatenda in three years, he had given up wondering about the turn in his life. He missed his family and sometimes, when he was alone and the others were asleep, he cried, forgetting he was fourteen years old and ready for circumcision. The grown-ups took their baths and when they left to go down to dinner, he felt so lonely he cried and Harry asked him in Shona what was the matter as the lamp burnt softly in the room to keep away the dark. The boy was not asleep as all of them had thought.

"Are you hungry?" asked Harry, saying he was, and then they did go to sleep. When they woke, Tinus had brought them a wicker basket full of cold chicken and freshly baked rolls, and Tatenda did not feel so lonely.

The next day Tinus and Seb had gone off to Colonial Shipping to make arrangements for the ivory only to be told Captain Doyle had left the company and the man in the office was not in a position to say any more. A man with a crooked face who looked familiar had turned away from them as they made their enquiries, leading them to believe Colonial Shipping was no longer interested in ivory. Seb felt the first twinge of alarm as he always did when people behaved out of context: ivory was the best trade to come out of Africa. In the middle of his conversation with the man who had not invited them into his office but stood at the counter, Seb felt a strong hand on his elbow. Tinus cut the conversation, and they were out through the door and back in the cab.

"That was the man, with his back to us, who tipped off Jack Slater outside Salisbury. With Doyle out of the company that manager was acting on your father's orders. Best we leave the ivory and get out of Cape Town and you go back to Rhodesia."

"Tinus, I'll go back with Em and Harry. You stay and marry Alison and sell the ivory somewhere else."

"And Emily's baby?"

"Then I'll go alone." When they reached the gate that led out of the docks it was closed and shortly after, the police arrived and Seb was arrested. Three days later Tinus and Alison had been married and Captain Doyle had sailed into Cape Town harbour with his new ship and the old crew of the *Indian Queen*.

SEB WOKE to his twenty-first birthday in cell number four of the central police station and he was cold and miserable and very much afraid. Being accused of a capital offence, he had been told, had prevented them from giving him bail, and he was to wait in cell number four with two blankets until a Royal Navy ship was able to take him back to England. There he would stand trial for the kidnapping of his brother's wife and son and there was nothing the colonial authorities in Cape Town could do but hold him in the cell.

The Prime Minister of the Cape, Cecil John Rhodes or the governor of the Cape Colony, had no interest in the case as the offence had taken place in England and that was the law and there was nothing anyone could do about it. It was clear to Seb that the idea of a man kidnapping his brother's wife and son left him beyond the pale. Emily had sworn on oath she had gone of her own accord, leaving her husband, and that her son was not her husband's but his brother's. She was now considered a slut who had committed adultery and broken her wedding vows, and none of this changed the fact they were sending Seb back to England. Privately, the man who ran the police cells, whose wife, he knew, slept with other men behind his back, thought Emily was as profane as the prisoner and if he had had his way, the slut would have been shipped back to England for a trial of her own, though under what statute he could not think. One of his Muslim friends said they stoned people in countries faithful to the law of Allah and that was what he would do to her. From that point, all communication had been cut between Emily and Seb and their nightmare took a turn for the worse.

In his cell, alone, early in the morning, the day after the wedding, Seb asked himself what he had done wrong other than to love a girl all the years he could remember. How could a father hate his son so much, a brother hate his brother, to bring him home in shackles when they both knew he was right and they were wrong? What could they want of him so badly that took away what was rightly his? For money? For Hastings Court? Pride and vanity? And what had his mother done to stop what she could see? If he was so wrong to be beneath the hanging tree then how much worse were all of them?

Through force of will and with daylight full through the small window above his head, he stopped feeling sorry for himself. He was right, and they were wrong, and right he told himself blindly, even foolishly, would prevail.

THE DOORBELL RATTLED IMPERIOUSLY for the third time and Arthur Brigandshaw knew he was trapped. For a week he had thought of suicide and found he lacked the courage. And now they had come for his house. He had nothing. There would be no food or shelter. They were going to throw him out on the street and his father was ready to laugh in his face. No one would give him a job. They would laugh, his friends, and walk away, comfortable in the trappings of their own money. The fourth ring sent him cringing to the back room, the small storeroom of the Baker Street house. He was quite alone. The last of his women had gone when the money stopped flowing. They had never wanted Arthur Brigandshaw, only his money. Huddled on the floor, the linoleum smooth, uninterested in his plight, he waited for the sound of breaking wood as they crashed down the door of the house he no longer owned. He would be thirty-four years old in a month's time, and he was penniless, and the fear of poverty ripped at his stomach. For the rest of his life he would live as a tramp, despised by everyone. The bell rattled again and Arthur was sick on the linoleum floor.

A voice from outside the house called his name 'Arthur' and Arthur wiped the stains of the sick from his mouth. Who would call his Christian name if they came sent by the bank? Maybe the shares had rocketed up as quickly as they had fallen down and he was still the man about town? Getting up off his bottom he avoided the puddle of sick and straightened his coat. Again, the man outside called his name and Arthur walked out of the small room to the top of the stairs.

"Just coming," he shouted, turning into the bathroom to wash his face.

From suicidal fear to desperate hope, Arthur trod the red staircase down to the front door of his house, fixed a smile of confidence on his face and opened the door.

"May I come in?" said Henry Manderville.

"My man was out when you rang."

"Bollocks. You're bankrupt, Arthur. The Charter shares went down another shilling this morning."

"Then why are you here, esteemed father-in-law?" said Arthur sarcastically. "Last I heard you were sunning yourself in Italy on our money. You haven't by any chance seen my wife?"

"I know where she is and who she is with." Henry pushed past Arthur and walked into the morning room.

"So you're part of the kidnapping," shouted Arthur, slamming his front door shut and following his father-in-law into the morning room.

"My first instinct is to knock your block off but then you would be of no use to me. You know better than me there was no such thing as a kidnapping and that young Harry is Seb's child, not yours. In the first place, we were both wrong agreeing to an arranged marriage. Sometimes they work, quite often in fact, and the flights of young love wither with familiarity. But to charge your own brother with a capital offence and have him arrested! That's murder."

"He kidnapped my son."

"She ran away with their son! Sebastian became a man and claimed what was his."

"The law is on my side."

"Yes, it is, which is why I am prepared to repay your overdraft with the bank in exchange for you withdrawing your complaint... You didn't consummate your marriage, did you, Arthur?"

"She wouldn't let me."

"Good, then the marriage can be dissolved. By the twisted luck of fate, you are going to be able to go back to your life of debauchery."

"I want the whole two hundred thousand," said Arthur thinking on his feet, the light of dawn flashing in his eyes.

"Yes, I rather thought you would and frankly I don't care. You can keep both Hastings Court and your money, but you can't have my daughter or my grandson."

Arthur began to laugh, quietly at first and then hysterically.

"Do you agree?" asked Henry.

"Of course. You sure you can give me the money?"

"My solicitor is certain, and he drew up the agreement."

"Father will spit blood."

"He may even come to his senses. After all, Sebastian is also his son."

"My father is as hard as nails. All he wants to do is come up in the world and he doesn't care how we do it."

Puzzled by the break into north country dialect, Henry gave Arthur the address and time to meet in the solicitor's office.

"You won't be late?" he said.

"Not this time."

Outside the closed front door, Henry Manderville shuddered as if someone had walked over his grave.

BOOK 3 – THE FIRST CHIMURENGA

1

SEPTEMBER 1895

For some months before his nineteenth birthday (the date given to him by Emily to celebrate), Tatenda had been yearning for his own people. Without a word to anyone, he left in the night and began his journey north from the farm on the banks of the Mazoe River. He headed north guided by the four stars of the Southern Cross, dissecting the pointer stars through the bar made by joining the two bright stars that never left the proximity of the cross. Careful that south was always kept at his back he began the long walk back to his people, the Kalanga, one of the smallest tribes that made up the Shona-speaking people.

Four years before, they had left Cape Town the day after Sebastian was freed from jail and taken the train to Kimberley. When Sebastian drove the lead ox wagon over the Limpopo River at the new crossing east of Tuli, and stated loudly that he would never leave the country the white men were calling Rhodesia, Tatenda felt the first shiver of fear for his people. These white people who had saved his life had come to stay and stay as masters, never as equals. And when, six months after they first arrived in Salisbury the man who said he was Emily's father joined them, Tatenda knew the days of freedom for the tribes of the Shona were over. The father they called Sir Henry had brought a friend from England, and the friend had brought a new wife, and this man they called Gregory Shaw told everyone he was going to have ten children and a farm so big that not one of his neighbours would see his chimney smoke.

They had settled on the farm on the banks of the river twenty miles from

Salisbury that the new government had given them. The trees had come out of the ground, ploughs had gone into the soil and as the game ran from the falling trees, the white men shot them for fun and only sometimes took the meat into Salisbury for sale. And then the first house went up and the first fences and the first white policemen in uniform visited the farm they were calling Elephant Walk. A few of the Shona people came out from hiding away from Lobengula and were given jobs on the farm. Each week they were given a ration of maize meal, a cup of salt, a bag of beans, and as much meat as they could eat along with a place away from the white man on the river to build a hut and plant some pumpkins. After generations of fear the people thought it was paradise. For most people, their freedom was worth giving away for food and shelter and protection from the stabbing spears of the Matabele, the Zulus of Shaka, who had raped and pillaged their way north to the ancient lands of Monomotapa.

Wherever possible, Tatenda had followed the game trail that took him north through the long dry grass that was often higher than his head, dotted with treacherous anthills hidden in the grass and tall msasa trees that traced their newborn leaves against the black heavens. When the moon went down, the millions of stars in the heavens were not enough to show him the way and he stopped under a tree and listened. The warm spring night whirred with the constant call of insects and frogs and far away a lion roared and made him shiver and clutch the puny protection of Harry Brigandshaw's .410 shotgun that he had stolen before he left Elephant Walk. Over his shoulder was a full cartridge belt with everything from number six birdshot to the heavy buckshot that if he got close enough would kill a duiker or a klipspringer.

The guilt of stealing Harry's precious gun was his only sorrow, mingled with the deep fear of loneliness and the fangs of wild animals. The late September sky was clear and layer upon layer of stars domed above his head deep into the black heavens, and he prayed to his ancestors to intercede with God to protect and take him home. Then as the lion roared nearer and was answered by another animal further to his right, he prayed there was a home that some of his people had escaped to from the Matabele terror. Not even once did he think of the new God Sebastian's reverend brother had made him swear to follow. The lions were too close for pleasing other people and other gods and before the night was out, he was calling to his ancestors in fear, his voice thin and shaking. Only with the light of day did he stop his shivering and remember he was a man going to join his people. Gathering his wits he went on his journey, using the sun's position to guide him north; with the night stars, he would check his position accurately the way Tinus had taught them to walk through the bush.

The new leaves on the msasa trees were russet brown and the red of ox-blood mingled with the pale green and yellow of limes. Birds were calling for their mates, telling them where they were in the new day of courage. A buzzard rose on the warm thermals up into the new blue sky, calling plaintively with aching sadness to the new day below. Alone he watched the bird turn and turn higher, calling with the same sad sound of melancholy that filled his heart. It was the first time in his life he had been alone and he looked back to the south whence he had come and he saw his warm bed, and breakfast on the table, and seven-year-old Harry, nearly eight, calling out to find some new excitement in a small boy's world. He almost went back.

The years of good food and the hard training of Tinus Oosthuizen had turned the thin boy into a strong man who came as high as his teacher's shoulders. His thick black hair was cut short to his skull and his face in the white light of morning was aquiline and spoke of some Arab slaver in his ancestry. His eyes were coal black, his lips thin for a Kalanga and his small ears almost as pointed as a lynx. The strong forehead sloped back to the short cropped hair and his head was domed at the back like a calabash. Using the hunting skill of the Boer, Tatenda worked his way through the long elephant grass and pushed the long barrel of his .410 through into the clearing and shot the small impala grazing beside the safety of its mother. The bush echoed with the shot and birds and animals scattered from the powerful sound. Quickly, Tatenda cut the half-dead animal's throat with the knife given to him on his eighteenth birthday by Sebastian. With skill and concentration he skinned the buck, placed a haunch over the coals of his new fire, and cut the rest of the meat into strips to dry in the sun and fill the single saddlebag that thumped against his thigh as he strode the bush. In the far distant heat haze, he could see the foothills of the mountains to the north. Having eaten and filled his bag with half-dried meat he went on his journey.

TATENDA FOUND the elephant trail that had been used for thousands of years on the third day of his flight and even the burden of going north was taken from his mind. The annual migration of the herds moving one behind the other took them south out of the Zambezi River valley a month or more after the end of the rainy season, depending on the grazing in the valley. The great bull led the mammals up the escarpment to the high ground and then down to the well-watered plains that stretched to eternity. The journey back was north and the rugged outcrops that sloped up to form a high ridge looking down into the distant valley. Among the great outcrops there were many places to hide, and pockets of fertile soil scooped into the rocks to grow millet and pumpkin away from the scavenging impi of Lobengula. The afternoon of the first day of his longer stride on the beaten trail he heard the horsemen far enough away to hide behind an anthill in the tall grass off the trail. He watched the four well-armed men ride south down the trail with a purpose. They were prospectors, judging by the picks and shovels strapped to the horses' rumps, but they were not looking at the ground. Their backs were straight, and they laughed as they went on their way, unaware of Tatenda twenty yards into the bush clutching his puny shotgun.

The next morning he was forced off the trail again by two horsemen, white policemen in the uniform of the British South Africa Police, one of whom he recognised as the man in charge of the open bush to the far north and to three miles south of the Mazoe River and Elephant Walk. It was this man's job to keep the peace, and he was heading south with the same purpose as the prospectors. That afternoon two more white men cantered past looking neither to the left nor right.

On the seventh day, he reached the foothills and followed the winding trail of the elephants through and around the outcrops of granite. Some of the boulders were hundreds of feet high, thrown down as he knew by the gods in anger when the tribe of man was sent away in wandering bands sacrificed to the mercy of beasts. Now his people had gone back to the place of the desolation and his search began as he climbed higher and higher watched by eagles and vultures from their nests. The trail swallowed him and he went on and round. Whole trees grew from splits in the mighty rocks, searching down with their roots for soil and sustenance. Leopard watched him from ledges high in the broken outcrops, so far away they looked the size of Harry's cats, basking in the late September sun, only retreating to the cool interior of the lairs when the colour of the sun in the morning changed from white to yellow and waves of heat rose from the bald heads of the giant boulders. With the heat of the day and rising thermals the clouds built in the rainless sky only to fade in the colder night. Rock rabbits scurried again in the cool of the morning and they reminded him of the plight of his people. By the end of the tenth day, when he was approaching the top of the mountains that ranged away to west and east, he had seen no sight or trace of his people, only the white men moving south on their horses.

That evening he stood next to a small stream that had found its way out of a cleft in the mountain and plunged in gentle fury out into space and down to the canopy of trees two thousand feet below on the floor of the Zambezi Valley that stretched as far as he could see. Despondent, he sat on his haunches and wondered if all the people of his tribe were dead. To his right, down a gentler slope to the valley floor, he could still see the elephant trail. As he sat and looked down into the great distance, he caught the first whiff of fetid breath, the first smell of foul air trapped for centuries. Facing him as he turned to find the source of the sickening smell was an old, gnarled, tangled tree not ten feet from his face. Leaving the stream behind him to continue its endless plunge over the cliff he found the small opening to the cave behind the tangled roots of the wild fig tree. Pushing his saddlebag and gun ahead of him he squeezed his way into the cave, disturbing a small rock that dropped inside and echoed its way deep into the bowels of the mountain.

For half an hour he waited until his eyes were accustomed to the dark. Little light found its way into the cave that spread into the darkness thirty feet below his feet. He was on a ledge and to his right, crude steps were cut into the rock leading down to the bone-strewn floor of the cave. However much he wrinkled his nose to catch the smell there was no trace of fresh dung or living cat, and he climbed down into the cave to see where it went, convinced the steps had been cut by his people.

The witch had watched him stand. All the time she stroked the soft fur of the crouched leopard, the yellow eyes fixed on Tatenda standing on his ledge, the predator waiting for the witch to let him go. The animal's stomach rumbled with his excitement. The witch felt the leopard's tail twitch against her back and smiled in the dark in deep anticipation. The distance between the leopard and the man as the man took the crudely cut steps to the cave's floor was eighty yards. The man's movement made the tail thrash and still, the witch stroked the leopard's head, calming the deadly instinct. The witch was waiting for the light and when the ever-rising sun high outside the mountain that encased the cavern reached the small entrance to the hole, hundreds of feet above the cavern floor, a bright white light beamed clarity on the ancient bones and the witch let go of the leopard to find the brief light that the witch used to terrify her people. In the shaft of light, the leopard stopped, commanded by a click from the witch's tongue.

At the moment the leopard showed its face it spoke, the yellow eyes fixed on Tatenda.

"This is the ancient home of Kalanga," spoke the leopard. "Who are you?"

The light and the leopard disappeared at the end of the sentence leaving

Tatenda rooted to the spot. With fear savaging his brain he did not hear the double-click of the witch's tongue calling back the leopard, her throat sore from her ventriloquy that had thrown her voice to issue from the leopard's mouth. As silent as the leopard, the witch withdrew further into the cavern, listening for the terrified departure of the stranger who had entered their sanctuary. When it came, a long moment after the sun passed over the hole in the roof, she smiled with toothless satisfaction.

The moment of pure fear, honed by thousands of years of superstition, made Tatenda shiver in the heat of the sun, his rigid hands still clutching the gun and saddlebag. The wind had come up and blown into his face taking away the smell of ancient death. A black eagle circled soundlessly, ignoring the man on the road below. Taking a down current, the great bird dropped vertically to the face of the escarpment, searching the jutting rocks for prey. The wind made a thin whistle passing through a rock cleft above Tatenda's head, and the sound of the normal wind soothed his shivering and stopped his urge to run out and dive towards the eagle soaring down below through the spray that was all that was left of the plunging stream. Dropping to his knees the ancient man within him, now dressed in European clothes, called for his ancestors to intercede with God and take the terror from his mind. He plunged his head in a running stream thirty feet from the lip of the escarpment, crawling further into the stream that dragged him slowly to the plunge, the current gentle with its balm, the rock floor smoothed by the years of rushing water. Luxuriously as he faced his ancestors, Tatenda turned on his back, still floating inch by inch to his death at the end of the stream, his body bumping the bouldered floor of the riverbed. A man was standing on the last rock beside the plunge with the saddlebag in his left hand and Harry's shotgun in his right, the belt of cartridges across his chest. A jackal skin hung from his waist and hid his genitals.

"You better come out of there," he said in Shona. He was about Tatenda's age.

"You spoke to the leopard," he said as a statement. "I have been following you for two days. The white men are leaving the country. It is time for the struggle. You are Kalanga or the leopard would not have spoken."

"Those things are mine."

"Where did you get them?"

"From the white man."

"You have been with the white man?"

"For many years after the Zulus killed my family."

"And now you have come home. Good. We are going to kill the white men and women before the soldiers return. It is said so by the witch. The

Kingdom of Monomotapa will come again and we will walk as men without fear in our own land, masters again of our destiny. The witch has spoken to the ancestors and they give us the word of God. We must kill the white people." Carefully, so as not to lose his balance and with the gun set aside on the rock, he put down his hand and helped Tatenda from the water.

THE WITCH WAS SATISFIED with her work when Tatenda, still terrified by his ordeal, was brought into the village that backed away from the labyrinth of caves, a sanctuary known to the Kalanga priests for centuries. The witch was head priest, and she knew she was the most powerful member of the tribe, smelling out anyone for death by clubbing if they disagreed with the instructions she fed to the people through the paramount chief. Each tribe that made up the Shona-speaking people were ruled by a paramount chief and each chief was controlled by the powers of the witch-priests. And for the first time in centuries, their words were being challenged by the white men and their God of love and forgiveness. The witch had travelled for nine days to attend a secret meeting. The word had reached the witch-priests that the white man's army was moving to the south for battle with the Boers. The Matabele and Shona people became of one mind. Together they would destroy the white man and drive them back across the Limpopo River. The witch-priests at their meeting agreed to unleash a war of liberation.

The witch watched Tatenda while she stroked the leopard's head. She was old and wrinkled, her breasts hanging in long black leather pouches to her navel. No one sat near her out of fear and the self-knowledge of her power was intoxicating. She had been a girl of three when she was taken for training by the witch before her. For forty-seven years, there had been no other contact with the people except through her power of fear and the magic she had learnt from her predecessor. Sometimes she laughed at the stupidity of people but the sound was silent in her throat. Sometimes she threw the laugh high into a tree at night, the cackling shattering the peace of the people and sending fear deep into their genitals. Whenever the chief questioned her words of suggestion, she used her power of magic, the tricks of her trade the other old crone had taught her before she died from the poison the witch had slowly fed into her food. The witch knew that power, absolute power was the most intoxicating experience of human life, and she was not going to have it usurped by these white people who did not belong in her country.

· · ·

THE MAN they called Gumbo after a Matabele assegai shattered his hip when he was twelve and left for dead, limped towards Tatenda who was standing alone next to the chief's hut where he had been taken. Tatenda watched the man approach. The gun, bag and cartridges had gone from Tatenda's possession and the limping man was smiling like someone who had just done a favour.

"The women gave you food?" asked Gumbo.

"No. I have not eaten."

"You will. There is food since the white people stopped the Matabele stealing our food."

"Then why do you want to kill them?"

"You have heard?"

"Everyone talks about a war of liberation. You chase out the white man and the Matabele will raid your cattle again."

"They are our friends. The chief says they are our friends. An enemy of my enemy is my friend."

"The Matabele need you after Jameson defeated Lobengula and chased him out of Gu-Bulawayo. The Matabele impis came to the walls of Fort Victoria and slaughtered our people in front of the eyes of the white man. Jameson made up an army and rode against the Matabele."

"And he rides again to chase the Boers out of Johannesburg to give the gold to Rhodes."

"If you succeed, you will live in fear of the Matabele. War is the only business. There are many Englishmen with powerful guns. I have seen them. You chase away a few and more will return. There is plenty of land for everyone. I have walked for days through the bush and you were the first black man I saw. White men, a few on horses going south."

"When the chief gives the word, we attack the farms and mines of the white men and when they come out of the forts, we will kill the men and then go to the forts to kill their women and children. They will have great fear of us. They will not come back."

"You are well informed." The knowledge of Doctor Jameson and Johannesburg had impressed Tatenda.

"I am the chief's son and they call me Gumbo. What is your name?"

"Tatenda."

"Gumbo. The man who limps. That is me."

"Gumbo. Be careful. Tell your father. I have lived with these white people for many years. They will never go away."

"Then why did you leave them?"

"To find my own people."

"Precisely. People live with their own. They feel comfortable. We also do not wish to live with these white people who treat us as slaves."

"It is better to be a slave of the white man than dead or hiding in the mountains like a rock rabbit, frightened of the birds. I have come to tell you to come out of the caves. The white men will protect you. There is a life of joy again for us."

"Do not say that. The witch is watching. You will have to fight with us."

"I will not."

"Then she will kill you. You have heard the voice of Kalanga's leopard and the priests are instruments of the leopard." Thinking of the leopard Tatenda shivered in fear, and the witch watching smiled to herself. 'Fear is the best controller of man,' she told herself, and for good measure threw a cackle at the msasa tree above Tatenda's head.

ONE HUNDRED AND thirty miles away to the south clouds had built up all day. The heat and humidity were oppressive. For the third time that day Emily snapped at Harry and sent him crying out of the house, which sent four-year-old Madge into a tantrum and stretched Emily's nerves to breaking point. All the men were out in the lands and Gregory Shaw's fancy wife had not come back from Salisbury in three weeks. Despite Gregory's bragging, the lady was not pregnant and Emily doubted she would come back to the farm. Romantic farming in faraway Africa, from the comfort of the Savoy Grill in London, was very different to the reality of a house built from raw timber which the termites ate with relish, sending fine clouds of chewed wood from the rafters dusting every cup of tea and making Alison Oosthuizen sneeze until she was ready to burst. Even after three years on the tract of land they were grandly calling Elephant Walk, she longed for the solitude and calm of Hastings Court and cursed the day she ever heard of Africa.

She loved Sebastian with all her heart but hated Africa with every fibre of her body. She was never free of bites whether tick or mosquito. Bats hung from the roof lattices that held up the open thatch, and twice she had found a dead snake in what they emphatically called the bathroom consisting of a tin tub that needed water lugged up from the Mazoe River. Even the joy of living with her father could not dispel the nightmares and if she ate wild boar again or venison, she would scream down what was left of their house. Even the buck ate the few flowers she had been able to grow in the patches of open land between the msasa trees, and Tatenda running off without a word to anyone had been the last straw, as the only other person who could speak Shona to what they referred to as the house servants, which even Alison thought was a bit of a laugh, was Harry and he was more than sparing with his workload. But above everything, it was hot, hot, *hot*. Giving full vent to her feelings Emily Brigandshaw screamed out loud and felt a little better. The noise shut her daughter off in mid-cry and brought Harry back into the house with an expression on his face that, under better circumstances, Emily would have registered as compassion.

Doing what every Englishwoman had done for a hundred years, she went into the kitchen and made herself a cup of tea from the permanently hot kettle that sat on top of the wood stove making the kitchen as hot as the oven even in winter. And to cap her misery, that the tea only slightly tempered, she was pregnant. Her only consolation was that nothing could possibly get worse.

Taking her second cup of tea into the garden they had created by cutting away the undergrowth between the trees for fifty yards around the cluster of three thatched houses, each of two rondavels joined by a corridor that housed the euphemistic bathroom and the kitchen, as well as a passage from the bedroom rondavel to the one they called the lounge, Emily found the wooden bench made by Tinus Oosthuizen and tried to think on the bright side of life. The door was open to a separate rondavel that gave Sir Henry Manderville his bedroom and she hoped nothing creepy crawly had got inside. It was the regular routine to check the inside of their beds for bugs and reptiles before climbing in between the sheets below the billowing white mosquito nets that hung from the termite-chewed rafters.

Then she smiled to herself and somehow felt better. Both her children had sidled up quietly and she told herself not to scream again, Harry and Madge were just as hot and Harry missed Tatenda. With the cup of tea set down beside her, she let too small sweaty hands slide into hers. In the last of their houses she could hear Alison talking to Barend in Afrikaans and for a brief moment, she heard the new baby cry. An ox bellowed somewhere far beyond the trees where the men were ploughing the land they had finally stripped of trees and tree stumps. Then the good thoughts rushed through her mind whilst sitting with her children, knowing the men were fighting for survival. The memory of the vindictive Captain, of her divorced husband Arthur, the marriage annulled for lack of consummation, the bitter cold and bitter loneliness of Hastings Court came back in violent memory, and when Harry next to her said it would all be better when the rains broke, she began to cry silently with joy.

"Mummy's just being silly," said Harry to his sister. To her mild surprise and for the first time that day, Madge failed to ask why.

"Come; it's time for your books young man. Go and bring them out here."

"Can I listen, Mummy?" asked Madge.

"Only if you don't say a word. Not even one why." The tinkling laughter of the children running back into the house for the books broke her dark spell, and even the floating fly she flicked from her tea failed to break her newfound mood of confidence. Harry was right. Everything would be better when the rains broke.

BY THE TIME the sun went down, blood-reddening the sky high into the cumulus, the four men were exhausted. They had been in the lands before the sun was fully risen, with breakfast and lunch brought to them where they worked with the six black labourers who had come looking for work and lasted more than a week. Half the black men coming out of the bush for work found the white man's idea of working from sunup to sundown unacceptable and went back into the bush to find a place by a river where they could build a hut, find a wife, and put her out to till the ground around the anthills. There was food in the river and food in the bush and a hut to sleep in away from the wild animals which were all they needed; working six days a week in the sun was no work for a man. When they left, most of them tried to steal something for their trouble and after three years building the houses, trying to plant a crop, trying to keep the cattle alive and away from tsetse and tick, even Tinus Oosthuizen admitted to himself that this part of Africa was tougher than anything he had found before. With a wry smile, he now knew why the country that looked so green was so underpopulated, even without taking the Matabele raiding parties into account. The only thing that thrived in that part of Africa was the game and the game brought the tsetse fly and the ticks.

The small labour force went off to find their huts by the river and the white men trudged back with the three oxen that had been pulling the ploughs through the ground that was hard as iron, every weight they could think of balanced on top of the two-furrow plough to push the discs down into the grass-tangled soil. They had managed to finish one acre of badly ploughed land all day. When they reached the houses, they were relieved to see Alison had organised the herding of their thirty head of cattle into the kraal away from the night predators that hunted from the thick bush. The ritual each day was the same. Everyone headed for Tinus Oosthuizen's house and the long veranda along the riverside of the house, stretching the length of the corridor that linked his two rondavels. In a tall mukwa tree hung three heavy canvas bags that caught the wind. The water seeping through the tightly woven canvas evaporated with the brushing of the wind and cooled the spring water in the bags and in the bags were bottles of quinine, the tonic water they believed counteracted the bite of the mosquito and malaria. Even the Afrikaner, Tinus, enjoyed the Englishman's way of drinking gin. After three or four stiff ones the daily slab of venison was easier to chew.

GREGORY SHAW WAS NOT certain if he preferred his wife away in Salisbury. The twenty-one-year-old flirt he had met in London had no resemblance to the twenty-four-year-old who had found nothing to her pleasure other than being the centre of attention and making everyone around her miserable. Maybe the idea he had given her of a mansion on a great estate had been a little farfetched and his descriptions of life in Africa more vivid than truthful. Maybe he had constantly compared Francesca to Sing. But whichever one way you looked at it, the woman was a bitch. There was no fool like an old fool, he told himself when it was too late. Taking the large gin and tonic with grateful hands from Sebastian Brigandshaw he took a good long swig and sighed with pleasure... There were some things that never changed.

"Now that tastes good," he said, and they all laughed. Gregory Shaw said the same exact thing every night just as the sun fired arrows of light at the blood-red clouds that mirrored themselves a few hundred yards down in front of them in the surface of the Mazoe River. Within five minutes it was pitch dark and the only light came from the hissing kerosene lamp on the table. From outside they heard the first roar of the lion, and the horses, out in the kraal with the cattle, whinnied with fright.

SIR HENRY MANDERVILLE had never been happier in his life. He enjoyed the physical work and the challenge of doing something for himself. Inheriting title and wealth removed the incentive a man needed to do more than go through a pre-arranged life in the same house with the same routine. The daughter he loved as dearly as his late wife was three yards from his chair, his grandson and granddaughter were trying hard not to go to sleep on the couch he had helped to make with his own hands, his son-in-law was holding his pregnant daughter's hand and the moths and diverse insects were being kept away by the tightly meshed wire screen. Outside the frogs and crickets screeched louder than the London Symphony Orchestra and the cattle lowing in the kraal had calmed the horses. The world of The Captain, of money and power, was as far away as the moon. The people he loved were safe in front of him and the gin and tonic tasted better than any gin and tonic he had drunk in his ancestral home.

SEBASTIAN BRIGANDSHAW WAS SO TIRED it was an effort to finish his second drink and when he went to bed, he knew he would not sleep and his mind would think round in circles. He was twenty-five years old and of the men on the veranda, he was the youngest by many years. His father-in-law was happy to work all day and think no further than what he was doing, knowing someone would give him food and drink for his labour. Gregory Shaw talked about a mansion but never how the money was to be made, and if he did have all the money he said he had in England, why hadn't he brought a team of builders from Fort Salisbury and built his house as far away as possible and kept his destructive man-eating wife away from a happily married man?

Tinus did what every Afrikaner did that he had come across, and that was breed children, letting Africa take care of their future. Practically he was brilliant, but when it came to the mathematics of their financial survival, he left it to his young friend.

By the time the rains came in five to six weeks, Sebastian calculated they would have thirty tilled acres to plant, to feed three and a half families and have enough over to expand. Even if every black man out of the bush wished to work forever, it would be no good as there was no food or money to give them. Over and over again his mind calculated how they were going to survive on thirty acres. He must have tensed again as Emily squeezed his hand, and that brought him back to Fran and whether he should tell Gregory what his wife was up to. Sebastian had no previous experience of women but his primal instinct told him Fran Shaw was trouble, trouble for him, trouble for Em, trouble for everyone. She was bored, and a bored woman with too much sex appeal in the middle of the bush with four men was not something any of them would know how to handle. He just hoped her affair in Fort Salisbury with Jack Slater lasted, the same Jack Slater Jeremiah Shank had wanted to arrest him for abduction back in 1891. The kerosene lamp spluttered on the carcass of a moth that had crept in under the door. Maybe four stiff gins instead of three would let him sleep. Looking at his children fast asleep on the couch, he was doubly envious. Nothing, he told himself for the umpteenth time, came easily in life.

. . .

THEIR WHOLE WORLD had shrunk to the light of the kerosene lamp. On the fly screen a giant shadow of a moth was dying in agony and outside it was pitch black. Alison, in light on one side of her face, handed them plates of cold meat and salad, the lettuce and tomatoes from the wire cage built by Henry Manderville to keep out the buck and wild pigs. They had stopped talking while they ate and all the children were fast asleep on mattresses around their feet. The distant days of being an English servant were so far away, she found it difficult to think of herself as the same person. Tinus was the kindest, the sweetest man on earth and all she had ever wanted to do in life was look after her own children. Harry had been a darling, but he was not Barend or Tinka. When she finished her food, she put down the plate on the low table and looked again at her sleeping children, the flow of love so strong she could feel it leaving her body.

TINUS OOSTHUIZEN CHEWED the end of his pipe he had forgotten to light and his mind was far back in the past, the past of his people trying to cut a life for themselves in Africa. For a while, he had thought of telling Sebastian but decided the man had enough worries chewing in his mind to add one that was far more serious than anything they had faced. The ivory hunter turned farmer and husband knew the signs better than anyone else in the room. They were vulnerable.

The administrator of Rhodesia, Dr Jameson, had taken the police force out of the country to help the Uitlanders, the foreigners in Johannesburg, overthrow the Boer republic of Paul Kruger and put the vast gold reef back in the British Empire. Rhodesia, five years after occupation, was undefended, and the settlers like themselves were scattered on farms and small mines in pockets of twos and threes. He had caught the look of the black men asking for work, the gleam of avarice, the knowing smirk of contempt. With a story to keep the wild animals away from the houses, he planned a way to turn the buildings into a stockade. Content with the solution to his problem, he lit a match on the side of his rough leather boot and brought the flame to the bowl of his pipe, sending clouds of sweet-smelling tobacco up into the flare of the lamp. Over the light of the match, he smiled at his wife, the blue eyes showing gently through the flame.

2

NOVEMBER 1895

With all his bravado of ten children, no one had thought to tell her the man was impotent and a girl of twenty-four had her needs. The bloody farm made her sick. Those two self-satisfied women clucked all day around their children and had no conversation other than babies past and present, all the time looking as if something was wrong with her. And when they looked at their husbands with puppy-dog eyes, it made her sick. The only man she fancied was Seb and never once had he given a sign that he noticed her. Jack Slater was no oil painting but at least he was a man, even if he had developed a high degree of conscience after his first long burst of sexual gratification. Generally, men made her sick, they were so easy to manipulate. She had first checked up the wealth in the Shaw family and by a devious route even found out the extent of Gregory's private income. And how was she to know the trust would cut him off if he married a Catholic? Worse still, the stupid man had only found out himself after the event when they both cursed his bigoted great-grandfather who had made all the money and written the terms of the trust. Then the great estate in Africa came to the fore, and it had sounded fun and a girl with a bad reputation and no great future took what she could get. But stuck in the bush with sanctimonious morons and a husband who couldn't even get it up was more than Fran Cotton could take. They could call her Mrs Shaw all they liked. Until the captain from India got it up, she was still Fran Cotton. And if she heard him call out Sing once more in his sleep she would ring his bloody neck. Touching Jack Slater's back very slowly with the tip of her right index fingernail she woke him up and, before he could think of his conscience, she had him on top. They both forgot where they were in the dark and it was a full half minute after their mutual climax before they came back to earth.

"You're a damn good fuck, Jack Slater," she said.

"And you're Greg's wife."

"You weren't worried about that a minute ago." And then she laughed. It made her feel happy and in control when she laughed at them.

"You'd better go home, Fran," he said seriously. This time she had been in Salisbury for three days.

"I know. You are becoming a bit of a bore. A good fuck but a bore. It really is such a shame."

"You're a bitch, Fran."

"Just after copulation, it's rude to call the girl a bitch. But you're right, Jack. I am a bitch and you can't say we haven't had some fun, you sanctimonious hypocrite. Why do people always sound so righteous and act so wrong? Funny thing is, they even convince themselves they have atoned for their sins. Probably why my ancestors became such devout Catholics. Fuck all week and pray all Sunday. What a religion!"

"Don't blaspheme."

"There you go again, Jack Slater. Up on your high horse. Someday you should try and look at yourself through my eyes and then you won't even dare talk about God. Now, do you want another quick fuck to keep you going for another week?"

Ten minutes after the door slammed, Jack Slater wished he had taken up her offer.

DOCTOR LEANDER STARR JAMESON, physician, confidant of Cecil John Rhodes, destroyer of Lobengula, King of the Matabele, and Administrator of Rhodesia, was not amused. The new administration office was at the top of the main street they were calling Jameson Avenue and half an hour after Fran drove her horse and buggy up Second Street on her way back to Elephant Walk, the man in charge of keeping him informed reported the liaison.

It was so hot Jameson's mind was boiling from oppressive heat along with his plans for invading the Transvaal. Outside his open window, a gig scuttled down the street sending dust high into a sky heavy with cumulus that every day gave the promise of bursting rain.

And now he was forced to think of Jack Slater who was going to be left in command when he rode for Johannesburg the following day. Far away came a roll of thunder which made him get up and look out of the window over the small Jacaranda trees he had planted on both sides of the dusty street. Far away beyond the new town he was trying to build, high up between the stacks of clouds, which were pitch black underneath and fluffy white at the top, forked lightning was flashing down the side of the thousand yard-high billows towards the dry earth. It was five in the afternoon and while he was standing with his back to the room, looking quizzically at the electric storm, a servant came to his office on bare and silent feet to light the lamps. When all four were finally lit Jameson turned round to face the problem of Jack Slater's affair with a married woman and left the storm to rumble and crackle with forked fire far away behind his back over the rooftops of scattered houses that were the beginning of his new country. He was going to bring this new country the three C's promised by Dr Livingstone, missionary and explorer of Africa.

Civilisation to stop the tribes killing each other; Christianity and the only true God; and commerce, that would bring the tribes out of fluctuating poverty to where a man could plan his life better than one day at a time. If only the petty foibles of individuals would keep out of his way, the trivia that took up so much of his time. If the man was so obsessed by his sexual lust, why couldn't he find a wife other than one that belonged to someone else? Captain Shaw may have left India under a cloud, but he was still a British officer and a gentleman. After thinking through the problem for nearly five minutes he was unable to find a solution. When it came to women, Dr Jameson was out of his depth. As he looked in brief despair out of the open window, a crack of lightning hit an old tree the builders had left for shade, splitting it in two, the crash of thunder booming instantly above his head. 'If only it would rain,' he said to himself for the umpteenth time that day.

Fran had stopped for a pot of tea at the new Meikles Hotel and was sitting outside on the veranda that overlooked Third Street and the road back to the farm when the crack of lightning and crash of thunder frightened her out of her wits. Even the well-dressed man with the well-cut beard and silver-topped cane at the next table jumped. They both nervously laughed together at their mutual fright. The man stood up and bowed to her as if to introduce and reassure. As he did so another violent fork of lightning cut the dark sky, but this time the crash of thunder made them laugh together without the nervousness. The man was dapper and wore a diamond ring on the small finger of his left hand. He was alone, and the diamond was larger than anything Fran had seen before in her life. The flash of the big diamond was in surprising contrast to the tattoo of an anchor below the elbow of his left arm. The man had taken off his jacket in the desperate heat and was wearing a short-sleeved shirt that came to his elbows.

"That should bring the rain," he said in a cultured English accent that to Fran was somehow not quite right... Maybe the man was a foreigner, she told herself.

"I hope so."

"Are you staying in town, Mrs...?"

"Shaw. Yes. I will be. Probably. I had intended driving the buggy home."

"Is your home far, Mrs Shaw?"

"Twenty miles. My husband will be worried about me, I'm sure."

"I'm sure. Shopping always takes longer than one thinks. The hotel will give you a room for the night and tomorrow morning we'll make a pleasant drive into the country. Would you like me to inquire about a room? I have a little influence as Thomas Meikle kindly borrowed some of my money to build his hotel. Maybe you would join me for supper, Mrs Shaw? My name is Jeremiah Shank, at your service."

The dapper man had put on his jacket and bowed to Fran. Making sure the expression did not show on her face, Fran's intuition told her the man was English, not foreign, and the accent of culture had been grafted on to an altogether different kind of vine. Which was why the man had quickly put on his jacket: the only thing he could not hide from his past was the anchor on his arm. Maybe this was what she was really looking for, she told herself, and with her best and most sensuous smile she put out her right gloved hand and accepted the invitation. If nothing else it would make that sanctimonious hypocrite Jack Slater feel jealous and Fran Shaw liked making men jealous. The little man smiling at her might have a crooked face but she was sure this one was genuinely wealthy and almost certainly a self-made man.

THE ONLY WEAK link in Jeremiah Shank's armoury was well-bred women. On his way to the bar, he had seen Fran Shaw sitting on her own and had changed course for the table just behind her back, inwardly grimacing at the idea of ordering a pot of tea. The crash of thunder had given him just the chance he was looking for. Timing had always been the key to his success, timing and waiting. Sometimes the prey was out of reach, like the two truckloads of ivory in the siding at Cape Town station, but the lack of opportunity to steal the ivory had sent him north earlier than he expected, and in Kimberley, on his way back to Rhodesia with the price of delivering

Sebastian Brigandshaw to the police, he had stopped off to look at the large hole in the ground. He was curious to see how Cecil Rhodes had bought up so many claims and combined them to make one big profitable dig without the walls and squabbles in between. Barney Barnato, a Jewish cockney pugilist, had done the same thing. Barnato was rich and Rhodes was so rich he could afford to buy himself a country.

Many of the small diggers found their capital running out before they found the diamonds. Like a man playing poker for big stakes, Jeremiah forgot his land in Rhodesia. Casting his carefully cultivated accent, he plunged into the big hole and made friends with the sweating diggers. First, he lent them money to keep them going, saying he had won the cash at cards. Then he waited. On the same day six months after he arrived on the train from Cape Town he called up the loans on thirty-four claims. With half his capital still intact he was able to employ a gang of blacks to dig down far enough into the blue rock to find the diamonds. Nine months later he was rich. He left the first digger who had fallen into his loan trap as manager and rode the mail coach for Salisbury. Behind, he left three thugs to watch the manager. The thugs received ten per cent of diamond sales, as did the manager. Like cat and mouse, they found it better not to steal. And to add to the mix Jeremiah had appointed one of the local policemen as a spy.

The estate of twenty thousand acres seventeen miles south of Salisbury was his main interest, as a man who wished to be a gentleman needed land. By the time he found himself entertaining the very sensuous Mrs Shaw in the exclusive dining room of Meikles Hotel, with the punkahs high overhead doing their best to stir the air, the first truly beautiful home in Rhodesia had been built on the north bank of the Hunyani River and Jeremiah's great estate was fenced and three thousand head of cattle roamed the bush inside the perimeter. Looking at the woman across the perfectly starched double damask tablecloth he was not sure whether he wanted to bed the woman as a whore or take her as a wife. There was no doubt in his mind that the accent emanating from Mrs Shaw was the genuine article, born and bred for generations, something all his elocution lessons had never been able to give. Idly as he watched her over his glass of Cape red wine, he wondered how much it would cost to buy out Shaw. Jack Slater was easy. The man had a conscience and once he was acting administrator he would have to give up the delectable Mrs Shaw. Jeremiah agreed with Cecil Rhodes, every man had his price.

Halfway through the meal and three glasses of red wine to the better, the lady began to tell him what he wanted to hear, though it puzzled him why Elephant Walk was so short of money. If he hadn't stolen the two wagonloads of ivory, what had happened to the money, unless it had gone down the same bottomless pit of Captain Doyle and his dream of a fleet of ships? Jeremiah felt a proprietary interest in Sebastian Brigandshaw as the boy had been the source of his wealth. He knew the crew of the *Indian Queen* had left Colonial Shipping to start a new line, and he suspected the capital had come from Tinus Oosthuizen and young Sebastian Brigandshaw. It never failed to amuse him how easily a fool and his money or a fool and his diamond claims were separated. The story of Shaw losing his inheritance, which he heard after the fourth glass of wine, really tickled his fancy. Likely the last of the ivory money had gone down the same rat-hole, Captain mighty Doyle... With a bit of luck, the ship had sunk with the whole damn crew. Jeremiah always found satisfaction in other people's adversity.

The lady was on a roll. Even Shaw's inability to fuck his wife came up politely in the conversation. Jeremiah, at the end of the supper, prided himself on the fact the lady had no idea he knew more about his shipmates than the shipmates knew about themselves. He ordered a balloon glass of Rémy Martin brandy and a cigar, and sat back in his chair, replete with food and conversation. It was such a nice feeling to be superior to everyone and the *maître d'* had been particularly obsequious, wringing his hands in compliance at every opportunity.

If there was a thing a woman or man liked doing best it was talking about themselves and Fran Shaw was no exception. By the time her coffee and liqueur arrived, a delicious glass of Benedictine, she was well on her way to being drunk and failed to pick up the gleam of interest in her supper companion's eyes when she mentioned anyone from Elephant Walk. She thought the interest was in her, and even managed to delicately slip in her problem with Gregory so the man would not feel constrained when he made the pass she was sure was coming.

The house in England outside Godalming had been in the family for centuries though the land they owned had shrunk to five acres and the firm of Holland and Cotton, solicitors, had been the source of family income since her grandfather had come down from Oxford with a Law degree and not very much else. But he was a gentleman and a gentleman's word was his bond and the local gentry felt safe with him as they did with her father, and there was still the old house to prove where they came from. Many of the clients were related to the Cottons as the pool of gentry in the county over the centuries had been small. The firm made the family a comfortable and respectable living. There were two boys and Francesca in the family, the name coming from her parents' three-week honeymoon in Tuscany. The boys were older, which was fun, but by the time Fran was sixteen she had met every one of their boring friends and the thought of marrying one of them and burying herself in the country for life was appalling. The one good pursuit that went with her background was playing the piano. Using the female charm she found so powerful she persuaded her doting father to send her to the Royal College of Music in London. She was a very good pianist, there was no doubt about that, but her real reason for going had been to get out of Godalming for good so she could start to do some living. They found her a respectable house to lodge in near the college and off she went, knowing her real future lay in her power over men, not in the way she played a Beethoven sonata. After Godalming, London was so exciting. She played the piano with such joy, she was soon the most popular girl in her class. Even the teacher thought she had a future. The only thing she missed from Godalming was the dogs, four highly strung Red Setters.

Her first love affair was with a flautist who wasn't very good at playing the flute but had the sensual looks of Lord Byron and long soft curly hair the colour of ripe corn. He was nineteen and the only man she was to love for the rest of her life. They talked about beautiful things, beautiful music, beautiful poems, beautiful flowers, and most often of all they talked about the beauty they saw in each other. Unfortunately, the flautist had a short attention span and after three months he went on his beautiful way. She saw neither hide nor hair of him again.

Making sure she chose the weak carefully, she pursued and crushed a long list of young men. Any that might have been suitable and looked likely to propose marriage were quickly warned of her reputation by her so-called friends. One of her friends was heard to say in a rare erotic moment that Fran Cotton was growing mushrooms on her bed sheets and all but one of her friends had no idea what she was talking about. 'Damp sheets, darling, damp sheets.' Then the unimaginative laughed nervously. By the time Gregory Shaw came along, a rich man of the world who would take her out of England and away from her reputation, she was looking for a husband. She had graduated from the Royal College and occasionally played the piano at soirées in expensive houses where the hostess was more interested in her playing than her reputation. It made her independent and avoided the problem of her going back to Godalming.

A yellow sunlight woke her in the morning and for a split moment, she had no idea where she was. She was hungover which was not unusual, drink having drowned her sorrows many times before. She was relieved to find there was no one else in the strange room, and then she remembered where she was and the evening with the dapper man with the crooked nose came back to her. To save her life, she could not remember his name. She pulled the cord for the maid, dropping a flap on the kitchen board one story down below that sent a servant up with a tray of tea to room twenty-four.

The tea soothed her parched throat while she contemplated the next move in her life. She could either go back to England and be ostracised by polite society, or go back to Elephant Walk and her husband. There was Jack Slater, but intuition said he was a spent force. She thought of work, but no one needed a pianist in a frontier town... They wanted a piano player who showed off more than her chest and who could sing. Against an audience that wanted lustful vaudeville in a town starved of women, Mozart had very little chance. Very often in life, Fran had found it necessary to take the best she could find out of many evils. With her horse fresh in the hotel stable, it would take three hours to drive to the farm. Maybe this time he would be pleased to see her. One never knew.

When she drove the horse and buggy away from the hotel, there was no sign of the man whose name she could not remember. It was cool in the morning and surprisingly the breakfast had settled her young stomach.

She began to sing as the horse trotted along. The servant from Elephant Walk, the one thing they all insisted went with her on her jaunts into Salisbury, sat silently. He was always more surly at the end of their stays in the town, and as the man could not speak English and Fran could not speak Shona, there was nothing she could say to break his mood. It made the men on Elephant Walk think they had done the right thing by giving her protection, and this made her laugh. If a lion wanted to eat them, Fran rather thought there was nothing either of them could do. It really was a very strange life for a girl from Godalming, she told herself, as a herd of buck scattered into the trees. Far over on the horizon over the tops of the msasa trees, the cumulus was beginning to build.

For the first time, Fran had no real idea what she was going to do with the rest of her life.

THE MAN on the bench seat next to Fran was convinced the war of liberation would be over in a week if everyone acted at the same time, Matabele and Shona. The stupid white men at Elephant Walk did not even know the difference between a Matabele, a Zulu from the south, and the scum that made up the scattered tribes of the Shona. His impis had been picking over them quite satisfactorily until Rhodes stole the land from his King Lobengula and Jameson rode into Gu-Bulawayo with armed mounted men and machine guns. There was nothing then they had been able to do but retreat to the north and await their time for revenge.

The man they called The Crocodile for his ability to snap with deadly effect when others thought he was asleep, had commanded the impi that killed Alan Wilson and his Shangani patrol in 1893 and knew the taste of victory. Enough of his warriors would always destroy some whites as, like Wilson, their guns eventually ran out of ammunition.

Infiltrating Elephant Walk had been so simple he had wanted to laugh. He was the induna of the Matabele, general to Lobengula, King of the Matabele. They had thought him a useless savage and given him a job digging up trees for a few beans, salt and meat from game that belonged to Lobengula: Lobengula, who now lay dead in his cave wrapped in the skin of a great black ox, buried with all the dignity that was rightful to the son of Mzilikazi, induna and general to the great Shaka, King of the Zulu. Silently Zwide recited the praise song to Shaka, followed by the song to Mzilikazi, followed by the longest one of all and spoken first by Zwide at the burial cave, the praise song to his own king, Lobengula. At the time the furrows on his face were deep with concentration. Then he thought of the gold and ivory, the boxes of rifles buried with the king, and smiled. The Matabele would rise greater than ever before.

The luck of being chosen to ride with the whore into Salisbury had only been what was due to him after the great trek from the mopane forest south of the Smoke that Thunders, which the whites were calling Victoria Falls. The journey had been dangerous but profitable. Now he knew that Jameson had left for the south and the country was theirs for the picking. Even the indignity of being a servant to a woman had been worth this knowledge.

All he now had to do was convince the stupid Shona to act in unison by making all their bickering tribes work together. He, like Mzilikazi, a descendant of Zwide the great chief of the Zulu, would lead the Matabele back to their glory. And once he had chased away the whites, he would see about the Shona. They would be his subjects as they had been the subject of Mzilikazi and Lobengula, praise their names.

He would slip away when he reached the farm. Quietly he wondered what the woman next to him would say if she knew he understood English, a task of learning placed on him by his king and learnt from the white hunters that buzzed around the king's kraal like blowflies on a kill. And the great white hunter Tinus Oosthuizen had not even recognised him away from his headdress of crane feathers and the skin of a great leopard he had killed with his own hands. Now dressed in dirty shorts and a shirt discarded by a miner for one week's pay, he was not surprised. Anyway, the whites said all blacks looked the same. They really were very stupid.

· · ·

IT TOOK a trained soldier to realise quickly the stockade being built around the garden and houses was more than a fence to keep out wild animals. The trees they had stumped out to plant crops were being strategically placed between two sunken posts, tree trunk layered upon tree trunk, the sets of sunken posts conveniently cut at the width of a fully grown msasa tree with the stump and canopy chopped off. The uneven nature of the trees left spaces for gun barrels. Against the far side of the tree fence, Tinus was stacking thorn bush but leaving sight holes at convenient intervals. Gregory Shaw had waited for his opportunity to talk to Tinus alone, away from the women and children.

"What's going on, Tinus?"

"I forgot you were a soldier. I can't really say. Instinct. The way the blacks look at me. We Boers have been in Africa a long time and never once was it easy. The man looking after Fran in Fort Salisbury is a Zulu. What's a Zulu doing in rags looking for work? And he won't look me straight in the eye. The Zulus have quite different features to the Shona."

"I can't tell one from another."

"You will... He's also got a bullet wound in his right thigh. Probably a couple of years old. Jameson has taken out the police and military and it makes me nervous. Why didn't someone tell Jameson that rushing into Johannesburg with a few armed men won't have the Uitlanders clapping their hands and joining the revolution? Those foreigners are a mix of every European race with a lust for gold mixed in with opportunist Australians and Americans. So, Kruger won't give them the vote. Who the hell wants the vote, anyway! They want the gold. And if I know what our esteemed administrator is doing on behalf of Mr Rhodes, you can be sure our Oom Paul Kruger, President of the Transvaal Republic, knows more about the plan to steal the Rand goldfields than I do. Which brings us back to us, which is the main point in question. Without armed soldiers patrolling the country, we are vulnerable. This is a stockade, Greg. To fight behind."

"I rather thought so. Do you need any help?"

"Check my lines of fire. Look for blind spots. All this may be a waste of time, but it makes me feel less nervous."

The first rolling thunder of the day rumbled from the hills to the north as the horse and buggy drove through the path they had cut through the trees.

"When it rains, that road will be impassable," said Tinus. "I want a word with that Zulu. I want to know who put a bullet in his leg."

Overhead the base of the cloud was black, the heat more oppressive than the day before. Lightning flashed nearer and nearer as Gregory inspected the fifty yards of the built stockade. He should have gone to his wife whatever she had been up to in Fort Salisbury but could not face the contempt in her eyes. He had known her reputation in London, there was no getting away from that, and the bad reputation had been part of her attraction. The side of him that wanted her to stay away was swamped with relief at her return. If only she stopped laughing at him, his impotency would go away. There was nothing physically wrong with him; it was all in his head. There had been many girls before Fran in London and none of them had left wanting. To make it different, to make it more important, to show that he was different to all the other men he heard about who had hopped in and out of her bed, he had waited till after they were married and that was the disaster. He had even stayed sober, the man of the world showing his young bride the great carnal pleasures in life. And then it had happened. Nothing. A piece of rope would have done better, and then she had laughed. Peal after peal of laughter, and they had gone to sleep in twin beds without consummating their marriage. A week later the family solicitor pointed out the terms of the family trust. He was left with a twenty-one-year-old wife and nothing but a swathe of virgin African bush. He had told Henry about his impotence and Henry had said to wait and that was three years ago and he was still waiting. And he was forty-one years old. Looking through the last rifle hole he wondered if what he wanted was a fight. Just as the first big raindrop dolloped on the side of his cheek he heard Harry yelling at the top of his seven-year-old lungs.

"Mummy, it's raining! Mummy, it's raining!" And everyone ran out of the houses. Within three minutes the heavens opened and everyone ran back inside, breathless with excitement.

"Home just in time," said Fran, thankful for the diversion. When she turned to give the black man an instruction where to put her case and the shopping, he was gone. She shrugged. The stable boy had taken the horse and the houseboy was told to bring the parcels in out of the rain. Then she joined in the celebration. Immediately the temperature had begun to fall. If the parcels got wet, the parcels got wet. Most important of all, it was raining. And she was inside the house without a scene.

The rain lasted a torrential hour and was a great relief. The lamps had been lit, and the drinks poured, and Gregory had said, "That tasted good". Everyone had noticed his wife sat on the opposite side of the room but they all carried on a polite conversation. They talked about the rain, they talked about the children. The subjects of politics and Fran, seething in each of their separate minds, they kept to themselves. They even laughed more than usual, which was a sign of the tension. Outside the wind was still blowing through the trees, but the thunder was so far away only the dogs could hear. Two of them were cowering under the dining room table, both of them short-haired ridgebacks, the lion dogs they were now calling Rhodesian ridgebacks. The light from the kerosene lamp picked out their frightened eyes and Tinus smiled. The dogs preferred to face a wounded buffalo than rolling thunder far, far away and he wondered if the fear was built into all of them from the great distant past. The two fox terriers, the danger alarm clocks of Elephant Walk, came from a different ancestry... Both were rolled out on their sides full of food and fast asleep... The problems of man at that moment were very far away.

IT TOOK Zwide all night to find the kopje and the jackalberry tree close to which he had buried his rifle. Driving through the trees, next to the whore, he had taken in the stockade and the thorn bushes to stop an assegai attack and knew on the instant the white men were not as stupid as he thought. For the first time in his manhood, he felt the cold stab of fear in his belly. The whore's husband was looking through loopholes in the stockade with an air of confident familiarity and the big hunter was looking at Zwide. For a brief intense moment he prayed to his ancestors for help and a fat drop of rain hit the back of his hand. He saw the big man look up at the sky and the whore's husband stopped checking the lines of fire from the stockade. The whore, sensing the rain, thrashed the reins on the back of the horse and the lurch forward gave Zwide the excuse to fall out of the open-sided cab. The whore, intent on the horse and the road, did not turn as he looked back at the buggy. Having made a previous reconnaissance like any good soldier, he knew which way to run and by the time the heavens opened with the torrents of rain, he was two hundred yards into the msasa trees heading northwest on the blazed trail that would take him to the Martini-Henry rifle, one of the guns he had taken from the buried cave of King Lobengula, the lid of the box replaced carefully to show no tampering. The two ammunition belts that crossed his body were stuffed with cartridges. With the coming of the rain, the light went completely and Zwide stopped in his track, fearful of losing the blazed trail made by breaking small green twigs on the lower branches of the trees.

He was shivering with a mixture of cold and fear and sometimes, when the wind blew the trees a certain way after the downpour had finished, he could catch glimpses of the light from the house. In the middle of the night the clouds cleared, and the new moon showed the broken branch next to his shoulder where he had stopped when the light went out. All night he waited and only in the yellow light of morning did he begin the loping run of the Zulu through the trees, running fast on the blazed trail.

By the time Tinus came looking for him, he was five miles away and still running at the same speed with the rifle and ammunition strapped to his back. Zwide ran all morning and only when the sun rose to its full did he stop by a stream for more than a drink of water. He was hungry but more exhausted and, safely wedged in a tree, he went to sleep for the rest of the day woken only by the rain. Below the tree, alone and oblivious to danger, a male kudu was browsing the green leaves. The bullet hit the kudu's heart, the animal's leisurely browsing turning to the throes of death. By the time Zwide climbed down from his tree the animal was stone dead. With the knife he had cached with his rifle he cut open the animal's belly, searching for the kidneys and liver. With warm blood dripping from his jaw, Zwide ate his fill and conquered his fear. With the skin of the kudu covering his body, he spent a warm dry night under the overhanging rock of a kopje. In the morning he walked the long stride eating up the miles on his way to the hills behind the ruins of Gu-Bulawayo, twenty miles from the new town the whites were calling Bulawayo (as if they had not stolen enough from his people). In the hills of the Matopos, he would plan the massacre of the whites in the greatest of detail.

WITH THE PREVIOUS night's rain having soaked the ploughed lands, the men and the six field labourers planted the corn each using a short-handled Dutch hoe to cover the kernels with two inches of topsoil. The straight lines, three feet apart, were made with stretched twine between pegs. Each planting down the line was one foot apart, and Seb was satisfied the reaping between the stands of maize corn would be uniform and ripe cobs would not be left in the lands. Three kernels were placed in each hole to have three chances of germination. The field officer from the Charter Company had told them what to do without charge. The hope was, the grass turned into the virgin soil would provide enough fertiliser for the corn to grow to the height of a man's head with one or more cobs on each stand.

Tinus had briefly looked for the Zulu early that morning and put the man out of his mind, concentrating on the more important task of farming. The man had probably run off when he saw the rain to stop being put in the lands... It was a backbreaking job which Tinus, with his great height, suffered from more than the others.

An hour before dusk, with the black clouds threatening more rain, Tinus left the planting with his .375 rifle and went looking for game. He walked northwest into the bush as the game to the south and east had become shy from constant hunting. The bush was thicker to the north and the game more difficult to track. As the first drops of rain splattered down on the leaves of the trees, harbinger of the deluge in the west where the squall of rain was already slanting down in a thick wedge of water, Tinus shot a female impala at eighty yards, killing the animal with one shot. Running across the clearing through the elephant grass that had been flattened by the previous night's storm, Tinus recovered his kill and slit the animal's throat. The last reflexive pumps of the animal's heart spurted rich blood from the jugular vein. When the flow stopped, Tinus hoisted the carcass onto his shoulder and began to trot in the direction of the house, quickly finding a game track that led in the right direction.

Tinus kept the wind on the same side of his face while the carcass and rifle jigged on his back. He could hear Harry yelling at his sister about something which made him think of Barend and Tinka. Then he thought of Alison and smiled again. She was a better Boer wife than he could even have imagined. Into his fourth long stride down the game trail, he saw the first broken twig and stopped in his track. From years in the bush, his unconscious mind had registered the unusual. Kudu pulled down on the leaves and never broke a twig that bent upwards. When he found the second bent twig, the leaves still green, the break still fresh, he knew what he had found. Then he saw the spoor of bare feet on the ground leading northwest and looked back over his shoulder to the trail.

"That's no ordinary Zulu," he said out loud, "that man knows what he is doing."

3

MARCH 1896

our months later, when the main rains were over, the Reverend Nathanial Brigandshaw, missionary to the tribes of the Shona, made his half-yearly duty call on Elephant Walk. Bess, his wife, had been left on the mission as the reverend thought it appropriate to keep his wife away from the appalling scandal that overshadowed the English community in and around Fort Salisbury. It was quite clear that Captain Shaw was unable to control his wife, and it was up to the Reverend Brigandshaw to have a stern word in his ear. Whatever would the natives think, Nathanial thought in constant alarm? The Bible was quite clear. There should be no adultery and coveting of other people's wives, and if the English could not set a proper example, how was he to bring the word of Jesus's church to the black people and have them obey the word of God? And by all reports, the woman came from a good family!

The reverend drove himself, not wishing to make a black man his servant, and was surprised to find a strong gate made from thick tree trunks barring his way into the family compound. On either side of the gate, thorn bush had been stacked around a high stockade that ringed the properties. Tethering the horse to a post he used his brown malacca cane to knock imperiously on the gate door. After five minutes and thoroughly frustrated he shouted on the top of his voice and Emily, his sister-in-law, slid back the bar and opened the heavy gate.

"Morning, Nat. What are you doing here?"

"Visiting of course. What does it look like?"

"Flock not behaving like Christians, I suppose?"

"Not this one anyway." Even after the main rains, it was hot and sticky and the reverend's stock of charity was low.

Emily said nothing and waited with the high door open until her brother-in-law drove into the compound. She found him a sanctimonious hypocrite and only good manners prevented her from telling him so. She would never forgive him for siding with Arthur. Now, obviously, poor Gregory was going to get it in the neck as Emily doubted if the great missionary to Africa would confront the source of the problem. If he did, she rather thought he would come off second best. Fran had the ability to turn a criticism of herself into a character assassination of the critic. Fran always attacked, never defended.

"While you are rubbing down your horse, I'll go and find Sebastian. I'm sure he'll be delighted to see his brother."

"What's going on here?" said Nathanial, missing the brief whiff of sarcasm.

"Tinus thinks the natives are going to revolt."

"Does he now? How quite ridiculous. They are delighted we have come to protect them and bring them the word of Jesus Christ. Absolutely delighted. They shall be saved, I tell them. They shall be saved. Remember that, Emily."

"I'll try, Nat... When your horse is all tucked in you can go up to the house whilst I look for Seb." The idea of Nat looking for himself was not part of his image. He liked his flock to come to him as supplicants; it made him feel he represented God in a better light.

Walking away on her small feet to the back gate that led into the lands, she wondered how it was possible for one set of parents to have such different children. Keeping the smile to herself, she noticed Harry scooting away before he was cornered by his uncle for a lecture on God and the bad habits of small boys. It was going to be a difficult afternoon and evening, she sighed to herself. As she turned through the back gate she saw her son disappear into the trees with his new shotgun. As he did so, he turned and waved. Then she began the walk beside the straight line of maize that stretched green and tall, acre after acre, the perfect sight for sore eyes. Idly she wondered how long Harry would stay in the bush.

SEB SAW his pregnant wife from a distance and stopped chopping at the thick tree root and put down his axe. His back ached, but he was happy. The thirty-acre crop of corn was better than expected, especially where the anthills had been flattened and spread as far as possible from the great nests built by billions of ants over hundreds of years, the soil rich in their excretion. There was one good cob from every hole, sometimes two or three plants where more kernels had germinated. And he had an idea that would make the corn far more valuable than sending it to the flour mill in Salisbury for turning into mealie-meal, the staple food of the blacks. Seb waved to his wife and walked to meet her. Farming for Sebastian was highly rewarding; the result was tangible; he could place his hand on the fruit of his hard work, and it made all the years of pain worthwhile.

Emily had stopped when Seb put down the axe. The unborn baby kicked hard. Putting both hands on her belly she sat on an old tree stump that had been left to mark one hundred yards of maize and calmed the baby. She was twenty-five and as she looked back to making love with Seb beneath the great oak tree, it seemed the girl of sixteen had nothing to do with the pregnant mother sitting on a tree stump beneath the African sky. Above, the clouds were white and patched evenly in the powder-blue sky. A dove was calling across the land of maize from the top branch of a msasa tree, calling to its lover, the call saying to Emily, 'How's father? How's father?' time after time. It was their joke, hers and Seb's, and when the bird first called in the morning, Seb would answer, 'Father's fine today', and they would laugh like the children they no longer were. A powerful man, richly tanned by the African sun, thinness and ponytail long gone, the corn-coloured hair bleached white by the same sun that had turned his face to the colour of mahogany, the clear blue eyes the only feature recognisable from his youth. All her frustration evaporated as he strode down the lines of green maize, grinning from ear to ear.

"He kicked," she called and waited on her tree stump. He kissed her gently, having taken off her broad-brimmed hat.

"What are you doing here, Em? The sun's terribly hot. Trouble?" Anything out of context in Seb's life usually meant trouble and, with the debacle of Jameson's raid into the Transvaal so new, he was instantly on his guard. Dr Jim had surrendered to a Boer commando outside Johannesburg ten weeks earlier along with the police and military sent from Rhodesia. Chamberlain in England was said to be furious with Dr Jameson and Cecil Rhodes. Jameson and the leaders of the abortive raid were being sent to England for trial. Rhodes denied any connivance. The rest was murky and laced with rumours. The relations between the Boers and the British had reached close to the point of war.

"Trouble in a way, but not the sort you are thinking about," said Emily. "Tinus's great revolution has not started and Chamberlain's trying to calm the Boers. Your brother is here. You'd better warn Greg. The Reverend Righteousness is high on his horse. Harry's gone off with his new gun and I'll take a bet our daughter has joined him."

"Bess?"

"No Bess. Poor Bess has been left alone with the children. God, your brother tells me, is standing guard."

"It's Nat that needs some sense knocked into him, not Greg. You go on back to the house and I'll join you later."

"Don't leave us alone for too long. He considers me a fallen woman. The looks of disapproval are almost a physical slap in the face."

FOR AS LONG as Seb could remember, Nat had never been wrong because Nat was on the side of the Lord. Calling up God as his defence had begun soon after the seven-year-old Nat's first Sunday school. From that moment on, according to James Brigandshaw, Seb's second eldest brother after Arthur, Nat had found his vocation. James, the soldier in the family, said brother Nat had so indoctrinated himself that he actually believed that every word in the New and Old Testaments was the gospel truth. The man had the ability to turn the Bible to his advantage every time he found himself in an argument. There was always a quotation to squash any rebellion. Simply, Nat on behalf of God was right. The only thing the three brothers ever agreed upon was that Nathanial was an insufferable boor and one day God would forsake him. To Nat, the brotherly animosity was another living proof of his path to God. They were his cross to bear.

As Seb walked back to the farmhouse two hours later, he could find no pleasure in the thought of his brother's visit. To make matters worse, Fran was not in Fort Salisbury as the military situation was too volatile for her to travel. Five good stiff gins would probably serve his purpose and, working on the principle that safety lay in numbers, they had all agreed to meet the reverend in Seb's house for sundowners. At the last moment, Seb's father-in-law conveniently pleaded sunstroke and Henry Manderville went to bed. In the rondavel that made up the lounge, they sat and looked at each other. Harry was still in the bush having released his sister to the pangs of hunger. Alison sat protected by her children, the baby fast asleep in its crib by her side. Seb suspected Fran of early drinking and Gregory had his mouth clamped shut. Tinus, as usual before dusk, was patrolling their northern river perimeter on horseback. Emily sat busily darning socks. It was to this captive audience that the reverend delivered his monologue. He was used to giving sermons where nobody answered back.

With Tinus and Harry still not home, Emily lit the kerosene lamp and Seb poured the drinks and for the first time in months, Gregory Shaw failed to say his drink tasted good.

They were all waiting for Fran and Greg to be castigated when Tinus came into the room looking grim.

"Get your rifles," he said. "Twelve people have crossed the river. Maybe more. Fresh spoor and they came from the north."

"Looking for jobs," said the reverend.

"Not in that quantity. Is your wife alone on the mission?"

"Of course."

"Then you are a damn fool."

"Blasphemy I will not allow."

"You'll allow a lot more than blasphemy if they kill your wife and children. Don't you see it, Reverend? Jameson, the destroyer of Lobengula, has been destroyed himself. The Matabele want revenge and the Shona will be told to help. This is Africa, not the East End of London."

"They love me on the mission."

"Don't you believe it. They hate your guts. And mine. We've stolen their country, don't you remember? And please, none of that nonsense about civilisation and Christianity."

HARRY LOOKED through the window and saw his uncle on his knees, his hands clasped together in supplication. He was shouting at the ceiling and a fine mist of termite dust was falling in the room, caught like a sunbeam by the white light of the kerosene lamp. Harry felt the giggle come up from his belly. Madge saw him through the windows and pulled a face, safe in the knowledge that Uncle Nat's eyes were shut tight and would stay shut tight until the tirade had finished being sent up into the rafters. The rest of the family and friends were trying not to look at each other and then the baby woke up in the crib and added her voice to the prayer. Aunty Alison tried to calm the baby to no avail and in the uproar, Harry let out his silent giggle. Uncle Tinus got up in his agitation and knocked over the small table spilling his glass onto the floor and Harry's giggle began to build to hysterics. Uncle Tinus then told the reverend on his knees to shut up to no avail and Harry had to stop laughing because his belly was hurting.

Then by mistake in his excitement, he dropped his .410 shotgun on its butt and the gun went off with a shattering noise as Harry had forgotten to put back the hammer after sighting a bird. The shot went up in the air, much to Harry's relief. Expecting his father to come running through the door to find him dead or give him a cuff around the ear, he was surprised to see the reaction in the room. The reverend shut his trap and leapt to his feet and the baby stopped crying and for a terrible moment, Harry thought he had killed the little thing. Uncle Gregory fell flat on his face on the floor pulling Aunty Fran with him. Uncle Tinus leapt for his gun, which was leaning against the wall next to the table with the food, and in his hurry knocked everything on the floor. Sister Madge, who had seen what had happened, was laughing with tears pouring down her face which didn't help Harry's mother who thought Madge was crying. Only then did Harry find himself looking into the clear blue eyes of his father with the thin pane of glass his only protection. With the gun on the floor, Harry decided to make a run for it back into the bush and ran full speed into the arms of his grandfather. Five minutes later Harry was sent to bed without any food and thought it all unfair. By the time he was allowed out into the calm of the morning, his Uncle Nat had gone on his way and Harry was quite happy at the way it had all turned out. Going back to the window, he looked, but there was no sign of his gun.

A WEEK LATER, on the 24th March, the Matabele went on the rampage, slaughtering isolated policemen and families scattered across mines and farms in Matabeleland. Zwide was furious. The attack had been planned for the 29th, the night of the Big Dance when the moon was full. At first, the reports were satisfactory and the whites that had not been slaughtered fled into Bulawayo. Soon the regiments would attack Bulawayo and Zwide would be king. The only blight on his euphoria was the Shona. The cowards had not joined the uprising.

On the 25th March, Frederick Selous, the greatest hunter of them all, rode into Bulawayo to organise the defence. He had brought the Pioneer Column, including Henry Manderville and Gregory Shaw, to safety at Fort Salisbury in 1890 and he was not going to lose the country in 1896. Commanding horsemen armed with Martini-Henry rifles, most of whom had handled guns in the bush for years, he led the counterattack against the Matabele regiments. The mounted cavalry was outnumbered fifteen to one, but they were mobile and their shooting was deadly accurate. They also had unlimited ammunition. By the time Cecil Rhodes came in with a relief column from Salisbury, the Matabele had lost the initiative.

With the Charter Company shares plunging in London due to expectation of a costly war, Rhodes, unarmed and alone, met the indunas in a cave in the Matopos mountains that overlooked Bulawayo. Zwide was not among them. Once again he had gone north and, while the end of the rebellion was being negotiated, he sat in the cave with the bones of Lobengula and the remnants of the black ox hide. Only on the second day of his exile did he begin to move the gold and ivory out of the cave. Alone, it was to take him weeks to move the treasure to its new hiding place. The guns, given out to the regiments for the rebellion, were surrendered to the whites as part of the amnesty. The Kingdom of Matabeleland had ceased to exist except in Zwide's bitter heart. There would be another time. Leaving his headdress and leopard skin with the treasure, he went back to Bulawayo and found himself a job chopping meat in a butcher's shop.

BY THE TIME Zwide was cutting up his first white man's cow, the witch was ready. Everything had gone according to plan: the last of Lobengula's regiments had been defeated, Jameson was still in England facing trial, and Rhodes himself had gone to Bulawayo with a relief column. The land of the Shona was ready for the war of liberation. The witch, a wrinkled old hag to those who chose to see her, smiled to herself. Never once had they trusted the Matabele emissaries.

The witch had collected the mushrooms over many years, dried them and ground them to powder. The orange-topped mushroom with the white underbelly was rare and precious, used only once in each generation to retain its power of mystery. Smoked from clay pipes, the powered mushrooms would stop the rust of the assegai and turn the white man's bullets to water. Across Mashonaland, the witch doctors were preparing their medicine for the Chimurenga.

When the moon was full, the Shona would burst out of their caves and hiding places to kill every white man, woman and child that had stolen their land. The Kingdom of Monomotapa was to rise again, the power of a witch and chief once more unquestioned. The new god of the white man would be destroyed. Once again the people would hunt the sweet rivers and plains of their forefathers and there would be peace among men. The yoke of foreign domination would be gone forever.

Satisfied with her preparations, the witch went deep into the cave to feed her leopard. When alone with the satisfied animal she prayed to her ancestors to intercede with God to give them deliverance, the most ancient cry of man.

TATENDA HAD learnt to say nothing. Once, he had told Gumbo, the chief's son, about the great ships in Table Bay with guns bigger than a buffalo. But when he talked about the telegraph that sent messages from Cape Town to Fort Salisbury as quickly as they spoke, Gumbo lost interest in a story that was obviously so stupid. The noise of Cape Town still rattled in Tatenda's ears, a mocking echo. He thought of the steam trains pouring black smoke across the veld, the great snake clattering onwards and onwards along the white man's rails. He thought of the pictures they had shown him of London, the capital of the world, of skyscrapers in New York across an ocean wider than the veld and great boats the mighty Zambezi could never float. There were pictures of the Queen and miles of soldiers all with guns, and he wanted to tell his people but he feared the witch and the voices from the trees. He feared the leopard would tear him limb from limb and he watched them go when the moon was full and clutching his puny gun he did what he was told and when he reached the Mazoe River, he crossed with the others and smoked the pipe and found the courage of a lion and they ran forward to attack the white man certain in their belief the white man's bullets would turn to water.

Right across Mashonaland, the struggle had just begun, the first war of liberation.

BY THE END OF JUNE, the trees around the stockade had been cut and cleared leaving an unobstructed field of fire. Every one hundred yards in a circle around their stockade, Gregory Shaw had driven in stakes to give their guns the range. At night they took it in turns to patrol the perimeter and listen for the rattling of the stones in the tin cans he had strung between the white-painted posts. Stacks of tinder-dry wood had been placed within throwing distance of twenty yards from the stockade that could be lit as an extra deterrent if needs be. Each of the firing points had been tested to ensure they enfiladed with each other. There were no gaps they could see in their defence.

At the mission on the other side of Fort Salisbury, Nathanial went about God's business ministering to his new flock. His three children played in front of the house on the dry dirt floor among the chickens and goats. His wife treated the sick and tried to teach the children English. Nathanial knew everything was a mess but denied the knowledge even to himself. Everything he had ever done in his life since he was seven years old was the will of God.

The morning Tatenda smoked his pipe, none of the children came to the school. The clinic was empty of sick. The reverend and his family were alone. Bringing them together in the improvised church that served as a classroom, he began to pray. Never once did he doubt the wisdom of God. To Nathanial, each life on earth was destined for a purpose as without a purpose there could be no point in life itself.

JEREMIAH SHANK HAD BUILT his house on the Hunyani River of stone, each block cut square and mortared into place. The square windows filled the front of the house looking down the slope to the river, and the trees had grown tall from their roots deep in the damp earth below the flowing water. Atop the two storeys of the house rose a tower that was higher than the house itself. By turning the steel cogs, the dome of the roof came open and showed Jeremiah the great heavens he had watched in awe from the pitching decks of ships. The vastness of the heavens fascinated the man. When the dome was wound open, the telescope looked at the clear night sky, layer after layer, past the Milky Way to the universe beyond. Night after night in the sanctuary of his tower, Jeremiah looked up at the stars and his soul went out to the heavens.

On the wall behind the swivel seat of the telescope hung a naval cutlass that had been handed down to him by three generations of seamen none of whom had come to any good, all succumbing to whores and rum, and all, so far as the family could remember, dead of syphilis. At twenty-eight he had stopped the rot and, with the right woman, he would breed a new family of Shanks who would stand tall in the corridors of power.

Jeremiah had seen his dinner companion twice since the night they had met on the Meikles Hotel veranda, and still he bided his time. He had looked carefully at other prospects in the new colony and found nothing that would fit his bill. With three generations and the sustenance of his wealth, the Shanks would have bred out their bad blood and replaced it with the best in England.

The old Jeremiah Shank had told him to run like hell at the first talk of rebellion back to Kimberley and the source of his wealth, but the house and all it meant was more powerful. Kimberley was a grubby mining town and only the elite were allowed membership of the Kimberley Club. Even Barnato with all his wealth was denied because he was a Jew. On the banks of the Hunyani, from the tower that looked out over the great plains of Mashonaland, Jeremiah saw his destiny. Only land was the mark of a dynasty, only land gave a man the true sense of power and privilege.

. . .

"THE MOON WILL BE FULL TONIGHT," said Jack Slater in the Salisbury Club.

"The Matabele were going to attack on the full moon, the night of the Big Dance," said Captain James Brigandshaw of the Queen's Light Horse. "You think there might be some fun with the Shona? Surely not. Even they can see what happened to the Matabele facing disciplined cavalry."

"Rumour has it the Mwari are telling their people our bullets will turn to water, that the spirits will guide them."

"What nonsense."

"We know that, Captain Brigandshaw, but a superstitious savage will believe his oracles. One of the many of man's stupidities. Look at the Mahdi in Sudan. History is littered with people running to their deaths. The Muslim if he dies in battle in the name of God goes straight to heaven. A heaven with sweet rivers and lush green grass littered with sumptuous women. Half of the aristocracy of England ran off to the Crusades. Religion mixed with politics is a powder keg. You should tell that missionary brother of yours to get his family to safety."

"He doesn't know I am in Africa. I was only ordered back from India after the Matabele rebellion and then the regiment argued about my secondment to a colonial force run by a company."

"India was the same with Clive and the East India Company."

"My argument, Slater. My argument. There are three of us in Africa, you know? There's the black sheep we don't talk about."

Jack Slater's mind went straight to Fran, and he tried to change the subject by ordering another round of drinks.

"You ever met Sebastian, old chap?" asked James, knowing perfectly well. The fact his brothers were in Rhodesia had been a reason for his posting. His brief mentioned Slater's involvement with his brother's warrant of arrest.

"Once, I believe."

"And you didn't arrest him. Snotty little kid, I seem to remember. Fortunately, I was away at boarding school and then in the army. The only thing we all agreed was Nat being a crashing boor. Don't you worry, Slater," said James, going back to his original subject, "let them all rise up. No one ever defeats the British. Remember that."

"Are you going to see him?"

"Who?"

"Sebastian Brigandshaw."

"Of course not. He's the black sheep of the family, didn't I tell you? Father never mentions his name and mother does what father tells her to do... One of these days I am going to get married," he said, going off at a tangent.

At the idea, Jack could only think of Fran naked in his bed and he hoped that no one would come to their table to make him stand up.

"You've gone a bit red in the face, old chap," said James and thought for a moment. "We don't have many troops if they do go wild. Most of the chaps were in that bungle with Dr Jim. If you're going to steal something for Queen and country, do it properly. The man's an imbecile. Made the British look a damn fool. That kind of bungle leads to war, you mark my word. A friend of mine in India fought with the Boers against the Zulus. The Boers don't dress up for war like we do but they shoot damn straight. Glory be, there's enough trouble keeping the natives under control without squabbling with each other. William of Orange came across from Holland so there's no reason we can't get along with the Dutch. Asked nicely, the Boers will want to join the empire. We can guarantee their safety. What's a few rules and regulations when you don't have to worry about a horde of savages going on the rampage? Joseph Chamberlain knows what he's doing. The colonial secretary was a businessman before he went into politics.

"My father says everything comes down to money and money can only be made when everyone behaves themselves. Take the British out of India and the states would be at each other's throats in a week, to say nothing of the Muslims hating the Hindus. The British administration provides law and order as it does here. Then people can trade without hindrance. Seems so damn simple yet everyone wants to face off at each other if the other chap's a bit different. Dread to think what the world would be like without the Pax Britannica. You mark my words, the Boers will come into the empire if they want to do anything with their precious republics... You know any nice girls in this town, Slater?"

At the mention of girls, the face of the acting administrator went bright red and James Brigandshaw had to look away to stop himself from laughing. He idly wondered who the girl was who brought on the hot flush... At least there was one woman in Rhodesia who could cause a stir. For a while, they lapsed into silence, thinking their separate thoughts. James idly stirred his coffee before carrying on speaking his thoughts out loud.

"There's always some fanatic or politician who sees the chance for power. They always say they do it in the name of the people, but you mark my words, they do it for themselves. Throughout history wicked men, dressed in the clothes of saints, have searched for a popular cause to give themselves power. To a few men power is so addictive they will kill millions to get what they want. The joke, old chap, is they always kill in the name of the cause, in the name of God, in the name of the people. That's why the world needs the British Army. To stop all that nonsense."

"You don't think it's us seeking power?"

"Maybe. But it works. We make sure law and order prevail in the empire. Now, a last toast." James Brigandshaw raised his glass of port. "To the Queen, God bless her."

"The Queen," said Jack Slater with a wry smile, raising his glass. "The Queen, God bless her."

"You know, Slater, it's wonderful to be an Englishman."

With the glass tipped back, Jack Slater's eyes came on a line with the open door and the round worried face of Billy Witherspoon and he recognised trouble. He immediately excused himself from the table and walked across the dining room to his aide. Everyone in the room followed his path, some turning in their seats to do so. There were only men, as women were not allowed in the Salisbury Club. Witherspoon's face could just as well have shouted the news and Jack signalled the man to turn his back on the lunchtime trenchermen. To counteract the horrified look in the eyes, Jack smiled and maintained his measured step. It was quarter past two in the afternoon and outside the club the sun was shining. He took Witherspoon by the elbow into the street and marched him past three of Dr Jameson's jacaranda trees before he would let him speak. Then he listened.

"Three accounts almost simultaneously of massacres on the mines and outlying farms. They struck with the full moon. The blacks are openly calling it the Chimurenga."

"What's the Chimurenga, Billy? Speak English!"

"The war of liberation. One of the police posts was attacked and two men hacked to death. The other man rode in with the story."

"Right. I want everyone into the capital. Easier to protect them. They can rebuild a home but can't come back from the dead. Get the message on the wires, Billy."

"And those without telegraph, the farmers and miners?"

"Will have to be told personally. Those are my instructions. Now go, Billy. But don't run. Englishmen never panic, so my lunch companion would have me believe."

"Where are you going, sir?"

"Back to the club to finish my coffee."

James Brigandshaw watched the acting administrator with approval as the man made his way back to the table. Everyone in the room had stopped talking.

"Bring me some more coffee, steward, and a glass of port. Captain Brigandshaw will have the same. Now, Brigandshaw, where were we before I was rudely interrupted?"

By the time the coffee and port arrived, the members and their guests had gone back to their conversations and Jack could answer the quizzical look on the other man's face.

"Finish your coffee slowly and then ride like hell to your brother's mission," said Jack quietly. "The natives are calling it a war of liberation. They are on the rampage."

"What fun. Largely, India was dull."

"It's in the other direction but when you have brought your reverend brother to safety, I'd be obliged you warn Sebastian Brigandshaw."

"Listen, don't worry about him. Nat, yes, he'll probably be on his knees telling God how good he's been. Seb might be our black sheep, old chap, but he always knew how to look after himself. Anyway, father said under no circumstances was I to make contact or he'd stop my allowance. I'll go alone but I'll take an extra gun on the rump of my horse. Watch your askaris, Slater, or whatever you call your native troops in this part of Africa. If it was me I'd take the guns away from them in case they are tempted. People are inclined to obey whoever holds the gun. Sort of fundamental situation, old chap. Nat will be surprised to see me."

"If he's still alive, Brigandshaw."

"Of course he will be. God's protecting him. Didn't he tell you so? Thank you for the lunch, Slater. My other piece of military advice, which I understand is what I am here for, is to patrol the outskirts on horseback. Then you know where they are coming from if they try anything silly. And tell the settlers to give their servants the night off and to lock the doors with the dogs inside. All fundamental but usually works. We only have twenty thousand British running the whole of India. Makes you rather think, doesn't it? You were rather impressive just now, Slater. Most impressive. Now, if you'll excuse me I'll be off to visit my brother. Three lovely children, I'm told. Never met them except the youngest in the cot. Yes, I'd better get married and have some of my own. Toodle-oo, old chap."

THEY HAD WANDERED around all morning looking for someone to kill, disorientated by the drug they had smoked in the clay pipe, passed from man to man until the smoke was finished. On the second smoke, Gumbo spilt the pouch in his excitement and the powder fell among the grass. Tatenda had choked each time he drew on the pipe and by the time they came back to the Mazoe River and followed its course, the drug had worn off. They had asked him about his white masters before he knew their intention and had gladly described the cluster of houses looking down towards the small river that cuts through the hills to the plain and the rich red topsoil cleft by the flooding waters over millions of years. In the red soil, the maize grew tall now the white man had chopped down the trees and the first sight of Elephant Walk was the lands of green maize he had helped to prepare and the guilt made his stomach sick. The village in the valley came back to him, the vultures on the ground, himself looking at death sprawling between the huts of his family. Alone he might have died, eaten by the wild animals.

They smoked the last of the powder to turn the white man's bullets to water and turned the corner of the last stand of tall green maize and took in the flat open land, cut clean of trees, the long grass burnt black. The stockade was flung thickly around the houses he remembered and Tatenda, half drugged by the sparsity of their smoke, saw the error of his ways. Vividly the drawings came back to him.

On Sundays, when Tinus Oosthuizen observed the day of the Lord, Harry would ask the big man to show him the books in the big wooden chest and, though the words meant nothing to Harry, the pictures drew a babble of questions. With Harry on one big knee, the leather-bound open book on the other and Tatenda looking over the broad shoulder, Tinus Oosthuizen would explain the meaning of the pictures, what the drawings meant in the context of the story the boys were unable to read. Most often, the pictures were of wagons drawn round in a ring with thorn branches in the gaps and between the great wheels of the wagons. Inside the circle were boys hiding among the piles of sacks and boxes, the bigger boys loading the guns, the guns passed to the women in long dresses and then to the bearded men firing through the spokes of the wagon wheels. Puffs of smoke were all around the laager of the wagons and black men like himself, some with guns, most with spears, were attacking the wagons, headdresses topped with feathers, courage written on their faces and in front of the wagons piles of his people dead, and he understood.

Tinus Oosthuizen had thrown a laager around the houses and through the holes in the fence would point the barrels of guns and the bullets would not turn to water and the witch was wrong and Tatenda had no wish to die.

In awe of the prospect, Tatenda hung back as Gumbo led the charge across the open ground with the white-topped sticks at regular intervals. When Gumbo reached the first post a gun fired from the stockade and the bullet tore through Gumbo, tearing out a piece of his back. Horror struck as Tatenda watched his friends, in turn, reach the posts and die and when they were all down on the black ground, blackened by the burnt grass, not even grass to protect them, he turned and ran back to the river. He dropped his gun and cartridge belt before jumping into the river to fight the rain-filled waters to the other side. When he reached the bank, water coughing from his lungs, his brain clear of the drug from his effort, he began to run through the trees with no idea of where he was going, the horror of death screaming in his mind as he ran and ran.

HALF AN HOUR later the doves had recovered their wits from the fusillade of sound. It was an hour before dusk and the dove-calls carried over the silence and then the crickets began to sing and the frogs croaked from the river, and far away up the river a fish eagle called its plaintive cry.

ON THE OTHER side of Salisbury, the doves were silenced by the cantering horse and James Brigandshaw hoped he had taken the right directions expecting a church spire above the trees, and then he found the sign written on a plank of wood, *St Mary's Mission*, and the horse broke through the trees along the rutted path and chickens scattered with the goats but no one came to greet him. The surrounding silence was tangible; the late sun through the trees on the weathered buildings a yellow glow. A slight wind had come and banged a door somewhere inside the building. Safer in the saddle than on the ground, James pulled his rifle from its holster in front of his right thigh and sent a bullet into the firing chamber and rode the animal up to the veranda of what he took to be his brother's house. Away from the house was a shed and by the side of the shed, two horses were grazing quietly. James rode around the house looking through the windows and then across to the shed. Inside his brother and sister-in-law were still upon their knees while the children played quietly between the school desks. The boy had the cantankerous look of The Captain while the girls bore no resemblances to his family. Everywhere else there was not a sign of a soul. James got down from his horse and walked into what he perceived to be a church. Then he coughed to draw their attention.

"You may kneel and pray with us, James," said Nathanial looking round. "The Lord has answered our prayers. The Lord has spared me for His work."

"You don't think the deliverance might have had something to do with a soldier riding hard, old chap? But please, right about now I have to ask you all to be going. There is a native uprising and you are all to be brought into Salisbury. I believe, old chap, the acting administrator, nice chap name of Jack Slater, has declared martial law so you'll be a good fellow and do what you are told. Dead missionaries stir up much anger in London and we have all we want right now."

"Who's the funny man?" asked the boy standing up from behind a school desk. "Why's he wearing a red coat?"

"He's your uncle James from India," said Bess, trying to get up.

"Kneel, Elizabeth," snapped Nathanial. "Now is the time to give thanks to the Lord. The Lord in his wisdom at the time of our need has sent our brother from India, a true miracle, a true miracle. Pray, Elizabeth, pray. The Lord is surely powerful."

James strode across the floor and yanked his brother up onto his feet and looked straight into his eyes. "It'll be pitch dark in an hour. Two hours to Fort Salisbury, maybe three with the trap. I will rope you into the trap if needs be. There's a nice big church in Fort Salisbury where you can do all the praying you want tomorrow morning. And I came from England, not India. Mater and Pater send you and yours their regards."

"Have you seen Sebastian?"

"Of course not. He's the black sheep of the family. Now, please get a move on before I lose my temper in your nice little church. Where is everyone?"

"They ran away."

"Exactly. Now come along, Bess, and give your brother-in-law a kiss and get the children into the trap while I harness the horses."

THE DUSK HAD COME and gone and inside the stockade the dogs were quiet and outside in the pale colourless light of the full moon, the corpses of men lay where they had fallen. Sebastian continued his round of the stockade listening for the cans to rattle, his hunter's senses pitched to screaming point. Once, with Tinus, a leopard had leapt at him out of the night, a snarling fetid mouth and claws flung out from the reaching paws. Instinct had thrown up the gun and he had fired, dropping the cat dead at his feet. He still had the skin of the male leopard in the house behind him where his children slept. The night was quiet. Small fires burnt at intervals. Looking up he saw the black heart of a passing cloud. The dogs lay still around the fire, content with the company of a man, and Sebastian bent down to stroke their heads in turn, two Rhodesian ridgebacks and two fox terriers, meeting their eyes in the light of the burning fire.

At midnight he gave the guard to Gregory Shaw and walked across to his house and pushed open the screen door to the veranda. He checked Harry's bedroom, and the boy was fast asleep. In the bed next to him, with the sheet flung off, Madge was asleep in the protection of her almost eight-year-old brother, and his heart swelled with pride for both of them, and when he found his room, Emily was asleep on her side and he got into the bed and within a moment he was fast asleep.

All through the night the leopard chased him, running and running from tree to tree. When he woke, the day had come and when he got up and looked, the bodies were still strewn on the blackened earth. The flies had found the corpses and beyond the blackened grass, the bush was alive with song and the orange glow of dawn flamed the sky above the trees and the scattered clouds were belly-red, and from the river Sebastian could see their glow reflected on the surface of the river and beside the river, buck were drinking.

THE BREAKING DAWN found Jeremiah Shank asleep in his swivel chair, the dome of his observatory open to the day, the stars fading quickly to obscurity. Below the tower, four black men were looking in at the closed windows of the ground floor and one of them went across to the farm sheds where the grain was stored. When he came out a yellow glow was in the heart of the building and directly behind, some three miles away, there was a similar glow from St Mary's Mission.

Jeremiah woke to the sound of breaking glass from below and got up to look down at what was happening. The small windows around the base of the dome were open to catch the cool breeze and Jeremiah put out his head to see the back of a man disappearing into his house.

His shout of, "Hey, what the hell are you doing?" was received from below by the discharge of an old muzzleloader knocking the man below onto his back, the shot ricocheting off the stone wall, making Jeremiah pull his head back into the tower. Now he could hear the man breaking furniture in the drawing room and rage began to build. Taking down the ancestral cutlass from the wall he threw down the scabbard onto the floor. Outside he could see the barn burning and rage took possession. Slamming the door open, the small man with the crooked nose came down the spiral staircase, cutlass in hand and shouting. He crossed the passage to the main staircase.

The man at the bottom of the stairs, high with dope, came rushing up the carpeted steps with his assegai ready to kill. Behind him, a second man stood below the banister and fired his gun at the white man. The bullet hit a portrait of somebody else's grandfather. As the shot struck the dark portrait, Jeremiah's naval training made him cut hard and he backhanded at the first man's neck, severing his head. The second man took the curved blade in his belly, the thrust coming up and twisting, taking out the man's bowels on the red staircase. The third man was running away towards the smashed windows when the cutlass cut through the back of his neck. The fourth man who had lit the fire in the corn shed was standing at the front door trying to get it open when the door leapt inwards and the handguard of the cutlass hit him in the face, knocking him back down the five steps. He put his arm up to fend off the cut. Perfectly balanced, Jeremiah changed the position of his feet and cut open the right side of the man's neck.

In front of him, the fire was burning in the store shed as the fury drained from his mind. Only then did he shiver.

HARRY FOUND the .410 shotgun by the river and did not understand why it was there. When the sun was overhead he watched his father bury the five dead men. Tinus said a prayer in English and the *Taal* while Harry from a distance muttered his own prayer in Shona so the dead blacks would understand.

BOOK 4 – SHIFTING SANDS

1

JULY 1897

A year to the day since Jack Slater hanged the leaders of the first unsuccessful Chimurenga, Captain Doyle of the *Indian Queen*, who first took Sebastian into exile, walked into the office of Baring Brothers in Threadneedle Street three hundred yards from the Bank of England. He was fifty-five. The dark suit he was wearing had been carefully tailored in Savile Row and was matched with a high stiff collar and black cravat. He had been perfectly shaved by an expert barber who had also cut his hair to hide the hole in his right ear lost to frostbite sailing the Horn as coxswain to The Captain in '64. There was no mistaking the weather-beaten lines on his face that told the most casual of glances the short, stocky man entering the offices of the first merchant bank in the City of London was a sea captain. No one took any notice as sea captains had been coming to the City for generations to sell their ships and cargo on the Baltic Exchange, insure them with Lloyd's of London, and raise capital from the likes of Baring Brothers. It was the sea captains and their like who had made Britain the greatest trading nation on earth with the largest maritime fleet the world had ever known.

In London, to appease President Kruger of the Transvaal Republic, Doctor Jameson had been tried and jailed for his abortive raid on Johannesburg but the foot soldiers were sent back to Rhodesia where calm returned to the colony. Cecil Rhodes, who had engineered the Uitlander rebellion to take over the Transvaal, resigned as chairman of the Chartered Company and as Prime Minister of the Cape. Captain Doyle in his new suit was convinced the stand-off in the Transvaal would lead to war with the Boers.

In hushed tones, Captain Doyle was shown into the private office of the senior partner. The man behind the sparse desk was tall and thin with a sharp nose, hooked slightly to the right. The man's skin was swarthy, inherited from his parents and not from the sun. In front of him on the desk was the current balance sheet of African Shipping, owned fifty-one per cent by Captain Doyle, and the balance shared equally by Sebastian Brigandshaw and Tinus Oosthuizen. By the time Captain Doyle sat down opposite the sharp-nosed banker, African Shipping owned five modern steamers and was in direct competition with The Captain's Colonial Shipping.

"Do your partners concur with your plans?" asked the investment banker.

"My partners are far away in the middle of Africa."

"Do they know your plans?"

"No, but I control fifty-one per cent of the company and have a valid power of attorney from both my partners over their shares. The shares given to my original crew have been repurchased by the company when they left our employ. There is a partnership agreement binding the remaining officers and crew by controlling interest, their shares part of my fifty-one per cent. They have all been greatly rewarded for their loyalty to me when I left command of the *Indian Queen* and Colonial Shipping."

"We shall want your partners' agreement."

"You shall have it. A surprise to them I expect. They think I have one ship. When I sent them the first set of accounts, Sebastian said he neither understood a word written on the paper nor wished to understand. They both gave me their full trust. They have a large farm, you see, in Rhodesia."

"You don't correspond?"

"By Christmas cards once a year."

"Very quaint... Why did they invest in you?"

"They thought they owed me a favour. Or rather, Brigandshaw owed me a favour."

The man with the sharp nose did not blink, the dark eyes boring into Doyle's soul. The seaman stared back without flinching, a faint smile reflected in his eyes. They were summing each other up, the lender and the borrower.

"Is this Brigandshaw a relation of the Chairman of Colonial Shipping?" asked the banker, his perfectly manicured hands now resting on either side of the open balance sheet.

"He is The Captain's youngest son."

"There was some scandal."

"There was."

"Does The Captain know of his son's shareholding?"

"No."

The silence ticked along with the clock that stood over and behind the banker's leather-bound chair. Captain Doyle knew there was nothing more for him to say, everything was there in front of the banker. The clock reached twelve-thirty and chimed the half hour. The dark eyes had not blinked and the faint smile half evaporated from Doyle's eyes.

"If we are to underwrite a share offering in your company, Captain Doyle, I would like to take you to lunch. At Barings we have found over the many years it is important to invest in people. Facts and figures are important but it is people who make them a success. I have a table booked at my club. Shall we go? I do hope you like oysters as they are rather good at this time of the year. Over lunch, I would be glad if you would explain how the son fell out with his father. Fortunately, my children have followed me into the bank. Barings has been a family affair for many generations.

"You will also tell me why you think Joseph Chamberlain, our esteemed Colonial Secretary, will bother going to war with bearded farmers of Dutch descent. Because if you are right, the shipping requirements to the Cape will be enormous. Should, and I repeat should, we take a position in your company, does twenty per cent sound equitable? We like to share in our clients' success. The flotation will bring us eight hundred thousand pounds, enough to double your fleet. Maybe one of your farming partners will wish to sell their shares. Sleeping partners are very useful at the beginning. Afterwards, they tend to be rather expensive... Was it raining when you came to the office?"

"No, the sun was shining."

"How pleasant. England has many surprises... We made a great deal of money financing the Napoleonic Wars. Done correctly, wars can be very profitable. But only for some; Rhodes still controls the Chartered Company even though he resigned as Chairman. Strange man, Mr Rhodes. All that gold in the Transvaal. Tut-tut, Captain Doyle. Maybe you are right. All that gold should belong to the empire, seeing we British financed the exploration and the shaft sinking. You think they will find gold in Rhodesia?"

"No."

"Neither do we... I think if the sun is really shining we shall walk to the club. What do you say, Captain Doyle? You look a fit enough man for a walk."

.   .   .

JEREMIAH SHANK CUT open the oyster, lifted the shell to his mouth and expertly tipped the contents down his throat. The shells on the oblong plate were spread over seaweed and ice with wedges of Spanish lemons at either end. Without looking at his lunch partner or saying a word he ate through to the thirteenth oyster and slithered the freshly killed fish from the half shell into his mouth. Then he sighed with pleasure and smiled at the banker.

"Perfect. Simply perfect, old boy," said Shank in an accent honed to near perfection that would have fooled anyone other than old Harrovians, old Etonians and other members of the public school elite. The man next to him had been educated at Winchester and inwardly winced at being referred to as 'old boy' by a man who had crawled out of the bowels of a ship. The bank was always thorough when it came to lending other people's money and knew the full career of one Seaman Shank. Even the more recent episode with the cutlass was recorded on the file of the Kimberley Diamond Corporation that would shortly offer its share to the public.

Unaware of his *faux pas* Jeremiah accepted a portion of halibut from the waiter in the City Carlton Club and added the white sauce from the boat the second waiter placed at his elbow. Each lunch companion complimented the other on the perfection of the chef's cooking and toasted the success of the flotation. The banker all the time was trying to imagine the small man next to him killing four natives single-handed with a cutlass. The revolting little man might have saved his own skin in a fit of bravery, but ever since the banker met the diamond magnate he had wanted to plant his fist in the man's crooked face, and the right drooping eyelid added the macabre to the revulsion. Aware of Rhodes's interest in Kimberley Diamonds, he had kept his primal urge under control and smoothly concluded the transaction. The lunch, unfortunately, was obligatory.

'What a day!' Jeremiah thought to himself. 'First, I told Cecil Rhodes to go to hell and now the Queen's bankers have given me the financial power to compete with anyone in Kimberley.' There was no doubt in his twenty-nine-year-old mind that he had finally arrived. With so much money how could Fran Shaw turn him down? He would buy himself a townhouse in the capital and allow the rich and famous to court his company. With Fran at his side, they would never guess his origin. Feeling replete and satisfied with himself he allowed his eyes to roam around the exclusive dining room of the Club and came eye to eye with Captain Doyle seated three tables to his left. The man who had discharged him from the Indian Queen without a Certificate of Character was staring at him with obvious contempt, and he wanted to get up and tell the weathered old sea captain that Jeremiah Shank was now the chairman of a major diamond corporation when the further implications made him stop in his tracks.

"YOU SEEM to know that man lunching with my brother," said the senior partner of Baring Brothers to Captain Doyle.

"He was a member of my crew. What's he doing here?"

"Exactly the same as you, Captain. Borrowing money and offering shares in his company to the public."

"He's a nasty piece of work."

"Probably. But so are most self-made men, current company excluded of course. Your friend is chairman of the Kimberley Diamond Corporation. If you have some spare cash, you should buy some shares next month. Rather good investment I would say."

"You know his background?" asked Doyle.

"Of course. Even down to the fact you failed to give him a Character Certificate. What the Royal Navy would call a dishonourable discharge. But the man has a way of making money which is what it's all about, if you come to think of it. Would you like to join them for coffee?"

"Not on your life."

"I see. Probably best. My brother says from the first time he met Shank he wanted to hit him on the nose. You will understand fighting in the club is strictly frowned upon. Now, a glass of port and you and I will go back to my office and sign the papers. Pleasure to do business with you, Captain Doyle." Idly, he wondered how many shares in African Shipping he would sell to the chairman of Kimberley Diamond Corporation. Men and their vanity were so easily manipulated, he told himself for the umpteenth time.

Captain Doyle left with one glare back at Shank as he followed the senior partner from the club. London society made him uncomfortable, and he was glad to be out in the street and sunshine. As they walked to Threadneedle Street, he wished he was back on the deck of a ship and for a moment regretted his decision to expand, forever on shore away from the passion of his life, the great sea oceans of the world. He knew selfishness was not always possible... The debt to Sebastian Brigandshaw and Tinus Oosthuizen had to be paid.

"THE ESTEEMED MAN with my brother is Captain Doyle, the man rather rudely staring at you as he left the club. You should buy some of his shares,

Mr Shank. Do you know the man?" asked the junior partner of Baring Brothers, enjoying himself.

"Never seen the man in my life before."

"Seemed to know you, Mr Shank."

"Had me for someone else." For a brief moment, the accent had slipped and the younger brother only just managed to suppress a smile.

"African Shipping, sir. Wonderful investment. Captain Doyle believes there will be a war in the Transvaal. This Kruger, so he says, is a man of great pride and will never back down and give in to Chamberlain's demands. You see, there are more immigrants on the Witwatersrand developing the gold mines than Dutch burghers, and most of the newcomers are English. If Kruger gives them the vote as Chamberlain insists, he will lose control of the government and nobody likes to do that. With a pro-British government in the Transvaal, they will wish to join up with British Natal and British Cape and your Mr Rhodes will have the chance of his lifetime to build a railway from the Cape to Cairo. Does sound rather nice, opening up so much country to British trade. Snag is, the Boers will be back where they came from under British rule and that is what they trekked away from in the first place. Do you know Mr Rhodes? I'd very much like to know his opinion."

"We have met in Kimberley. Kimberley is a mining town. Small, you would say."

"And what was the opinion of the shortly disgraced Mr Rhodes?"

"He never gives an opinion that doesn't make him money. How many shares can you get me in African Shipping? The logistics of fighting a war six thousand miles away would require a fleet of ships bigger than anything afloat at the moment."

"Which is why African Shipping is laying the keels for ten modern ships." Silently the younger brother forgave himself for exaggerating. The keels would only be laid after the successful flotation of the shares.

"Buy me as many shares as you can."

"Certainly, Mr Shank."

For the next few minutes Jeremiah Shank was silent, thinking of the consequences of war. His education had been minimal but his mind was crystal clear. Writing letters and adding up figures were for people he employed. It was the thinking that made the money. He could read and that was all the formal education he required; the rest he was born with. War. He could not get it out of his mind.

"You seem distracted, Mr Shank."

"Excuse me, sir, but I must go."

"Not another glass of port?"

"Could you order me a cab?"

"WHERE DO you want to go, guv?"
    "Anywhere... I want to think," said Jeremiah.
    "Nice day for thinkin' I'd say."
    "Shut up, cabbie."
    "Anything you say, guv."
    The horse, left to its own devices, began to make its way home out of the City of London across London Bridge and the River Thames. In the back, oblivious of the river, Jeremiah was thinking, taking different thought lines, different businesses, but each with the new ingredient factored into the equation. War. And how could he, Jeremiah Shank make money out of a war in South Africa? How would it affect his diamond mine? His estate in Rhodesia, where the rebellion had been laid to rest by swift public hangings? Food. He thought of food for an army. He thought of how long it would need to be fed. He thought of horses and how many remounts would be needed to stay in the field. He thought of the Boers and how long they would fight, and remembered the day he had broken into a cold sweat with dead bodies around him, the strength, anger and rage drawn from him by men trying to take what he had built. The Boers would fight for their own with the same bitter rage.
    Even with the afternoon sun shining into the cab he shivered again at the terrible implications. And this time the British would be fighting men with modern rifles who knew how to shoot a buck dead with one shot from seven hundred yards, dropping the bullet in the animal's head using the wind. 'Ships. Horses. Cattle,' he repeated to himself. Kimberley would be safe as part of the Cape. The Boers would never dare invade British territory. By the time the horse trotted over the cobbles into the East End of London, Jeremiah Shank was richer than Croesus. Not once had he looked out of the cab, his mind's eye searching Rhodesia to buy horses for breeding, cows for breeding, men to work his great estate. But above all, he was going to buy a controlling interest in African Shipping and throw the great Captain Doyle back in the sea.
    Only when the horse stopped outside a council house in Bermondsey did Jeremiah come back to the present, and when he did and looked out of the cab at the mean street and the meaner houses, he knew with a fright exactly where he was, a place he had told himself for fourteen years that he would never go back to. Three semi-detached houses down from where the

horse had stopped was 37 Pudding Lane and outside on the mean step were two boys he strongly suspected of being his brothers.

"Bleedin' horse, came right home," said the cabbie into Jeremiah's horror. "Bought the 'orse from some bloke around 'ere, see."

"I'm taking a walk."

"Not 'ere you aren't, guv. Don't like toffs, 'ere about."

"I know my way around."

"Not 'ere, guv, please. Bleedin' 'orse done it, ain't he? All I got, this 'orse an' cab. Take away my licence they will, losin' toff in Bermondsey. Come on, guv, where you really want to go?"

Jeremiah gave him a half-crown and told him to wait, walking down the familiar cobbles with the familiar sounds and smells. Old Smiler was still selling his cockles and whelks as was Mary with the same pushcart and her jellied eels. Come the winter, both would be selling chestnuts hot off the coals, Smiler and Mary thick in their old coats and mittens, red fingers bitten by the chilblains and gas lamps hissing in the fog, and far away the foghorns sounding from the river. There were two boys playing on the street with nowhere else to go, and as he walked past the boys he had never met, both gave him a look of fear mingled with hatred and the street was just the same. He stopped, turned and looked back at the boys on the step and stared them down, making them break and run back to the front door that opened on old hinges. A big fat woman yelled at him, "What you want?" and slammed the old door shut with the boys inside and the brass knocker clanged once more after the door was shut in final confirmation.

And when Jeremiah reached the cab, the cabbie was ashamed to look at him as the fare was crying.

THE DAWNING CAME moments after the door knocker clanged for the second time; the top hat and cane, the well-cut suit, the spats covering the shiny shoes had masked the man at first glance. Opening the living room curtain an inch she saw the nob get into the cab, not thirty yards from where she stood on the bare wooden floor, and the man was crying, the one eyelid drooping half shut, the crooked nose the way he had been born. She watched the last forlorn look at 37 Pudding Lane. Ethel Shank let go the curtain: to some extent, there was even justice in the fine clothes. Then she thought how sad it was that Jeremiah, the name Fred had wanted, looked like her brother and not the man who was really his father.

"Mum, why you crying?" asked the youngest.

"Never you mind," she said and tried to put the image of the first in her litter out of her mind.

LORD EDWARD HOLLAND, known as Teddy to his many friends, was lucky not to see the fat, blousy woman peeping through the corner curtain. There was no resemblance to the sixteen-year-old chambermaid who had taken his fancy, a luscious lass from the docks of London who had come to Bramley Park to earn her way in life. Teddy had left Eton and was waiting to go up to Cambridge to read philosophy and was bored at home for the first time in his life when the flashing eyes, big bust and solid thighs caught his attention. At first he had ignored the signals, until his libido overcame his better sense of decorum. The girl was a servant and should have been below his dignity but it was a hot summer, and there was nothing else to distract his attention. So when they found each other alone in the copse behind the ornamental lake, a walk he had always taken in summer to think of life, he did not imagine it as an ambush but a magical chance that would not come again in a hurry. She had looked at him with liquid eyes and led him into the bracken where he proceeded to lose his virginity to surprisingly expert hands. And like all men, he never forgot the first woman in his life.

For a month they trysted in the bracken until Teddy went up to Cambridge to find out how much people in general and women, in particular, enjoyed his company. Invitations flowed for the holidays and Teddy only came back to Bramley Park at Christmas to find the chambermaid gone. Embarrassed to make enquiries that would raise eyebrows, he tried to put the girl out of his mind, wondering with a feeling of guilt if anything had come from their lovemaking. He was the third son of the Marquis of Surrey and with two older brothers, the title was never going to be in his hands, only the money from his over-rich American maternal grandfather.

The title went back to Richard the Second of England who bestowed it upon his half-brother, the king's father having married a widow. Along with the peerage went a large estate, but by the time Teddy's father came along the only thing left was a very old title and nothing else. The marquis, having taken up carpentry to earn a living, emigrated to the States where, to the young man's surprise, he was met by a New York newspaper reporter who had picked up from the passenger list one John Holland, Marquis of Surrey. When the reporter had looked up the name in *Debrett's*, he knew he had a story. Despite all the talk of being a Republic, American people, especially the new rich, craved the old world of aristocracy and inherited privilege. The paper man did his research and by the time his syndicated article came out across America, people might have thought a King of England had come to take up residence in the one-time colony.

Sensibly John Holland explained his financial predicament to the reporter at the beginning to find himself booked and paid for in the best hotel, clothed and paid for by the best tailor in New York, and launched on the unsuspecting but totally gullible New York society set. Like Teddy, his father was a very likeable sort of chap and was soon on every society lady's list, especially the ones with daughters. The rich can buy anything and soon after his arrival, John Holland was bought by the iron man for his only daughter. The iron man was stupendously rich as every iron rail laid across the vastness of expanding America came from his foundry in Pittsburgh, Pennsylvania.

Bramley Park was bought back by the man from Pittsburgh and John Holland was reinstalled in the family seat that his father had lost to the creditors. The iron man lived long enough to see the birth of a grandson who would inherit the ancient title to his great satisfaction... Somehow it made all that money worthwhile. John Holland to his pleasure found himself not only back in the ancestral home but one of the richest men in England, thankful to give up his saw and spirit level. Being a man of good faith he sent the paper man a large personal cheque, and set about breeding a family and living the way he had wished to be accustomed.

When Teddy the third son turned twenty-one, he inherited half a million pounds and went off on his travels, having finished with Cambridge. But all the while through the rest of his life he felt a twinge of guilt over never finding out what happened to the chambermaid, the chambermaid who never grew older than sixteen in his mind.

A WEEK after Jeremiah had made the cabbie whip up the horse to get out of the East End of London, the prospectus of Kimberley Diamond Corporation was published in the *Daily Telegraph* and ended up on the silver tray next to Teddy's letters. Teddy was taking his breakfast under the elm trees, the same breakfast he ate every morning, summer and winter. Bacon and eggs with one sausage. The mid-August day was perfect, the scent of flowers strong for the early morning, and there was a slight dew on the perfectly cut grass where the lush green foliage of the elms prevented the sun from reaching the lawn. It was the kind of morning that felt grand to be in England.

At forty-six Teddy felt well satisfied with his way of life. His elder brother was off in the colonies governing some country Teddy had never heard of until his brother's appointment. His second elder brother was still in Egypt waiting with the British Army to revenge Gordon's death at Khartoum. He was on Kitchener's staff and had been for some time. The remainder of Teddy's siblings, all girls, were married, even the ugly one with all her money, catching an impoverished baron, and Teddy was left to enjoy Bramley Park. He was a little round in his stomach but still handsome in a mature kind of way, so he told himself. He had never married, and he was happy.

During his philosophy studies at Cambridge, a phrase in the Old Testament had been drawn to his attention which he never forgot; 'it is better to live on the roof than inside with a nagging wife'. The professor had explained that even in those days wives had the habit of nagging their husbands and the Jews were lucky to have good weather and roof gardens to get away from the wives that nagged. Every time he was on the brink of proposing to a nice young girl, he inspected the girl's mother in his mind and every time decided that when it came to the mother, he would have found himself living on the roof. The professor of philosophy had correctly pointed out to his students that most girls came looking and behaving like their mothers, a phenomenon that had gone on down through all the years of the human race. Nature decided the future whatever people tried to do about it.

Glancing at the letters, Teddy picked up the *Telegraph* and as was his habit turned to the financial page to check the value of his stock. Satisfied at the rise of his chartered shares, he glanced at the page opposite and was caught by the words Kimberley and South Africa. He had made good money from his South African shares and began to read the prospectus. When he reached the list of directors and read the name of the chairman, Jeremiah Shank, he wondered why the name gave him such a jolt. After pondering for a long time he remembered. Twenty-five odd years earlier a card had come to him in the post with a London postmark. An uneducated hand had written his address on one side and the two words 'Jeremiah Shank' on the other. For the fun of it and the strange coincidence, Teddy decided to buy shares in the Kimberley Diamond Corporation. By the time he had finished his breakfast and phoned his stockbroker in London, his friends had arrived for the morning game of tennis. It really was a very pleasant way of life, he told himself.

CECIL RHODES WAS aware that a diamond had no value other than its scarcity. The diamond was a token of a man's respect and the more money he spent on the jewel, the greater his respect. If Rhodes could ensure the gift not only retained its value but appreciated, and if Rhodes controlled all the diamonds out of the ground, he would have a product that would last for centuries. The intention was a total monopoly with his company carefully controlling the supply of rough diamonds to the cutters, always slightly less than the public demand. In times of depression Rhodes would stockpile rough diamonds; in times of boom, unload his stockpile. In Kimberley, where he began, the only major company not in his possession was the Kimberley Diamond Corporation. He had made an offer before the public listing which had been rudely turned down. Now he was going to gain control of the company through the open market. Aware that Baring Brothers owned twenty per cent, their usual fee for underwriting the risk of a mining company, Rhodes knew that if he dropped the value of the shares below the listing price, he would force Barings to sell at a loss and further depress the value of Kimberley shares. When he thought buying would not increase the value of the shares, Rhodes would buy and force Shank to buy his own shares to prevent a catastrophe. Rhodes had more money than Shank or anyone else in the diamond trade, which was why in a financial fight he always won. With Barney Barnato's membership of the Kimberley Club had gone the takeover of Barnato's mining company as Rhodes knew every man had his price: a minor son of a minor English vicar had made one of the empire's two great fortunes.

The day the public was offered five million one-shilling shares at one shilling and fourpence each, Rhodes sold two million shares he did not own, expecting the shares to drop from the selling pressure so he could buy the shares for less than the price he had sold them. Only a spattering of spectators from the public bought shares and Rhodes would have had his way if Teddy Holland had not come into the market on the second day with a buying order for one million shares, his stockbroker having advised him to wait. As a result, Teddy paid sixpence a share. Barings, seeing a major buyer in the market, bought instead of sold. The shares rose to tenpence, still well below the listing price, so Teddy bought another million and the price rose to one and six. When Rhodes was forced to buy his two million shares so he could deliver the scrip, he paid Teddy Holland three shillings a share, which made the mining magnate shrug his shoulders.

Teddy had made a fortune on his hunch and decided to follow it through. He wanted to meet this Jeremiah Shank whose name was such a coincidence. Jeremiah, knowing the name of the buyer who had saved his financial life, was only too happy to meet his benefactor and find out why the man had bought the shares but before he met the man for lunch, they sold all his and Barings shares to Rhodes at half a crown. Jeremiah personally walked away with a little under half a million pounds, enough to turn his Rhodesian estate into paradise. At last, Jeremiah Shank was a true country gentleman.

THE LUNCHEON at Bramley Park was the highlight of Jeremiah Shank's brief life, and spoke of a position in society he had never dreamed. A coach, emblazoned with the crest of the Marquis of Surrey, met him at Godalming station. The summer weather had turned mild and wet and the lunch was served in a conservatory that looked out over the country estate of the Marquis of Surrey. Politely, Jeremiah with his best accent, enquired the acreage of the great estate and was told there were nine thousand. A flutter of pride surged through Jeremiah's stomach when he mentioned his twenty thousand, take a few here and there. Having made so much money out of each other the remark went unnoticed, or so Jeremiah thought.

"What is the value of your African estate?" asked Teddy politely a while later.

Jeremiah gave him a figure.

"That's the difference, of course," said Teddy.

Realising he had been put in his place, Jeremiah changed the subject and at half-past two the coach was announced and off he went on his travels.

THE RAIN HAD STOPPED when the man took his leave and the coach went off down the long driveway on its way to the railway station. Teddy took his thinking walk to the copse behind the ornamental lake. Next to the lake, an ancestor had built a gazebo where Teddy took refuge when the rain came down in earnest.

The mild shock of finding such a young man as his lunch companion was quickly overcome by a strong desire to punch the man on the nose. It was the look of him. Nothing he said, the idea of African acres soon squashed by the price. The nose had a twist to it and the drooping right eye was surly. Teddy had asked the young man if any in his family had any connection to Bramley Park and received a blunt no. Teddy put it all down to a fortuitous coincidence. When Shank had asked him why the interest in Kimberley Diamonds, he had been frank. If he had not thrown it away, he would have shown him the postcard.

When the rain stopped, he walked back to the house. Three of his friends were coming down from London for the weekend to play tennis and bridge and Teddy put the matter out of his mind. A pair of pigeons were making a wonderful noise in the elm trees, cooing at each other.

THE FOLLOWING MONDAY shares in African Shipping were offered to the public with Jeremiah buying as many as possible.

With Fran on his mind, he booked a passage back to Africa, this time travelling on a ship he partly owned.

The two boys on the steps and their mother banging the front door stayed in his mind all the way to Cape Town. If he claimed his mother after so many years, he would jeopardise any chance of Fran and buying a house in the West End of London. His money would be no good to him. If he sent them money anonymously, there was still a chance of being found out. Finally, he rationalised they were better off as they were with Fred Shank humping his coal to the houses and emptying the sacks into the scuttles. He could still see his father with the blackened face and the old sack on his shoulders to rest the hundredweight loads. The man was a worker, there was no doubt about that. On Fridays, Fred had one pint of beer in the Boar and Bear and the rest went to Jeremiah's mother. They were a strong family; Fred had his pride and Jeremiah's mother kept the house clean as a new pin. There was a board school around the corner for the boys and the girls if any of them wanted to learn. The community in the East End looked after their own. Being born within the sound of the bells from Bow Church, and therefore being a Cockney, had a ring of pride. No one mucked around with a Cockney.

By the time he took the train north, Jeremiah had convinced himself the family he had run away from to go to sea when he was fourteen, were better off as they were. He could still smell the roasting chestnuts and taste the jellied eels. Nothing he had ever eaten since could touch old Mary's jellied eels. They were all right. His family were all right.

2

DECEMBER 1897

*F*ran Shaw had reached the stage of boredom where she did not care anymore. Jack Slater had not been confirmed as administrator of Rhodesia and it was rumoured that their affair was the reason he had been sent to Kimberley as a manager of De Beers Diamond Corporation, Rhodes's main source of income. Gentlemen did not have affairs with other gentlemen's wives as it set a bad example for the rank and file. Even her brief sexual gratifications had been taken away and Gregory was still impotent with her. There was a rumour a girl in the secretarial pool in Salisbury had reversed the problem and that a second girl had shown the problem was cured, but the more Fran tried to show interest, the more her husband shrank away. It was all so unfair. She was labelled a whore for sleeping with Jack Slater while her husband had become a folk hero among the white community for overcoming his impotence in trying circumstances. The men sleeping around were rather good chaps unless they violated another man's property. If she had any money of her own, she would have gone back to England a long time ago, but like everything else in a marriage, the woman had to ask for everything she wanted, and husbands were disinclined to give their wives a fare home when for the sake of their pride they wanted them to stay. Everything and everything came back to what the man wanted. She might as well have been a sack of flour.

Envy had never been part of her make-up but when she watched Emily and Sebastian with their three children, George having been born three months before the Mashona rebellion, she was violently jealous followed by remorse and sadness. Why could she not have a man in her life, one man that was all she would ever want in her life, a man and children, children who loved each other and showed both love and respect to their parents? Just like the family in the house next to hers. And Alison and Tinus were close enough behind in their serenity. Never once had Seb or Tinus looked at her, as a woman, though she had to admit to herself she had tried to make them look.

Down by the river on her own, she began to cry her tears of self-pity... There was something wrong with her. There had always been something wrong with her. She was a horrible person and no one in the whole wide world cared whether she was alive or dead. In the middle of the river, a fish jumped in the mist of her tears while the river never stopped flowing.

THE TRAIN that brought Jeremiah Shank back to Rhodesia carried a large wooden trunk addressed to Sir Henry Manderville, Bart, Elephant Walk, Mazoe District, near Fort Salisbury, Rhodesia. When the railwaymen moved it from the goods wagon to the dirt strip that ran along the railway line opposite the single-storey goods shed, it was so heavy they thought it contained lead. The wooden trunk, strongly bound with iron hoops, was moved to the goods shed where it waited for a week. Secretly and for months, Sir Henry had been enquiring at the hatch on the roadside of the goods shed and when he was shown the big trunk sent all the way from England, he was as excited as the day he married Emily's mother. With help, the trunk was lifted up onto the farm wagon and off they went on the long road back to Elephant Walk. The ridgeback dogs had come into town to guard the farm purchases in the open wagon and stood guard on either side of the trunk. Having sniffed for smell they lost interest and put their paws up on the side of the open wagon to check everything passing by. Regularly they crossed from one side of the wagon to the other to make sure nothing was missed, neither trusting the other. The drought had taken a grip on the countryside and where it should have been green in December, the grass was brown and short, beaten to the ground by the endless beat of the sun.

In his excitement, Henry had quite forgotten to do the rest of the shopping.

The dogs were off the back of the wagon well before it reached the gate to Tinus's stockade and raced down the track at full speed, ignored by the horse and Henry. Sitting on the high box of the wagon he watched for the fox terriers and smiled when they rushed out of the open gate, yapping to save their lives. The pairs of dogs crossed, ignoring each other, and the terriers tried to jump into the back of the wagon without success, barking all the time. Henry smiled, the comfortable smile of having just arrived home.

Harry, his eldest grandson, came out to see what all the noise was about. Inside the stockade, tame Egyptian geese were honking at each other. Having rushed inside, the ridgebacks rushed out again nearly knocking over Harry for the second time, and all four dogs raced off into the bush chasing each other, the fox terriers constantly barking. The men were in the fields, but Alison, heavy with her third child, came out of her house at the same time Emily pushed open her back door that led out from the kitchen.

Fran heard the noise but, having had her fourth stiff gin, stayed inside. There was never anything of interest so far as she was concerned. She let the book she was reading slide off her knees and took a long swig at the gin, slightly diluted with water and coloured pink with aromatic bitters. People sometimes asked her what the books were about, which at the end of the day she rarely knew. The one she was reading had the illustrious title of *Clover Blossom*, on the front the imprint of a Regency buck. When the dogs stopped barking she picked up the book from the floor, thought she found her place, and carried on reading, soon being no part of Elephant Walk.

Outside around the wagon, staring at the wooden trunk with the iron bands, were six-year-old Barend Oosthuizen, his two-year-old sister Tinka, Harry, his sister Madge who was the same age as Barend, and younger brother George, who had toddled precariously between the msasa trees that shaded the lawn.

"What's in the chest, Grandfather?" asked Harry.

"Where's the shopping, Father?" asked Emily, her arms crossed in front of her chest.

"Oh, dear. My word. Look, I forgot. I've waited a long time for my books and here they are."

"Open the chest, Grandpa," demanded Madge. "We want to see."

"All right then. Everyone up in the wagon. We need lots of men to lift the box onto the ground so we'll have to have a look where it is. Barend, come up here quickly and give me a hand. The stationmaster gave me two keys, one for either side of the trunk, and the wire cutters will soon have these iron bands out of the way."

"What kind of books?" asked Harry losing interest.

"Let's have a look, shall we?"

Emily helped George up onto the wagon as the dogs came tearing back into the compound, sending the geese running and honking for their lives, heads stretched down the end of their necks as far as possible. Ten minutes later the chest came open, the big lid pulling back to reveal the treasure while letting out the smell of old leather. All the children looked inside with puzzled curiosity.

"With these books," said Henry proudly, "I will be able to identify all the butterflies and birds, putting them into their right categories, and the ones no one has seen before, we will give them names and my friend at Oxford who sent all this will register proper Latin names with the Royal Society. When I have finished, I will start with the insects."

"It'll take you a lifetime, Father."

"That's the idea, Emily. That's just exactly the idea. A man needs something to do with his life. I did manage the post office, but the stores had to wait. Once I had the trunk nothing else entered my mind. Two letters there were. From England. Both the same, I would say. One for your husband, Emily, and one for Tinus. Now, who would be writing to them from England?"

"Are you going to read all those books, Father?"

"Of course I am. Now, children, I have a very good idea. Why don't we empty the chest one by one and you can put the books into the centre of my room on the floor and I can look at each one as it comes out of the trunk? Now, just look at this one. An encyclopaedia of the world's butterflies with drawings. I bet they haven't got half the ones I've collected. Children! Where are you going? Emily, my dear, it appears we are failing in their education. Hunting the bush, yes. Collecting specimens, no. And reading books is going to be right out of the question. I don't believe my grandson can read."

"George is a little young," smiled Emily.

"I was referring to Harry, Emily."

"I know you were, Father. Now give me the letters. When the others come back, they can lift the trunk into your rondavel and that way we won't have a mess all over the place. Well, not immediately."

Emily put the two letters in the front pocket of her apron and walked across to Alison.

"How are you feeling?" she asked.

"Tired. Be glad when this one is out on its own in the world."

"Letter from England for Tinus. One for Seb. I think they are both from Captain Doyle."

"Shall we open them?"

"Better not. You go and lie down. I'll shower the children."

Alison looked at Emily walking back to her house and smiled. How things changed in life. She took the letter back to her house. Inside, the cat was eating a rat on the dining room table, purring loudly. Too tired to care, Alison put the letter next to the cat and the rat and went to lie down. To the sound of the children squealing under the cold shower in the little outside enclosures they had made of grass, she fell asleep, her hands clasped over her swollen belly. She was smiling.

GREGORY FOUND Fran drunk in the one armchair and, taking a clean set of clothing, left without a word. The small shower enclosures, one for the men and one for the women, allowed a man to shower while looking over the top of the thatch-grass. The water was tepid from the day's sun. He added a jug of hot water to the large bucket and with the rope that looped over an arm of a tree, hoisted the contraption above his head and tied the rope. A piece of rubber hose was attached to the bottom of the bucket and dangled over his head held straight down by the weight of a large iron rose.

Reaching up he turned the spigot above the shower rose and warm water began to wash the day's dirt from his body. Were it not for Fran drunk in the chair he would have whistled a tune. Tinus, in the ladies' shower with Seb outside standing guard, was singing in the *Taal*, a tune his grandfather had taught him from the Great Trek. Halfway through he switched to English and an even older song of his mother's Scottish clan, the McDonalds. He was in fine voice, and forgetting himself Tinus began to whistle 'Greensleeves' the song some said had been written by Henry the Eighth.

"Shut that up, you Sassenach," came from the next shower and all three of them began to laugh.

"Hurry up both of you," shouted Seb. "I need my gin."

THE UNOPENED LETTERS sat on the low table on Tinus's veranda that he alone called the stoep. Gregory had given his apologies for Fran, saying she was tired, which everyone knew was a lie. The sun had set leaving a red sky behind the msasa trees and for the first time, Emily noticed Tinus had left his gun in the gun cabinet. When not in use the guns were chained so the children, Harry in particular, could not take them out. Gregory said his obligatory 'that tastes good'; Henry said cheers and went back to his book while Alison related the story of the cat and the dead rat on her dining room table. Barend tried to twist Madge's hair and received a loud, unladylike smack which made him grin; he had caught her attention. George was fast asleep on a rush mat near the screen door. Slowly the pressure lamp took over the light as colour faded from the night sky. Far away there was a rumble of thunder, the unspoken hope in all of them that it would bring some rain. Food was set out on the big table that had been moved onto the screened veranda for the summer. The tension of war that invaded their lives for so long was gone and the only blight on their happiness was Fran and Gregory Shaw.

The experiment of using the maize corn to fatten the cows, Seb's great brainchild, had worked and the farm for the first time was self-sufficient. Thirty black men were now empowered and housed in their own compound, each family given an area to build a hut in the same tradition their own chiefs had perpetuated through the centuries. All signs of fear had left the farm and food was assured for everyone. They could hear drums beating from the native compound, a sure sign of content.

"You'd better open them," said Alison.

"Doyle saying he's gone bust," said Tinus.

"Doesn't matter," said Sebastian picking up his letter from the low table where in his mind's eye it was burning a hole. The huge hand of Tinus came forward and picked up his letter. The letters were opened in silence and Henry put down his book. Everyone waited. Seb looked up for a moment and then started again. Tinus had finished reading and was staring at the ceiling, the lamp throwing strange shadows from his full beard up over the dark cavities of his eyes. Silently he passed the letter to his wife. Seb finished the letter for the second time and gave it to Emily. Tinus began to chuckle from deep in his big chest, the shirt buttons fighting to stay attached to his shirt.

"What's going on, old boy?" asked Gregory.

"Very simply," said Sebastian, "my partner and I are very rich. Em, give him the letter. Alison, pass yours to my father-in-law if you don't mind, Tinus. Presume they have made you the same offer?"

"Sixty thousand pounds sterling. Who are these Baring Brothers?"

"The largest merchant bank in London," said Henry, scanning the letter passed to him from Alison. "My word, that really will put the old pirate's nose out of joint." And then everyone began to laugh at the reference to The Captain, the reason for all of them being in the room.

"Are you going to sell?" asked Seb of Tinus quietly.

"Of course I am. Look, Seb, a farm can belong to only one person in the end. We both know that. My dream, far back in my mind as I knew I would never have the money, is to buy a wine farm in the Cape. Ceres in particular. Every Boer wants a wine farm in the Cape with a long Cape Dutch house and a cottage down the road by the sea. Why don't we both buy farms in the Cape?"

"Funny how money upsets everything," said Fran Shaw, pushing open the screen door. "Someone better give me a gin. You either have too much or too little. Splits up the jolly old family, see." She was quite drunk and Gregory put her down in his chair.

"Funny how often the truth comes from babes and drunks," said Gregory too quickly. There was a long silence. "No, Fran, I apologise. That was quite unnecessary. Appearances, Fran, appearances. Always so very important. No, on second thoughts let us go home. Will you excuse us, everyone? Good night."

"Take some supper," said Alison.

"Sorry. But I don't feel hungry. Henry, old boy, I'll see you in the morning. Such a long way from Florence don't you think? A long way from Chittagong. A long way from Nottingham. Fact is, I'm a long way from anywhere."

WORKING on the principle that talking about a bad situation makes it worse, Emily turned to the children.

"Come along, children, it is well past your bedtime."

"Mummy, I'm still hungry," said Madge trying to keep the whine out of her voice.

"You've eaten enough for three grown people."

"Harry," said his grandfather stepping into the breach, "come along and I'll tell you another story of the first Mandervilles who landed with William the Conqueror."

"Oh, tops. Come on, Madge, Grandfather's going to tell us a story."

"Barend," said Tinus, "take your sister back to the house." He spoke in the *Taal* and without a question, Barend took his sister by the hand. "Both kiss your mother and aunt before you go... Good night."

"Father," said Emily, "can you pick up George? He's fast asleep."

When Henry had taken his grandchildren and Barend and his sister had gone to their house, Emily turned to Alison and Tinus, "What are we going to do?"

"Nothing," said Tinus.

"She's drunk. Unhappy. He's miserable."

"Never tell a person the truth about themselves. First, they will secretly hate you and secondly, it will not do any good. We can be kind to both of them, Em. All we can do. Married people have to go to each other with their problems."

"If only she had some children," said Alison.

"Would you like me to serve supper?" said Emily. "My father will be a long time with the children. He loves to tell stories."

"He should write them down for the future," said Alison, quickly following the change of subject.

"He has his butterflies," said Emily, relieved the crisis was over, "and now he has all the flowers and insects to contend with."

As Emily got to her feet with the others to go to the dining room table and their cold supper, a crash that sounded like broken pottery echoed across the houses over the beat of native drums throbbing constantly from the compound down by the river.

FOR THE FIRST time in his life, Gregory Shaw almost hit a woman but upbringing and training stopped the deadly impulse. Turning away from the woman who had thrown the jug, he was sick with horror at what he had almost done. He knew that if he was not a gentleman, he was nothing. Outside the fox terriers were barking, a hollow sound in the empty night.

Sobered by the broken jug and the brief threat of her husband, Fran began to shake. She tried to tell the dogs to shut up but nothing came out of her mouth. Gregory had his head bent away from her and the horror of what he was doing came to her and with it understanding. He was crying. Silently. But he was crying and for once she began to think about someone other than herself.

"Greg, I'm sorry."

"I nearly hit you."

"I know."

"That is so terrible. You know that. A man hitting a woman."

"It's my fault. I married you because I thought you were rich."

"It's my fault. I thought a wife so young would bring back lost years."

"And extinguish her memory."

"Maybe... Are people always selfish?"

"Always, Greg. If they think otherwise they are lying to themselves. Even charity is given for self-satisfaction. Each must have what the other wants to balance. Harmony comes with balance I think, though mostly I don't know what to think."

"You want to go back to England. I have nothing but my share in this farm and that doesn't amount to anything if you want to be rich. Divorce and where will you go? I didn't know about the Catholic clause, and with my dreams rushing around me I wouldn't have cared. Digging farms out of the African bush is hard, Fran. There are things here we didn't know about in England. Rinderpest. Too much rain. Drought. War. Did you know last night a leopard ate the head from a calf while it was being born? Smelt the blood of birth. Tinus had to shoot the cow. No one has ever tamed Africa and maybe no one ever will. Even Nat had his church burnt to the ground. His school. Everything he thought he was doing right. But Africa didn't want his God any more than his education."

"Will the money come back if we divorce?"

"I don't know."

"Don't you want to find out?"

"No. What I have is here. I'm too old to change my life. Fran, I'm almost forty-four and most of my life has gone."

Quietly Gregory went down on his knees next to the cold fireplace and began to pick up the pieces of broken porcelain from the rush mat. Outside the dogs had stopped barking. In the still of the night they could hear Henry Manderville's voice storytelling his grandchildren and for a moment they both listened through the open windows. Then the drums stopped and without the rain the frogs were silent. Even the whirr of crickets was dampened by the dark of the moonless night.

"He loves his grandchildren," said Gregory.

"Oh, yes. They have something to give each other, you see. The balance. They are his future and he is their past. He likes talking the stories and they like listening. It's all about them. Their family. They all belong to the same thing... Don't blame yourself. I was a fool long before I met you. Probably always been a fool. Part of what's being told out there I wanted... Family, children, belonging, but something else said there was more and I went looking. I enjoyed everything on the surface and you were to be the rich prize of my success. There was music but that was only on the surface. Do you know, I have never heard an original note of music in my life? When I took my LRAM I cheated on the composition. I thought of Mozart and changed some of the notes because there were so many of them. I was so good at fooling people and myself that one of the teachers thought I would go into composition. Become a composer. For a brief flight of fancy I believed him, fool that I was. We are what we are, Gregory. Thank you for not hitting me. I deserved it. Can you bear to give me a hug?"

"Of course, you fool."

"Maybe only babes and drunks do tell the truth."

"You're not drunk anymore."

"No, I'm not."

THE LETTER from Captain Doyle that was meant to precede the offer from Barings Brothers arrived a week later. For the families living in isolation, the idea of the white tribes of Africa having a war with each other was ludicrous. When Gregory laughed out loud at the idea of untrained farmers squaring up to the British Empire, he received a look from Tinus that was murderous. Quickly apologising, he had quite forgotten the man he worked with all day long was not an Englishman.

"Tinus, you don't really think this Kruger wants a war... Why?"

"To keep him in power. To keep his Boers from the grip of the British. My grandfather trekked away from the British, away from the Cape and British rules and regulations. The only rules the Boer accepts are those in the Bible. A Boer, his family, his Bible and a rifle. That's freedom. Individual freedom. Democracy ties the hands of a man like that, always telling him to do the will of the majority. There are more Uitlanders, foreigners, than Boers in the Transvaal digging for gold. The right of every white man to vote will give them the power and join the Transvaal to the British, what my grandfather risked everything to get away from. Captain Doyle is right. If the British force Kruger to enfranchise the Uitlanders, he will fight."

"But he will lose in a week," said Gregory.

"The veld is big and wide. The Boer knows every kopje and every Boer can kill a buck with one shot from five hundred yards. Those British red coats with the nice white sash that crosses over the heart will make a good target. Don't laugh at the Boers, Gregory. You will regret it."

"But you want to go to the Cape," interrupted Sebastian. "That's going back in your family history."

"My mother was Scottish. My wife is English. I live here under British rule. Don't judge the Boers by me, Seb. Some would say I am a detribalised Boer, ruined by English influences. No, Seb, you can't dissuade me. I'm selling. Having my wine farm."

"The children will miss each other," said Emily, keeping the fear of loneliness out of her voice.

"Yes they will but soon new families will arrive in the Mazoe Valley. The rich red soil will bring them. With your dividends from African Shipping, Seb, you can buy out my share in Elephant Walk."

"When are you leaving?" asked Sebastian sadly.

"When these English bankers pay me my money."

"And war with England and the Transvaal. Which side will you take?"

"I will take no side. The war will be far away from my wine farm. Look, Emily, you and the children will visit. When Barend grows bigger, he will want to come to his father's old hunting grounds. We will always be related to each other, if not by blood then by memory. I can send you the equipment you need. Newer strains of livestock, bigger cattle. Come, this isn't the end of our world together."

FRAN WATCHED her husband and understood. She had given up drinking during the day having embarrassed herself in front of her friends. Instead, she waited impatiently for the first drink on Tinus Oosthuizen's veranda. Gregory's back had straightened. The eyes had lost their hesitancy. For one brief moment of hope, she thought his impotency would leave with his new strength. The man was a soldier who had lost his job and the thought of war had brought him alive again. In a war, they would need his skills. In a war, petty convention would be drowned in necessity. In a war, Gregory Shaw would be a soldier again, a real soldier with a uniform, a real command, a purpose for his life. She never spoke what was in her mind but they both knew; war would be good for both of them. In front of her eyes, the ageing husband had become a young man again. For a moment she was even jealous.

THE ONE THING Henry Manderville feared most in the bush was snakes. For lions and buffalo, he carried a gun with a good chance of acquitting himself. Snakes were waiting for him hidden in the grass, and no amount of expert reading could convince him his footfall vibrating through the earth sent most snakes running faster than he would have wished to run himself. High gaiters and leather trousers were his answer to the phobia, and he carried a long stick with a short fork at the end for imprisoning the upper halves of snakes firmly to the ground with the idea of walking around the pole to make his escape.

Every day he left with the rising sun, the butterfly net firmly attached to his haversack, the hoop behind his head, the handle bouncing on his bottom; a wide-brimmed hat turned down at the front kept out the yellow light of the morning sun. For all intents and purposes, he had given up farming in pursuit of his new obsession. All over the rondavel were books open and shut.

The riverside acacia was chock-full of birds and butterflies from very large fish eagles to small songsters that had no English names. The butterflies flitted from flower to flower, small ones like the cabbage whites he had known in England to creatures with long tail feathers more like kites than butterflies. All the problems of the world had left his mind to live free with nature, and Henry had never known such contentment. All the wonders of the world were around him in the trees and bush, the long elephant grass, the reeds by the river, gurgling water, the hum of bees and the calling of the birds. Best of all, he told himself, there was not one sign of man, only animals watering peacefully from the river.

At midday when the sun was too hot to venture from the shade of the tall acacia trees, lacelike in green leaf and sharp with thorn, Henry collected water from the river and in the protection of rocks washed clean by the river in flood, he made a fire and boiled water for his tea. Down by the river, where a swirl of water through the rocks had given him the perfect hiding place, he collected his bottle of milk. A man without a sweet tooth, he drank his sugarless tea and prepared to catch his lunch, a ritual that provided Henry with short bursts of excitement as well as long periods of hunger when the fish wouldn't bite. On fishless days he refused to eat in punishment, and left the buttered bread in its waxed paper to be eaten the following day.

During the heat of the day, with his back to a tree trunk, he read the books from England stashed in his haversack. When the white light of day yellowed with the sinking of the sun he foraged for his specimens, and with the last rays of the sun burning the sky red, he trudged home a happy man.

Back in the compound they smiled at him, gave him a drink on the veranda as was their ritual, and told him of their day. Sometimes he showed them what he had found but not always.

YOUNG HARRY BORROWED a pair of British Army field glasses from Uncle Gregory and spent a long and hungry day viewing his grandfather from the sanctuary of a shaded outcrop of rocks across the river. He was fascinated by the leather pants that had been lovingly made from the skin of young bushbuck carefully cured in salt to softness. The butterfly net gave his grandfather a halo with the morning sun in his face and Harry expected him to be doing great things with so much equipment: the gun, the forked stick, the pole and net, the haversack bulging with content. By the time the light had gone from yellow to white Harry was bored but, being on the other side of the river in full view, if he stood up, he could see his grandfather settled down comfortably with his back to a tree reading books.

Earlier he had viewed through the glasses a close-up of the triumphant capture of a butterfly that had left Harry wondering what it was all about. The secret place for keeping the milk cool was revealed, the fire curled smoke from behind a rock, and for a very short while, the catching of a large fish was worthwhile but spoilt when grandfather went about cooking the bream over the hidden fire instead of catching lots of them for supper. The smell of cooking fish wafted over to his hiding place and sent saliva washing down his chin. At some point he fell fast asleep and woke to search for his grandfather with the field glasses, only to find him staring upwards, stock still under a tree where he stood for a long time until a bird came out and flew off down the river. Harry could see and almost hear the sigh of contentment. Later, when his grandfather was off into the thick bush where Harry couldn't see him anymore, he escaped back over the river and ran back to the compound where he raided the meat-safe with the small holes in the zinc to let the air flow through and was caught by his mother cutting chunks of cold meat off last night's leg of venison.

"Where were you for lunch?" asked Emily.

"Watching Grandfather. Uncle Gregory says Grandfather's gone potty. Mummy, what's potty? Is it catching butterflies and standing still for hours under trees looking up at birds? 'Cause if that's potty, Grandfather's potty."

"I think Uncle Gregory meant eccentric."

"So Grandfather's eccentric?"

"Oh yes. They say a lot of Englishmen left out in Africa become eccentric. Even some of those who go to India."

"I'm an Englishman. Do you think I'll become eccentric? I hope not. I don't like catching butterflies and staring into trees." Harry thought for a moment with his mouth full of meat, chewing. He swallowed. "But I wouldn't mind those bushbuck trousers."

"I'll make you a pair," said Emily smiling.

"Will you, Mummy? Oh, tops. You're the best mummy in the world."

"No she's not," said Madge from the open door. "She'd have smacked me for stealing the meat... Mummy, what am I going to do when Barend goes away?"

ALISON, with a basket of washing from the communal line, heard the last part of the conversation and walked on to her house. She put the basket down in her kitchen and sat thinking, far away in her thoughts. The baby was due in three weeks' time but her mind was elsewhere. Ominously, Barend and Tinka were quiet in the back of the house; Tinus had not yet come in from the lands. Rightly, she told herself, she should get up and start setting cutlery and crockery on the long table out on the veranda.

A gecko was climbing up the screen that was meant to keep the flies out of the kitchen, the small sticky feet-pads allowing the lizard to defy gravity. Like the spider of Scottish legend, she watched as the gecko stalked and killed the flies that were trying to get through the finely meshed screen, and wondered where her life would have been if she had not climbed out of the window at Hastings Court and joined the runaways on their odyssey to Africa, to an African farm cut off from the realities of her known world.

It was difficult for her to imagine the young woman who had taken the job of looking after Harry. If she had not loved little Harry so much, she would not have run off in the night; if her brother had not gone to sea; if her parents had not died; if she had not become a child's nurse, a servant in all but name; if she had not let Tinus have his way before they were married. Now they were going again. Leaving Harry, Emily and the enigmatic Seb who worried about all of them, the weight of the world resting on his shoulders. Now she had two, almost three children, and a husband richer than anyone she had ever known in England except The Captain. Idly, she wondered if the old pirate, as Grandfather Henry called him, ever missed his grandchildren. She doubted it. That old man had money on his brain, morning, noon and night. How strange that Madge, granddaughter of the owner of Hastings Court, old, old money in an old, old house, was worrying about the grandson of a jobbing gardener and not a very good one by all reports, Alison's education coming from the board school and the lucky interest of a primary teacher.

From being servant and mistress she and Emily had become friends far from the rigid rules of English class. There had just been the four of them in the bush with a common destiny... And then the children... Then again, like destiny, the potty grandfather and his unhappy friend. Sadly, overwhelmed by loneliness, she thought again of leaving her friends, more family than friends, and she understood. There was comfort in their companionship, lost as they were in the middle of the bush. They relied on each other; that was it. Their own preservation relied on each other and even Fran had found it was no place to fall out with the people she needed, no time or place to argue. Alison sighed. She would miss them all so much.

And when she looked for the gecko, it had gone.

3

JUNE 1898

*B*y the end of June, a year after the first Chimurenga, St Mary's Mission had been rebuilt except for the church. Earthly attractions came before the house of God. The mission comprised a small dispensary managed by Bess, a school run by Bess and Nathanial, a large kitchen and dining room, two dormitories and, after long theological debate, an open area with goal posts at either end. The church, when it was built, would be of great proportions as befitting Nathanial Brigandshaw's real mission to Africa: the mission of saving souls from the domination of eternal hell, consumed but never dying in the fire of the Devil, the eternal pit of damnation for those who did not accept the one true God and his only son, Jesus Christ. The stone church would rise above the charred remains of sacrilege, the spire visible to the heathen pagans for miles around, the Cross of Christ high and triumphant, throwing its light over the darkness of Africa, bringing that light to everyone who believed in the Trinity of God the Father, God the Son and God the Holy Ghost. Three great kilns were burning the bricks and the House of God, when it rose from the bush, would be so powerful that no mortal man would ever burn it down.

With his long black skirt touching the dry earth of Africa, Nat strode his domain with the great energy of a man doing the work of God.

THREE MILES AWAY, the man who had made all this possible by paying for it was gazing down out of the window of his tower across the Hunyani River at the throngs of horses being tended to by his black grooms under the eye of Jack Jones, a man listed in England as a deserter from the British Army. Jeremiah Shank had recognised a soulmate in the men's bar of Meikles Hotel when the ex-corporal Jones had told him to stop the crap and to use his proper accent. As in everything Jeremiah did in his life, he turned the incident to profit. Anyway, he was too short to start an argument, and the Welshman was looking at his face with the expression of a man looking forward to doing harm.

"'Ave a drink, mate," said Jeremiah throwing his elocution lessons out of the window, having first looked around the small bar to make sure that he would not be recognised. The barman was a black man dressed up in a red fez and a white jacket whom Jeremiah knew would have no idea of the difference between French and English. When the barman failed to understand the order, he gave his customer a short menu to point to where the bottle labels had been miniaturised in the margin. As Jeremiah had found since he had first come into money through working for The Captain, free drinks turned men's opinions quicker than fists or guns. "Nice to talk proper," said Jeremiah sliding the beer to his new friend. "Rumbled me, mate. Jeremiah Shank at your service. Tell me, my old codger, what brings you to the colonies?"

Seven beers later Jeremiah had the story. The Welshman had hit an officer for mistreating a horse and, instead of waiting to be locked up for insubordination, he had thrown away his fifteen years' seniority with the Welsh Guards and caught a train for Liverpool. For three years he had roamed around America, made friends with a gold prospector in California and followed the American to the gold fields of Monomotapa where they had found nothing, splitting up the night Jeremiah had found Jack Jones in the men's bar of Meikles Hotel.

"You want to come and work for me, Taffy?"

"Why would a good Welshman who likes horses better than men want to do that, I ask?" The man was quite drunk.

"'Cause after Cecil John Rhodes I'm the richest man in this bleedin' country."

"Now are you, man? Well, that does make a difference. Fact is, I'm broke."

"I know, my old cock. But I also know you know all about horses and that bit does make me interested. Pick you up in the morning outside the hotel at ten o'clock."

"Yes, guv."

Later, in the best room in the hotel, Jeremiah smiled to himself. Only at the end had he reverted to his posh accent and only at the end had the

Welshman called him guv. Jeremiah Shank was really learning about the power of money.

The investment in St Mary's Mission was as calculated as any business decision. There was nothing in Jeremiah's background to offer his peers so he decided to dazzle them with good deeds. When it came to sending out the invitations to the ground-breaking ceremony for the reverend's church, the drawings for which together with the cost were more like a cathedral to Jeremiah, he understood why so many people in history had gone in for charity. A rather nice piece of paper had been printed with the masthead proclaiming the St Mary's Mission Foundation, while discreetly at the bottom were listed J Shank Esquire (Chairman) and The Reverend N P J Brigandshaw. Even years later Jeremiah was unable to find out what the P and J stood for but at the time he only saw the initials, and was so impressed with the Esquire after his own name that he forgot to ask, the opportunity slipping away forever.

To ask Fran Shaw meant inviting her husband, which brought up the question of asking the younger brother he had heard referred to as the black sheep. That was when the reverend was talking to the army captain who so consciously looked down his nose at Jeremiah Shank. In the end, everyone at Elephant Walk was sent gilt invitations and Jeremiah wondered if the black sheep would remember his face and the part he played with Jack Slater and the police in trying to have Sebastian arrested with the ivory. There was always a risk in everything, Jeremiah told himself.

THE INVITATION to Mr and Mrs M J M Oosthuizen arrived three months after they had left for the Cape, the new baby keeping them in Rhodesia until it was old enough for travel, Alison still hoping Tinus would change his mind. Tinus, she found, like so many men had a one-track mind, and all the guile in the world failed to change his direction. For Alison, it was the worst parting she had ever faced in her life.

Sir Henry's invitation was soon lost among the litter of books and specimens that infested his one-room rondavel, Harry convinced that some of the bugs were still alive.

Sebastian looked at the invitation with surprise. It was the first social engagement to which he and Emily had ever been invited, the taint of their elopement keeping them off the government social list. The thought of meeting his second brother after they had been in the same country for so many months made him smile; nasty names and rumours were always reported back to their owners even in the African bush.

For Fran Shaw, the name in small print at the bottom under Foundation Directors rang a distinct, faint bell in her mind but failed to connect to a thunderstorm on the veranda of Meikles Hotel. Bored to distraction with her life despite Gregory having squared his shoulders at the prospect of war, she was happy to send off her reply accepting the invitation regardless of the fact she had not been to church for years. After all, the church had always been a social event as well as a communication with God.

THE LAWNS down to the Hunyani at Holland Park were immaculate, and where the msasa trees had been left standing on the way to the river small flowerbeds ringed their trunks giving a splendid splash of colour amidst the dryness of the leafless branches, rain having not fallen for months. In between the trees, black men in bare feet, starched white uniforms, and red fezzes with black tassels hurried between the multitudes of guests. Earlier everyone had watched a visiting English bishop scoop out an inch of hard dry soil with a silver trowel presented by Jeremiah with the bishop's name on the back as the presenter. Drops of water were thrown at the dry patch of the cleared bush by the sweating bishop dressed in his full regalia.

In a cluster around the tiny scooped-out hole in the ground, a crowd of overdressed Europeans were being watched with amazement by a crowd of Africans who had come for the free lunch and had no idea what all the fuss was about. Thankfully the group of Europeans sang for a while out of tune and then got into their carts and drove away from St Mary's Mission leaving the Africans to the fine spread of food, most of which none of them had ever seen in their lives before. There was some dissatisfaction at the lack of maize beer at such a festive occasion but the black people in a few short years had become accustomed to the less pleasant habits of their new masters. One of the young boys named Amos by Nathanial, who was to play a major role in the future of the mission, said that half a celebration was better than none at all, even though he was far too young to drink.

The three miles from the Mission to Holland Park had taken the guests half an hour and young Amos would have been amazed to see how much liquor was flowing between the trees and their neat ringed flowerbeds. There were trays of champagne and Pimm's No. 1, silver trays of light and brown sherry, the latter a euphemism for sweet as no English lady of culture could ever bring herself to ask for a sweet sherry. Trays of canapés to go with the liqueurs were handed round and all before the main luncheon to be served on the terrace of the great house.

Guiding the red-fezzed black waiters with military precision, Taffy Jones was dressed as a major-domo and used the social skills he had learnt as a part-time waiter in the officers' mess of his regiment. Taffy had been enjoying himself up to the point when Major Brigandshaw, recently elevated by the British Army, took a glass of champagne from a waiter's tray, turned and looked straight into Jack Jones's eyes.

"Don't I know you from somewhere?" James Brigandshaw was splendid in his red uniform and medals and for a moment the ex-corporal thought it was all over. Then the major gave him a wintry smile and turned back to the only good-looking lady, the really good-looking lady in the whole crowd of them, and for the rest of the day, Jack Taffy Jones intended keeping well away from the man in the crimson uniform.

Thankfully out of earshot he missed the comment of James Brigandshaw to Fran Shaw.

"That man's been in the army. Probably Guards. Tall enough. Now I suppose I'd better go across and talk to that reprobate younger brother of mine. Father said he'd cut me off if I paid him a visit but he never said anything about talking at a church function, though frankly this looks more like a garden party at Bucks Palace than a religious dedication, and if someone doesn't get that poor bishop out of his robes he's going to expire in the noonday sun even if this is meant to be the winter. You want to come across and introduce me to Seb? Probably won't recognise me, you see. Only thing we all agreed upon at home was that brother Nat was a bore, harmless but a bore. Thank goodness no one let him give a speech at that ground-breaking ceremony. If you can call ground-breaking digging up an inch of soil. That poor bishop, he's so fat and the ground so low. You know, I told your husband there's going to be a war with the Boers in the Transvaal over the right to vote and he became rather excited. Said I'd inquire about a new commission. You see, he left Chittagong of his own volition."

"How do you know, Major Brigandshaw?"

"You'd be surprised how much the British Army knows about everyone. Including our host."

"Do tell. He's such a mystery."

"Not if you know the facts."

"Now you are teasing and you'd better stop as here comes the man in question. I'm sure I've seen him before somewhere, but bless me I can't remember."

"Probably just as well," said James under his breath. To James, women were either naïve or plain damn stupid. Or was she playing a game? Deliberately, he left her talking to the host as he moved off to join his younger brother in what would be their first conversation in many years. As he walked he was amused to see the tall major-domo move away in the opposite direction. Mentally he marked down a need to find out more about the man.

To Jeremiah's surprise and annoyance, the woman for whom he had gone to so much trouble failed to recognise him and was about to stand back, waiting for a formal introduction.

"We have met, you know," he said in his best British accent. "Fact is, we had supper together... There was a thunderstorm, you remember?... Meikles Hotel."

"Oh dear, are you the same man who paid for my room?" Then it all came back, including the memory of her hangover, and she blushed. "Then I must thank you for being so kind. Storms are so terrible in Africa."

"You reached home safely the next morning?"

"Yes, I did... Do you think the church will look splendid?" she said, changing the subject.

"I hope so, seeing I'm paying for it. Maybe we will both remember each other the next time we meet."

"I do hope so. Holland Park is such a lovely home. What's in the tower?" she said, looking up.

"My telescope. That dome opens to the sky. At night the sky is very beautiful."

"You spend a lot of time looking up at the night sky, Mr Shank?"

"Yes. Would you like to see the heavens, Mrs Shaw? Now, if you'll excuse me I have so many guests and the bishop wants to leave."

Still annoyed, he turned his back and left her standing alone. Even the best-laid plans come to nothing, he told himself, and put the matter out of his mind. Halfway towards the bishop he stopped and looked back and their eyes met at thirty yards. When he reached the bishop, he was smiling.

The crimson major had reached the bishop two paces ahead of him and was whispering something in the Right Reverend's ear that made Jeremiah stop. The bishop beckoned over Nathanial Brigandshaw and seemingly passed on the message.

"No pagan witch doctor is going to intimidate me," said Nat sharply to his brother.

"They are calling her the Prophet, brother. In Shona of course. Tried once to pronounce their word. Very difficult. The man who speaks English says as near as he can think it means prophet. She has a pet leopard and frightens the wits out of people who come too close. Withered old hag by most reports. We think she had something to do with the rebellion but we kept away from hanging a woman. She was the power behind the Kalanga rising and probably ordered the burning of brother Nat's church. Often the people who start all the killing are far away from the event when it happens. Fanatics themselves, they breed a deadly fanaticism in their followers. Rather like 'who will rid me of this priest', if you'll forgive me using Henry II as an example, Bishop. The smaller people in life have a smaller vision and take their leader's words rather too personally. Anyway, this old crone has prophesied that when they burn down your church in the second Chimurenga, and that one I can pronounce, it will send all us British back to where we belong. A Chimurenga translates as a war of liberation. So like the apes at Gibraltar, brother, you'd better look after your new church when it's built. Can't have these prophecies coming true, can we?"

"Why don't you arrest the crone and hang her as a witch?" said Nat.

"Burning witches at the stake is rather out of fashion, old chap."

"But if she started the rebellion?"

"If everyone went back in history and started hanging the perpetrators of rebellions, I rather think one half of the world would be trying to hang the other half. Let sleeping dogs lie. The rebellion is over."

"She's a heretic," Nat almost shouted.

"Not according to her belief, so I am told. She just has a different way of looking at it all."

"That's blasphemous, James. And in front of the bishop. You should be ashamed of yourself even thinking such a thought. We have come here to save the blacks, not throw them back in the hot fire of damnation."

"My apologies, your Lordship. 'Twas not my own belief, I spoke only the witch doctor's. They say she believes in one God but has a different way of speaking to Him. Through the intercession of her ancestors. I am no theologian just an ordinary soldier. No, the army will do more harm by hanging the prophet. There are few of us and many of them. If we want to do any good for them, as we all profess and believe, we must get along with them first. And hanging their high priest would have the opposite effect. Even Constantine didn't hang all the pagans at once when he tried to convert them to Christianity... Ah, there you are, Seb. I've been meaning to talk to you. How are you after all these years? You know, you're grown and I don't have the same wish to box your ears anymore. Fact is, I'd probably have my own ears boxed by the look of you. How's the great white hunter? Emily, how are you? Now, is this my nephew Harry?"

"And I'm Madge," said a young voice next to him. "And this is George. Why haven't you come and visited us, Uncle James?"

"Now that's a long story, young lady."

"I can listen."

"Well, if you're going to do that, we'd better go over to that chair under the tree so you can sit on my knee."

"Can George come as well?"

"George can come too. But first, let me take away your father as I rather think I owe him the explanation first."

"Even if I am the black sheep of the family?" said Sebastian smiling.

"Father was going to cut off my allowance."

"I know. How's Mother?"

"I rather think she would like to have sent her love."

"But she didn't."

"She's frightened of Father... Is that Sir Henry over there with a butterfly net?"

"Grandfather's gone potty," said Harry.

Even the bishop smiled at the sight of Sir Henry Manderville down by the river with a butterfly net in one hand and a large glass of Pimm's in the other.

"You have done a great thing building a church," the bishop said to Jeremiah Shank.

"Not built yet, Bishop."

"Yes, well. Now, if you'll excuse me. The day has been long for an old man."

BEING the eyes and ears in Africa of the British Army, James was amused to watch the exploits of the merchant seaman who had managed to have himself ostracised by the Merchant Navy, no mean feat in James's book. Not long ago in British naval history, those who went to sea for the king had to be persuaded into service. James ate the man's splendid spread of food on the man's terrace, extracted himself with difficulty from the grip of his niece and rode off in the afternoon back to Fort Salisbury. He waved at Sebastian from atop his thoroughbred horse and let the animal have its lead.

It was a beautiful day, and he had not eaten or drunk too much to spoil the pleasure of the sunshine and the bush. James was a man who enjoyed the open spaces and rather thought he would have been a gentleman farmer if he had not decided to join the army. He hoped Sebastian understood that a British officer in a good regiment was unable to live without a private income. There were always problems in life. Having decided in his own life to avoid the problems of marriage he would have enjoyed getting to know his brothers' children. They all seemed happy, which was what really mattered.

With the intention of finding out why Shank had called his farm Holland Park, and to check the unlikely rumour being wafted around by the little man that he was related to Teddy Holland, James made a mental note to also enquire about the tall major-domo and then let his mind drift away from military intelligence.

He chuckled to himself. Not once had any of the brothers mentioned that pompous ass, Arthur, all day. What stuck in James's craw when it came to Arthur was that every time the ass made a mistake, it made him richer. The shares in the Chartered Company that should have sunk Arthur out of sight were making him richer than ever. Since the collapse of the Matabele and Shona rebellions, and Rhodes's move over the Zambezi to explore for minerals, the shares had more than doubled. Then he shrugged. His father had done even better out of the same shares and that was the source of his private income. His horse shied for a moment as it caught the scent of a lion. James pulled his rifle from its holster and for the rest of the journey kept his eyes on the way ahead. Africa, as he knew, was always full of surprises.

THE RUMOUR HAD STARTED when Jeremiah told the bishop that he owed his great wealth to Lord Edward Holland, third son of the Marquis of Surrey. The idea of building a church so tall its spire would dominate the surrounding bush for miles had originated with Nathanial Brigandshaw when the bishop was doing the rounds of the new church of the province of Central Africa, which at that stage had more to do with imagination than practical achievement.

In the lounge of the Meikles Hotel, with the punkahs stirring the heat, Jeremiah overheard the conversation at the next table as it was his habit to listen to other people's conversations. It was both a hobby and a valuable source of information. Being neighbours, he had met Nathanial on a number of occasions and had given money to the Mission. The idea of building a church the height of St Paul's Cathedral out of local brick in the middle of nowhere fired his imagination and provided a way for his redemption and entry into colonial society. Even a knighthood seemed a possibility with the right amount of charity and connections. Jeremiah had soon realised that money was a scarce commodity, and those who dished it out liberally were forgiven their sins and the sins of their fathers. Under the weight of enough money, anyone could acquire a heritage to which they would like to aspire. Looking for his opportunity he waited, and when

Nathanial looked up from his animated conversation with the bishop, Jeremiah was standing at his elbow.

"Do you require more funds for your Mission, Reverend?" he said.

"Mr Jeremiah Shank, the bishop-designate of the Church of the Province of Central Africa."

"How do you do, Bishop. Now, I hear a rumour you want to want to build a church and of course I would be happy to oblige. My benefactor Lord Edward Holland enables me to be generous."

"You are related to Teddy Holland?" said the bishop, smiling at the prospect of raising a large sum of money for the church, the prerequisite for the creation of his bishopric.

"On my mother's side," blurted Jeremiah before he could stop himself talking.

"Maybe when you have the time, we can meet again."

"I am always at the service of the church. As a director of this hotel, I wish you a pleasant stay. I presume you are staying with us?"

"You work in the hotel?" said the bishop, about to change his tune.

"Of course not. I merely lent them a large sum of money. I have my estate, Holland Park, but three miles from the reverend's mission. My investments and donations are handled by Baring Brothers in the City of London, bankers of note. I am sure you will have heard of them, Bishop?"

"Of course I have, dear sir," replied the bishop.

It was the first time anyone had heard a name given to his estate on the Hunyani River and Jeremiah, in it up to his neck, thought he had taken another step on the road to his reinvention. All he hoped for was that Lord Holland never heard a word of it and the great distance between Africa and England would dilute the story before it reached Bramley Park.

With the bishop's card put away in his breast pocket, he walked out of the lounge of the hotel. Outside, Jack Jones was waiting with the horses.

"Money, old cock," said Jeremiah, pulling himself up into the saddle, "is a drug they never get enough of. Silly old fart. Had the sod eatin' out of my bleedin' hand."

"Who?"

"The bishop of something or other. Now, let's go down to Annie's shack and get drunk, my old soldier. A man still has to enjoy 'imself."

"One of these days, guv, you'll put the right accent in the wrong place."

"Probably."

ANNIE WOULD HAVE LAUGHED out loud were she not aware that the small man with the crooked nose was sensitive about his height. The long and short of it were standing at her entrance. Outside Meikles Hotel and the stone house with the observatory overlooking the Hunyani, Annie's shack was the most elaborate house in Rhodesia. Despite the prudish setbacks imposed by British colonialism, the establishment flourished.

Moving graciously across the room, she greeted Jeremiah Shank. The tall man next to him was given the nod due to a servant and the three of them moved through the throng of men and young girls to the gilded bar in the centre of the great room, the crystal chandelier sparkling above with the lights of a hundred candles. Being late, June fires were laid for the going down of the sun when the bush temperature would plummet.

"Valentine is away for a while but I am sure she will be back in time to have a drink with you, Mr Shank. And what great work has bought you into town?"

"I'm building a church to the greater glory of God. It will rise in the African bush, the cross so high no man will be able to touch it and everyone will see the light of Christianity for miles and miles."

"I never know, Mr Shank, when you are being serious or pulling my leg."

"I never joke about my maker," said Jeremiah humbly. "My man here will have a whisky and so will I. Doing the Lord's work is a thirsty business."

"Are you staying in town tonight?"

"Yes, I am."

"Please enjoy my hospitality."

"I will."

When Annie reached her office, the smile had left her face. "Tell Valentine to have a bath and get ready. The little man is back again."

By the time Valentine appeared, bathed, perfumed and perfectly groomed, no one in the room would have guessed her age at thirty-five. The round dark face was smooth of wrinkles, her stomach small and flat, her smile radiant. Had she been born other than in the slums of Cape Town, she would have been an actress instead of a whore. Her red dress reached the floor spread wide by ten petticoats, her bosom pushed almost out of the top of her dress, an unblemished firmness the colour of milk coffee. Behind her head, the long black hair had been gathered and caught by a silver clasp in the shape of a lion. No other ornaments touched her body and the smile she gave Jeremiah caught him in the genitals. Even as she put her white-gloved hand out to be kissed, his eyes were fixed not on her dark and sparkling eyes but on her cleavage.

"Kind Mr Shank, how nice to see you again," she said in a strange accent that was part of her lure... To give her conversation, Annie had taught

Valentine how to read. Ever since the understanding of the written words, sweet romances had been a balm to her work. Always now she pretended she was someone else, the heroine, the lady with the glittering future and the perfect love.

Many years before in the hovel that had been her home in Cape Town, a young sailor had come ashore. The Englishman was unworldly, an officer and a romantic, treating Valentine like any lady he would have met in England. By the time his ship sailed, she had a dream forged in her mind by the midshipman. She was going to escape her poverty and go to the tropical island the boy so vividly described, where fruit fell from the lush trees, fish were caught by hand in the warm shallows and people loved each other. From the day he left she began to save her pennies in pursuit of the vast sum of money she needed to make her dreams come true.

"Are you mine tonight?" asked Jeremiah.

"I'm always yours, dear Mr Shank."

"Call me Jeremiah."

"Really, Mr Shank... Why, isn't this Mr Jones? How do you do, Mr Jones? I do so hope you are well."

BOOK 5 - WAR

1

OCTOBER 1899

*T*he heat was oppressive, the bush dry as tinder, brown grass broken down by six months of drought. Brown trees leafless, no colour for miles except for the high blue sky showing between the columns of cumulus that reached to heaven; insects silent waiting for the rain and God's salvation; October, the month the new Rhodesians were calling the month of suicide, when tempers snapped and friends fought with each other. And through the silence from far away came the whooping joy of Gregory Shaw as he forced his exhausted horse the last hundred yards towards the stockade of Elephant Walk. He shouted his news. There was a war. At last, there was a war. And this time it was definite. The Boers had given the British an ultimatum.

The wild geese honked away from the shouting noise and pounding hooves, flying up and over the stockade. The dogs barked and a cow in labour joined her moos to the sudden mayhem. Sebastian Brigandshaw pushed open the screen door of his house having woken heavy-headed from his afternoon sleep, the mid-day too hot for anyone to work. The door thwacked shut behind him and the sun pierced his brain. Across the dry brown lawn between the msasa trees ringed by flowerless beds, white froth was lathering from the mouth of the exhausted horse.

"You're killing that bloody horse," he shouted, further annoyed by his own swearing.

"What's going on?" called Emily from inside the house.

"Gregory. He's gone mad. Look, you fool, you can't ride a horse like that in this heat. You'll kill the poor beast and we don't have good horses to spare. What on earth's the matter with you?"

"Kruger's given Chamberlain an ultimatum to move the British troops from the Transvaal border. The Boers, for God's sake, Seb. The Boers have given us an ultimatum."

"Us, Gregory?"

"The British."

"Then they are all fools. A third of Rhodesians are Boers. You mean we're going to fight each other?"

"Not here."

"Sorry, my friend. I don't have your enthusiasm for killing people. Don't want to kill the animals anymore except to eat... You'd better rub that animal down before you do anything else."

"Don't you see, Seb? I'll be back in the army where I belong. Your brother promised if hostilities broke out."

"So now when you see Tinus, you're going to shoot him?"

"I never thought of that."

The door clunked shut behind Seb, leaving Gregory alone. The dogs stopped barking. The tame Egyptian geese stayed down by the river and from far away towards the Zambezi escarpment came a distant roll of thunder. And when their compound returned to its quiet, Seb knew something had changed for all of them. The white tribes of Africa were going to war with each other. They were going to destroy each other and everyone else that came in between.

"The bloody world's gone mad again," he said, slumping back onto the bed next to Emily.

"Please don't swear, Seb. The children will hear you."

"Sorry, Em. Not thinking in this heat. First we fight Lobengula, and when we've chased him to his death, we put down a rebellion. Now we are going to fight each other. Marvellous, absolutely marvellous. Don't we ever learn?"

"They won't make you go in the army, will they?"

"I have not the slightest idea. And just when the money from African Shipping was helping to build the farm, this had to happen."

"Are the new ships ready?"

"Yes, they are."

"Then Captain Doyle will make a great deal of money. Everything the army needs has to come from England... You think Gregory's horse will be all right?"

"Yes, Em. He loves that horse. In his excitement, he just wasn't thinking."

Ever since the start of recorded time men have been excited at the start of a war and disgusted by the end."

THE SINKING SUN was shooting red fingers of fire up the sides of the giant cumulus. The wild geese had come back from the river for their evening feed of corn. The dogs were chasing the children, and the children were chasing the dogs, the fox terriers barking with renewed excitement. On the fly-screened veranda in a comfortable chair, Henry Manderville had his legs spread out straight in front of him and Seb was pouring a glass of claret. Emily had put out the cold supper and the one servant had gone back to his hut for the night. The sound of drums was coming from the huts of the Africans down by the river and the smell of woodsmoke drifted up from the cooking fires. The thunder had gone away but not the oppressive heat that sapped everyone's energy except the children's. Their laughter was pleasant in the moment of sundown. Nobody spoke. Seb poured his wife a glass from the bottle. They waited, no one touching their drinks. One of the ridgebacks scratched at the screen door and Seb got up to let her in. The dog's water-bowl was on the veranda and the dog was thirsty.

When he got back to his chair and turned to sit down, a figure was standing outside the screen door silhouetted by the glow of the sinking sun. The man was in uniform. He placed his hat under his right arm as he entered the room. For a moment Seb was unsure who had come to visit until the man moved into the light and the kerosene lamp showed him the face of Gregory Shaw. The uniform was blue with a wide white stripe down the length of the trouser. The tunic of the uniform was buttoned to the throat, and the cloth stretched ominously under the armpit that cradled the hat. From the knee down the light exposed the yellowing of age of the white strip. The leather cavalry boots were immaculate. Atop the stiff neck of the pale blue uniform with the red piping, Gregory gave them a wan smile. Fran came into the veranda, letting the rest of the dogs and Harry follow.

Seb was about to say something when he caught the pleading look in Gregory's eyes. Instead, he poured two more glasses of claret and proposed a toast.

"The Queen, God bless her." Everyone including Harry got up and repeated the toast.

Gregory refused to sit down and Seb understood why, the old stitching having enough trouble under the armpit.

"What's the uniform, Greg?" asked Seb.

"Ninth Bengal Lancers." He looked about the veranda in the half-light, the profile of his face caught and lost by the kerosene lamp. "Plumer's sending reinforcements to the Transvaal border tomorrow and I'm riding in early to offer my services. Luckily my number two uniform has a little more stretch." He tried a stride with only small success. "Put on weight, old boy. You know, it's eleven years since I wore this uniform... You think they'll need me, Henry?"

"Quite sure they will. Every man in a war. Damned impressive, Gregory, if you'll excuse the expression, Em. That one ribbon's for bravery, what?"

"Northwest Frontier in '79... This one'll be all over by Christmas. Why I'm in a hurry."

"Makes sense. Bit of exercise do you good. Sebastian, be a good chap and give the captain another glass of claret. He's finished that one."

Later on, Gregory took his food standing, and no one laughed.

FAR AWAY IN the cold of the Franschhoek Valley, the sun had not set but the yellow light of late evening had turned the colour of the surrounding hills to soft purple. The news of war had reached the valley an hour earlier. A servant was busy lighting the big fire in the smoking room that led off from the long central room of the Cape Dutch house. The children were across the valley with friends and ever since the news had reached them, brought by a jubilant neighbour shouting obscenities in the *Taal*, Alison had wanted to be sick. Across the room, her man was standing silently looking at her. Tinus was forty-two, almost three years younger than Gregory. The big beard was streaked with grey and the belly that stretched his shirt was soft with good living. After the years in the bush, domestic life had been good to Tinus Oosthuizen and even one day away from his children was too long. Though he was looking at his wife, he was thinking of his brother and nephews in the Transvaal.

"What does this mean to us?" asked Alison into the silence. They could hear the tick of the grandfather clock in the dining room despite the door being closed. The fire flared for a moment and the look on her husband's face came back from its faraway place. She had fed the new baby half an hour before and the boy was fast asleep. He was called Christo, and the easiest of all her children.

"It means my people are at war with your people. The boundaries of the Boer people do not stop in the Transvaal or the Orange Free State. We are a nation wherever we are. The Cape, Natal, Rhodesia."

"Your mother was a Scot."

"My father was a Boer, and that is what counts."

"What will you do?"

"I don't know, Alison. I am a Boer living in a British colony under British rule and my people are at war with them. My people will expect my help."

"Will you give it to them? What about our children? They are more English than they are Boer."

"That's why they are with the du Plessises. To learn they are Boer. That is their heritage."

"But why does it matter so much?"

"Because man is tribal. Would you like to be German?"

"No, of course not."

"Then why must my children be English when they are Boers?"

"But how can President Kruger give the British an ultimatum? The British Empire controls the world."

"And that's the point, my wife. Kruger does not want them to control the Transvaal and put all his gold in the Bank of England."

"It's about gold?"

"War is always about gold. Gold in one form or the other. Gold and power and usually they go together. Part of life's mosaic and the pattern never changes."

"I'm pregnant again."

"I am pleased for us."

JAMES BRIGANDSHAW HAD BEEN LISTENING to his colleagues in the British Intelligence service for half an hour, never taking his stare away from the pig eyes of Cecil Rhodes, the most influential of the rand barons who through his diverse and interlocking shareholdings controlled a major portion of the gold on the Witwatersrand. The man's eyes were bloodshot and he wheezed with a chest complaint, but never once did he return the stare. It was an hour past midnight and Kruger's ultimatum had not been met, with British reinforcements reaching the borders of the Transvaal instead of withdrawing as Kruger demanded. The small, landlocked state of the Transvaal with its armed militia of farmers was at war with Great Britain, the most powerful nation on earth. Outside on the streets of Johannesburg, everything was quiet. The foreigners, mostly British, Uitlanders in Kruger's terms, were inside their houses doing nothing as they had done when Doctor Jameson tried to precipitate an uprising in 1896.

James, like his colleagues, was dressed in civilian clothes and had yet to enter the conversation. Rhodes had not spoken a word. In the stable next to the two-storey building on Sauer Street where the meeting was taking place, well-fed and rested horses were waiting to take the British officers out of enemy territory. All but James were going south to the Cape Colony.

The argument had been going round in circles ever since it had begun.

"You'll excuse my interruption, gentlemen, but you are all missing the point," said James. "This war has nothing to do with voting rights, though if those other than Boers were permitted to vote, this war would be unnecessary as we British would be in the majority if you exclude the blacks, an interesting point in a discussion on rights but best leave that one alone. Please, do not let us be beguiled by our own propaganda. What a politician says to gain his point is rarely the reason for that point. The British government has cried eloquently that there can be no taxation without representation. Sounds rather nice, doesn't it? Very righteous.

"We British are right and this man with the full beard, this farmer from the veld is wrong. The British cabinet probably doesn't give a hoot for the British miners in Johannesburg. They want the gold to be British, to hell with the people. They are hypocrites but heaven forbid we ever say that in public. But the fact remains. They want the gold. Now, to tell Mr Rhodes and the other mine owners to close their mines and stop paying Kruger is folly. To blow up our own mines is even more ridiculous. Let Kruger have his supply of gold for as long as it takes the British Army to invade and reach the mines. Don't tempt these burghers to sabotage the mines and set back British gold production for years to come."

"He will use the gold to buy arms and kill Englishmen," said a British captain.

"Probably. Then we must hurry the army to Johannesburg."

"It may take months."

"It may take years. Remember the battle of Majuba, old chap. All I'm saying is, there's no point in blowing up one way or another the very thing we are fighting for. To fall into the trap of believing our own political claptrap would be foolish. Tell the press what you like but gentlemen, please, let us be honest with ourselves."

"You really think this war is about gold?" asked the same man.

"You tell me what else it is about, old chap."

"The mines stay open," said Rhodes standing up. "And if any man says I was in Johannesburg tonight, I will deny my presence. I never left Kimberley. Good night to you all." At the turn, Rhodes turned back to the men seated around the table. "Mr Brigandshaw, are you related to The Captain?"

"He is my father."

"I see. I really do see. Maybe you too, sir, have a double agenda."

"The result is always the same, Mr Rhodes. You said so yourself. At the end of everything it all comes back to money."

"And vanity, Major. Never forget vanity. A man's price can also be his vanity."

The door closed on the richest man in the empire and they all listened to his footfalls receding down the stairs.

"What did he mean by your double agenda, Major Brigandshaw?" asked the colonel in charge of the meeting.

"My father owns Colonial Shipping as you know, sir. Mr Rhodes thinks my father will make a great deal of money when the demand for shipping space exceeds supply as a result of this war and shipping rates spiral. And he is probably right. Politicians send the army to fight their wars to extend their political power but men of business, men in trade, reap the real profits. But how silly of me, gentlemen. I am sure you are just as aware of the machinations of men. President Kruger would have been left on his stoep in Pretoria for all eternity, obscure and happy, were it not for the gold under his ground. With respect, Colonel, but I sometimes find life a trifle indigestible but then maybe we should get to the horses before the burghers make a meal of us."

"This meeting is closed," said the colonel.

THE BOER PONY stood patiently waiting for James. The lieutenant-colonel and the two captains had let themselves out of the stable into the night ten minutes earlier. They had all shaken hands solemnly and then been wished a cheery toodle-oo by James. He was alone and took from his jacket two lumps of sugar and offered them to the pony. The velvet muzzle pulled the cubes from the palm of his hand while man and horse looked at each other with genuine affection. James had bought the small horse from Jeremiah Shank six months earlier to everyone's surprise. The animal was too small for most Englishmen's taste but James knew the Boers favoured the strong mountain ponies that foraged for themselves from the veld. A pony, a bag of dried meat, a Mauser rifle, two bandoliers of ammunition and a Boer could trek for months without looking for supplies.

The soft brown eyes of the horse watched carefully as James changed his clothes. Finally, he covered his face and cheeks with theatrical glue and affixed the beard in place. Placing the small saddle with the short stirrups over the pony, he checked the Mauser rifle and slid it down into the well-worn saddle holster. The first and second bandoliers were crossed over the dirty, well-washed shirt and half covered by a long jacket of homespun. The trousers were long and tough, like the leather boots, to fend off the thorn bush of the highveld. James hung the double saddlebag over the horse's rump and mounted. When he rode the horse down Sauer Street into the night, he was like any other burgher headed home to the farm after a visit to the sprawling mining camp of Johannesburg. If challenged he had learnt enough words of the *Taal* to pass as a Boer. There was nothing on James or the pony, including James's underwear, to suggest he was British. The nice touch, he thought, was the old bush hat with a wide rim he had stolen from a Boer who had trekked up to Rhodesia in the never-ending search for a pot of gold. The man had left the hat on Annie's bar while he went out to relieve himself, too drunk to notice the theft.

ON THE THIRD day of his journey, James could smell himself. The Great North Road, a misnomer for a bush track deeply rutted by the wheels of heavy carts, was empty of people, but either side the open veld was teeming with springbok, gnu, elephant and giraffe. Never before had James been so content with himself and on the fifth day they rested beside a river, he and his pony. Beneath a tall acacia tree, the war that he had been part of provoking was as far away as the moon he could still see in the morning sky, and he wondered sadly why so many men and women could never be content with themselves. The long brown grass, broken by animals and heat, stretched away to hills far distant in the haze of summer and the white clouds placed in the blue sky never moved, patterning the bush with shadows and darkening patches of the great hills.

Alone in the wilderness of Africa, he made himself a fire and boiled a pot of water for his morning tea and drank it without sugar or milk while the pony, free of saddle and rifle, drank at the river.

On the second day, they reached the Limpopo River, brown and muddy, more pools than a river, waiting for the new rains to send it flowing smoothly to the east. The crossing was easy and James was back on British soil.

FOR SIR HENRY MANDERVILLE, there were more important things than politicians arguing with each other to protect their political turf. The crate containing Mr Crapper's invention had arrived three months earlier and mysteriously sat alone in the centre of the vacated rondavel that had once been his home. Young Harry had looked at the wooden crate many times, asked many questions, and received but one reply, 'Wait and see'. Soon after the arrival of the crate, a hole had appeared in the back of the bathroom wall, in the house that had once belonged to Tinus Oosthuizen, and then for some time nothing further had happened. Three weeks before the Boers moved into Natal and the Northern Cape, a trench had appeared behind the hole in the wall that led to a deep pit, oblong in shape, that was filled with large rocks. Next to the trench, a wooden tower grew to the height of the thatch with a platform and on top of the platform, after considerable effort and with the help of every black man on the farm, Harry's grandfather had plonked a tin tank. For the first time, Harry was told a secret.

"That tank's going to contain five hundred gallons of water."

"But how, Grandfather, are you going to get the water into the tank?"

"Wait and see."

The scene of the action for Harry then moved down to the river where a hand pump had been installed as long ago as Harry could remember to pump water to the compound, five hundred yards away up through the bush, the stockade and between the msasa trees ringed by the flowerbeds, a laborious process but better than carrying up buckets of water. Down by the river, another wooden tower had taken shape and on top of this one, again with great difficulty, Harry watched his grandfather plonk a contraption that went round and round for no purpose every time the wind blew. 'Wait and see,' was all he got. A series of cogs and chains, this time Harry judged with extreme difficulty, were built up the tower and down to the water pump. Many strong arms had worn the wooden handle smooth by pushing the long piece of wood from right to left for two hours each day to give the households water. The chains were attached to a cog that protruded from the centre of the contraption, going round and round another cog at the bottom of the tower, just above the pipe. At the same time as the chains were going round in sympathy, James Brigandshaw was removing his false beard with difficulty, having had a swim in the Baby River without being eaten by a crocodile. Then Harry's grandfather connected the last chain to a new piece of machinery he had joined to the pump instead of the handle.

"Come and see young Harry, come and see."

Together they strode up the path while the wind squeaked the cogs and chains behind them and when they got to the ground-level water reservoir, centre of the three main houses and to the right of the rondavel, water was spilling in spurts into the tank.

"But who's pumping the water?" asked Harry.

"The windmill," said his grandfather, gazing up at the tank behind his house with satisfaction. "Today we are going to open the crate."

"Wow," said Harry. "Can I go and tell Mummy?"

"Of course you can."

It was obvious to Harry that his grandfather felt very pleased with himself.

EVERYONE HAD BEEN INVITED to the opening of the crate that had now been brought out onto the lawn from the rondavel. Harry looked around, bursting with excitement. His eight-year-old sister Madge was trying to look bored with her plump arms folded in front of her chest while George was running after the fox terriers, one of which had lifted a leg against the crate when it was first put on the lawn. The dog had then lost interest. The ridgebacks were lying down in the mottled shade of a msasa tree, only their eyes moving to catch everything that was going on. Two of the cats had gone up a tree to keep out of harm's way. Aunty Fran was looking vaguely interested but distracted as Uncle Gregory had still not come back from Fort Salisbury. Harry wished he was six years older so he could go off to the war with Uncle Gregory, still not sure which army he wished to join. Harry's father was watching the proceedings with mild amusement and his mother was more concerned with three-year-old George running off with the dogs. Looking at his mother, Harry was sure he was soon going to have another brother or sister but no one had told him anything as usual.

A crowbar was inserted into the wood behind one of the nails by Harry's grandfather and with a mighty crack a piece of wood broke off from the crate. The only new thing Harry could see was straw but as the crowbar swiftly did its work, the wood came apart, the straw was pushed aside and a white, porcelain tub was brought out of the wreckage and stood on the lawn in all its glory. At the back, at the bottom, Harry noticed there was a large pipe in the shape of a 'U'. The other side of the crate revealed another porcelain piece with a separate white lid and to the side in a slim compartment were two round pieces of wood, one with a large hole in the middle. Then everyone went off and had tea. The biggest anti-climax in young Harry's life was over and twice he gave his grandfather a filthy look.

For two days Harry's grandfather was closeted in the bathroom with two black men. Out went old bricks and earth that had made the floor and in went the bowls along with piles of river sand and cement. On the second day, the 'U' pipe appeared out of the hole in the wall at the back of the bathroom where it looked down the trench. A new water pipe was taken in through a small hole in the wall. The water pipe from the river was changed and connected to a pipe that went up to the tank on its stilt and just before lunch, Harry heard water splashing into the tank high up on its tower. Harry was nothing short of astonished.

Just before tea, the whole family was called into the bathroom. Above the big bowl, the smaller white bowl with the lid was fixed high up on the wall with the small, outside pipe bending into the top at the side and a larger pipe leading down underneath. A chain hung from the other side on its own. Harry's grandfather was looking very smug.

"Witness, everyone, the first pull and let go in the whole of Rhodesia other than the ones in Mr Meikle's hotel." And without any further ceremony, Harry watched his grandfather pull the chain and water rushed down the pipe into the bowl and flushed out the back through the 'U' pipe. Only then was Harry Brigandshaw truly impressed for the first time in his young life. Everyone else began to clap.

That evening on the veranda, soon after the sun had gone down, Harry perceived his grandfather to be tipsy. The whole evening turned out almost as festive as Christmas.

BY THE TIME the invention by Mr Crapper had flushed its first wares into a freshly closed French drain, James Brigandshaw arrived in Salisbury on a very tired pony.

"I say, old boy, you really do look a mess," said Gregory Shaw before James could even unsaddle the pony of its burden. "Bit of incognito? Did that myself in Afghanistan. Must have been '76. No, '75. Damn tribesmen wanted to infiltrate British India. Easier of course. Put a thing that looked like a sheet over your head and off you went. Surly bunch those Afghans... Never said much so language wasn't a problem. By the time they came up the Khyber Pass we had the guns trained on them. Always been a one for military intelligence after that. Usually gives the enemy a nasty surprise."

"Gregory, what on earth is that uniform?"

"Ninth Bengal Lancers. Number two, of course. The number one was too tight under the armpits. Put on a bit of weight."

"We'll have to change that uniform."

"Into what?" said Gregory, doubtfully.

"Mashonaland Scouts, I thought we'd call them. Colonials. All colonials who know the bush. Tommy out from England in his new 'khaki' uniforms will be no match for the Boers who have hunted the land all their lives, whatever the War Office wishes to think. General Sir Redvers Buller the new GOC should know. He fought with the Boers against the Zulus when the white tribes of Africa knew that to divide themselves was suicide... You give me a hand with this pony. How long have you been waiting for me?"

"Two weeks and a day. Came into Salisbury the moment the ultimatum expired. You mean, I can have my commission back?"

"Not exactly. The Scouts will all be troopers. Like the column you came in on with Sir Henry Manderville. I am going to raise them like a Boer commando where the leader gets elected by the rest of the men... You think that young brother of mine will join? Apart from Frederick Selous he probably knows the bush better than any other Englishman. He may be the black sheep of our family, running off with Em and all that, but we'll need him in this war. And the other Rhodesians. I'm going to mount them on ponies just like this one and push right into Boer territory. Rather like those wild tribesmen were trying to do to you in India before you got on top of them. Can you imagine the information we'll send back to military intelligence?"

"Your brother won't join."

"Why not?"

"Doesn't like killing animals anymore, let alone people."

"This is war."

"You've forgotten one big thing, Major Brigandshaw."

"What's that?"

"His best friend and mentor is a Boer."

"Don't be silly, Tinus Oosthuizen is a British subject."

"But he's a Boer. Like a lot more of them here in the Cape and Natal."

"Don't be ridiculous. They won't fight for Kruger. Far too well off."

"Your nephew, young Harry, wants to join the army if he was only older. Heard him tell his mother. What was chilling was the boy asking Emily which side he should fight on, the Boers or the British? His best friend is Barend Oosthuizen, apart from a black kid called Tatenda, and Barend has sworn an oath with your niece to marry Madge when she turns sixteen. No, I don't think Sebastian will join your Scouts. The worst kind of war is a civil war, and that's what this one is going to be... This poor horse is whacked, old boy."

"So am I," said James, "Let's get a drink before I report. The pony can stay at the water trough and have a rest."

"You going to drink like that?"

"We'll go to Annie's. She won't mind. I had a bath in a couple of rivers. You should have smelt me coming over the Limpopo. Could even smell myself, old chap."

. . .

ANNIE'S SHACK WAS FULL. Instinctively, in the face of war, men were looking for women with whom to reproduce themselves.

Having left the pony free of its burdens, the saddle on the pole next to the hitching post, the saddlebags slung over James Brigandshaw's shoulder, the rifle under his arm, they had walked the last half mile.

Now he looked around the whorehouse and smiled to himself. All men had the ability to appear what they were not, to lie about the truth, to give the impression they were people anyone would wish to know. But James, smiling to himself, knew better. At the end of the bar was a man masquerading as a gentleman. Talking to him was a man who James should arrest for deserting the British Army. Three semi-drunks down the long bar was the ex-administrator of the territory, back from Kimberley and looking for a job, who had been the lover of the wife of the man in the strange uniform who, even though he was too old, was going to be a scout. And to James's total surprise, alone and drinking whisky, sat the baronet who had sold his daughter and known the bitter taste of retribution.

Jack Slater saw Gregory Shaw and, despite the strange uniform, recognised him and looked away. How strange, James thought, that husbands were always the last to know.

The cuckolded husband's eyes were elsewhere.

"Leave him alone, Greg," said James, restraining Gregory. "Henry has his problems."

"What's he doing here?"

"Getting drunk, probably. And if he sees us, he'll ask himself the same question. War does different things to different people. The young want to fight them, thinking of glory and gratitude... Probably their ancestors have bred into them that getting old is not a good thing, though they don't know that yet. The lonely think of companionship. The men women scorn, think of medals that by some miracle will make them attractive. Some are just nasty and like to kill. That Jeremiah Shank over there saw the money before most of us saw the war. He'll be even richer at the end of all this. He owns more horses than any man in Africa. His strong arm is Jack Jones who hopes, misguidedly, that I know nothing about him and he would like to run away but can't. War changes things and in change there is opportunity. And loss. Oh yes, Gregory, there is loss. Lots of loss, always loss, and still man has gone to war for as long as he can remember. Why do we do it? Who knows? A flaw in man? Is there a God, Gregory, who made us and made us with a flaw? Or is Darwin right?... We evolve and war winkles out the weak and makes the species stronger, more able to survive? Twice on this journey, alone from Johannesburg, under the stars of heaven, I thought too much of the meaning of life, and the more I thought, the number I made my brain. Once I thought my mind had left my body and gone to the stars, but then a nightjar called and brought me back, and I don't think I will be able to do that again, and if I do I will never come back and that will be the end of my body. Can a mind live on its own? Are there millions of minds up there on their own thinking away? You see, this is what war does to me. It makes me think. And makes me nervous. Now, to your health, sir, and to the Mashonaland Scouts. Ah, here comes Henry. Do you think he will want to join the Scouts?"

"Why don't you ask him?"

"Sir Henry Manderville, how are you?"

"A little drunk and a little lonely. Thank God for a familiar face."

"Do you wish to join the Mashonaland Scouts?"

"Probably. Being among so many strange people makes me more lonely than being on my own. Is it a sign of weakness to be lonely? Or a sign of guilt? I am very lonely tonight and very glad to see you both. I have been thinking about my wife. Have a drink, gentlemen. A beer to slake the thirst and then a drink. The piano player is going to play again, and he is very good. We'll drink to the piano player and, as the saying goes, 'please don't shoot him as he is the last one we have got'. Even a bad piano player is better than no piano player. Like most things in life, we never get what we want but make the best of it. No one wants this war except those foolish youngsters over there, but we'll make the best of it. It will be another part of our lives whether we like it or not... Now, listen to that. Isn't he terrible? Maybe we should shoot the poor man and put him out of his misery. Maybe not. Blood on the piano can dampen the spirits. Let the appalling thumping noise continue and allow me to buy my friends a drink.

"My friends! Such lovely words. Very possessive. As if you belong to me. Which you don't. Annie tells me it is cheaper to buy the whisky by the bottle and if you get one with the top uncorked, you may get what you are paying for instead of the gut rot that tastes the same after the fourth drink. Knew a man once who swore he could identify any whisky away from the bottle. Man was a liar of course. Mr *Barman!*... Give us a bottle of whisky for my friends. Gregory, old son, that uniform is too bloody small for you but have a whisky. When the world goes potty, there's only one thing a man can do. Get drunk... Isn't that my friend Mr Shank over there? The friend who tried to put young Seb in jail? My fault of course. Always my fault. Haven't you always found, Major Brigandshaw, that when it comes to the bottom of anything it is always your fault? And poor old Jack Slater. Now he's no longer the top dog he drinks alone. Unfair, Gregory. Go and ask the poor man over for a drink. No. Now I remember something. Leave him alone to stew in his own juice. Do you think it is possible to stew in one's own juice, Gregory? Ever since I sold Em to The Pirate I've been stewing in mine. Yes, I'll join the Mashonaland Scouts whatever they are, just to get away from myself. First, we'll drink the bottle. Have a party... Stupid really as no one has ever been able to run away from themselves however hard they try."

2

NOVEMBER TO DECEMBER 1899

$\mathcal{K}$arel Oosthuizen felt inside the back of his trousers and scratched his hairy arse. After a few moments of intense pleasure, he levelled his Mauser rifle down at the mining town of Kimberley and fired a random shot. At midday, even the dogs were off the streets. From a thousand yards, it was too far for him to hear the whine of the ricochet. Down the Boer line, someone else fired a shot, followed by complete silence.

"Why don't we attack the place, man?" said Karel in the *Taal* to the man three yards away.

"'Cause khaki will stick a bayonet in your fat belly. They can't get out and we can't get in without a lot of dead burghers. We wait. Soon they run out of food and come and talk to us. I have a cousin who worked on the mine. Maybe he's down there."

"The whole khaki army will arrive soon and chase Piet Cronjé out of the Cape. Come, man, we got to fight this war and not scratch our arses. Tiens went off this morning. Just left. Wants to plant his mealies."

"We're all free men. We volunteered. Man has to plant his crops. What's the point of having the land if we don't plant the mealies?"

The siege of Kimberley was in its fifth week. From behind the Boer artillery, two cannons fired over their heads and both men raised their heads to watch the explosion. Satisfied with the plume of smoke, followed by the explosion, Karel rolled onto his back, got his hand inside his trousers and scratched his balls. From down in the town came a second explosion, and a shell screamed over their heads and crashed into the open ground five hundred yards behind them.

"Where'd they get ammunition?" screamed Karel. "They don't have any more ammunition."

"There've been rumours," said the burgher on the other side. "Rhodes had his explosive people at De Beers making him shells. Looks like for once a rumour was right. Maybe we dig a trench. Nothing else to do. You miss your wife, Karel?"

"I don't have a wife. Let's go and make lunch on the other side of the kopje. We've fired at them. Nothing more till sunset. You think the British Army is really coming up to fight, Cronjé?"

"Just another rumour."

"The last one was right. General Buller is a famous soldier. Cronjé calls himself a general, but he's a burgher like us. Rumour has it his wife's with him in the supply wagons. You ever heard of a war where the general has his wife to hand to cook his breakfast? Now, Kruger, he was a general, but he's the President. Why're we fighting this war?"

"You want to be told what to do by the British? Make you speak English, man. Tax you and send your money to England. The British win, you take your hat off to an Englishman. We win, they take their hats off to us."

They walked back over the kopje and looked down at the crater made by the De Beers shell.

"Tomorrow, man, I'm digging me a trench," said Karel into the silence.

"That gun could kill us," said a man.

Karel Oosthuizen, a nephew of Tinus Oosthuizen whom he had never met, was twenty-five and already as big as his uncle. He could play the game of tossing a two hundred pound mealie sack back and forth over a flat wagon with his elder brother and laugh at the force of the sack hitting his chest. A fat smack from his flat hand could send a man clean off his feet. To keep up his strength on the farm, he ate six pounds of meat and twelve eggs every day of his life. His mother's full-time job was feeding her husband and her seven sons, the poor woman never having had a daughter to help her with the chores. And now all her men, including the fifteen-year-old, were out on commando and she was left with ten natives to run the farm further back down the Vaal River. Thirty years before, the Oosthuizens had fought the natives for the land, and Karel worried about his mother, a woman of five foot two inches with only her tongue to keep control. When they all rode off to the call, they had thought to be back by Christmas. Smuts had suggested giving the Uitlanders the vote after five years of residence in the Transvaal. Five years was a long time. Five years would make them think like burghers. Then the war would be over and Karel could go home to the farm to look after his little mother and maybe look for a wife. The farm which his father had taken by riding around the perimeter as fast as he could in one day, was big enough for all the brothers and there was more land to be had to the north across the Limpopo where Rhodes had opened the hinterland. He was going to find himself a wife just like his mother and breed himself a family, a very large family.

He had forgotten about Sarie, Frikkie's woman, the one son in the family older than himself. Sarie was pretty in a funny kind of way but she was a poor white from the slums behind Pretoria, and Karel's mother treated her just like a black. The two little girls had not even been entered in the front of the big family Bible that had come up on the Great Trek. They were not married, Sarie and Frikkie, Karel knew that. The great sin and Sarie were never spoken of, and Karel's mother had never yet spoken to the poor girl, even when the girl was giving birth to the twins, not six months after coming on the farm. Sarie was a brave girl and put up with everything for the sake of the twins: they were five years old now but Sarie had had no more children: something about a breech birth and Sarie nearly dying when the twins were born, but it was never talked about. Rather like his grandfather Martinus, who had married a Scot and gone to live in Graaff-Reinet in British Cape Colony even though his father, Karel's great-grandfather, had been on the Great Trek. There had been talk in the Transvaal branch of the large Oosthuizen family that the Scots woman taught her children English before the children learnt the *Taal*.

Karel's brothers and father were with General Cronjé and his army who had gone out to block General Buller and his British generals from entering the Transvaal. There were many burghers with Cronjé and a detachment of the State artillery, the only professional soldiers in the whole Boer army. Karel had been hunting far north of the farm with three black men and when he came back with the meat, his kin had already gone out with the local commando. Karel rode off alone to war and when he reached Pretoria, they sent him down to Kimberley to lay siege to the diamond town. There were his mother and Sarie and the two girls on the farm with the blacks and all over the Transvaal it was the same and he wished the war would be over and life back to normal.

Taking his large pot of stewed meat and mealie meal away from the others, he sat on a rock and looked again at the large shell crater in the ground and it made him think. Families who fought with each other were always the ones that destroyed themselves. Were the Englishmen in Kimberley really his enemies? Only by killing each other would they make each other enemies for a very long time. Karel shivered in the heat and finished his pot of food, spooning up the mush into his large mouth and dripping the gravy down his rich brown beard. High above them all, caught on the thermals that had drifted the birds away from the Vaal River fifteen miles to the northwest, a pair of African fish eagles were crying their desolate call, seven-foot wingspan open to lie on the warm currents of air, the *kwee-kwee* cry, the last lament in the great blue sky dotted with puffs of white cloud, the birds oblivious of man's insanity down below. Karel watched the great black and white birds, the tails white and shifting to keep the birds right with the thermals, the white heads calling with pain and joy to each other, and he watched them for a long time as they turned and drifted north back to the river. When he could hear their calls no longer, he was sad.

SARIE MOSTERT WAS twenty-two years old and the mother of the twins, Klara and Griet. For all of her life, the world had been hostile and the only weapon she had found for survival was her flashing eyes that once past fourteen years old, and directed at a male, went deep into his soul and then straight down to his genitals. In clothes, mostly dirty, that covered everything except her toes, the brown, soft eyes were the window to the body under the bodice and skirts.

In the slums of Pretoria, away from the single-storeyed houses with the hospitable stoeps, it was common to find whites poorer than the blacks as when the blacks ran out of money, they went back to their kraals to grow mealies and pumpkins round their thatched huts and run cattle in the endless bush or hunt. The whites had nowhere to go and no skills to live in the bush and sometimes the missionaries took pity on them, but not always. Good upstanding whites resented their poor relations for showing a bad example to the blacks and hoped they would go back to the slums of Europe.

Sarie could neither read nor write, and from the age of six had learnt to steal her food and clothes and share them with no one. Her mother had died of influenza when she was eight when the virus decimated the overcrowded and underfed slums, and Sarie's father had disappeared soon afterwards, for which she was thankful. All she had ever received from her father was a hard, flat hand and a rough tongue. No one had cared about him or Sarie's mother and no one had cared about the little girl with the flashing eyes. Survival was the only force Sarie understood, and the need was so strong, stretching back to her primal forbears high in the forest trees, that disease passed her by and blind cunning brought her the bare necessities of life.

In the bitterly cold nights of winter, newspaper provided the means for her survival, wrapped around her body, her feet and her face, ignored by all but the scavenging dogs. The dogs were her best and only friends and she had them lie down next to her, sometimes a mangy dog on either side whimpering from the cold but slowly giving each other the warmth of their bodies. Then they slept, woken by the cold cruel morning of another day when the scavenging started all over again, the little girl, dirty, smelly and hungry followed by two, three, sometimes four dogs, the dogs just skin and bones. From the dogs she learnt that eyes talked better than words, a whole world of soft expression and understanding. Her dogs spoke to her of sympathy, of guilt, of hope, and when she stroked them gently on their muzzles, they looked at her with the purest love which made all their struggle worthwhile. They were her family.

In the spring and autumn, she and the dogs left the slums early in the mornings, past the silent streets of the other world, the snores of comfort rumbling from closed-door houses, barked at but left alone, out into the country, barefoot Sarie trotting with the dogs. Ten miles into the veld, the dogs foraged for rats, big, fat, grain rats the size of rabbits, the dogs instinctively hunting in a pack, flushing and running down their quarry. Sarie used a stick on the guinea fowl, waiting for the birds to go up in the sparse trees to roost at dusk, softly climbing the trees to the sleeping birds and knocking them down with a swift sharp sweep of her stick, the dogs full of rat, content and away from the bird hunt. In the falling light of day, the small girl made her fire and roasted the birds and ate till at last her tummy was full. Then, with the fire piled high to keep away the predators, she slept curled up next to the dogs only waking to feed the fire. In those days and nights, she could reach out and touch her happiness, at night look at the stars and smile, in the day, dream by the side of a stream. Sometimes she sang, a beautiful sound, and the dogs' ears pricked up to hear the music and all their eyes were smiling.

Every day when the sun was high and hot, she searched the fur of each dog for ticks, their ears and eyes, back and legs and then, rolling them over, scratched their bellies as she looked. When man, black or white, came close, the dogs bared their teeth, circling the girl with protection. When she swam naked in the small rivers and streams that watered the highveld, the dogs lay flat on their stomachs, their snouts stretched forward, and watched her, their eyes full of amusement. None of the dogs swam however much she called. They were the sweet, warm days.

Sarie watched where the monkeys and baboons had eaten berries from the trees and only then did she eat, her knowledge a deep instinct in her genes like her fear of snakes. The years went by full of feast and famine until the girl grew into a woman and the eyes of men grew hungry. She had made some human friends in the slums and some of the farmers, black and white, waved at the dog-girl even if they kept their distance from the hounds. She was part of their world like the veld and sky.

BILLY CLIFFORD WAS twenty-two when he first saw Sarie Mostert. He had woken with the dawn and gone out on the stoep of his father's house in Church Street, the main road that ran through Pretoria. The Cliffords rented the small house while his father, a railway engineer from Dublin, helped build the railway line from Pretoria to Delagoa Bay to give the Boers access to a seaport without going through British territory. Shaun Clifford, Billy's father, was a patriot and knew the pain of being forced to live under British rule. Any native who wished to stay free of the British was a friend. Billy was in the Transvaal to visit his parents, having graduated from Trinity College, Dublin, with a degree in English when the dog-girl walked past in front of the stoep, silent on bare feet, flanked by her dogs and carrying a tall, thick stick. He stood up to get another look at the strange sight in the African dawn, but the dogs growled and he sat back down again. Billy was bored, there being little to do for a young, Catholic Irishman in the heart of Boer Calvinism. His mother was with the Catholic nuns most of the day doing her good work, and his father was off in the swamps of Portuguese Mozambique building his freedom railway line for the Boers. Billy's mother was happy to have his father out of Ireland: Gladstone's Home Rule was not enough for Shaun Clifford. Independence for Ireland with the English, all of them, back over the Irish Sea, nothing less; and he'd fight for it and die for the cause if that was what it took.

Every morning, Billy rose with the dawn and sat in the big wicker chair on the stoep and looked for the dogs and the girl, afraid to go inside and make himself a cup of coffee. It was something to think about, something to do. All the neighbours spoke not a word of English and Billy had no Dutch. He had promised his long-suffering mother to stay for six months and was trying to start his writing but nothing came, only damp bad copies of the writers who had gone before him, the ones he had so avidly read for his degree. The two girls were married with children of their own and the big brother had left long ago to make a fortune in America and no one in the family knew if he was alive or dead. Billy's brother had never been a man of words and used his fists to inflict his will. Billy feared the worst but kept his thoughts from his doting mother, whose life had gone out when her oldest child had sailed out of their lives without even a look back over his shoulder. So the days dragged by and his mind stayed blank and by the end of his third week in Africa, he did not even wish to read. After a week of fruitless early mornings, Billy gave up and listened to his boredom made worse by having no idea what to do with the rest of his life other than to write which he couldn't, his mind as blank as the white pages, his imagination stuck in the nub of nothing. And to make it worse he had no money, Irish nationalism being far more important to his father than allowances for a work-shy son.

"You should have been an engineer like me, Billy my boy. Told you that. You can't make anything with words a man can eat." And then he had gone off into his swamps and left Billy with his mother.

Alone, always alone, Billy rode his father's horse out into the African veld, the animal unable to go with his father down into the lowveld for fear of the tsetse fly that killed domesticated animals. Alone, he rode each which way the horse would go, caring nothing for the journey. Billy rode fast and well, happy to have the boredom beaten out of his bones, and just before the stallion lathered, Billy would bring the horse back to a canter and then to a trot, and with the slower rhythm the boredom would creep back onto the horse next to him when even the wild animals were no distraction.

THE DOGS, used to zebra and buck running away from them across the veld, had heard the horse but kept their heads down, looking at Sarie naked in the cool water of their stream. The old dog that had been with Sarie nine years was fast asleep under a tree, occasionally yelping at his dreams. A pair of crows lifted out of the tree and flew off downstream before calling back at the interruption, the crows having seen the man on the back of the horse. And when Sarie came out of the water clean and fresh, her nipples hard and pointing, she climbed up the bank of the little stream and looked up into the green eyes of Billy Clifford high up on the stallion's back. While Sarie kept looking at him, the dogs rose up as one with their hackles and the horse shied, dancing a full circle before Billy brought the animal back under control.

The surprise for Sarie was not her nakedness but the reaction of her pack of dogs. Sliding off the stallion's back Billy turned his attention to each of the dogs, ignoring her. Without a snarl, they lost interest and went back to their own pursuits.

"Have you got your clothes on?" asked Billy with his back to her after the dogs were pacified. With his right hand on the stallion's neck gentling the horse he repeated the question. Then it dawned on him: she spoke no English and he spoke no Dutch. Then he heard the giggle, and they laughed out loud together and Billy's boredom flew away high up into the sky. A week later without using one word with each other they were lovers, and the dogs took up the habit of trotting behind the big stallion, Sarie perched on its rump, legs astride, her arms clinging round her lover, her face pressed to his back.

THE PERFECT HAPPINESS lasted six weeks. Shaun Clifford, returning from the malarial swamps for a short visit to his wife, was not a man to spend money on a son to have a girl in rags from the slums of hell as a daughter-in-law. The scandal, to which the lovers remained oblivious, was presented to Shaun by his wife the moment he returned and sent him into a blind temper. Billy had been away one night and had left Sarie by their river to return to his mother and found his father and two of the neighbours on the stoep in Church Street. The neighbours left quickly without a word and Billy's world crashed around him. A man without money was at the mercy of his father.

On the third day of their terrible separation, Sarie walked barefoot back through the town with her dogs, past the stoep in Church Street, past Billy, wordless in the grip of his father's arm, but their eyes met and hers smiled at him, the treasure for his years to come, and for the first and only time Mr and Mrs Clifford saw the mother of their granddaughters. The train left with Billy the next morning at the start of his journey back to Ireland and what appeared to him as the rest of his lonely life.

ON THE 28TH NOVEMBER 1899, Koos de la Rey and three thousand five hundred burghers opened fire from slit trenches for the first time in warfare and decimated General Methuen's British soldiers. Whilst advancing over open ground towards the Modder River ten miles south of Kimberley, Karel Oosthuizen's youngest brother, Piers, fifteen years old, was riding onto the family farm upriver to make sure his mother was safe, permission having been given by General Piet Cronjé for the boy to leave the Boer army that was moving down from Mafeking to confront Buller's generals. Sarie was the first to see the lone horseman. For a moment she watched, thoughtful of it being her man, Frikkie, until she recognised Piers. The twins kept close to her as they waited. Elijah came out of the barn and was the first to talk to Piers. Quietly, Sarie took her daughters inside to the room they shared behind the house, a small shed built by Frikkie as near to the main house as his mother would allow. Next to her shed were the servants' sheds, bigger than Sarie's with vegetable gardens and extra rooms for the black children, the children that were not allowed to play with the twins.

Sarie listened from behind her thin walls as Piers told the mother his news. Only when she heard that Frikkie was alive and well did she relax, as without her benefactor she knew the old woman would throw them out onto the open veld. In her hostile world, she had learnt how to protect her babies, the treasure of her life. The war, which she no more understood than the world itself, was coming closer. The following morning Piers was gone. Sarie sighed and smiled at her children. Whoever won the war would make no difference to Sarie Mostert. Even the blacks had a better status than a poor white with no husband and two illegitimate children. Again she smiled to herself. Life could be worse. There was a roof over her head and food every day for the three of them and the girls were full of health and energy, green-eyed like their father.

ELIJAH WAS a Xhosa and far away from his tribe and the place of his birth on the coast next to the confluence of the Indian Ocean and the Kei River. He had ridden the perimeter at breakneck speed with Ezekiel Oosthuizen, the father of the seven boys, the young Elijah leading the spare horses so the circle they rode all day was wider than any other of the Boers laying claim to their land. The two men had ridden from sunup to sundown to complete the ring and proclaim the farm they later called Majuba in celebration of the Boers' victory over the British in the first Anglo-Boer war. He was an old man now and could no longer count a herd of springbok at two thousand yards but his sons were strong and their sons were strong and the great farm they had pegged out thirty years before had been good to them and never once had any of the families, black or white, known hunger. With a Sotho wife he had bought for five cows given him by Ezekiel Oosthuizen, life had been content until now. Elijah knew the history of the tribes that fought for and occupied the territory south of the great Zambezi River, and the terrible years of the Lifaqane when tribes slaughtered tribes in an orgy of self-destruction. Before the Lifaqane, his wife's people owned the very land that made up the farm Majuba, a source of pride and irritation for his sons and grandsons who still dreamed of the power of their ancestors.

Elijah watched Piers ride away to his new war and was sad that at the end of an old man's life, where an old man should sit under a shady tree while his granddaughters brought him beer to drink, it was all going to happen again. Elijah had never seen an Englishman, but he knew of their power and their defeat of the mighty Zulu. Now they were bringing great ships full of soldiers to Africa and they would crush the Boers as they had crushed the Zulus and they would never go home again, and in the end, the war would come to Majuba and Elijah, and peace and prosperity would be gone for him forever. From what Piers had told him there was going to be a great battle between the Boers and the British that had nothing to do with the blacks. Elijah shook his head in sorrow. When two lions fought each other in the king's cattle kraal many cattle died, trampling each other unless they could break out of the kraal and run away from the fight. In despair, he looked around him and knew there was nowhere to run. He and his family would just have to wait and see. Talking quietly to himself, he went across to his pony, threw a blanket over the animal's back and rode away from the small group of buildings onto the open veld to find his sons and grandsons who were hoeing the acres of maize they had planted with the first rains a week after the white man had ridden out to war.

When he told them Piers's story, he expected them all to worry about their families just like he had been worrying ever since Piers gave him the news of the impending battle. Instead, everyone but Elijah became excited and stopped hoeing the land and went off in a huddle away from the old man and Elijah feared even more for his children. For a brief moment, as he looked, he thought Kei, the youngest of his sons, named after the great river near where Elijah had been born, had grown six inches. On his face was a look that looked so far it had no distance. There was always one dreamer in every family and for the first time in his life, Elijah admitted to himself he was an old man. There was a new bull in the kraal and nothing he could do to protect the bull from its own destruction. His son wanted to fight both of them, Boer and British, and win back the land of his ancestors.

A WEEK LATER, when Koos de la Rey was this time digging a twelve-mile trench in front of the hill at Magersfontein, the British having brushed aside the Boers on the Modder River with their overwhelming numbers, Kei rode north from Majuba on the best pony left on the farm. In the saddle holster in front of his right knee was the Mauser rifle Karel had taught him to use, left behind by Ezekiel Oosthuizen to protect his wife. Kei had smiled to himself at the idea. The little woman would have knocked herself over backwards if she had fired the gun. Over his shoulder rode cartridge belts from left to right and right to left. In his saddlebag over the pony's rump behind his short-stirrup saddle was a month's supply of dried meat. Beside them trotted a dog that had never left his side since the day Sarie had given him the best of one of her litters. The dog was skin and bones but could run all day beside the pony, a long pink tongue hanging from its jaws.

Once off the farm, Kei felt powerfully elated, drugged by the adrenaline of freedom. He was going north with no certainty of his destination except that north was away from the white men who were going to destroy themselves and leave him free for the rest of his life. From a distance, Kei looked like any of the Boers out on commando, and when a British patrol away from the railway line fired at him, his surprise turned to anger as he spurred the pony and cantered away from the danger, bent on his one-man crusade of launching a black rebellion.

On the 9th December, when Kei was riding north thirty miles west of Mafeking, Karel, despite the rumours of the British advance to relieve Kimberley, was enjoying his war. Long ago the brothers on the farm Majuba had run out of new stories to tell each other, and the fresh ears that sat spellbound while Karel told them the highlights of his life made the camaraderie around the campfires the best days he could ever remember. That Saturday night they sat around the fire smoking their clay pipes while a burgher from Potchefstroom told them how he had fought a lion with his bare hands. It was a good story and well told and no one around the fire believed a word of it, which was why Karel had never told them the story of his elder brother Frikkie, the biggest of the Oosthuizen family. Waiting politely for a lull in the conversation to see if his new friends had something better to say, Karel entered the conversation. Behind them, Kimberley was quiet and further to the south nothing had been heard from the British guns for days and some of the burghers were convinced de la Rey had chased Methuen back over the Modder River on his way to the Cape.

"Frikkie, that's my brother Frikkie, the really big one in the family," began Karel, pleased by the titter that ran around the fire at the idea of an Oosthuizen bigger than Karel himself. "Frikkie shot a pair of leopards that had been killing our calves on our farm Majuba, sometimes eating the calves as they came out of the womb, the smell of the birth blood bringing the leopards down from the hills. We skinned the big cats and the pelts still lie on the floor in the farmhouse.

"Well, a day later, we were checking on the cattle, me and Frikkie, when a leopard cub, not six weeks old, came walking towards us and we knew that yesterday we had killed the little fellow's mother and father. So Frikkie picked up the cub and put him in front on the saddle which was nearly a mistake as the horse didn't like that at all. To a horse, a leopard smells just the same at six weeks old. When we got home, there was one mistake we did find... The cub was a girl, not a boy. Frikkie tried feeding the cub cow's milk, but the milk was too strong and only when we watered it down would the food stay in the cub's stomach. So Frikkie had a new pet and his dog went off and sulked but the leopard thrived and week by week grew bigger. By the time the cub was three months old, wherever you found Frikkie you found the leopard. Inseparable, quite inseparable.

"The year before Sarie came on the farm with all her dogs, Piet van Tonder from the next farm invited all us Oosthuizens to his wedding, and Mrs van Tonder, Piet's mother, makes the best *mampoer* in the Transvaal. Kicked like an elephant, so they said. When we got ourselves dressed up in our Sunday suits with the nice black hats, we were ready to go, up there on the horses, when the leopard who was used to following Frikkie around the farm made it plain she was coming too, which father said would cause a problem with the van Tonders and the rest of the guests. So Frikkie got down from his horse and walked back onto the stoep of the farmhouse, pushed the leopard inside and locked the front door, and off we went to the wedding in high spirits, the sun not up an hour.

"It was the best wedding I ever went to and that *mampoer* of Mrs van Tonder's was the best I ever tasted and lucky the horses knew how to ride us home as the only sober ones were young Piers and Ma, Ma never having touched a drop in the whole of her life. But when we got back, there was the leopard sitting on the stoep outside the front door, and Frikkie was so annoyed the animal had got itself out of the house he gave her a big fat *klop* round the side of its ear and sent the leopard off into the bush to sulk. Then Frikkie fumbled with the key and just before Ma was going to take the big key and open the door, the key clicked the lock open and in we went to the sitting room and there in front of the cold fireplace was Frikkie's pet leopard. It took just a moment before Frikkie understood what he had done and then he passed right out, poleaxed flat on his face on the floor. You see, the leopard my brother Frikkie had reared from a cub had just come on heat."

"What happened to the leopard?" asked the man from Potchefstroom after a moment of silence.

"Which one?" asked Karel, and everyone but the man from Potchefstroom laughed.

THE NEXT DAY BEING A SUNDAY, no one took their rifles to look down on besieged Kimberley as both sides had agreed at the beginning of the war that Sundays were the Lord's day and hostilities would be suspended. Karel was enjoying a cup of coffee an hour and a half before sunset when they all looked at each other with fear and then a certain amount of indignation.

"But it's Sunday!" exclaimed the man from Potchefstroom. "We're Christians. We don't fight each other on the Lord's day."

From ten miles to the south the distant cannonade built up, and a cheer rose from the town of Kimberley. For an hour and a half, Karel listened to the terrible artillery barrage and knew instinctively who was firing the guns. The war that was going to be over by Christmas was not going to be over for a very long time. A vicious stab of fear wrenched around in his stomach. The British Army had arrived in Africa and was less than ten miles away from where he was no longer enjoying his coffee, and Karel knew that Oom Paul, President Kruger, had made a terrible miscalculation by declaring war on the British. Karel, as he listened and listened to the bombardment, felt very small and vulnerable. Then came the silence soon after dark. For half an hour there was no sound from the battle raging to the south and then they all saw a great light shining up at the sky, the first time any of them had seen a searchlight. For the rest of the night, no one slept and very little talk was heard among the burghers. By the time the long night had passed for them in fear and light revealed their faces to each other, Karel noticed the man from Potchefstroom was nowhere to be seen and when Karel looked, he found the man's pony gone. He knew the horse well as it stabled with Karel's pony and was the only one with a white blaze down the front of its face. They were all free to come and go as they pleased and for a moment Karel was tempted to saddle up and ride away back to Majuba and bury his face in the welcome skirts of his little mother, but then he told himself he was a man and not a small boy and walked back to his friends. No one talked about the men, many of them, who had left in the night.

All through the night, Karel had been thinking of his father and brothers who were with General Cronjé and Koos de la Rey at Magersfontein ten miles to the south. The terrible bombardment the night before, the lone searchlight and the endless silences of the night, told him they were all dead, and even though he knew from reliable rumour that a long trench had been dug in front of the complex of hills, through which ran the railway line to Kimberley from the south, he was sure no one could have lived through the bombardment. Any moment he expected to see khaki down below and checked yet again his gun was loaded. There was fear in everyone's eyes and no one spoke.

As suddenly as the guns had stopped the night before, a sharp crack of rifle fire came to them from the south and three of the men stood up and threw their hats in the air.

"They're Mausers," shouted Karel in his excitement and relief, and everyone down the siege line began to cheer.

By noon the word had reached Kimberley the British had been stopped, but the battle raged. The siege was tightened to make sure the British could not break out and join the battle. All day long cannon and rifle fire came to them on the wind and after dark, word reached Kimberley. The British General Methuen had not broken through the Boer trenches and thousands of British were lying dead on the battlefield, cut down by accurate Boer rifle fire from the safety of their trenches that had protected the burghers from the exploding shells the night before. Trench warfare had won the battle for the Boers and the next day cheers ran again around Kimberley and hats were tossed in the air. Lord Methuen, the British general, and his army of thirteen thousand men were retreating back to the Modder River, and when at lunchtime Piers found Karel with an order to join the family commando at Magersfontein, there was only one brother slightly wounded by British shrapnel and the rest of his family were alive and well.

With mixed feelings of relief and fear, Piers rode out with his brother from the siege lines.

3

DECEMBER 1899

*T*wo weeks later and two days before Christmas, Billy Clifford sailed from Southampton on the *Dunnottar Castle* with Lord Roberts, the new British commander-in-chief who was being sent to South Africa to replace Sir Redvers Buller. On board were bevvies of fellow war correspondents. Winston Churchill, who at the age of twenty-six was being paid two hundred and fifty pounds a week by his newspaper, a sum ten times greater than Billy's salary from the *Irish Times*, was not on board, having been captured by the Boers. But as Billy reflected impatiently as the liner separated from the tugs, his father had not been the British Chancellor of the Exchequer and his grandfather the Duke of Marlborough any more than he had stood for parliament at such a tender age. Billy was excited at the prospect of following a war but he was even more excited at finding Sarie. Ever since freeing himself of his father's chains by becoming a journalist and finding a way of using his degree in English, he had been saving his pennies to one day sail back to South Africa and find the girl whose memory still burnt in his heart like the all-consuming fire of hell.

Using his brief weeks in the Boer capital of Pretoria as his credential for following the war, even white-lying his knowledge of what the Boers were now calling the language of Afrikaans, he had wheedled his editor into giving him the job at the salary of twenty-five pounds a week.

As the boat sailed down the English Channel into the Bay of Biscay his heart beat faster, and instead of war and bullets all he saw in his mind's eye as he looked over the rail at the ship's wake was a cool stream, a blue sky and the most beautiful girl he had ever known in his life.

WHILE BILLY WAS DREAMING about Sarie, the Mashonaland Scouts were crossing the Limpopo River from Rhodesia into the Transvaal. The water flowed around the bellies of the horses and Henry Manderville fired his Lea-Enfield twice into the river to dissuade the crocodiles from attacking the horses. The temperature was well over eighty degrees and being first light as they crossed, the tsetse fly was cruel to men and horses, the bites at neck and wrist like red-hot needles. The horses, at Henry and Gregory Shaw's insistence, were salted having been previously bitten by the tsetse, infected and recovered. Even though the heat so early in the morning was intense the Scouts were covered from head to toe, their slouch hats pulled down over their faces, their hands protected by gloves. Even then the flies found flesh.

Henry's uniform was the same one he had worn on the Pioneer Column that had occupied Rhodesia. Gregory, a much thinner Gregory after weeks of intensive training, had discarded the trappings of the Indian Army and was dressed in the same patchwork dark grey and black that camouflaged well with the bush. The nine horsemen, led by Major James Brigandshaw, were the first under Colonel Plumer's command to cross into enemy territory. Their instructions were to sabotage the Boer railway line from Pretoria to Delagoa Bay three hundred miles to the south through enemy territory.

FROM THICK BUSH half a mile upriver, Kei watched the soldiers ride their horses out of the river. When they were out of sight, swallowed by the heat haze, he pointed his pony at the water and crossed into Rhodesia. With him were four other black men on ponies like his own and like Kei, they were armed with stolen rifles. Two of the men were from the Sotho tribe, one Ndebele and one a Matabele. Across the river, they made camp and rested. Then they rode on north towards the old capital of Lobengula, King of the Matabele, careful to avoid people, black or white.

Kei's odyssey had begun when his meanderings crossed the direct line between Kimberley and Bulawayo and he surprised four black men at their campfire. Kei watched them from the time the sun went down until the moon gave him enough light to see what he was doing. To his surprise, the four men around the fire conversed in Afrikaans. After three weeks on his own he was lonely and missed his family back on the farm Majuba, but his pride stopped him turning the pony round and riding home, the wrath of his father a strong reason for keeping his resolution. The four men were renegades like himself but each had a good horse and a rifle of a type never before seen by Kei. Judging from the distance and the timbres of their voices Kei thought the four men his own age. One was much taller than the others and paced around the fire at regular intervals. His nose was long and straight like his chin. One of the men, when he got up on the other side of the fire, had a gap between his legs even when he walked standing straight. Their rifles, like Kei's, were in bucket holsters that were lying around a tree away from the resting horses. That night there was no sound or sense of wild animals. When the meat began to roast on the open fire, Kei's mouth watered. The question he asked himself as the night darkened and he waited for the moon was how to introduce himself into the company of the four men without being shot.

When he judged the men to be asleep around the fire and there was enough moonlight for him not to tread and crack every piece of fallen wood on his way to the fire, he made his slow approach. The big man with the straight nose had taken his rifle to the fire where it lay next to him on the ground. Just beyond the firelight Kei stopped and braced himself, his Mauser pointed at the big man's chest. In the same language the four men had been speaking around the fire, he pleasantly but loudly wished them 'good evening', at the same time moving forward so the big man could see the gun pointing at his chest.

The words from the night woke all four men instantly. The bow-legged man was first to scream and run away into the bush imagining the Devil. The big man, equally frightened by the voice of a ghost from the night, left his rifle on the ground and ran away with the rest.

The remains of the roast bush pig that had been left on a tripod next to the fire were the best food Kei had eaten since leaving Majuba. Three times he called into the night and each time heard more crashing further and further away into the bush. With the Mauser across his legs, Kei waited for the dawn, having removed the bolts from their four guns. He also checked their horses. When everything was safe, Kei whistled for his dog. With the animal on guard next to him and wood stoked on the fire, he slept till morning, waking to a wet rough tongue licking his face.

Two hours later the dog barked long before Kei heard anything. The dog's intelligent face was pointing northeast, and the ears were pricked to catch the slightest sound. The big man was the first to break cover.

"Good morning," said Kei in Afrikaans. "As you can see I am not a ghost. And thank you, your meat was delicious."

The four men had worked in the Big Hole at Kimberley digging for diamonds when the town had come under siege. They worked on a gang deep in the earth for a wage that gave them food and something to save so they could go home and buy cattle and with the cattle buy themselves wives, put the wives to work in the fields, their sons to looking after the cattle, and drink beer under the shade of a tree with their friends. The main way to wealth was to steal some of the diamonds they found in the earth to sell to elicit buyers for a small fraction of their worth. The process had been going well for all four men when the Boer army had besieged the town and food became more valuable than diamonds.

A week before Kei had joined them, the four men had been armed by the British, told to slip through the Boer lines at night and drive as many cattle back to Kimberley as they could find. The mine owner for whom they worked had promised a reward that would make them rich once the British had won the war. The big man being a Matabele of pure Zulu descent had no doubt in his mind the British would win. Shaka, as the mine owner called the big man, was to lead the foraging party, hiding their holsters and guns under blankets draped over the horses' necks. With the British and Boers in agreement that the blacks were to be kept out of the war, they would be safe. Once through the Boer lines, which they found easy as the besiegers sat around their fires at night and black men were black men who belonged to neither side, Shaka and his three companions never looked back. With four rifles and four hundred rounds of ammunition, Shaka had a better plan for getting rich.

Shaka had been one of the last to see Lobengula, King of the Matabele, alive, and had seen the indunas take the sick old man up into the hills, the great king lying in the back of an ox wagon. Two days later the indunas came back and slaughtered the biggest black bull in the king's herd that had been driven in front of the army as it retreated further and further into the mopane forest away from the British in 1893. Everyone then knew the king was dead, and the regiments lost heart. Two days before the king's wagon had gone, the wagons loaded with crates of rifles and the king's treasure of ivory, and some said gold, had been taken somewhere into those hills below the Zambezi River: this was the prize Shaka had convinced the others to help him find.

When the band of five men crossed the Limpopo River and moved off into the great mopane forest, Shaka felt at home.

"Their soldiers are going south," he told them. "We will have no problems. Maybe with the gold and ivory and the king's guns, the Matabele will rise and kill the British. It is always better to kill a man when he is looking the wrong way."

"Are you sure you can find the hills?" asked Kei, seeing the endless trees ahead of them.

"Of course I am," said Shaka. "Have we not crossed the Limpopo? Are we not in the land of the Matabele? The king's treasure is over there," he said, pointing at the nearest tree.

If nothing else, Kei told himself, he enjoyed their company. The country was vast and day after day as they rode north they saw not a living soul nor even a ghost.

WHILE THE FIVE men and the dog were making their journey through the mopane forest, two hundred and thirty miles to the east Jeremiah Shank was entertaining Francesca Shaw to dinner at Holland Park. The dining room table was long, and they sat at a distance of twenty feet from each other with a servant behind each of their chairs who kept filling up their glasses. Somewhere Jeremiah had heard it was the way things were done in English country houses, and he always imagined that if Lord Edward Holland had had a wife, he would have dined in such a way at Bramley Park. Jeremiah, at last, and for the first time, was trying out how it would feel to have a well-bred woman at the far end of his table.

The husband had conveniently gone off to war and Jeremiah had found the object of his desire taking tea in Meikles Hotel, of which he was still a director. Explaining that Jack Jones was on the farm to provide a chaperone even if the Welshman was a man, he asked Fran to drive with him to Holland Park. On the journey, when the lady asked him how he came by the name of Holland Park, Jeremiah kept up the myth that his benefactor, Lord Edward Holland, brother of the Marquis of Surrey, was a relation. Intent on the road and looking ahead, he missed the look of amusement that came over Fran's face. If there had ever been straight talk between a man and a woman she would have told him outright his money was all that mattered and defunct aristocrats were not part of her plan. To maintain the fiction she let out an impressed 'really' and kept quiet.

To Fran's surprise, now that Gregory had ridden off to war, she felt a twinge of conscience as the time was well after lunch and there was little chance of returning to the hotel that night. The only thing going for the little man next to her with the crooked nose and drooping eye was his wealth, the strongest aphrodisiac Fran had ever known. The biggest surprise after weeks of army training was Gregory finally making love. Thinner and fitter than she had ever known her husband, and man again now he was going to war, he had made love to her the night he came back to take his departure, leaving Fran with the first real puzzle to come into her marriage.

Being a woman who always looked ahead, she had accepted Jeremiah's invitation to look at his horses as men at war very often got themselves killed. When the charade of the dinner was over and Fran quite tight, she was taken into the music room where she found a medium grand piano with the lid up, the stool out and Jeremiah ready to listen. After some tentative notes, Fran found herself playing the piano for the first time in a long while and, drunk though she was, she lost herself in the music. She played for half an hour to the silent bush out through the open windows and never once did Jeremiah interrupt.

Still a little drunk she hung her head over the keys and wondered what in the name of God was she doing in the middle of the African bush away from the old house in Godalming, away from being the daughter and granddaughter of a country solicitor in a country that had not seen war for years. Now here she was with a strange man, common as dirt, being unfaithful to a man who for right or wrong reasons had ridden off to fight for the country of his birth. Helped by the wine, tears flowed down her cheeks, hitting the black and white keys, and for those moments the house and Africa did not exist, only that part of her which had been created by so many English ancestors. She felt an arm on her shoulder and a hand in her hand and she was led away from the piano, out of the room and up a spiral staircase, past a dark portrait of someone's ancestor with a bullet hole in the painting, to a tower with a roof that wound open and a telescope that looked up at the stars and all of heaven.

"It doesn't matter none, luv. It don't matter none," he said to her in what she recognised as his true voice. And then she was seated in the chair and she was up there, part of the heavens, and for over an hour he talked about the stars and showed her where she was looking, and when they went down to his bedroom and made love, there was nothing wrong and the crooked face no longer annoyed her and the sounds of Africa were background to her pleasure. And then she cried properly before she went to sleep.

But in the morning for Fran Cotton, the world was hard and cruel the way it had been before. The false voice was back, the eyelid drooped, the nose was crooked and the man she had vowed to live with for the rest of her natural life was off hundreds of miles away still riding out to war.

WHILE FRAN WAS WATCHING Jack Jones break in a horse destined for the

British Army, twenty miles on the other side of Salisbury, eight-year-old Madge Brigandshaw was putting the finishing touches to her tree house, obeying a primal instinct from her distant ancestors to build her home high off the ground away from the predators. Harry, nearly twelve, back from boarding school in Cape Town for the holidays and bored stiff, was giving his sister a helping hand while almost four-year-old George got in the way as usual. With war having cut the railway line, Harry was not sure when he would be going back to school, and with not even his grandfather to supply a mild form of amusement, Harry was trying to grow up fast so he could run off and join his uncle in the war. To Harry's great relief, Tinus Oosthuizen had not joined the Boer army and even though Barend was the same age as Madge, Harry had spent most weekends on the new farm in the Franschhoek Valley thirty miles from his school. Alison, with the ulterior motive of seeing Harry, had written to Emily recommending the school that was run by the Church of England: many said it was the best in the Cape. With Seb's dividends from African Shipping he could afford the boarding fees, and were it not for the unpredictability of his father, Seb would have sent the boy to England for his education.

Sebastian watched his children and the son that was almost a man and wondered where the years had all gone. Alone on the farm, he employed over one hundred black people, and were it not for the war and his feeling of guilt, he would have been as happy as any man was able to be in a world that no one could ever predict.

"A penny for your thoughts," asked Emily, seven months pregnant with their fourth child.

"The war, Em. Am I being a coward? Even your father is down there with a gun in his hand."

"Why do men always want to fight?"

"Maybe they have always had to fight for what they wanted and then protect what they got. So long as some are rich and some are poor, man will fight. He thinks it such a short life to prove his worth. And all that striving is mostly worthless in the end. I mean, what's the point?"

"You think we made a mistake coming out here?"

"Probably."

"You think I should have stayed with Arthur!"

"How can I even think of that? We should have told them you were pregnant with Harry."

"When you were out on the high seas, kidnapped by your own father? Frankly, The Captain wouldn't have cared a damn. Whichever way, the boy was his grandson. Your father is so vain he can't see the wood for the trees, and your mother is scared stiff of him. Don't worry about the war, Seb. It'll be over once General Roberts launches his offensive and the Boers like Tinus will be happy as part of the empire. It's Christmas tomorrow and likely Fran will come back from Fort Salisbury. She has a soft spot for the children, you know that. And your brother will come over from the mission and he always brings a train of people and we will all have a lovely time."

"You are always so enthusiastic, darling Em."

"There's no point in being otherwise... Children! Please come down for lunch."

"What's for lunch?" Harry called down.

"Come and see." There was one sure way of getting children out of trees. She smiled and put her hands on her belly to feel the baby kick.

THE TRELLISED VINES were heavy with small green fruit that stretched in lines at the level of a man's head as far as the eye could see. The valley was green and perfectly ordered, interspersed by the gabled homes of the wine growers and the clusters of labourers' houses. All around the Franschhoek Valley towered the mountains, purple in the varying light, the vast protection for the valley people from the other world.

Alison sat on her stoep on Christmas morning in the first light of day listening to the squeals of her children opening up the stockings she had hung in the middle of the night at the end of their beds, full of silly things. An orange for colour, a box of Christmas crackers, a water pistol for Barend and a small doll that rolled its eyes for Tinka. Christo was mercifully still asleep. The morning was cool with a gentle breeze from the Berg River and the first cup of tea she had made herself in the brown pot she brought from England was always the best one of the day. To add to her pleasure the new baby was not making her sick in the morning. Tinus had been fast asleep with his mouth wide open making a fluttering sound more than a snore, and none of the servants had risen from their beds. Morning birds called to each other and the smell of damp soil from yesterday's rain was rich. Down in front of the raised stoep, some ten feet above the lawn, the house built on a slope, the ducks were swimming in the large, lily-filled pond, the flowers sweet and smiling. Her new home was the most beautiful place she had ever seen, and instead of being a children's nurse in someone else's establishment she was mistress of the house. Alison Ford, she told herself, had come a long way after climbing down the ladder at Hastings Court. Maybe only youth did things like that, never fearing the consequences. Halfway across the valley, six feral geese were flying in a perfect skein, the heavy beat of their wings alive on the wind. Halfway through her second cup of tea Christo woke and the moments of peace were gone and Alison's day began.

THE SUN ROSE HALF an hour later at Elephant Walk and Sebastian had taken his worries down to the Mazoe River. Behind, through the msasa trees and the stockade from the Shona rebellion, his family was still asleep. Further downriver at the compound there was little noise on this day decreed as a holiday. The day would be hot and humid, the main rains having broken a week earlier. The fox terriers were still asleep at the foot of Harry's bed but the two ridgebacks had followed him down to the river five hundred yards from the stockade, quiet but alert to the day's potential. The river was flowing strongly from the good rains and brought with it the debris from the banks upriver. It was Christmas Day and Sebastian wished everyone a happy Christmas, which brought his mind back to England and the house The Captain had built, the winding avenue of oaks planted by his father that hid the horse but not the rider, and he wondered why life had sent him so far away. He wondered what he would have been doing on this Christmas Day were it not for Em and the cruelty of his father. He had never thought of a career, so engrossed had they been with each other. Every year in Africa, on her birthday and for Christmas, Sebastian had written to his mother telling her the news of her grandchildren and never once had she sent him a reply. She had other children more important than the black sheep. Looking back, he thought he had loved his mother, and she had loved him back.

The wild geese began the morning run over the trees, honking at each other in full flight, and in front of his toe a dung beetle was pushing a ball of horse dung relatively the size of a house. Seb watched the beetle for a full five minutes before the insect got it wrong and the ball fell down the riverbank into the water where it was rushed away on the current. The beetle stood still for a long moment before going off to roll another ball of dung, the primal instinct to procreate by laying its eggs in the dung too strong to accept defeat.

And then the worries came back to Sebastian, and he had to look at them all over again. James, who at that moment was leading his troop further into enemy territory towards the railway, had said the war was about gold but Sebastian was not sure. Life was never that simple. Despite their isolation, Sebastian was as well informed as anyone even if the newspapers were many weeks old. The books he ordered came to him in crates and he devoured them page by page and mostly more than once. It was his recreation and many an hour of deep pleasure was spent in a wicker chair under the shade of a mṣasa tree reading the knowledge accumulated by man. The reason for the war in Sebastian's mind was jealousy, hatred of British arrogance, dislike of the man at the top but most of all, the wish of other nations in the world to destroy the British Empire and take the trade for themselves. The argument was about power and if one of the smallest nations in the world could beat the British Army as they had done in South Africa, the empire itself was vulnerable and the world was a dangerous place for Englishmen.

Ever since Bismarck had herded the German states into one country, England's power on the continent had been challenged and now the Kaiser, Wilhelm II, had sold the Boers Mauser rifles and was building a navy to challenge the British. Russia had spent years intriguing against the British in Afghanistan, peering over the frontier passes and coveting the wealth of India down below. France for as long as France existed had been the enemy of England. And America, the one-time British colony, had almost gone to war with England in 1895 over the border between Venezuela and British Guiana. Only the Royal Navy, twice the size of the next two navies in the world, held the wolves at bay, wolves now looking at England as a wounded animal where an army of amateur soldiers could defeat the largest British army ever sent overseas. For Sebastian, the problem was not the gold on the Witwatersrand but the survival of the empire, the survival of Britain itself, and Britain had very few friends.

A simultaneous attack at the same time by three or four of her erstwhile and present enemies would bring down the greatest empire the world had ever known with everyone fighting for a piece of the disintegrating prize. Roberts on his way out from England had to win the war and quickly, before England lost her credibility. But for personal reasons, Sebastian was unable to go out and fight for the country of his birth as there was no way in the deepest recess of his mind that Sebastian could go to war with Tinus or any of his tribe. Without Tinus Oosthuizen, Sebastian knew he would have been very little in life. Not only did he owe the man for his wealth and his life on more than one occasion in the bush, but he also owed him for a friendship that had seen and protected a young man with no wealth and a young man in jail and in fear of his life. The families loved each other, and that was the end of it. They could even call him a coward if that was what they wanted.

Even through the trees, he heard the gate being pushed open in the stockade. Dogs barked and the two ridgebacks raised their heads for a brief moment, recognised the fox terriers, and went back to dolefully contemplating the flowing river. A late owl dropped from a tree on the riverbank and glided across the river.

"Brought you some tea, Dad," said Harry sitting down next to his father on the fallen tree trunk. Sebastian turned and smiled at his oldest son, the one true cause of both of them looking at the African river. The dogs went off together in their endless pursuit. The tea from the flask tasted good with just the right amounts of milk and sugar.

"You mind if I have some?" asked Harry. "Mother's still asleep."

"Happy Christmas."

"Happy Christmas. I didn't get a stocking again this year."

"Of course not. Your mother should have stopped when you were six."

"It's not so much fun growing up... Dad, when are you going to the war?"

"I'm not, Harry."

"But why? Uncle James and Grandfather have gone and Mother says he's too old but he went."

"Because of Uncle Tinus."

"But I told you, Uncle Tinus is not going to fight for the Boers."

"I hope not but when people start killing each other's families, they take sides."

"But you don't want to take sides."

"Oh, I'm on the English side because I'm English. Same way Tinus will be on the Boer side because he's a Boer. But we don't want to fight."

"Where's Aunty Fran?"

"I'm not quite sure. Salisbury. Meikles Hotel, probably."

"I like Uncle Greg but I don't like Aunty Fran."

"You mustn't say things like that, Harry. It's rude."

"Are you a coward, Dad?"

"I hope not son, I really do." Sebastian tried to put his arm around his son's shoulders, but the boy moved away.

Without another word between them, they waited for the dogs and then walked up to the house for a breakfast of cold meats so that the house servants would only have to come to work for the big Christmas lunch at three o'clock in the afternoon.

"This one's not going to be easy, Tinus," he said to himself as he went through the gate.

The rest of his children were running across the lawn towards him shouting happy Christmas and Em was waiting for him on the veranda with a smile.

"Happy Christmas, my darling."

"When are we going to open the presents?" demanded Madge.

"When Uncle Nat and Aunty Bess arrive with the children."

"I wish they'd hurry up," piped George.

When away from the children, Sebastian told her what had happened down by the river. Emily shuddered.

"I'm not going to war," he promised her again.

"It's not only you I worry about. There's Alison and Tinus. Tinus, he's the one to worry about. Hasn't he got a pack of nephews in the Transvaal?"

"I rather think he has."

"Harry's the least of our worries."

"He thinks his father is a coward."

"Well, you're not."

BY ELEVEN O'CLOCK on Christmas morning Ezekiel Oosthuizen, the father of the seven sons, was in a spiritual trance. The Boer army under General Cronjé had been slowly moving south to confront the British. Ezekiel, dressed in a black frock coat and top hat, harangued his congregation from a rise, the great red beard, the colour inherited from his Scottish mother, covering his chest, the old, blackened teeth feeling the spittle of his words. Not a man in the crowd seated down the slope from his feet took their eyes from the preacher, the light of the sun making the man larger even than life.

"God has chosen us," he thundered. "God has chosen us to give light to the dark, to bring His word to the wilderness and God shall not be wrong. We are the chosen people, chosen by God to bring the light to Africa and if we trust in God, the English will go back over the sea. Fear not, the English. Fear God. Trust in God, my people, and God will deliver us. Let us pray for our redemption and may God bring the plagues upon our enemies."

Ezekiel fell to his knees on the hard stones that littered the rise constituting his pulpit, the Bible clutched in his right hand, and with all his might and soul prayed to his God for the deliverance of his people. Head bowed on his chest and feeling nothing from the stones, he kept them on their knees for half an hour and only then did he rise, renewed in spirit, mind and body. The crowd, awed by their own renewal with God, silently went their ways and with them all seven sons of Ezekiel. All that was his life and the future of his life was moving mile by mile towards their destiny.

When the euphoria of his religion had drained from his mind, the pain the stones had inflicted on his knees was excruciating and once again he was a burgher with a gun.

There had been no sight of the British for two weeks and the cooking fires had been burning from before dawn, the oxen roasting in the sun, the smell rich on the gentle breeze. The women who followed their husbands and sons tended the cooking and with church over for the day, the men gathered amid families and friends. Leaving his sons, Ezekiel walked away on his own to think and worry about his wife left alone on the farm; old Elijah would be loyal to him but he was not sure of Elijah's sons. From a distance he watched his boys, four from the wife who had died giving birth to his only daughter who had died with her mother, and the three from his little wife who ruled them all with her tongue. Ezekiel smiled with pleasure.

He had left Graaff-Reinet at the age of nineteen, the year Tinus was born, to seek his fortune to the north and the two brothers had never met. For years the family had thought him dead, killed by the natives and never once had he been able to leave his new farm and make the trek south into the Cape.

For a long while, Karel looked across at his father.

"You think he's all right?" asked Piers, the youngest in the family.

"He's old, Piers. Probably too old for a campaign like this. He has a lot of memories. I think he's going through some of them up there."

"He's probably missing our mother," said Piers.

"Are you?" asked Karel gently.

"Just a little."

"We'll look after you."

"I'm glad you're back with us, Karel."

"So am I. Now go and take your father some coffee. Take one for yourself."

As the battle drew closer and Tinus's brother contemplated his own mortality, Billy Clifford, on board the *Dunnottar Castle*, was wearing a yellow paper hat at the journalists' table while he ate his roast turkey and chestnut stuffing, the bird as dry as a bone.

"Put some more gravy on it," said the man next to him. Everyone was listening to a journalist relate the story of Winston Churchill in the cavalry charge at the battle of Omdurman that had taken place the year before in the Sudan. After his capture defending an armoured train, Churchill was the war correspondent's hero. "He wrote a book on it called *The River War*," said the journalist. "Man can write, no doubt about it. The best family connections in the world can't teach you how to write."

"Want some more claret, Clifford?" said the man next to Billy. "Helps wash down the bird. Why we British subject ourselves to dry old turkey every year instead of roast beef of old England, beats me. Tradition, I suppose. There's a lot be said for tradition. Lets you know what to expect. Don't like surprises myself."

"He's a splendid talker."

"Who?"

"Man talking about Churchill. You know, this will be the first war where we journalists can have today's news at tomorrow's breakfast table. Communication like that is going to change the world. Brings everyone closer. Gives us a lot of power. We can change a war while it's in progress by reporting the facts. Before, the war in the colonies was over before the British people heard anything about it. Public opinion. We control public opinion, mark my word. And the men who control the opinions of the public will in future control the world."

With the last words, the *Dunnottar Castle*, sailing in winter weather off the north coast of Africa, began a slow corkscrew roll and Billy's lunch companion lost interest in the conversation. Only the raconteur failed to miss the beat in his story while around the dining room, some diners were getting up from the tables and leaving the room before they made a bigger exhibition of themselves. Billy thanked his sailing days at Trinity College and persevered with the leg of the turkey. When he looked up again from his plate, the man next to him had gone and the raconteur, sensing there was something bigger than Winston Churchill at play, brought his story to a conclusion while the steward put down another balloon glass of brandy next to his cleaned plate.

"Where's the plum pudding?" called the raconteur, looking around with happy expectation, causing another man to get up and leave the table.

Billy, happy with the thought of being two days nearer to Sarie, raised his glass to no one and everyone and drank down his claret. He too was ready for the plum pudding.

AT THE END of his two-hour sermon, attended by his family and seventeen blacks who had not understood one word, the Reverend Nathanial Brigandshaw made them all kneel down and once again pray to God, for a victory of British arms over the people who had deigned to give the empire a military ultimatum. His son with the uncanny resemblance to his grandfather, The Captain, had been fast asleep for an hour of the sermon and Bess had had to wake him up to get him down on his knees. The two girls had developed a way of blanking their minds while still staying awake with a look of absorbed concentration and were their father's favourites. Bess, seated between her daughters, always used her husband's sermons to plan the coming week and hoped he would talk as long as possible. It was one of the few periods in her life that she had to herself as no one was allowed to talk to her. The clever part of her long reverie was to pick up some of her husband's keywords subconsciously so she could answer his questions afterwards. The reality was a new church in the middle of the bush that allowed words to bounce off its walls without the slightest human comprehension.

The seventeen faithful blacks having sat comfortably through the ceremony were led off by Amos, now fourteen, to partake of what the whole thing was about so far as they were concerned. After giving the faithful their Christmas lunch, the reverend left the mission with his family for the drive in the trap to Elephant Walk and Christmas dinner with his wayward brother, complaining all the way how much he did for his family. By the time he drove through the open gate in the stockade, he was righteously indignant.

Harry, watching them arrive from the safety of the river, wondered why his father put up with it all. Uncle Nat was the biggest bore in the world.

"Poor Aunty Bess," he said loudly as he began the walk up to the house.

The good news this year was the relations came alone. Harry's next surprise was Aunty Fran going out first to meet the visitors having only herself arrived back on the farm an hour earlier. 'The world of grown-ups,' Harry told himself, 'works in strange ways.' His stomach rumbled halfway to the house and when he smelt the roast, water rose up in his mouth. By the time he greeted his cousins, he was actually whistling.

HARRY'S PATERNAL GRANDFATHER, six thousand miles away lording it over the estate of Harry's maternal grandfather, was wearing a smirk and had been for the last two days. The Christmas lunch was being served in the old dining hall at Hastings Court where for centuries Harry's ancestors had eaten their dinner. The old oak table, pitted with circular lines of age where the grain of the wood had worn away, had been in the family longer than the room and was pitch black. Three places were set, one at each end of the long table for The Captain and his wife and one in the middle for Arthur, the heir apparent.

Arthur, at forty-two, had grown fat from idleness and debauchery but still kept his eyes on the main chance of inheriting his father's fortune. The boredom of three days with his parents would one day (and for Arthur, the sooner the better) have its compensation. There had been no conversation at the table as none of them had anything to say to each other. If Arthur's mother opened her mouth she was contradicted by his father, and when Arthur wanted to say something to his father, it was always rude. Mother and son had learnt to keep their mouths shut. Somewhere earlier in the morning, they had somehow wished each other a happy Christmas before going off to church where Arthur had fallen asleep, gently and quietly. All through his sleep Mathilda had been in two minds whether to leave him be or wake him up, not sure which was most likely to bring the disgrace to The Captain's attention. Seated in the front in the Manderville family pew they were conspicuous. Mathilda had looked around, found more of the local gentry asleep than awake, and left Arthur alone, the other principle of her troubled life coming to the fore: when in doubt, do nothing. She had seen the smirk on her husband's face, a self-satisfied smirk, and feared a deep displeasure. To stop the turmoil in her mind, Mathilda thought of her bower by the artificial lake, the ducks on the water and the birds in the trees, while trying to think of something nice that had happened in her life.

The silence at lunch grew intense while Arthur stuffed food in his mouth and drank everything poured out by the servants, always pointing to the emptiness of his glass. Mathilda had never drunk alcohol, always needing her wits about her to survive.

Even with fires burning at either end of the dining hall, the great room with its raftered ceiling and walls festooned with swords and battle axes was as cold as charity. The hall, a place designed for feasts, was not a place for solitary eating, and high up in the corners darkened by centuries of wood fires the click and clack of knife and fork threw down echoes from the past. Against the tall, leaden windows, some plain, some coloured, a cold sleet beat on the small and ancient panes and the wind howled. Somewhere further in the old house, a door slammed making Mathilda shiver. And still, The Captain smirked.

Arthur, well drunk by now and muffled in his overcoat despite his father's ridicule, the east wind biting at his back from under the old oak door, his long sleeves soaked in gravy, wondered when his father, dressed for an August climate, would tell them his news. Again he pointed to his claret glass and inwardly laughed at the stupidity of life. He knew, he knew, he always knew.

The Captain, with a cold and lifeless hand, tried to tap his wine glass and dropped the spoon, the silver clattering to the cold stone floor. The sound brought echoes from the corners of the ceiling and the sleet pelted harder on the coloured panes, held in small triangles by ancient lead.

"I have an announcement," said the old sea captain in the moment of his triumph. "The Queen, God bless her, has seen fit to bestow upon me a baronetcy in her New Year's list of honours. As from the 1st January in the year of Our Lord 1900, I will become Sir Archibald Brigandshaw, Bart. I give you the toast. 'The Queen. God bless her.' Lady and gentleman, you may now retire to the fire."

Like a gust of foul air, Arthur's containment finally burst, and he laughed so loud echoes fought with echoes in the rafters. His father was finally trapped; he could leave the money where he wished, but the title would always be his.

"You're drunk, Arthur. You may leave us," said The Captain.

Throwing back his chair, his overcoat caught in the high back and sent it crashing to the floor. Arthur reached the panelled door and with great control turned back to his mother and father.

"Congratulations, Father. It was what you always wanted. My mother, the future Lady Brigandshaw... It is a great day for our family. I am so proud."

For a long while, the parents listened to the sound of their son's feet on the stone of the old passageway. Finally, they were left with the sleet and the wind. Somewhere far back in the time of man, someone was laughing at them. Then they looked into each other's empty eyes.

UP IN HIS room with a fire roaring up the old chimney, Arthur fell back on his bed and he was smiling. Everything in life was for sale, even a baronetcy. With the newspapers screaming patriotic twaddle after early British setbacks, with the sieges of Ladysmith, Kimberley and Mafeking a personal affront to every Briton, The Captain had offered free cargo space on his entire fleet of ships to carry war materials to South Africa. In a fervour of gratitude, a grateful government about to lose its power unless it did something quickly, and grasping at straws, accepted so generous a gesture of solidarity from a member of the public. What Arthur wanted to know as he poured himself a cognac from his secret supply was the new shipping rates after the one freeload.

"To the Pirate," he said, raising his glass to the ceiling, remembering his one-time father-in-law's epithet for The Captain. "May you steal forever more and leave it all to me." Then he fell back on the bed and began to snore, the empty brandy glass falling to the carpet.

4
___

JANUARY 1900

*B*illy Clifford spent the first morning wandering the streets of Cape Town looking at every woman hoping to see the face of Sarie. *Dunnottar Castle* had come into Cape Town harbour with the dawn in a calm sea with Lord Roberts met at the docks by Milner, the British High Commissioner for South Africa. Billy, knowing Sarie was a thousand miles to the north living on the streets of Pretoria with her dogs, told his hopes and dreams to calm down and wait.

He walked along the foreshore to the docks and showed his press pass to the guard at the gate. Every wharf was unloading equipment and men, while ships waited their turn to come into the harbour.

Billy walked up the gangplank of the *Dunnottar* to his cabin to pack in peace and finished the job as slowly as possible. He gave the cabin steward a shilling to carry his two bags and sea chest on shore and took a walk along the silent deck for the last time. Next to the *Dunnottar*, a new vessel was unloading war materials from the bowels of its holds, the fore-and-aft deck hatches open to the Cape sun, two cranes diligently working, hooking up the netted cargo and swinging the crates onto the wharf and the waiting goods train. Billy, leaning over the wide wooden rail, idly watched the sergeant-major in charge of loading the railway wagons that by nightfall would be headed for the front. The new vessel showed two tall funnels, raked to let the soot from the burnt coal pour over the vessel without reaching the iron decks. There were wisps of smoke from the funnels. Billy read the name, *Indian Queen*, London. Then he turned his attention to the vessel across from him unloading with the same urgency. Between the ship's funnels hung a banner: *cargo delivered free*. All down the side of the ship was the name Colonial Shipping.

Billy shook his head as he looked around at the multitude of ships... If his friends from Pretoria saw what he was seeing, they would know the inevitable. The sheer weight of numbers was going to crush the Boers. Here, in Cape Town harbour, was the outcome of the war. Taking a notebook and pencil from his pocket, Billy began to write his first war article for the *Irish Times*, skilfully blending Ireland with the Boer. The Irish knew; it had happened to them so many times before. Wars were won with money in pursuit of money, soldiers the last resort of politicians, force the last resort of the bully.

Looking across the crowded harbour in the January sun, Billy knew this bully was big and mean.

ON BOARD THE *INDIAN QUEEN*, the third of the same name, Captain Doyle turned his attention from the unloading to the ship across the way. With the telescope brought into focus, he recognised the stocky figure on the bridge down to the pinkie finger missing from the man's left hand. For a brief moment, the recognition and memory were good. Onboard and along the dock there were more members of the press than military, and the man he was watching through his telescope was the centre of attention.

"Good luck to you, Sir Archibald," he said loudly. "Bosun. Keep your eye on the unloading. I'm going ashore. Two more days by my reckoning."

"Isn't that Captain Brigandshaw on the *Manderville*?"

"Yes, it is."

"Hasn't captained a ship for years, I'd say. What's he doing here?"

"It's called publicity, Mr Wells. Publicity. Take a look through my telescope. That's now Sir Archibald Brigandshaw, Bart."

AFTER WEEKS IN THE SADDLE, Gregory Shaw would have comfortably fitted into his Indian Army uniform. Major James Brigandshaw had led the troop of Mashonaland Scouts deep into Boer territory where most of the male population had gone to join Cronjé who was approaching the Modder River. The British skirted the isolated farms and had ridden down into the lowveld close to the Portuguese border of Mozambique. The vegetation had changed, and the heat intensified. Twenty miles from Komatipoort inside the Transvaal they cut the rail three days after Lord Roberts had taken the train north to direct the relief of Kimberley and to attack the Boer army of Piet Cronjé. Having been taught at the Royal Military College at Sandhurst to make a reconnaissance before any attack, James set out to watch the railway line bringing supplies from Delagoa Bay to the Boers. All the trains were heavily armed.

"They'll have spare rails to replace any we twist," said James to Henry Manderville as he watched a train winding its way through the trees and rock outcrops before starting the climb up to the highveld. "Take them less than two days to sort out any mess we can make. It's the bridge or nothing."

"Or we knock out a train today. Run like hell and knock out another fifty miles away next week. They can guard the bridges but not all that railway line. This side of the kopje we can roll boulders onto the track and the train driver will only see them when he comes round the bend when he won't be able to stop. Derail the engines without even using our explosives."

"After the second rock pile, they'll come looking for us."

"Then we lead them all over the bush and come back to the railway line to do it again. The more men looking for us, the less to fight Methuen."

"You and Gregory can lead us round in circles and not get lost?"

"Your brother would be better but I can try. Knowing where you are in the bush is more instinct than science. But unless nine men can kill the guard on the bridge, you'll never blow up the bridge. For my say that bridge is out of the question without artillery."

"All right. Good. Let's put some rocks on the rail and see what happens. They might even think it was a rockslide the first time. We'll need to cut a tree to give us a pole to lever out the boulders."

The following night they camped in thick mopane forest next to a giant baobab tree that was hollow in the centre and big enough for all nine of them to sleep comfortably away from the rain. In the centre, they made a fire for cooking. High in the dark dome of the hollow tree, Henry counted seven sets of eyes by the flickering light of the fire. The bats, hanging upside down, were wide awake.

Less than a mile away, the giant boulder that had needed the leverage from three tree trunks to be put onto the line waited around the blind bend, shielded from sight by a small hill the railway engineers had sliced to make way for the rails. Outside under a tree dripping from the last rain, Gregory listened for a train from the south. They had dropped the boulder onto the track after the empty train from the north had passed. There was movement all around him, scuffles and grunts as the wild pigs foraged for food. Just before Gregory heard the train, a baboon let out a blood-curdling cry, followed by another as a leopard killed. The train was probably ten miles away and as he went into the tree to report, the rain came down in a flat deluge and the sound of the train was lost in the squall.

"They're coming," said Gregory.

Leaving the horses tethered around the fire for protection, the troop moved out to see whether the boulder would derail the steam engine. Unless fired upon, they were to remain silent. On the back slope of the hill, they waited. The brief deluge of rain had stopped and the sound of metal on metal dominated the bush. They could hear the engine labour as it began the slow climb, pulling what they knew was a long line of full wagons.

"It's not going fast enough," whispered Henry.

"They can't hear you over that racket," said James. "May not derail the train, old chap, but they won't get past. Bloody big rock that one."

From his vantage point, James could see the sparks from the engine and the shape of the boulder silent on the line. Then he heard the crash, and the bush was shattered by noise and fire as the engine toppled onto its side, spewing hot steam. Through the steam, James saw the mouth of the furnace and heard the screams of the driver.

"Time to go, gentlemen. Take the Boers a while to put that fellow back on the rails."

Silently, they moved back down the slope, slithering in the wet. Back in the mopane forest, they waited for dawn while they listened to the noise from their train wreck. In the pitch dark, it had been easier to cut the railway line and follow it to the boulder than to find their baobab tree and the horses in the mopane forest.

In the first thin light of morning, Henry led them back to the big tree. The fire had burnt down, and the horses whickered at them with relief. As they ate breakfast, the bats flew back to roost inside the baobab tree.

"We do it again, one week from today," said James, "then they'll know and come looking for us. But I'll tell you something: after tonight, we may defeat the Boer in battle, but if he comes at us the way we fought, it'll take us a month of Sundays to winkle him out."

FIVE HUNDRED YARDS on the other side of the Mazoe River from the houses where the trees had been stumped out, the valley up to the foothills was lush with green fields of tall maize undulating in the light breeze. Sebastian, viewing the culmination of his hard work and the toiling labour of his workforce, smiled with satisfaction... Farming, he told himself, was the only job where you could see the end result. The rich, red soil and the good rains had grown the stands of maize higher than his head and already in the middle of January, the plants were beginning to tassel. With the price of maize meal double with the demand down south, Sebastian calculated that for the first time in all these years, Elephant Walk was going to make a profit large enough to compensate for the losses that had accumulated in the previous years.

"That section," he said to his black foreman, pointing to his left at twenty acres, "is for your people. What you don't eat, you sell for your own profit. That is your bonus, all of you, for the year. If you want, I will sell the surplus for you and give you the money. So long as I run this farm, hard work will always have its reward. Tell the gang, work is finished for the day."

Walking back and crossing the top of the weir they had built across the river, he hoped the man understood his broken Shona. Harry, sitting under the thick foliage of a msasa tree, was reading another of his grandfather's books while he waited for the British Army to capture the railway line north of Kimberley so he could go back to school.

"You want to do me a favour, son, and explain to Sam what we agreed about the twenty-acre land? I tried, but I'm not sure he understood half of it and I want to be certain. A man must know why he's getting a bonus and how much. Sam will have to distribute this year but in future I want each family to have their own rows to cultivate from the start. Whatever they sell, Sam will get an extra ten per cent from me in cash. Everyone in life must have an incentive, however big or small."

Harry nodded to his father. "I'm going out with the gun to shoot guinea fowl."

"Good. Haven't eaten one for all of three days."

"You miss Uncle Tinus, don't you, Dad?"

"And not only because he was the only one who was good enough to shoot a buck at seven hundred yards."

"You could do it."

"I've told you, Harry, I've given up killing. Some of those elephants still haunt my dreams."

"I wonder who's winning the war?"

"No one. No one ever wins wars. I even feel guilty about taking the extra price for the maize. We will give some of the crop's proceeds to charity."

"Not to Uncle Nat!"

"No, not to Uncle Nat. We'll think of something we can do ourselves."

"Aunty Fran's been sick again."

"Has she now?"

"Yes, she has. And Mother says she's going to have the baby today."

"Your mother's not due for another month."

"Today, she said. Had enough of being fat. I think Aunty Fran is in the family way."

"How do you know?"

"Father, please. I've seen a lot of babies come and go around here. I'm twelve in April and what's more, my voice is about to break."

"Who told you that?"

"A boy at school... Father, how does a voice break? Sounds terrible. Will I be able to talk?"

"You'd better ask your mother."

"Mother said to ask you."

"Not now."

"Will you tell me before going to war?"

"I'm not going to war. And Harry. Take the smirk off your face. I rather think you know more than you're saying about this voice-breaking business."

"I rather think you're right. When are we going into Salisbury to hear the war news? Roberts and Kitchener must have arrived in South Africa by now and General Buller can stop blowing hot and cold. You have to fight a war to win it. Can't sit on the fence. He never commits more than a few of his troops at a time."

"I'm sure the general knows what he's doing. Who told you all this?"

"I read, Father. The newspapers. The wonderful thing about reading is you know what's going on."

"Good. I'll give you a book on the voice thing."

"I've read it. Two, actually. Housemaster caught me in the library and gave me a wallop."

"Then why ask me and your mother?"

"Oh, I don't know."

"You're smirking again, Harry. Go on and get your guinea fowl before I give you a wallop. We'll go in tomorrow. I want your mother to see the doctor. Don't forget to talk to Sam."

"Can we all stay at Meikles for the night?"

"Yes, we can."

"Even George?"

"Even George."

"It's not fair."

"Nothing in life is fair, Harry. You'll find that out soon enough."

EARLY THE NEXT MORNING, when Harry was talking to Sam, Sarie Mostert opened the door to her banished hut and knew something was wrong. All four of her dogs were quiet but alert. There was no one about and she could feel the emptiness of the farm. The children came from behind and each put a hand in hers and the three of them listened to the silence.

"Elijah," she called into the stillness, and then to herself, "Not even Elijah, that's bad."

"Go inside," she said to her twins. "The blacks have gone."

"Where've they gone, Mummy?" asked Klara.

"How must I know?"

"Are they coming back?" asked Griet.

"No, I think they're not."

"Who's going to work the farm?"

"We are, best we can."

"But I'm only five."

"Griet, you're going to have to be like a man on the farm. Pretend you're seven or eight."

"Can I be seven or eight?" asked Klara.

"Of course you can, silly. We're twins. If I'm seven or eight so are you."

"Then, Mrs Seven-year-old, please take your sister and go and feed the pigs and then come to the kitchen."

"You think Ouma has gone?"

"She'll be there."

INSIDE THE KITCHEN, the mother of the three youngest sons of Ezekiel Oosthuizen sat stone still. She heard the white trash Frikkie had brought back from Pretoria open the door and still she refused to speak. Not being married was an abomination. The children and the mother had not even been christened, that much she had found out from her eldest son. And now the war had left them alone. God had deserted Helena Crouse who was now Helena Oosthuizen. God had left her alone in hell. Biting back tears of fear, her white knuckles gripping the edge of the kitchen table, she turned and glared at the white trash that was putting wood in the side of the stove below the big kettle to kindle new flames. The girl was dirty to the core, unclean in the sight of God, and how her Frikkie had brought a whore into his home was a matter for Frikkie and his God.

The girl came towards her as was the rule and put out her hands for inspection, showing the nails first and then the calloused palms, outwardly clean but inwardly filthy. They neither looked at each other nor spoke as was the rule, and with the flames of the wood adding to the heat of the new day, the kettle began to boil. From outside she heard the pigs snorting and grunting, squeaking with pleasure, and knew they were being fed and wondered who was feeding them, and then she knew. Elijah, faithful Elijah had come back to serve her as the tribe of Ham were ordained to serve in the Bible. Patiently she waited to hear the deep voice of Elijah chiding the hungry pigs, and all that came to her through the open door was the piping sound of the whore's children, bastards till the day they died and went to hell to join their mother in the fire of eternal damnation. Then the truth dawned slowly and surely... The bastards were feeding her pigs.

The irony of the woman's comprehension was not lost on Sarie as she put the freshly made pot of coffee on the kitchen table, the table scrubbed almost white by the blacks. She had wiped the pot to make sure nothing spilt and the four mugs, two big and two small, waited for the woman's attention next to the bowl of sugar. No one had milked the cow so the small pot of cream was missing from the table. The small woman was as neat as a pin, even so early in the morning, the full black dress that fell past her ankles buttoned to the middle of her neck, just below the green velvet ribbon that matched the green eyes. Sarie, always generous to a fault, thought the woman must have been pretty as a girl. While she stood waiting for her coffee, she heard the girls come back from the pig pens and guessed correctly the moment when her dogs would bark with pleasure and the twins would start chasing the dogs in circles. The feeling of joy and wellbeing swelled inside... Everything she loved in the world was happy. And then the feeling sank, and she turned her head away from the woman now pouring coffee as the pain of memory pricked behind her eyes as she thought of Billy.

Taking the two small mugs in one hand and her own in the other she went out of the kitchen as silently as she had come. The dogs raced off away from the children, two of them trying to jump on each other's backs while the one with the black and white tail nipped at her sister's back legs trying to herd them, a throwback instinct to some lost pedigree. As always Sarie warned the twins the coffee was hot and as always the hot coffee bit their tongues. They sat together on the bench under the mango tree and slowly drank the sweet coffee. Behind them, a morning dove called and called.

THE WOMAN LOOKED at them through the kitchen window. The girl was simply dressed with the puff sleeves almost to her elbows, the gown faded with sun and washing. A flush of jealousy saturated her body bringing out sweat under her armpits and down the cleavage between her breasts. She had tried so hard to give Ezekiel a daughter to replace the one her predecessor had lost, dying herself. With a will stronger than iron she controlled herself. The girl's hair was pulled back and showed an oval face with a small sweet mouth and small pink ears, and the smile the girl gave to her running dogs and then to her daughters wrenched at the tight fury of her jealousy. The girl was pretty, she could see that from the safety of the kitchen window, and the bastards, swinging their shoeless feet under the bench, were as pretty as any little girls Helena had seen in her life. And then a terrible thought came and lived for one brief moment... If only the little girls were her grandchildren and Sarie her daughter.

ACROSS THE CLEAR HIGHVELD, Sarie heard the jangle of the horses' bits and knew the reason why the blacks had fled into the bush. The twins heard the faint sound and stopped playing with the dogs. The morning dove, high in the blue-green trees behind the buildings, stopped singing. The bush waited, and the dogs turned to face the danger. Sarie told them to wait and all four dogs sat down on their haunches. Sarie could see the woman looking across at them through the closed kitchen window.

"Maybe this time we will have to speak to each other," she said, giving her thoughts the sound of her voice. The dog with the black and white tail turned and looked at her.

"What is it, Mummy?" asked Griet.

"Horsemen. Probably soldiers. Go and tell Ouma. She has to be ready."

"Who are they?" asked Klara.

"I don't know."

Neither of the twins moved from the shade of the mango tree. Sarie watched down the track. When the slouch hats of the riders rose from the ground into view and then the horses, the dogs, frightened by the number of horsemen, turned and ran back, their eyes pleading with their mistress to run with them away from the unknown.

"They're Boers," said Sarie. The dust around the horsemen swirled between the animals' legs and over the rifles in the saddle holsters, enveloping the motley group of men dressed as they would have been to go to work on their farms.

"Children, go into the room... Now!"

Sarie stood up from the bench and waited.

"Whose farm is this?" demanded a man as the horses stopped in the yard, all but the leader getting down... The man found it easier to intimidate people from a height.

"Ezekiel Oosthuizen."

"General Cronjé requests food for his army."

"Requests or demands?"

"Same thing. Are you Mrs Oosthuizen?"

"Of course not."

The man sniggered. He could see white trash wherever he found it. "Where are your blacks to help us round up the animals?"

"They ran away."

One of the unmounted men had found the pigs. The squealing and honking started all over again. Sarie hoped her dogs were far enough away and out of sight. By the time the ordnance wagon rolled into the yard the pigs were trussed, the bags of grain from last year were in the yard and Sarie was still alone under the mango tree. She counted the bags of grain and knew they had left them nothing. The chickens squawked as they ran for their lives and still the woman stayed in the kitchen looking out of the window.

"I'm sorry," said the man, "it's the war. Same for all of us. There is going to be a big battle. Many men will die. You will be alive. It's the war. Ezekiel Oosthuizen, the preacher, he will understand." The man leant down from his horse and chucked Sarie under the chin. "It's the war," he said again.

When the morning dove began to sing an hour later the farm was still and empty and Sarie sat on the bench under the mango tree. She was smiling. All four of her dogs, tails between their legs, were slowly walking towards her across the yard. By the time they reached her, she was on her knees hugging the dogs.

Inside the kitchen, still staring out of the window, Helena was paralysed with fear. All the sharpness of her tongue had gone with the pigs and chickens, the grain, the cows she had seen them herd away between the riders. To make it worse, the girl had stopped playing with her dogs and was staring across at her from under the mango tree. Only when the girl went into the hut she shared with her children did Helena break the spell of her paralysis. For half an hour she hoped the girl would come and tell her what had happened.

ELIJAH HEARD the dove and knew the soldiers were not coming back. Inside the maize field, his family crouched with their few possessions.

"It is time to go," he said to his three wives and four of his children. "The soldiers have taken the food."

"Where are we going?" asked his third wife.

"Home."

"This is our home."

There were fourteen of them hiding in the stand of maize that grew about the women's heads, the youngest child asleep, wrapped on her mother's back with a piece of cloth. Elijah and two of his remaining sons carried hunting rifles and water skins. It would take them many weeks to walk to the coast where the river washed into the sea.

"What about the woman?" asked his second wife who was the same age as Helena.

"It is better we go. There is no food. Her God will look after her. The preacher always said that God was on his side. You are my family. They were our masters. Now we must be our own masters and go back to the tribe."

"But I am not Xhosa," said the three wives together.

"You as my family will be welcome."

"We are afraid," said the senior wife.

"It's the war," said Elijah, "each must look after his own. We are going home. Come, before the dogs find us again."

And Elijah, with his gun at the trail, led them out of the maize field and by nightfall they were off the land he had ridden around so many years before with Ezekiel Oosthuizen.

"We could have stayed," said one of his son's wives.

"And your men would have been digging trenches for the Boers," said Elijah, "When the British come to take back Kimberley they would have killed your husband for helping the Boers. This is a white man's war. Let them kill each other."

TWO DAYS after Alison had a miscarriage with their fourth child, Barend came home from the neighbouring farm with his right eye shut and swollen and Tinus Oosthuizen knew that his peace and quiet was over. The boy's nose had been bleeding and his shirt was torn down the back. The boy was eight years old and already in the wars. His young sister looked at her father with acute disapproval.

"This is all your fault," said four-year-old Tinka and Tinus had to suppress a wish to laugh at the brazenness of the little girl looking up at him with her hands on her hips. Instead, he picked her up to get a closer look into the slate-grey eyes below the big eyelashes. "Put me down," she screamed and pulled his beard.

"What happened?" he said gently, putting her on the garden table that sat alone with a bench under the oak tree.

"Thys du Plessis beat him up."

"But Thys is twelve. His father would never let him fight an eight-year-old."

"Barend started the fight."

"Tinka, don't tell stories. A year, two years Thys will be a man."

"He said you are for the British. That our mummy's British. That your mummy was British."

Barend, talking for the first time since the beating, looked at his father. "I said you were for the Boers. That many Oosthuizens are fighting for the Boers. Then he said you are a coward for not going to fight like his father and I hit him."

"Has Magnus joined Scheepers?"

"There's going to be a big battle near Kimberley. The Boers have men down here looking for recruits. The British are sending train after train to the front with soldiers. Thys said Cape Town was full of British troops and it wasn't fair. If I was older, I would go and fight for the Boers."

"It's not our war, Barend. We are British subjects living in the Cape which is a British colony. Any British subject caught fighting for the Boers become rebels and are hanged if they are caught. The British Empire is the biggest empire the world has ever seen. We Boers are not only fighting Britain. There are Canadian and Australian troops with Roberts right now. Never start a fight you can't win, son, however right you are. It's the first principle of survival. Afterwards, you find a way to get your own back and if you are right, you will. The British are going to win this war however clever the Boers have been up till now, and any Cape Boers going out with Scheepers will be hanged by the neck."

"Then Thys was right. You are a coward."

"Barend, you are my son."

"No, I'm not anymore."

With his hand in his sister's and his dignity intact, the boy turned his back and walked away towards the gabled house.

"Oh my God," said Tinus sitting heavily on the wooden bench. "Now what do I do?"

As was his habit, Tinus walked, but the problem grew larger as he thought through the alternatives. In frustration, he longed for the solitude of the lone hunter before Sebastian had joined him in the hunt. The months of uncomplicated happiness were never as well appreciated at the time. There had been no one to look after or worry about other than himself, and the two blacks who followed his trail and cut the great tusks from the elephant carcass and sat wordless but comfortable with him at night around the fire, listened to the symphony of Africa without a worry in any of their minds, the great heaven of stars high above them, layer upon layer in the universe of God. And when the men spoke it was men's talk of hunting and finding food, and the problems of other people were nowhere in their minds. In the early times, he had stayed out in the bush for two years without speaking English or Afrikaans, as content as the herds of animals that roamed the great empty space of Africa. Now his wife was miserable, his half-made child buried in the earth, his eldest son was black and blue defending his honour, his daughter thought she hated him, the one half, the McDonald half, was fighting with the other half, the Oosthuizen's half, that made him who he was and the dilemma was tearing him apart. All he wanted was to be alone in peace on the banks of the Zambezi River with the fish eagles calling and the river running smoothly by his side.

At the stables he saddled his horse and rode out away from the house, trying to run away from his problems, but the further and harder he rode, so the problems stayed and festered in his mind.

After two hours and without a solution he turned his horse and rode back to face his troubles. There was life and death, these were certain; and then there was honour and duty, right and wrong, hope and despair, and these were the ones he no longer understood.

THE CURTAINS WERE DRAWN TIGHTLY, hiding the day, but light seeped into the big room with the great bed and canopy, and Alison felt more miserable than at any time she had ever known and the tears flowed on and on. All her life had gone with the child she yearned to hold and comfort but had buried deep in the dark earth like the tomb she wanted for her room to become in the depth of her pain. She wanted to die. If life made so much pain, she wanted to die. If so much beauty turned so quickly to so much pain, she wanted to die. The tap on the door was far away and then he was standing beside the bed and she hated him. The cause of her pain.

"Go away," she said, loud and clear and turned her wet face into the pillow, hiding her words. Her child was dead. There was nothing he or anyone else could do.

THE DAY MOVED on to its own conclusion and the sun set behind the mountains and the valley darkened with the shadow of the sun and the birds called; the black ibis flew high in flocks, their loud, harsh cries accompanying their flight. The light faded and the day was gone and no one came to his bench under the oak until it was very dark in the hour before the moon had risen and the stars had found their power of light. The words behind him came like the words of God, and for a long moment he listened before he turned.

"I have a message from your brother Ezekiel, Tinus Oosthuizen. Your people need you. A skilled hunter like you. You must come with us north. The *volk* is going north to fight... You can't stay here any longer. You know that yourself. You'll feel much better when you are committed. Magnus du Plessis and the others are waiting for us. The wives will look after each other. Bring your horse and rifle. When the moon rises we ride for Kimberley. Now, let us pray, you and I."

"Who are you?"

"GJ Scheepers. The British call us the Cape Rebels... Now, let us pray that God will deliver us and our people."

5

FEBRUARY 1900

hilst six thousand British cavalry led by the 9th and 16th Lancers with pennants snapping above the swirling dust were cutting through the Boer line of defence opening the way to Kimberley, Kei was opening the first box of Martini-Henry rifles that Zwide had helped to carry into the cave seven years earlier. Sarie's dog sniffed at the oily paper covering the guns and lost interest. The skeleton wrapped in a black ox-skin sat behind the rifles against the wall, and alongside was a leopard skin and an induna's head-ring. For all that day while General John French's cavalry was sabring the Boers and then riding the last miles to relieve Kimberley, Kei and his four companions, with flaming torches looking into every crevice and cranny, searched for the gold of Lobengula, last King of the Matabele. All they found of the king's wealth was three huge tusks of ivory left around the king's burial shroud.

At the mouth of the cave, the five men made camp looking north to the Zambezi River. Carried on the wind came the sound of continuous thunder.

"The spirit of the king is warning us to go away!" said the man the British had called Shaka. The Zulu was terrified of the ancestors. He spoke in Afrikaans, their common language.

"It's a big river," said the Ndebele.

"What big river?" asked Bow-legs, the Sotho.

"The Zambezi. I had a friend who had a friend who saw the river plunge over into the great hole in the ground, sending the river water into clouds. You hear the smoke that thunders."

The second Sotho shook his head in disbelief. "It is God speaking."

They were all silent as the sun sinking behind them poked yellow and red fingers through the clouds, leaving pale patches of duck-egg blue, clear and ethereal. Somewhere towards the sound of thunder, now a constant roar as the wind turned full in their direction, a lion roared and was answered from afar. As the sky behind them lost its colour, the lions roared on and on. Many birds in the mopane forest below the cave called to tell their partners where they were. When the birds of the day were quiet, the owls began to hoot. Kei fed the fire in silence and the flames rose, drawing light up the gnarled tree that had grown out of a crack in the rock and would shade their camp from the sun during the day. The dog Sarie had given Kei sat panting away from the fire at the rim of the light, its tongue hanging limp and dripping sweat.

While General French was drinking iced champagne with Cecil Rhodes in the Kimberley Club (the Boers having melted away from their siege trenches once the heavy cavalry had punched a hole through Cronjé's miles of defence), the five men agreed the black ox-skin covered the king and that the gold of Lobengula had never existed. They cooked the small buck Kei had shot and skinned at first light. By the time the moon rose, all five men and the dog were fast asleep.

When Kei woke with the sun on his face, the fire was white ash and the dog was nowhere to be seen. Expecting the dog to bound back at any moment, Kei led the five horses down to the stream that flowed out of the side of the hill and let them drink. Two eagles circled the sky silently looking for prey.

"Where's Blackdog?" asked Shaka.

"He'll be around," said Kei more confidently than he felt. Then he called for the dog at the top of his voice, the name echoing far into the king's burial cave.

After a while of calling, Blackdog trotted out of the cave looking pleased with himself. In his mouth was Zwide's head-ring which he dropped at Kei's feet.

"It's an omen," said Shaka. "The dog is telling us something. The ancestors have spoken to the dog. Why would an induna leave his head-ring behind, the symbol of his power? He would never do that at the time of the king's burial. He must have come back. And why did he come back? To take the gold. Any Matabele warrior will recognise the ring. There is gold or why did he come back and leave his head-ring as a symbol of his right? Whichever induna wore that ring on his head knows where he put the gold.

He moved it, you see, to stop anyone from the king's burial party coming back and stealing the gold."

"You think a Matabele will tell me anything?" asked Kei.

"They will tell me," said the Ndebele. "We are the same tribe."

TATENDA, Harry's childhood companion, had turned twenty-four at the time war broke out between the Boers and the British. After years of humping carcasses on his back, his shoulders had grown broad and his jet-black skin shone with rude health. The butchery had grown and was the largest in Bulawayo and if the pay was poor, the pickings were good and none of his friends went hungry. The new town of Bulawayo, some miles from the dead king's kraal, was flourishing, spurred on by British agents buying supplies for the biggest army that had ever left British shores.

When the word reached the butchery, spreading like wildfire down the wide main street, Tatenda knew that deliverance was not to come from a British defeat at the hands of the Boer. Kimberley had been relieved and Cronjé's army was caught in a loop of the Modder River. With Cronjé crushed there would be nothing to stop the British from capturing Bloemfontein, the capital of the Free State, and after that Pretoria, the capital of the Transvaal. Tatenda knew it was the beginning of the end and he cursed as the yoke of the British Empire dropped more firmly over his neck. Each day he translated the English papers for Zwide, never once thanking Emily for teaching him to read and write. With the first Chimurenga a distant memory, the bitterness of defeat had soured to a constant pain. All that kept him working was the knowledge of Lobengula's gold, the wealth that would one day buy them guns to win the second Chimurenga and chase the British out of Africa once and for all.

They had built their huts along a small stream a half-hour walk from Jack Slater's butchery, the one-time temporary administrator turned businessman. After dropping Harry's .410 shotgun and fleeing across the Mazoe River, Tatenda had wandered through the bush living as best he could, one of many fugitives fleeing the wrath of British justice and the certainty of being hanged by his neck from the nearest tree if they knew he had attacked the white man's compound. He ate locusts and mopane worms to keep himself alive and a year later thought it safe enough to look for a job in Bulawayo, far enough away from Salisbury and the Mazoe Valley. His bitterness in defeat came to Zwide's attention as nothing that happened in the black village that grew next to the new wealth in Bulawayo was lost to the old induna and quietly, without

Tatenda knowing the reason, he was told to walk to Jack Slater's butchery where he would find a job chopping and humping the white man's meat. Only after six months of hard work was he told that Zwide had been Lobengula's general and the seed of liberation still burnt in the general's heart. By the time French relieved Kimberley, Tatenda was one of three people who knew where Zwide had moved the king's gold and the gold was to be used to liberate the Matabele and the Shona from the grip of Cecil Rhodes. Under oath to the ancestors, Tatenda swore to keep alive the dream of the liberation... Emily's kindness in bringing up an orphan had been returned with hatred. To Tatenda, the kindness was patronage and if there was one thing Tatenda hated more than anything else in his life, it was being patronised.

JACK SLATER HAD WORKED out that administering a small part of the British Empire was not going to make him rich and, despite the social stigma back in England, he had gone into trade. After a brief fling working for De Beers in Kimberley, and a year after hanging the ringleaders of the Shona rebellion, he had resigned from the employ of Cecil Rhodes and found his way to Bulawayo where he had spent six months getting drunk in three out of the four bars, the Cecil having thrown him out for bad behaviour. He had grown a thick beard, his hair was down his back, and no one would have believed him if he had told the drunks he sat with that back in 1896 he had taken over the administration of Rhodesia while Jameson was fanning the flames of what was now the war raging south of the Limpopo River. Every old timer and quite a few young timers had stories of glory in their past when the alcohol made them brave and before they ran down the last of the evening into maudlin drunkenness.

By the time Kimberley was relieved he was thirty-three, called himself Jack Slattery for safety when he remembered, never wrote to his family in Tonbridge, and was rich and getting much richer. By the time he was forty, he would have enough money to go home, shave off his beard, find his family, revert to Jack Slater and buy himself a nice country estate in the middle of Kent. The Jack Slater when he finished would appear from nowhere and become a country gentleman and ride to hounds. With his wealth, he would then look for a rich wife, have a large family and forget Fran Cotton... He always thought of her as Fran Cotton, single, instead of Fran Shaw, married, to assuage the guilt of having an affair with a married woman that broke all the rules he had once so carefully lived by and had thought so essential.

The day Kei and three friends walked into Bulawayo trailed by a black dog, he had decided the only rule that mattered in life was being rich.

KEI HAD WISELY LEFT the horses and tack in an abandoned Matabele village with the guns. Shaka had been left behind to look after the animals.

The first Matabele to be shown the head-ring ran away without saying a word. The second tried to grab at the ring and was hit hard in the face by Kei's right fist. A day later one of the horses went lame and had to be shot. Blackdog, sensing the animosity, took to whimpering at the sight of strangers. On the fourth day, the Ndebele who had been asking the questions was found dead hanging from a tree. In the dark of the night, Kei, his three remaining friends and Blackdog left town making a trail pointing south and back to the raging war. Five miles from the nearest hut, Kei found a small stream that would serve his purpose. Leading the way in the light of a sickle moon he turned the horses north, the hanging and the dead horse convincing him even more of the existence of Lobengula's gold. Still in his pocket was Zwide's head-ring. The lust for gold was so strong he could see the yellow coins.

THE BOER LINE was stretched seven miles along the Modder River. Karel Oosthuizen, along with the brothers and father, had individually dug themselves in along the high lip that looked across the open veld and confronted the British. In the protection of the river bank, and close to the water, huddled the women and children and the bellowing oxen. At first, the British had sent cavalry against the flank which had been shot down by the well-entrenched Boers. With the wagons in laager and clear targets for the British guns, the bombardment began and Karel pulled his rifle down into the bottle-shaped hole he had dug for himself and backed into a bigger hole deep enough to withstand the British shells. In the dark and noise, there was no way of knowing if anyone else was alive. For days the guns blasted the trapped Boers and every time the artillery fell silent and Karel put his head and rifle out of the hole to defend an infantry attack, there were fewer and fewer burghers able to fight.

ON THE SIXTH day of the siege, when the Boers' laager had shrunk to two miles along the north ridge of the river, Billy Clifford watched the carnage through binoculars from a kopje half a mile on the south side of the swollen river and was sick to his stomach. If war was indeed an extension of politics, he wanted nothing of either of them. After two days of frontal attacks that had decimated British ranks, Roberts had arrived to take command from Kitchener and the little man standing close to Billy on the kopje had surrounded the Boers and bombarded them day and night with everything from pom-poms to twelve-pounders to 4.7-inch naval guns. Ammunition wagons exploded, towering mushrooms higher than trees rose from the exploding earth, green lyddite smoke drifted over the carnage and even though the rain had swollen the river and washed away the carcasses of oxen and men, the death stench was so strong Billy still wore a handkerchief over his nose and mouth. Below the north ridge, and hidden from Billy by the three hundred feet drop to the river bed, were the Boer oxen, women and children among the trees that drank from the river, and many of the shells fired at the Boer trenches on the high ridge had fallen short. For Billy the fearful bellowing of dumb animals was the worst of the horror as the seventh, eighth and ninth days continued in hell and then finally, the Boers had had enough and the white flag rose from the rubble of smashed wagons and earth and the guns fell silent.

On the tenth day, with Cronjé riding into the British lines to take breakfast with Lord Roberts and negotiate his conditions of surrender, Billy watched the confusion and was pleased to see some of the Boers slip away.

The battle of Paardeberg was over.

"Please God they give up now," said Billy to a correspondent from the *Cape Argus* who was standing next to him.

"Don't be silly. Roberts has won the big war but now comes the little one. Why do the British want our land when they have so much of their own? The British can have the rest of Africa for all we care."

"You are a Boer, sir?"

"A Cape Boer and for the moment a loyal subject of her Majesty the Queen. But when the hit-and-run guerrilla war starts I may be forced to change my mind."

"You think they'll go on fighting after the British enter Bloemfontein and Pretoria?"

"To the bitter end."

WHILE BILLY WAS WRITING his daily report to be cabled to the *Irish Times*, Karel found his pony hidden on a long tether in the hills north of the Modder River. At the end of the stretch of the leather thong, was a small mountain stream.

"Get up on the back," he said to Piers in Afrikaans.

"The horse will not carry both of us."

"He will for a while and then we will walk."

"Where are we going?"

"Away from the British. Come, young brother. We've both lost weight in the days of hell and my pony has been grazing good grass."

Neither of them mentioned their father nor their brothers.

THE WIDE-BRIMMED HAT cast shade over both Sarie Mostert's shoulders, the burning sun being directly over her head. Beyond and behind her the very earth of the farm was dead. Nothing moved. The tall blue gums behind the buildings, the mango tree above the bench, the brown, sun-scorched grass, the dust in the farmyard, nothing moved and the wind was far away. Even the old lady had stopped watching her through the kitchen window. Her only hope, the badly tended stands of maize, had gone in a bushfire and she wondered who was still alive in the world to have started the fire to flush out the game. Behind the mango tree, the pig pens and chicken run were as silent as a tomb. In the dark shade of the mango tree on the wooden bench, the six-year-old twins were playing a secret game. For half an hour neither of them had torn their mother's heart by complaining they were hungry.

Picking up the heavy water buckets after her short rest, Sarie pushed open the gate to the kitchen garden and sloshed water on rows of vegetables, wilted and half dead, scorched by the summer heat, the pieces of old sacking she had propped over the rows unable to stop the deadly penetration of the sun. There was no doubt in Sarie's mind. They were all going to starve.

After the fire, they had eaten for a day before the carcasses of burnt porcupine had rotted in the heat. Now the burnt black earth as far as she could see around the farm to the distant hills was empty and silent as the windless day. Even her dogs, who dug for the rats and moles, had given up the hunt. There was nothing to eat, not even grass or leaves from the trees. With empty buckets, she crossed again to the well where she stopped and listened.

"You hear that noise, Mummy?" asked Griet. "That's thunder. It's going to rain."

'Or guns', thought Sarie. "Before the sun goes down, we will go to the river and look for frogs and river snails."

Even the birds had left the burnt and barren land. Two of the dogs watched her. They were skin and bone. For three days she had caught nothing in her traps. She ignored the distant rumbling, not daring to wish for rain and the new shoots that would spring so quickly from the blackened earth.

KAREL AND PIERS looked over the burnt black earth that stretched to the patch of distant buildings, silent in the shimmering heat, the gum trees indistinguishable from the house and barns. The brothers were silent either side of the horse they had not ridden for the past three days.

"There's no one there," said Piers after a long pause. "You think there's just you and me, Karel?"

"Ma will be there. And the blacks. They're inside away from the sun."

"There are no cows or horses. Nothing's moving."

"We'll get to the river and rest the horse."

"All that rain we had at Paardeberg and nothing here. God has strange ways."

The crack of thunder brought up the horse's head.

"Maybe not. God is always watching."

"You think we should pray?"

"Not till we reach the river. Without water, this horse will die before the sun goes down."

"You think Pa and Frikkie are really dead?" asked Piers.

"Only God can be sure in all that carnage."

"And the half-brothers?"

"Only God."

"Pa said God would give us victory."

THE LIZARD WAS five feet long from the tip of its tail and it had not eaten properly since the fire. Lying on a rock in the trees overlooking the river, the reptile was quite invisible. The dappling of the brown burnt leaves blended perfectly with the mottled scaliness of the lizard. The round, bulging eyes swivelled and watched for the slightest sign of prey and the big pouched belly swelled and sank perceptibly but not enough to warn the twins. On the other side of the river, all four dogs were digging furiously in the river bank. Further downstream Sarie had found two small frogs the size of an English penny with red striped legs; the big frogs that made so much noise after the rains had gone. The only sign of life was a pied kingfisher that sat high on a tree looking hopefully into the barren water. Even the crickets were silent, oppressed by the heat.

With the patience of millions of years of ancestry, the lizard waited, its claws gripping the rock. The mouth came open in expectation and the tail snapped once as the reptile launched itself at Griet's back bent over the water.

The dogs saw the movement as the lizard broke cover and, yelping with excitement, charged from rock to rock over the river, warning the twins who jumped into the river as the pack hurled their bodies at the green and orange reptile. By the time Sarie ran up the river over the rocks all four dogs had locked their teeth into the scaly lizard. The twins looked back at the fight from a rock in the middle of the river and yelled their treble excitement to the noise of grunting dogs. In the hope of drowning the dogs, the lizard tried to run to the water, thrashing at the dogs with its tail. The children backed off and plunged into the river while the dogs strained to keep the lizard out of the water, the sand between rock and river slimy with blood, the dogs silent in their desperation to hold their prey. Going into battle with her knife, Sarie plunged the blade into the lizard's neck, which spurted blood over her arm. Sarie stabbed three more times before the lizard gave up the fight for its life with the dogs' teeth locked in its sides and the round eyes pleading with pain. Slowly, very slowly life went out of the reptile's eyes. Plonked on her bottom in the wet river sand Sarie looked at the bloody blade of her knife. Ten minutes later the fear had drained from her body and she got up to skin their prize. The dogs watched her patiently as she stroked the blade over a smooth rock. First, she gutted the lizard, cut off the gallbladder and threw it in the river. The entrails she gave to her dogs, the heart, the liver and the kidneys, then she skinned the lizard. By the time the sun began to sink, the rumbling from the sky had gone away and the reptile's flesh was hanging in strips from a thorn tree. Sarie walked down to the river naked. In her hand was a piece of lizard flesh. Looking across the fading light she smiled to herself and threw the meat. The pied kingfisher dropped like a stone and by the time Sarie was floating on her back, she could see the bird high in the tree silhouetted by the violent red of the sunset, the piece of flesh clutched firmly in its claws.

AT FIRST, Karel thought the flickering light of Sarie's campfire was a trick of the sinking sun reflecting the red and orange from the surface of the river. He watched carefully until he was certain.

"Piers, that's a campfire down the river."

"Khaki," said Piers.

"Khaki would make noise. Leave the horse and come with me."

·   ·   ·

FIRST, the bitch brought its head up from its paws and listened, ears cocked. She'd always had the best hearing. Then the dogs half rose from the dry sand and turned their ears towards the sound Sarie could not hear. Looking into the eye of each dog in turn, she made them sit. The twins were fast asleep between the dogs and the flickering firelight showed their sweet faces. They had made camp in the cup of a giant rock where sand had washed in a past flood. The sand and the underlying rock were still warm from the day's sun. Taking her knife, Sarie crept out from the rocks and hid in the dark of the thorn thicket.

Ten minutes later she thought she heard a sound. The light had faded from the sky and the new moon would not be up for three hours. The planets were visible but not the stars. A piece of log on the fire broke and fell into the flames, sending sparks high into the black of the African night.

BY THE TIME Karel looked down on the curled and sleeping twins and the silent vicious eyes of the bitch and the three dogs, Sarie had the knife to Piers's throat. Then Karel laughed from ten yards away.

"It's not khaki, it's Frikkie's woman, but she's not there. Those are her dogs and the girls."

Piers, with strong hard fingers on his windpipe and a knife to his throat, made not a sound. Then the fingers slackened and the knife blade went away.

"I'm here," said Sarie and gave Piers a sharp shove towards his brother. She was poor white and trash and still kept her place.

"Why are you not at the farm?" asked Karel.

"No food. Your army took everything they could, and a bushfire burnt the rest."

"Where's Ma and the blacks?"

"The blacks went. Your Ma's at the house."

"Alone?"

"She's alone."

"Elijah went?"

"Kei first and then Elijah. He was frightened by your soldiers."

"Have the khaki been here?"

"No English."

The bitch and the dogs were standing high on their feet and only sank back when they recognised Piers and Karel by the light of the fire.

By the time Sarie had cooked the brothers strips of meat over the fire, the twins had still not woken from their dreams and Sarie was wondering how much worse her life could become. Her one protection, Frikkie, was dead. Then she shivered. With the sun down an hour, the temperature had plummeted. She got up and fed the fire with river flotsam to keep her children warm. Idly she softly stroked the head of the bitch while she stared into the fire.

"Now what am I going to do," she said to herself. The two men sat on the other side of the fire away from Sarie and the twins. The girls were still fast asleep, curled up around the dogs.

HELENA OOSTHUIZEN WAS certain her family was dead, and she did not care anymore. Death was better than being left alone on the farm and she had neither the will nor strength to go anywhere else. Even the girl had now gone with the twins and dogs and only the sound of thunder penetrated the house. The curtains in the bedroom where she had loved and born her children were closed. She had given up praying to her God weeks ago as all that her God had given her He had taken away. She had made her peace and was ready to die alone. She was tired and long past the stage of being hungry. Helena hoped to fall asleep and never wake in the mortal world. Smiling from the thought of distant memories, she began to pray for the last time. When she slept, the smile was still on her face.

Karel found her in the late afternoon and thought she was dead. Touching the back of his big, calloused hand gently to the side of her face, his heart raced when the warmth of life flowed back to him. Then his mother opened her eyes and smiled.

"I knew I'd join you today," she said. "Where are the others?"

"Piers is looking for you in the other rooms. Pa is dead and Frikkie."

"But I am dead so where are they?"

"No, Ma, you are alive. The khaki shelled us for nine days and Cronjé surrendered."

"Then let me die. I was dying. I went to sleep to die."

"No you didn't, little Mother." Gently, Karel picked his mother up from the bed, a weight he barely felt. "You are still going to see your grandchildren."

"What is that smell?"

"A stew of meat."

"You brought me food?"

"No, Frikkie's woman."

"She went away."

"To find you food. A giant lizard. The strips are dry and will feed us until I can make a plan."

"The girl came back? Put me down. I can walk. If I am alive, I can walk."

"Yes, Ma." He was smiling.

"Now don't burn the stew," was the first thing she said to Sarie. The twins gave her one look and ran back into the yard where the dogs were chasing each other.

THE BOER FORAGING party had not taken the hay and left alone in the barn, the horse began to eat steadily. The soft brown eyes, wet with happiness and brushed by large eyelashes, looked into Piers's eyes and they understood and welcomed their dependency.

That night the thunder broke overhead and lightning picked out the barren veld. When the rain broke on dry earth, the combination scented the air with the smell of rich earth. The next day was overcast, the ground soaked with rain, and Sarie's rows of scorched vegetables came to life.

On the third day, Karel took the horse and went hunting up in the hills where the streams broke from the granite outcrops. At the end of a day's hunting, across the back of the horse's rump, came the carcass of a female kudu and together they butchered the animal into strips of biltong. On the seventh day, when green shoots were springing from the veld and the sky was still overcast, the children and dogs had forgotten their hunger and the way of things had returned to normal; Sarie living in her hut like a servant, the men keeping their eyes from her body, and Helena ruling them all with her tongue. Isolated on the farm, the war was far away. Piers dug and planted another kitchen garden and as the game came back to eat the new grass and legumes, food was plentiful and the store of dried meat hanging in the barn away from the dogs was enough to feed them for weeks; and all the time Sarie waited to be told to go on her way.

Alone, she thought of Frikkie and felt nothing but thankfulness for the care and gentleness he had shown to her and the children. There had been no love, only a common need, Frikkie for a woman, Sarie for a roof over her head. Every time she tried to remember his face, the big man changed to the sensitive face of Billy Clifford, and she cried for her lost love as much as her lost protector. She let the days go by one after the other and waited for the future to take care of itself.

MAJOR JAMES BRIGANDSHAW'S new orders were to reconnoitre south of the railway lines deep into Boer territory, checking British maps for accuracy. The Mashonaland Scouts, seven in number, were dressed in the same dark grey and black uniforms with slouch hats that Sir Henry Manderville and Gregory Shaw had worn when they occupied Rhodesia with the Pioneer Column. The only difference for Henry and Gregory was the new Lee-Metford bolt action rifles that had replaced the Martini-Henrys of Johnson's column. James was dressed in the uniform of the Queen's Light Horse topped by a white pith helmet.

For ten days they had travelled south and had long discarded the British maps as unintelligible. A few blacks had moved away from them in the distance and the Boer farmhouses had been left well alone. In their saddlebags were strips of dried meat and they no longer made fires even during the day. By the time they came upon Ezekiel Oosthuizen's farm they were two hundred miles south of the railway. James had ridden ahead of the seven troopers and had broken out of the gorge that cut through the hills where Karel had shot his female kudu. With powerful binoculars he searched the valley below, focusing on the farmstead for a long time. A fire had recently swept through the valley and James was pleased there were no crops for the Boer army to confiscate. Through the charred black of the fire came the faint hint of green and he marvelled at the resilience of the African veld. Even after the troop caught up to him, he still searched down below for signs of life. James Brigandshaw was a good soldier and never broke the rules of training. 'Impatience in war,' his training officer had said at Sandhurst, 'kills more people than stealth. The most important part of any attack is reconnaissance.'

"Not a sign of life, old chap," he said to Henry Manderville as they sat their horses next to each other, looking down into the valley. "Not a horse or a cow. Cronjé's men foraged far from the Modder River by the looks of it. Now down there is what I call an isolated farm. Wonder what they did for a social life? Middle of bloody nowhere, old chap. Least you and Seb can go into Fort Salisbury and have a noggin or two."

"Not even the sign of blacks," said Henry having taken the binoculars. "No food. This war's going to be harder for the women and children than the fighting men. And the blacks? Where have they all gone? Thought there was something under that tree in the yard for a moment but probably a trick of the shade moving with the breeze."

"They won't give up," said Gregory Shaw. "Too many people have been hurt. A skirmish you can forgive and forget. Not full-scale war."

"They'll pack up once we take Bloemfontein and Pretoria," said Henry.

"Hope you're right, old chap. Now, I'm going to watch that farmhouse for another hour and if there's still no sign of life, we are going to make it home. Bet you chaps could do with a bath and a cooked meal. That place is so isolated no one can get within five miles of us without being seen. At night we'll bivouac away from the buildings. It's now four hours before sunset. Perfect. Bath, hot meal and sleep among those gum trees behind the house. Gregory, have a look, old chap. You know the drill as well as I do."

THE HEAT PRESSED down on the iron roof of the farmhouse making loud cracks from the expansion of the metal. Inside Sarie's hut the heat was stifling, but with the window and door tightly closed all day, it was cooler than the shade of the mango tree. The twins were too hot to do anything else than lying on their beds staring at the ceiling. In recognition of the intense heat, they had stopped talking to each other. The dogs, kicked out of the hut, were spread under the bench in the shade of the mango tree next to a large bowl of water put out for them by the twins. The three dogs and the bitch had given up swishing their tails at the flies and their eyes were closed.

In the house, Karel, lying on the bed he had used since he could first remember, was trying not to think. From the room next door he could hear Piers snoring and mentally wished him happy dreams. As he thought of his family, the pain pricked behind his eyes and alone, away from prying eyes, he let the tears flow and the pain of loss seep through his body. Finally, like always, he began to feel sorry for himself, as if they had left him as head of the family on purpose. Trying to think what to do, his thoughts went in circles. There was going to be no escape as the British were going to win the war, and even if he came out alive they would take the farm from him and give it to one of their soldiers. When he slept the heavy sleep of day, his nightmare continued, convoluted and incomprehensible.

THE EIGHT HORSES walked slowly towards the buildings shimmering ahead of them in the heat haze bouncing from the iron roofs. For the last time, James put up his hand for them to stop while he watched the buildings. He could see the dark green top of the mango tree but the trunk and bench were hidden by the barn. James's binoculars looked straight at the drawn curtain of Karel's bedroom. All the windows he could see were curtained.

"The owners have locked up and gone," he said and waved them forward.

. . .

THE BITCH OPENED her eyes first. Then she got up and moved out of the shade and looked around the barn. The horses were three hundred yards away. Frightened, the bitch ran back to the closed door of Sarie's hut and scratched, waking her instantly. She opened the door and followed her dog to the end of the barn. On top of the shimmering heat and dust, she could see the slouch hats of the Mashonaland Scouts, mistaking them for Boers. She crossed the yard back to the house and went in through the kitchen. She tapped lightly on Karel's door and the snoring stopped. She tapped again.

"Soldiers coming."

"Khaki?"

"Boer, I think. Wearing slouch hats."

Karel came out of the room with his Mauser.

"How far?"

"Close. Three, four hundred yards. You can see them through your window if you draw the curtains."

Back in the room, Karel pulled a corner of the curtain. "Hold the curtains like that," he said to Sarie and adjusted his binoculars to focus on the horsemen.

"Sarie, go tell Piers to go out the back and up-saddle. The officer is British. The troop's colonial. They won't hurt you or Ma but they'll kill me and Piers. And keep your dogs quiet."

With the greatest of care not to move the curtain, Karel got his hand on the catch and very slowly opened his bedroom window. Taking two books he wedged open a gap at the bottom of the curtain and slowly pushed out his rifle, bringing it to rest firmly on the windowsill. He could sight over his rifle perfectly at the British officer. Patiently he waited for Piers to ready the horse. They were coming towards him over the veld very slowly, conserving their horses.

'Even two up we'll get away on a fresh horse,' he said to himself. 'Those animals have been riding all day.'

RIDING DIRECTLY BEHIND JAMES BRIGANDSHAW, Gregory Shaw was thinking of Sing and India and the face he saw was still clear and beautiful. In all the many years they had been apart she had never aged a moment. The sound of the Mauser travelled just behind the bullet which cut a neat hole through James Brigandshaw's white pith helmet tracing a slight furrow through his hair before shattering Gregory's skull an inch below his hairline. The picture of Sing in his mind and his life was expunged in the same moment. The body slid from the horse.

Behind the house, two Boers on a single horse broke cover and James watched them go. Then he took off his topi and inspected the neat hole in both sides before putting it back on his head.

They rode into the farmyard.

"We'll bury him under those gum trees," said Henry Manderville.

"Yes. That'll be a good spot but it doesn't really make any difference now."

"Who were they?"

"Deserters, probably. What a bad show. Shot by a deserter."

"But he was in uniform. He'd have liked that."

"I suppose so."

THE BITCH and three dogs had slunk off with their tails between their legs well before the horses stopped under the mango tree. Helena Oosthuizen watched the enemy from her bedroom window and stood in full view, hoping they would shoot her there and then and have it over with. Even the thought of Karel and Piers getting away left her soul empty.

Standing back from her window, Sarie watched James take off his white hat and acknowledge the old woman standing at her bedroom window. The body of a dead soldier was slumped over a horse and far down the track, she could see her dogs trotting away from danger. Now the stock of dried meat they had so carefully hung in strips from the roof of the barn would be taken by the soldiers. Without the horse and rifle, they would be hungry even if the soldiers did not ransack the kitchen garden; the plants after the drought were too small to be eaten.

"BE careful she hasn't got a gun," said Henry, still holding the reins of Gregory Shaw's horse. "In the wars with the blacks the women fought alongside the men."

"Is she alone? We can't leave an old woman alone. Think of wild animals, the blacks. Anyway, she'll starve. If the Boers don't surrender, we'll have to do something with people like this. Not the gentlemanly thing to leave women helpless. We'll have to bring them in and feed them. Just staring at me. I can feel the hatred and her men have just killed my friend. No, old chap, this is not going to turn out to be a good war. Curse the gold and diamonds. We'd have all been better off without them, Boer and British."

"Can't run an empire without gold," said Henry.

"Anyway, we're here now so we'll have to finish the job. Take a ride around the back but make sure she doesn't try to shoot you. You speak any of their language, Henry?"

"Not a word. Tinus spoke English from his Scots mother and anyway, the English never bother to learn other people's languages. Rather pointless, really. Sooner or later they all speak English."

"Don't get far without English. After you come back, we'll dig a grave for Gregory. Damn shame. Damn shame."

WHEN THE SOLDIER opened her door to look inside, she was waiting for him with the knife and the twins were under the one large bed.

"There's another one here," he shouted and closed the door. "Got a knife. Young one dressed in rags. Do they have white servants? What shall I do, sir?"

"Open the door and take the knife away," said James.

"Yes, sir."

When the door opened again, Sarie was standing with the twins holding her hands. Ignoring the trooper, Sarie let out a piercing whistle and watched the dogs far away stop in their tracks. Sarie whistled again, and the dogs trotted back.

'They can't be any worse than the Boer soldiers,' she said to herself and walked out into the heat of the sun, the twins on either side of her each still clutching a hand. Over by the gum trees, they were digging a grave.

6

JUNE 1900

*T*he chief of British Intelligence in South Africa inspected James Brigandshaw's topi with mild interest, poking his index finger through the hole in the front before handing the pith-helmet back across the desk. Colonel Hickman had arrived in Cape Town three weeks earlier and was red raw round the neck from his exposure to the African sun. His nose above the large, drooping moustache was peeling badly and the little red cheeks between the sideburns and the moustache were the colour of a ripe tomato. The whole face had fascinated James for the full five minutes of the interview.

"What are you staring at, sir?" snapped the new colonel, bringing James back from his reverie... Everything he had to say was in the report on the mahogany desk.

"Sorry, sir. Been in the saddle too many weeks. Mind wanders off."

"Officers whose minds wander off are a danger to their men, Brigandshaw. A danger to their men and don't you forget it. Trooper Shaw would probably be alive if your mind hadn't wandered. Shot by a deserter! Bad enough these Boers are uneducated with not a gentleman between them. But you, Brigandshaw. A British officer. A gentleman. Royal Military Academy of Sandhurst. And you lose a soldier shot by a deserter."

There had never been any point in arguing with a senior officer sitting behind a desk and James let the verbal abuse pass over his head, convinced the tomato nose was about to explode with the tomato cheeks.

"And *stop staring, sir!*"

"And will that be all, sir?"

"And no it won't! Sit down! You have not been dismissed. Luckily for all of us, this war is all but over with the British flag flying over Pretoria. So this nonsense in your report about protecting Boer women can be ignored."

"Have Smuts, de Wet and de la Rey surrendered?" asked James, showing interest for the first time.

"They will now Lord Roberts has taken Pretoria."

"The Boer commandos can muster twenty thousand men."

"They will surrender without Kruger and their capital."

"Yes, sir." He was going to say something about telling that to General Smuts and thought better.

"You may take some leave, Major Brigandshaw. You can go back to England with Lord Roberts if you wish to. General Kitchener will be taking command."

"Before the war is over?"

"Are you questioning your senior officers?"

"They may not have been deserters."

"What are you talking about?"

"The two that shot Captain Shaw."

"He was a trooper. Two up on a horse. Why didn't you ride after them?"

"Our horses were blown."

"There are going to be some changes around here, you mark my words."

"I would prefer to go north. I have brothers and Captain Shaw..."

"He was a trooper. Man lucky not to be cashiered. Consorting with natives. Can you imagine what would happen to the empire if every Englishman hobnobbed with the natives? We have to remain aloof to maintain our authority. You can leave now, Brigandshaw. Deserters, dammit. Shot the wrong man, I'd say. Report to me in three months, by when I hope to have forgotten this report. Shot by deserters. What on earth has the British Army come to?"

THEY RODE NORTH TOGETHER. Henry Manderville had been discharged from the Mashonaland Scouts on the grounds of ill-health. He was too old at forty-eight for the rough life of a soldier and with Gregory Shaw dead, the fight had gone out of him. Being in another man's company for so many years was a habit and for Henry, good habits were hard to break. He was too old to make new friends in the troop and too old to keep up with them in the field. They had tolerated the old man but never tried to make him a friend. And with the troop given leave, he was too old to follow them around the bars and whorehouses of the mining camp they called Johannesburg. His books and butterfly net called. His daughter and grandchildren called. Even his small home with the 'pull and let go' invention of Mr Crapper was all he wanted. He was tired and counted most of his life to be over. Most, nearly all of what he wanted from life was in the past and when he reached the farm on the banks of the Mazoe River, he was going to put his feet up, relax and think of his dead wife and live with her in his memory and let the rest of the world go by unnoticed. If people wanted to have wars and kill each other, they could do it on their own without the help of Henry Manderville.

"You know what, James," he said, "being out of uniform and going home is rather pleasant. And the fact is, I really do think of Rhodesia as home. So let's try not to bump into a Boer commando before we cross the Limpopo River. Do you really think this war is going to be over in the next few weeks?"

"No. All we did was capture Cronjé and five thousand men. The rest are undefeated. They don't need Pretoria and Bloemfontein to fight a war. They can play hide and seek with us in this vast country till the cows come home. And they won't forget defeating a regular British army at Spion Kop. Kruger's run off to Switzerland with the Boer treasury and the young men have taken command. We've lived off the land for months and made a damn nuisance of ourselves. And we have another problem. We either leave their women and children to the misery of starvation and the natives, or we bring them into camps and feed them ourselves. I can't get the eyes of those little girls out of my mind. They looked so alike. You think they were twins, Henry?"

"Most likely."

"Leaving white children all alone like that will give the natives the wrong idea. Wasn't long ago the British Army were protecting our people and the Boers from the Zulus and the Xhosas. This blasted war is bad for the white man's image. There's more to this than Boer and British. There's the native question, one that's far bigger for all the white men in Africa... I think we'll make camp by that stream over there. The sun's almost down. Be across the Limpopo tomorrow and then we can make a fire... It's beautiful, isn't it?"

"What?" asked Henry looking ahead to the river.

"Africa."

TWO MILES TO THE WEST, a group of Boer commanders had gathered to discuss the fall of Pretoria and to decide the future conduct of the war. Tinus Oosthuizen, slimmed down by months of dry meat and living in the saddle, had seen and watched the two men for half an hour through his binoculars as they dismounted by the stream and began to make camp.

"They look like Boers and ride like Boers on a short stirrup but why aren't they making a fire to brew the coffee?" he said to Magnus du Plessis. GJ Scheepers, the leader of the Cape rebels, was in the talks with the other generals, and Tinus as a chief scout was in charge of the sentries and responsible for making sure the generals were not caught off guard even though the Northern Transvaal was firmly controlled by the Boers.

"Maybe they don't like coffee. Maybe they are tired."

"Funny thing is even at this distance one of them reminds me of an old friend of mine. Just the way he walks."

"A lot of people walk the same way... You think we can resupply ourselves from the British?"

"Hit-and-run. Guerrilla war."

"The line's cut to Delagoa Bay. How can we survive? All right for us. Our wives and children are in the Cape where there's food and protection. What about the women on the farms?"

"The men can go home and rest, check on the places. Provided the natives don't rise up there won't be a problem... I want to ride down and check those two men."

"By the time you get there, it will be dark. If they're still there in the morning, we'll have a look. There's roast sheep on the fire tonight and I haven't eaten mutton for a very long time."

"I don't like animals behaving strangely. In the bush it means danger. And those two men down there should have made a fire by now to keep off wild animals even if they don't drink coffee."

"You worry too much, Tinus."

"What kept me alive in the bush for so long. In the bush, anything unusual is to be feared."

WITHIN MINUTES of the sun sinking behind the hills, the highveld temperature plummeted. Like cows chewing the cud, they both munched the dry meat until it was soft enough to swallow. The light went almost as quickly, leaving the taint of blue in the west behind the hills. Now it was pitch black to the east. Henry got up from the ground and fetched them both an extra blanket strapped to the rumps of their horses. A wind came up and cut through the blanket and their homespun jackets, cutting them to the bone. They could hear the shuffling of wild animals followed by the snort of a wild pig. The crickets, dulled by the winter night, were silent. The stars of heaven came out and then a higher level until they could make out the Milky Way dashed across the deep heavens like milk thrown far and high by a maid emptying the last of her bucket. Once, James imagined he smelt roast meat and told himself he had been too long in the bush. His mind moved from pleasure to fear as he heard the sawing cough of a leopard from across the stream.

"Was that leopard?" said James.

"Yes," said Henry. "From the trees on the other side. We should make a fire."

The leopard fell silent for the next half hour but neither of them could sleep. Again, James smelt the rich sweet smell of roast meat and this time saliva rose in his mouth and he laughed to himself. They heard the leopard cough once more and then the dark night exploded with sound as the leopard struck at a pack of baboons they had watched while making camp, the screaming of the babies more human than animal, the pack leaders barking out the danger as the pack scattered. Five minutes later the bush was quiet and this time James was certain he heard laughter, very distant laughter coming on the wind from the hills to the west. Diligently, with hands rock steady, James searched the hills and found the firelight winking on and off as the distant wind moved the boughs of the trees and changed his line of sight.

"That's a Boer camp," said James. "Henry, we need a fire. If they saw our camp they will suspect our darkness. First, we make a fire and then we move. They're roasting a bloody animal, for God's sake."

Up in the hills, Tinus was laughing. He had heard the far away baboons screaming for their lives and understood the reason for the panic.

"That brought some sense, Magnus. Now they light a fire. Lucky the baboons were easier meat. There's a leopard down there. Now I can go and have some mutton. Those are Boers. Stupid Boers, but Boers. Probably ran away when the British rode into Pretoria and don't know the bush. Tomorrow we'll go down and make them join the commando. On their own, they'll be dead in a week... Look at that. More layers of the heavens... Those two down there had me fooled for a moment. All that soft living in Franschhoek... I hope she is all right."

"My wife will be looking after her. Alison's strong. She'll be all right. All women have bad moods after a miscarriage. By the time you go home, she'll be fine again."

"When do you think we'll go home?"

"When we've won the war, Tinus. Now, you want some of that mutton or not? All the best bits of fat will have gone but there'll still be meat... They've built quite a fire down there. The leopard must be close to them."

BY THE TIME Tinus had eaten his fill of roast mutton, James and Henry were across the river. They could hear the leopard crunching the bones of the dead baboon and smelt the fresh blood. James shivered and for once in a long time wished he was back in England where it was safe and wild animals did not hunt in the night.

IN THE MORNING with the first light of day, Tinus inspected the burnt-out fire and smiled grimly to himself.

"Whoever it was, they left soon after lighting the fire and they went across the river."

"To get away from the leopard?"

"No. Look over there. In that tree. A baboon carcass hanging halfway up. The leopard will be back for the rest of his meal tonight. And you can see the tracks of their horses. Must have passed yards away from the leopard. Whoever camped here knew exactly what he was doing."

"You think they were British?"

"I'm certain. Headed north to Rhodesia. There are Englishmen in Rhodesia who know the bush as well as me. I trained one of them. Spies in Boer clothing."

"Two men can't do anything."

"Not by themselves. Get on your horse, Magnus. We must break the camp right now and trek. Split into small commandos. If the generals haven't finished talking now, they never will."

BRITISH INTELLIGENCE HAD learnt of the Boer meeting before it took place. There was always someone in need of money who was prepared to spy on his fellow man, always someone who had a grudge against his brother. By the time the British were in striking distance, the group had split into small commandos with instructions to harass the British as they tried to take control of the Transvaal beyond the confines of Pretoria and Johannesburg where the mines were working again for their mainly British owners... The unspoken purpose of the war had been fulfilled.

Tinus caught the rearguard with the wagons, killed the British soldiers with accurate rifle fire from seventy yards and looted the wagons of food, guns and ammunition before the advance column knew what had happened in their rear. Instead of trying to pull the ox-wagons and leave a slow trail, Tinus only took what his men could carry on their horses.

"There are going to be more British columns to savage. Speed and space are our friends. We can lead the British plodding round in circles for years until they all get fed up and go home. Everybody wants to go home in the end. We ride. The vultures are beginning to circle. Hit hard and run hard."

KEI HAD WATCHED from the time the Boers struck the supply wagons to the time they lumbered forward again, the British having buried their dead. The vultures were circling higher and higher on the thermals, empty of food. There were scattered remnants of the attack and when all was quiet, he came out of his hiding place in the kopje. The horse followed the rocky descent with sure feet, never once stumbling on the loose stones. Leaving his horse to graze on a loose rein, he scavenged the ground for anything that would be useful. There were tins of bully beef scattered where the Boers had looted, a British water bottle in its khaki casing and a pile of loose .303 cartridges which were perfect for his British rifle that had been taken by Shaka when the Zulu left Ladysmith. Blackdog cocked his leg at a looted British ammunition box and made his point before trotting over to Kei eating from the bully beef tin he had cut open with his hunting knife. The dog watched every mouthful going from the tin on the end of the knife, the black eyes liquid with hope and hunger.

"We are both going to eat our fill today, my dog. There are plenty of tins and there's only you and me. Only you and me."

They had been hunted down from the moment they left Bulawayo in such a hurry having found the Ndebele hanging from a tree after asking too many questions about an induna's head-ring and the gold of Lobengula. Shaka had gone off into the bushes for his morning ablution the second day after leaving their false trail, never to be heard or seen again. They rode all that day and again that night when the moon came up, Kei, the two Sothos and Blackdog, that never left his side. After two days they began to relax and Kei went off with Blackdog to hunt for food. When he came back at dusk with a small duiker over the rump of his horse, there was not a trace of Bow-legs or his companion. Man and horse had seemingly vanished into thin air. With the cold shiver brought on by the prospect of his own mortality, Kei decided his days of wandering were over. Despite the chastising he would get from his father Elijah, he was going home to the farm the Oosthuizens called Majuba. In the fading light of dusk, Blackdog and Kei had eaten raw meat before Kei checked the stars for his bearing south. With the sensation of eyes watching his back all through the night, he found a small cave where he had hidden the horse, posted Blackdog at the entrance and slept till the sun was high in the sky.

On the day after James Brigandshaw and Henry Manderville had crossed the Limpopo River going north, Kei crossed the same river going south, knowing full well he owed his life to the dog now eating its third tin of English bully beef, each hunk of congealed meat going down in one swallow. Looking at the graves of the British soldiers, Kei shivered again; wherever he seemed to go at the moment were dead men.

By the time they left with what Kei could carry, the vultures had vanished from the sky.

ANNIE'S SHACK was full and Valentine's dream of going to Mauritius close. Every time Jeremiah Shank had a row with Fran Shaw he came running to Valentine and, despite his bad habits, the rewards had been worth the pain. The moment the war was over she was going to take a ship from Beira and fulfil her dream of living happily ever after like the heroines in the books she read so avidly. A man sat down next to her and broke the picture in her mind.

"How are you, Valentine?"

"Why, Sir Henry! You are so handsome. So thin. I barely, sir, could recognise you. Be so kind as to tell me where you have been."

Henry Manderville, wincing inwardly at the mangled talk, smiled on the outside. He had always felt sorry for the girl and never wished to break the veil that separated Valentine from reality. He would have preferred to take a drink in Meikles Hotel but like so many perverse things in life, the gentlemen drank in the whorehouse and those who thought they were gentlemen drank in the most expensive hotel.

"We want some company and a drink, Henry," James had explained that afternoon when they booked their rooms. "Let's have a bath, get properly dressed and go down to Annie's shack. It's not the whores I'm suggesting, Henry, just a good chinwag and find out what's going on in the world. We've been in the bush for too long."

Valentine kept talking while he looked around the room with its chandelier dominating the patrons. Down the bar was Jack Slater and through the front door came Fran Shaw, followed a pace behind by Jeremiah Shank.

"I always have the urge to punch that man in the nose," said James sitting down on his left.

"Why didn't you pick up his lackey for desertion?"

"Forgotten I told you that story. Never jump to conclusions, Henry. There's usually a good reason for everything. An officer was mistreating a horse and Jones hit him. No gentleman mistreats a horse or a woman... Shank used to work for my father, did I ever tell you that? He was the one paid to put Seb in jail. But of course, you know."

"Does he know who you are?"

"Why would it matter to him he's so bloody rich? Made a fortune out of the army. Poor old Greg. She really put horns on him and with Jack Slater half-drunk down the bar this is going to be quite a night."

"Do you know everything about us?"

"Most everything, Henry. Most everything that's interesting. There's power in knowing a man's bad habits."

"What do you know about me?"

"Oh, Henry, why ever would you ask?"

"Because of Emily."

"Oh, that's all over. We're family. Arthur's a social outcast and my father has delusions of grandeur. Seb and Em are happy. If anyone has an argument with Shank it's Seb, and Seb ignores him... You think I should tell Fran now? Did she ever love him?"

"No. I don't think so... Married him for his money and when they found out she was a Catholic, the family trust cut him off."

"That was bad luck. Maybe you had better tell her, Henry, be a good chap."

FRAN UNDERSTOOD the moment she walked through the door and saw them at the bar. Gregory was dead. It was the way Henry and James were looking at her and just then the baby gave a kick, her pregnancy hidden by the voluminous skirt. From down the bar, a chair fell over and Jack Slater was looking directly into her eyes. With less than a month before the baby was due, she would have been unable to run even if she wanted. Behind her, Shank saw Jack Slater and with his factotum giving him protection, moved to her right between the entrance and the drunk Jack Slater. Annie came across to block the confrontation. Without a pause and with the best grace she could muster with the baby distorting her walk, Fran crossed the room. Valentine moved off the bar when she saw her coming and made Fran smile grimly. In the old days she would have sat down on the vacated bar stool but with the baby that was impossible. Both the men stood up as she approached and no one spoke. Shank had followed and stood behind Fran.

"Please leave us, Shank. This is family business," drawled James.

"She's with me."

Behind Jeremiah Shank, Annie had her hand on Jack Slater's arm. Jack Jones, aware that Major Brigandshaw knew him for a deserter, decided discretion was the better part of valour and quietly left the room; with the commission he had made for himself on the side selling the horses, he could afford to make a new life in Australia. When Shank turned round Jones had gone.

"I have some bad news, Mrs Shaw," said James formally. "Your husband was killed in action. He died instantly from a bullet intended for me. I am very sorry."

Everyone had heard and Annie dropped her hand from Jack Slater's arm in sympathy.

"I'm sorry, Fran," said Henry. "He was a good friend."

To Henry's surprise, small tears began to flow down Fran's cheeks. Unknown to them she was crying for the unborn child who would never know his father despite what she had said to Jeremiah Shank.

"Do you want us to take you back to the farm tomorrow?" asked Henry.

"No. No. I don't think I'll be going back to the farm. Poor Greg. He always tried so hard and only once succeeded."

"She's with me, cock, I told you," said Jeremiah.

'They always revert to type,' thought Fran, 'but when I'm old, I have no wish to be poor.' Then she turned to move out of the room.

"Please, Jack, leave him alone. I'm sorry. Sorry for a lot of things. But leave him alone as it just isn't worth the trouble. You're a good man, Jack Slater, and I'm sorry. You would have made a grand administrator of Rhodesia. Jeremiah, I think we should now go home. There is no longer any point in pretensions."

So FAR AS Seb was concerned the war down south did not exist. The new baby had been born in March and Harry had gone back to school soon after Kimberley was relieved and the railway line was open again. Until the war was over, he was to stay in Cape Town.

"A man without education has no future, Harry," Seb had told him at Fort Salisbury railway station. "Tell Aunty Alison and Uncle Tinus we miss them all on the farm. You've got some catching up to do. You may not appreciate working hard now but you will. I want you to go to Oxford and have what I missed."

"I want to farm, Father."

"So you shall. First look at the knowledge accumulated by the world and then come back to Rhodesia. A wise man can usually be successful in life, a fool, never."

The June sun was hot overhead as the oxen pulled the ploughs slowly through the rich red soil. By the time the first rains came at the end of October, five hundred acres would have been ploughed deep for planting. Seb knew the success of farming came in watching every detail; from sunup to sundown he rode round Elephant Walk checking on each job he had allocated in the first light of morning. He had never been happier in his life.

EMILY SPENT every day alone with the children and the servants. When Seb came back from the lands he had just enough energy to drink two quick brandies, eat his supper and go to bed. By the time Emily undressed he was fast asleep. Most evenings their conversations were so short there was nothing to remember of them while she lay awake next to him, the sound of the drums coming from the compound feeding her fear. Even the new baby slept in its cot at the foot of their bed without making a sound. The thing she missed more than anything was someone to talk to as mostly anything Seb ever said was about the farm; never once did he mention the war. Most mornings she felt more tired than when she had gone to bed.

THEY HAD STAYED in the hotel three days before Henry Manderville rode alone out to the farm. James Brigandshaw's leave was cut short; Boer commandos, small units of mobile men, were attacking British columns with impunity from the Transvaal, through the Free State and as far as the Northern Cape. Hit-and-run, swallowed up by the great expanse of Africa. The war was raging like a bushfire out of control.

The ride was pleasant even if a little maudlin, and many times Henry caught himself talking loudly to Gregory Shaw and hearing the answers in his head as clear as a bell. Never before had he talked so normally to the dead, not even his wife; Gregory Shaw, it seemed, was alive and well in his mind. After the maudlin start, the jokes began to play and by the time he rode in through the stockade built by Tinus Oosthuizen, he was happy as a cricket though a little surprised at the reaction of his daughter.

"Oh, Father, I've never been so pleased to see anyone in my life."

He had not even had time to get down from his horse.

JEREMIAH SHANK WAS MORE ANNOYED with finding his books fiddled than Jack Jones scarpering off to Australia; employees could always be replaced, money not so easily. Anyway, he told himself, the horses had been sold and the horseman no longer needed. If the man had asked him, he might have given him a bonus; it was the stealing that stuck in his craw and right under his nose. People come and go in life, he told himself, and this one had gone.

The Reverend Nathanial Brigandshaw would have nothing to do with marrying them as they had been living in sin the best part of six months, despite the money Jeremiah had given to build the great church rising steadily out of the bush, a monument to God and the power of the English evangelists in Africa. The civil wedding took place in the music room at Holland Park and everyone that owed him money or did business with the estate on the Hunyani River attended the wedding. The same day Jeremiah wrote to his mentor, Lord Edward Holland, backdating the wedding to make his son perfectly legitimate. No one else in England received a word. There was no chance in his mind the baby would be a girl. Impatiently he waited for the birth when soon after he would set sail for England and set up an establishment in the West End of London. The thought that The Captain had been made a knight of the realm was comforting. If a jumped-up Lancastrian could reach such heights so could Jeremiah Shank from the East End of London.

"Now, Fran, be a good girl and go and have my son quickly. I'm in a hurry."

The words were the first after the guests had left the wedding reception that had flowed out onto the lawns between the rose gardens.

Keeping her temper, Fran swore never, even in the heat of the moment, to reveal the father of her child; there was too much at stake; her time would come. There were a lot nastier ways of making a fortune than marrying Jeremiah Shank. Or so she told herself.

"WHO'S THE FATHER?" asked Henry. They were sitting under the msasa trees with the new baby on grandfather's lap. George was at his feet on the grass playing with the fox terriers and Madge had gone off on her own, bored with the adult conversation after the first excitement of seeing her grandfather. The ridgebacks were furiously digging up separate holes in among the cannas while the gardener was watering the flowerbeds with a hose fed by the windmill pump that cranked water from the Mazoe River. There had been no rain since the end of March and none was expected until October. The garden, watered by the river and Henry Manderville's ingenuity, was a blaze of colour.

"Gregory," said Emily.

"Are you sure?"

"Quite sure. Women talk, Father. Once the army let Gregory back into uniform, it made him a man. Fran was so proud of it. Funny thing is, she was so looking forward to him coming home and finding her pregnant."

"Then why was she living with Jeremiah Shank?"

"I don't know. After two months of Gregory leaving she just never came home."

"So Jeremiah thinks he is the father?"

"You think she would tell him a lie?... What are you laughing at, Father?"

"Greg would have appreciated the irony. Well, she's not the first person in history to hedge her bets."

"You think she would do something like that?"

"Money speaks louder than words and wars are dangerous. The way we behave is never the way we are taught to behave and we are rarely as nice as we would like other people to think... When will Seb be back from the lands?"

"When the sun goes down."

BOOK 6 - THE BITTEREINDERS

1

SEPTEMBER TO OCTOBER 1900

The British patrol reached Majuba farm at the end of September with orders to bring in anyone alive and burn the farmhouse to the ground. Lord Kitchener was no longer willing to let the Boer commandos find sustenance on their own farms. Without the farms, he reasoned, the Boers would be completely cut off and surrender; guerrilla war was a war of attrition which he was going to win, carving the bushveld into blocks, building blockhouses and fences and, like flushing grouse on a Scottish moor, beating the bush until the starving Boers ran into the fences to be cut down by machine-gun fire from the blockhouses. If the Boers would not surrender and behave like any civilised man when he lost a war, Lord Kitchener would scorch their earth so dry not even a grasshopper would find a living.

Sarie, working in the main house to prepare a meal for the old woman who had given up on everything including life, saw her dogs trot off with their tails between their legs. By the time Sarie heard the horses, the dogs were well past the gum trees. Smiling to herself, she wondered if there were enough vegetables in her kitchen garden to make the Boer commando a vegetable soup. The men always craved vegetables after eating dried meat in the saddle for weeks. Three times now they had visited Majuba farm and never stayed longer than a night. The men were thin and smelled of unwashed clothes but there was never enough time to do more than cook them a soup before they saddled up to keep ahead of the khaki. Only Cronjé commissars had taken all their food.

Looking out of the window still smiling to herself, she came eye to eye with a British lance-corporal.

"No horses," shouted a private from the stables.

The corporal smiled with satisfaction; there were going to be no bad surprises on this farm.

Leaving the food to burn on the stove, Sarie and the twins were forced into a horse-drawn wagon with the old woman who had not said a word. Sarie patted the wrinkled hand, thankful her dogs had had the sense to run off into the bush. The last two things she saw as the wagon rolled down the road, past the gums and out into the veld, was the bitch watching her from a hide, well hidden, while the first red flames of fire went up from the farmhouse and the outbuildings.

KEI'S ODYSSEY had taken him from the banks of the Limpopo to the banks of the Orange River, chased one time by the British, then by the Boers, his own people scattered to the four winds by the flames of war, until he finally decided to go home. To the north of the Limpopo were Matabele trying to kill him for the induna's head-ring tucked inside his knapsack, and elsewhere the ravages of war had stripped normality from the lives of everyone. For Kei, it was like living in a nightmare without the ability to wake up. The world of men had only the urge to kill each other.

Blackdog saw the tops of the gum trees on the horizon first and sniffed the air for confirmation. For the first time since leaving home, Kei felt his heart lift at the thought of family and friends. He would never find the gold of Lobengula so there was no point in thinking about that anymore. Alone he had left and alone he returned in the late September evening.

From the back of his horse, it was possible to see the burnt buildings long before they reached the gum trees. At the gum trees, the bitch came out to sniff the bottom of her offspring, mother and son wagging their tails as they circled each other. The three dogs watched from a distance. Kei called out if anyone was there. The sound dissipated in the silence. Dismounting at the row of huts that had been his home, he kicked at the burnt walls and the debris of fallen roofs, the iron roofs black from the fire. After half an hour of searching, Kei was convinced there was no sign of his family, dead or alive. On the bench under the mango tree, he began to cry like a small boy for his mother until Blackdog put his head in his lap and looked at him with all the understanding of having been there many times before.

Stroking the head of his dog, he got up from the bench feeling better.

"No point in staying here, Blackdog, no point at all."

Getting up into the saddle he turned the horse towards the far hills where Karel had killed the buck and rode into the dusk. Behind him followed Blackdog, the bitch and the three dogs. Somehow Kei was whistling.

FOR THREE MONTHS the two brothers had kept themselves out of the war, living off the bush as best they could, avoiding people. They had made camp in the hills they had known since childhood and watched the smoke rise from what had once been their distant home. Long before Kei rode up into the hills they had saddled up. From the distance, it was impossible to tell whether Kei was Boer or British. The dogs trailing behind the lone horseman were hidden by the long brown grass. In their haste not to be seen, Karel and Piers were only concerned with the danger from behind and were not watching the bush and birds for signs of danger.

The man on the big horse blocking their way was a giant with a full beard, mostly grey but with a hint of chestnut. The long, tangled hair was matted. The man and horse were perfectly still, the penetrating stare of the blue eyes bringing Karel up in his tracks. Behind the giant were seven horsemen. The elephant gun held by the giant was pointed at Karel's belly. Behind Karel, Piers swore out loud.

"That's good, you speak the *Taal*," said the horseman. "Deserters?"

"There's someone coming up behind us."

"It's a black man and five dogs. Don't you have field glasses? Who did you desert?"

"We escaped after Cronjé surrendered. Behind us is our farm. The British burnt it to the ground ten days ago. They took our mother. There was nothing we could do. We were in the hills."

"Why were you not on the farm?"

"The khaki had come before and I killed one of their men. They were wearing hats like you. All except the officer. I tried to shoot the officer first but killed the man behind."

"I must teach you how to shoot."

"We have been hiding for three months."

"Then now you can stop hiding. There is a British unit building a blockhouse to the west of these hills, in the plain. There are soldiers guarding them. What is your name?"

"Karel Oosthuizen and this is my brother, Piers."

"I am also Oosthuizen. Martinus Oosthuizen but people call me Tinus."

"Are you the white hunter?"

"I was many years ago."

"And your father was also Martinus?"

"You seem to know me, son?"

"You are our uncle. Our father, Ezekiel, was killed at Paardeberg, and was your brother."

THE CAMP WAS FENCED with wire and inside the wire were tents and the stench of too many people living too close together. Sarie helped the old woman out of the wagon and kept a firm hand under her elbow. They had been moving towards this place of desolation since leaving Majuba farm burning behind. Even in the slums of Pretoria, among the poor whites, she had never seen worse conditions. They were being herded into the camp like chickens. In tent thirty-four there were already three families of women and children and every one of them looked starving. Even Sarie with her ability to survive anywhere was going to find this British concentration camp a challenge.

"The first thing we do is keep clean," she said to the three of them huddled in their corner of the tent. "In Pretoria, the people who were slovenly died of illness long before they starved. We will catch our own water off the side of the tent and no one will eat without washing their hands. If there is no water, cleanse them in the soil, Mrs Oosthuizen. You are now my responsibility and I will not allow you to die, however the British wish to punish us."

That night, before she slept on the hard ground, she knew what it felt like to be locked in a cage. When she woke in the morning, one of the children was dead in the opposite corner of the tent.

THEY WERE DOWNWIND and the stench of war washed over them making Billy Clifford dismount so he could be sick into the long dry grass. The British patrol had found the copper wire cut, sprung into a coil and shining in the light of midday. It was hot, and the sweat mingled with his vomit in the grass. Within seconds, flies were feeding off the disgorged content of his stomach, making Billy heave again, sending a sharp pain up from his coccyx. The vultures had long been on the ground and the only sign of life was a lone man on a horse riding away from the half-built blockhouse. As the horseman rode out of the long grass some half-mile ahead, Billy shook his head to clear his vision and put the field glasses to his eyes, adjusting them carefully for range.

"I was right," he said to the captain. "There's a small pack of dogs following that horse."

"Wild dogs. Probably kill the man and the horse in the end. He's black. Scavenging. Poor sods are getting their end of the wedge."

"You're wrong on one thing. Those are not wild dogs. There's one upfront of the horseman and it's leading the way."

"You feel better, Clifford? After nearly a year out here thought you'd be used to it."

"It's the smell. Makes me realise what we are when we die. Dead meat."

"You don't believe in God, sir?"

"I come from Ireland, Captain Menzies. I have to believe in God."

The pattern had been the same for weeks. The British soldiers were dead, their stores looted. Even the searchlight had been to no avail. There were four men still alive, one without a scratch who had hidden under the bodies of his dead comrades.

"A bloody great giant he was, with another not much smaller. Come out of the ground in broad daylight. We was working we was. Puttin' the blocks in place when all 'ell let loose. Never even saw the buggers till they was on us. Crawled up they 'ad in bloody daylight. Came up right out of the ground over there."

"How many, soldier?" asked Captain Menzies.

"A dozen, maybe less. My rifle was down on the ground. Didn't 'ave time. That bloody giant shot three of my mates right through the head. They were gone in ten minutes. I watched 'em. Running with what they could carry into a fold in the ground and when they came out of the other side they was ridin' horses."

"And the black man?"

"'Im and his dogs was lookin' for food."

"So they weren't wild dogs?"

"Not likely. The black dog came and licked my face. I was pretendin' dead."

"You're lucky to be alive."

"Bleedin' right I am. Anyone got a fag? Those bloody Boers ran off with the cigarettes."

While they were burying the dead, Billy sat on a rock in the shade of the only tree within three hundred yards of the half-finished blockhouse. Someone had repaired the copper wire and he could hear the Morse code being tapped out to Kitchener's headquarters. For a long while he stared at the blank sheet of paper and then, with the writing pad comfortably rested on his right knee and his pencil licked in contemplation, he began to write his article for the *Irish Times*. He was pleased with his headline.

'A war feeding off itself breeding hatred for a hundred years.'

After he sent his column down the same copper wire, the Giant was on his way to becoming a living legend.

By the end of the week in Europe, every newspaperman was asking the same question: 'Who is he?' The one that found out first would have his column syndicated right around the world.

BILLY WROTE ARTICLE AFTER ARTICLE. In the camps across the highveld, the Boer women and children were herded in even greater numbers towards their destiny and the earth was scorched again. Chivalry and honour, even the reason for the war, had long been lost and Billy understood. The British had done it all before in Ireland. Or, as he said in his articles, man had done it all before and would do it again and again to the end of time: the one crop, the one crop that never failed was the one that was sown with the seeds of hatred.

TINUS WATCHED the rocky slopes with the trained eye of a hunter. Red-tipped aloes grew between the craggy rocks and lower down where the topsoil had collected in cups of rock, small trees clumped together feeding in the shallow soil. There was not a sound, the land was empty. Patches of white cloud stood motionless in a blue sky, and then over the high hills of the Soutpansberg, a pair of martial eagles flew down the slope to the Sand River, lifting on a thermal halfway towards Tinus. The white-bellied birds rose high in the sky calling their *kee-wo-ee*. It was perfect leopard country and Tinus wondered how many pairs of yellow eyes were watching.

Next to the river, the men of the commando were hanging their cartridge belts from the lower branches of trees. The saddles were on the ground, the horses drinking from the river. All the animals were English horses, the Boer ponies having perished in the pain of war. The one Tinus rode had been Jack Jones's favourite, the stallion that had sired many of Jeremiah Shank's remounts sold to the British commissary. The stallion was jet black with one white blaze on its chest in the exact shape of a diamond. Jeremiah himself, always superstitious, had bought him at a sale in Kimberley; they had called him Diamond. Tinus, equally superstitious, had not given the animal a name in time of war. After searching the countryside for the third time he dismounted and led the stallion down to the river. While the horse drank,

Tinus removed the animal's tack, leaving his Mauser against a tree within easy reach. Then, rifle at the trail, he walked the riverbank looking for crocodile.

"Someone watch the river," he called. "I'm going in." For the first time in weeks, Tinus was going to get himself clean.

As he sank into the flowing river, Magnus du Plessis saw there was not a trace of fat on his neighbour's naked body. Holding his Mauser ready to fire into the water he searched the opposite bank for crocodile as the rest of the commando stripped and ran into the river. Piers was the first to dive headfirst into the water. They were sixty, maybe seventy miles he estimated, from the Limpopo River, further away than he had ever been from his Franschhoek farm.

When Tinus had washed the private crevices of his body, he floated on his back and forgot he was fighting a war. Then he smiled and let his mind go back to his early life north of the Limpopo in the land of Lobengula, King of the Matabele. As he drifted downriver, he could see the great fat-bellied tyrant in his armchair under the jackalberry tree and the pots of maize beer being offered to the king. Then he thought of Alison and the children and his mind snapped back to the war, worrying about the other men's families in the concentration camps set up by the British to deny the Boer commandos the supplies from their own farms. Then the guilt of his family's safety disappeared when he remembered the price he would pay if caught by the British. There was only one sentence for a rebel. They would hang him by his neck until he was dead. The sharp crack of the Mauser brought him back to reality. He had floated more than a hundred yards downstream. Magnus du Plessis was running along the bank firing, stopping and firing into the water around his body. Then Tinus began to laugh at the absurdity.

"You'll bring every khaki for miles," he shouted, splashing the water.

"Bugger the khaki. There was a nine-foot crocodile halfway up your ass. Get out of the bloody water."

With powerful strokes, Tinus began swimming against the current with Magnus swearing at him from the bank.

"I know what it is," he said to Magnus when he got out of the water where the men were making camp. "I feel I'm almost home."

"Your home is a thousand miles away in the Cape."

"I don't think so, friend. My home is across the Limpopo River and I only found out just now. This is the real Africa. Eagles, crocodiles and swimming bare-arse in the river."

"You can swim bare-ass in the Cape."

"Not with a nine-foot crocodile halfway up… We're going to rest here for a week to give the men time to look after themselves. Then we go back to war. I want to bring a thousand men together to show the British the war will never be over without negotiation. We must make them negotiate, Magnus. It's the only way. Now, would you be so kind as to pass me my trousers?"

"Look at him," called Piers and everyone in the commando followed his upward gaze. The female eagle had caught a three-foot snake and was struggling to rise into the sky. Three hundred feet above the ground the bird let go and the snake, still writhing, plummeted to the hard rock below. Before the female could reach the dead reptile, the male swooped and snatched the snake with both claws. The female caught up and snatched at her prey, twisting and turning the birds in flight. The snake came apart just above the craggy rocks and the birds settled fifty yards from the men, the hooked beaks tearing at the flesh. Both birds were facing the men, staring them down with baleful eyes.

Later the birds flew off, rising slowly on the thermals, higher and higher into the African sky.

"IT WON'T WORK, SIR," said Major James Brigandshaw. "Or rather, it won't work for a very long time and by then the bitterness between the white races of Africa will last a hundred years. If we place their women and children in camps, we must look after them. In one of the camps, the children are dying of measles. Kill a man's child and he'll fight you for the rest of his life. Men like that won't negotiate."

"Are you, sir, contradicting a major-general with forty years' service?" said Colonel Hickman.

"The job of British Intelligence is to give the high command intelligence. I advocated bringing in their women but only to protect them instead. They are dying in British protection. Disease spreads in close confinement, we know that. We know we are not deliberately introducing disease to the confusion of the camps, but to the Boer in the field it will look like we are murdering his women and children."

"Major Brigandshaw! Are you accusing us of murder?"

"That is how other people will see this campaign, how they will see emptying the veld, burning their houses, chopping the veld up into areas and running a grouse shoot to flush out the Boer commandos."

"How else do we do it, Brigandshaw?" said the general, folding his arms across his chest. "Let us hear what the major would do if he, God forbid, was Lord Kitchener."

"I would hunt them. At the moment the small bands of mounted Boers run rings around us. They literally see us a mile away and avoid us if they wish, attack us if they wish. Never once are they under threat until they decide when to attack. These are not birds frightened by the beaters. These are intelligent men in their own bushveld. Unless the sweeping soldiers link arms in the night, the Boers will slip through the cordons; silently fight their way through, make a gap and then go back for their horses. The African bush is not a flat Scottish grouse moor."

"How, Brigandshaw, do you propose hunting these wily Boers?" The general was smiling.

"By sending out hundreds of small, mounted units with trackers. Make the Boers know the war is always just over the ridge, just through the trees. Make him feel like a hunted fox with the dogs baying for his blood. And stop the women and children dying in the camps. Whatever happens in the end, we British have to live with these people in Africa."

"Are you proposing native trackers? That won't do."

"No, sir. Rhodesians. Men who know the bush as well as the Boers. Men who also know they have to live with the Boers when the British Army has sailed back over the sea. We want hunters not barbed wire, pillboxes and camps for women and children. Hunt them at night as well as the day. Then they'll negotiate. A man can only take so much and then he cracks up. Ask the fox. The dogs get him nine times out of ten."

"An interesting idea, Brigandshaw," said the general, "but totally impractical. How do you supply these men all over the place? There would be no discipline. No, sir, we are a professional army and no professional army runs around like that. The Boers are finished anyway. Just a few stragglers. And don't forget, Brigandshaw, there are a lot of dead birds on a grouse moor. Wouldn't like to be a grouse on the twelfth of August."

Around the table, everyone but James began to laugh.

Colonel Hickman waited for the general and his staff to leave the room; James Brigandshaw thought the nose and cheeks were redder than usual but the merriment had gone out of the man's eyes.

"Close the door, Brigandshaw," he said and walked around the conference table to look out of the window. "Jacarandas," he said. "Very pretty. Don't have them in my English garden. The blue's the same colour as the African sky... You were right on one thing. This war isn't over by a long way. Think your idea will work?"

"I don't really know."

"Forgive me for laughing with the general. There's as much politics in the army as Westminster. Never does for the chief of intelligence to rub up a major-general the wrong way. Why we have rank. Works in the overall picture. Your leave's cancelled, of course."

"Rather thought so when you brought me down from Salisbury."

"Give me a written report on our merry band of hunters. Some of your Mashonaland Scouts, I presume. Well, you can forget about fighting with them. You're back in intelligence here in Pretoria. Those men you gave leave, better cancel, in case I like your idea. Who would set it up? Train the Scouts to 'liaise' with our commando units?"

"My brother."

The colonel turned from the open window and began to laugh. "He's a priest, for goodness sake."

"Not Nathanial. Sebastian. He's the black sheep of our family. A scandal when he was seventeen and ran away to Africa with an Englishwoman. Daughter of a baronet. He's thirty now. Lived in the bush all those years, first as an elephant hunter and then as a farmer."

"Why was it such a scandal? They married of course."

"Not yet, sir. The girl was married to my elder brother, Arthur. Marriage was annulled. My brother said the son was his."

"Which brother, for God's sake?"

"Sebastian. You see, Arthur stole Emily with the help of my father. Emily was always Seb's since they were children."

"And you want me to employ this black sheep?"

"Yes, sir. He knows the bush like the back of his hand."

"I should think he would, keeping away from the girl's father. What did the baronet do when this Sebastian ran off with his daughter?"

"He lives with them, sir, on the farm in Rhodesia."

The colonel glared at him and turned back to look out of the window. "Well, it's been done before in time of a war. Fact is, there have been quite a few black sheep who did quite well in difficult situations. Put it all in your report, though leave out your family's dirty linen. And there's one more thing. The *Irish Times* first made a hero out of one of these hit-and-run merchants. Gave him the *nom de guerre* of the Giant. The British and South African press have picked up on it and the anti-war lobby has made a hero out of him in the English press. He's been good for Boer morale which isn't good for us. Some say he was a white hunter up north. Others say he's a farmer from the Cape and a British subject. Probably a figment of the Irish newsman's imagination. Anyway, I want you to find out who he is. He rides a black stallion with a white blaze on its chest. One of our remounts most probably. Or again it's all a lot of hogwash. The worst thing that ever happened in this war was letting the press run around the battlefield. Instant story back in England. Not like the good old days in India when the problem was all over before they heard anything about it at home. Let a soldier fight his own war without interference. If the man exists, I want him killed. If he's a British subject, I want him captured. Then we'll hang him for treason. Stop a lot of the Cape cousins doing anything foolish. Men are less inclined to be heroes when they feel a noose around their necks."

"I've read about him."

"Good. So you know what I'm talking about."

KEI HAD FOUND an overhang on the face of a cliff and made himself most comfortable. At the back, he could light a fire so at night when the temperature dropped he sat in comfort with the five dogs sprawled on the ground and was content. If anyone saw the flickering light high on the cliff, they would think it was the spirits of the dead. Every night and one by one the dogs came to him for their fur to be searched for parasites. From the far side of the cave, the horse watched them with brown, liquid eyes, the horse's tack and Kei's rifle in the fire-thrown shadow of a boulder. The dogs had found the cave by following up the steep and crumbling path that climbed from the open plain, the path forged by the course of a now dried-up stream that dropped from the top of the cliff.

In the mornings from his eyrie overlooking the plains, he was king of all he surveyed. First, the dogs went out to sniff the morning air, followed by the horse. The sun rose out of a far-distant range of hills while the birds sang and Kei went to the spring and doused his face with cold water. And when the dogs reached the open grassland Kei sat on a high rock and watched them hunt while the horse grazed at the foot of the cliff.

On the Monday after James began his inquiries into the true identity of the Giant, Blackdog made the left horn of the bull curving out and around while the bitch made the right. Deep in the grass, watched by Kei from his rock, the three dogs waited in a line, their long bodies flat to the ground. Kei counted eleven springbok in the herd oblivious to the danger lurking in the grass. With the rising sun at his back, Blackdog led the charge, chasing the buck towards the dogs lying in the grass. The male springbok lowered its horns but Blackdog ran around him as the dogs in the long grass sprang at the smallest in the herd, tearing at its throat. By the time Kei scrambled his way down the path, the dogs had ripped open the belly of the young springbok to get inside and their heads were covered in warm blood.

Whistling for the horse at the foot of the cliff, he tossed the carcass over the horse's back, forcing the delicate front hooves between the tendon and bone of the back legs. Slowly, walking behind his horse, he mounted the path, the dogs left behind to eat the warm entrails of the springbok.

By the time the springbok was hanging by its back legs inside the cave, and Kei came out to whistle for his dogs, there were horsemen sweeping across the plain. The dogs were not sure which way to run as some of the sounds were bouncing back at them from the face of the cliff. The dogs ran the wrong way straight at the horsemen into short grass. The dogs stopped and though Kei could not see from the distance, he knew they were shivering with their tails between their legs. One of the horsemen pulled his rifle from his saddle holster, dropped to the ground and walked towards the cowed dogs.

Standing up from the cover of his rock, Kei shouted in Afrikaans, "Don't shoot my dog." The man with the gun ignored him and Kei began to shiver. "Don't shoot!" he called in a small voice.

Down below the man with the gun went down on one knee, putting the rifle on the ground. Kei heard the whistle and saw his pack of dogs rush the kneeling man to attack. Another of the men dismounted and ran towards the dogs who were now slobbering over the first man who was lying on his back in the grass with a dog wrapped in each of his arms. Blackdog leapt from the ground and landed on the chest of the second man, knocking him to the ground. The rest of the horsemen were shouting encouragement and a man on a black horse was signalling to Kei with his arm. Reluctantly Kei walked slowly down to the dried-up river bed, twice falling on his bottom. His rifle was behind him in the cave with his horse. The wind had come up and pushed towards him the rancid smell of unwashed bodies. The smell was slightly sweet, the distinct smell of white men. All the men were bearded with long dank hair, knotted and dirty. Bandoliers of cartridges hung across their bodies and their clothes were dirty and looked like rags tied together. Only the guns were clean. Kei waited his last moments of life at the foot of the cliff. He could see the two men walking towards him, their chests above the long, brown grass. The smaller of the two men began running towards him and Kei looked behind for a way to escape. Blackdog ran through the grass first followed by the bitch and then the man was hugging him. The bigger of the two men spoke from behind.

"Sarie's dogs. It is a miracle. And Kei. We thought all you blacks were dead. Even in the middle of a war, you can find your friends... These are Sarie Mostert's dogs, Frikkie's woman," he said to the big man on the black horse. Kei could now see a white diamond-shaped blaze on the horse's chest.

Then he began to laugh hysterically. He had run away from them and they had found him here in the middle of nowhere. Now he would have to run away again.

"How d'you get here?" asked the big man on the horse.

"I have a horse in a cave."

"And a rifle?"

"Yes, I have a rifle."

"Then you'd better join us. You won't get far on your own. And bring the dogs. Are they any good at hunting?"

2

MARCH TO APRIL 1901

*M*ajor-General William Gore-Bilham believed in comfort. Campaigning was part of the pleasure of being a soldier and in South Africa, he was enjoying himself. To make sure his stomach was kept in order he had brought with him the cook from his English estate along with one of the footmen, the butler being too old. In Cape Town, soon after he landed, the general had purchased two ox-wagons together with the requisite number of oxen. The one had been made into a splendid caravan with a double bed, cupboards and a toilet he could use so as not to expose himself to the African elements at night. Being a man of sixty-two he required the toilet three times every night and such a weakness was never to be shown to the men. The second wagon contained his personal possessions, a large bell tent, chairs, tables, crockery, cutlery, a stock of two hundred bottles of '72 Heidsieck Dry Monopole champagne, three hundred bottles of assorted burgundies, clarets and German hocks and a small upright piano that had travelled out from England with him on the boat. There were tins of foie gras, caviar, jars of Gentleman's Relish, his favourite pickles from his estate, and every penny of his considerable wealth had been inherited including his army commission in a good regiment that had been bought for him by his grandfather. There was a saying (that no one in the regiment would ever have said to his face) that it took three generations to make an English gentleman. William Gore-Bilham's grandfather, whence the family fortune had sprung, was anything but a gentleman, having built a fortune out of his workers, some as young as ten, toiling twelve hours a day, six days a week for enough money to feed themselves so they would not collapse from hunger at the looms. As the general rose in rank to colonel of his regiment and beyond, the size of his private income was more important than his skill as a soldier, the etiquette in the officers' mess more important than the ability to read a map. The general had felt guiltily glad when his grandfather died as the man's accent was appalling.

By the end of March the worst of the summer heat was over, the rains now intermittent, and the general was determined to fulfil the orders of Lord Kitchener and bring the Boer general back to Pretoria one way or the other. The man they now knew as Martinus Jacobus McDonald Oosthuizen had created havoc from the Northern Transvaal down to the Northern Cape, once attacking a British column with over two thousand men and disappearing into the veld without a trace. The man's myth was doing more for Boer morale than damage to the British Army, and it was going to stop.

The general's immaculate caravan was parked on the banks of the Crocodile River, equidistant from Pretoria and Mafeking one hundred and forty miles to the south. The general's headquarters, that surrounded the caravan, was in the bush thirty miles from the Bechuanaland border and all reports indicated Oosthuizen and a small band of Boers were between the general and the border. To the general's considerable satisfaction the Cape rebel was about to be caught in the dragnet of eight thousand British and Colonial troops that were slowly drawing the noose around his neck. Twenty armed sentries stood guard on the perimeter of the divisional headquarters while the troops were far away sweeping the rugged bush, slogging their way forward in the African sun under full kit, only the officers riding horses; half the men had been in Africa less than three months and most were red raw from the sun.

In the large bell tent set up under a sixty-foot high acacia tree, General Gore-Bilham amused himself by watching the crocodiles on the sandbanks that dotted the river down the long, steep bank from his bell tent. He was immaculately dressed as were his staff officers. Every man above the rank of major had laid a small bet on how long it would take the army to capture the rebel. Not one of them had any fear for his own safety as they waited for lunch to be served at the long, cloth-covered table set up under the rich shade of a cluster of river-watered trees. From somewhere they could hear the hippopotamuses grunting in the pools away from the main flow of the river. The sky was pale blue with just three small clouds lost in the firmament, but not one of the British had looked further than the height of the tree. Apart from the heat and the grunts of the hippo they could just as easily have been in Aldershot, the home of a large part of the British Army, southwest of London.

From across the river in thick bush, Tinus Oosthuizen could not believe his eyes. All the sentries had their backs to the river and according to his scouts, the nearest British soldier was ten miles from the Bechuanaland border, at least a six-hour slog from what he was watching through his binoculars. A man in a fancy red uniform was sprawled in a deck chair at the entrance to a round tent, seemingly engrossed in the flow of the river. Men in white jackets and white gloves were laying a long table and from so close, Tinus was able to count three wine glasses at each place setting; most of the officers were standing drinking what Tinus presumed to be sherry. They were dressed in an assortment of colourful uniforms nearly all with stripes of different colours down the outside of their trousers. Some of the officers wore sashes round their well-fed stomachs but none carried swords; the most lethal weapons within their grasp being the knives laid out in perfect order with the forks on the white tablecloth that dropped just short of the red dust of Africa. The elderly man from the round tent managed, with effort, to push himself out of the deck chair. When he joined the sherry-drinking officers, everyone stopped talking until a mess steward had sidled up to the right of the man's elbow with a silver tray and one glass in the dead centre. Without looking at the tray or the steward the man picked up the glass of sherry and began to drink, sending the rest back into conversation. Quietly, Tinus handed Magnus du Plessis the glasses.

"How on earth did that lot of twits conquer a quarter of the world?" said Tinus.

"They may look like twits but they're going to eat a better lunch than us."

"Maybe not. We'll attack at the end of lunch when they're all full of food and wine. Karel, I want you to take thirty men upriver; Magnus, you take thirty downriver. I heard it said that at the end of lunch they clear everything off the table and bring out the port and then someone stands up to propose a toast to the Queen. When he stands up, it's the signal to take out the sentries. When you have their full attention, I'm going to swim across with the rest of the commando. My guess is that's their divisional headquarters and the fat old fart who came up last for his sherry is General Gore-Bilham."

"What about the crocodiles?"

"Don't splash. By the time the crocodiles have taken an interest, we will all be across. I've checked them all on the sandbanks. Most have their mouths wide open and are enjoying the sun. If one goes for you mind its tail, not its mouth. Kei will stay on this side of the river with the dogs and the horses."

Within thirty seconds of the mess vice-president standing to propose the toast to the sovereign, eighteen of the sentries were dead, shot through the head by a marksman who could shoot the eye out of a flying eagle three times out of five. The thorn thicket surrounding the river camp had given perfect cover to the Boers. By the time the officers and their general were aware of what was happening, a giant of a man dripping river water was standing at the foot of the table.

"Sit down, gentlemen. You are prisoners of war," he said in perfect English.

Twenty minutes later, having eaten what was left of the lunch, the Boer commando pulled back over the river. The tents, the general's caravan and the field kitchen were left burning. The fat general and seven of his senior staff were manhandled across the river, along with thirty of the best horses.

While the British Army was still pushing towards the Bechuanaland border, Tinus led his men and their captives in the opposite direction, stopping ten miles from the Crocodile River.

"Take their clothes down to their socks and underwear and let them loose," Tinus said in Afrikaans.

From the height of his horse, Tinus watched the British being stripped of their dignity.

"You are now free to go," he said to the general in English. Then the mounted Boers and the spare horses trotted off into the bush.

When he looked back from a rise, the British were still standing in their underwear. "Welcome to Africa," he said again in English, knowing he was too far for them to hear. 'They will have sore feet and blistered bodies from the sun but will probably live,' he said to himself. When taking them prisoner he had taken three British water bottles for each officer. Even in war, there were rules in the African bush.

BILLY CLIFFORD, who was writing a series of stories for the *Irish Times* on the great British sweep to capture the Giant, was the first to reach the divisional headquarters attracted by the flames that burnt high in the sky, the smoke visible from fifteen miles; the thorn thicket that had allowed the Boer marksman to reach within fifty yards of the sentries had burnt in a rush of heat, the fire feeding on itself in the heart of the dry thorn bush. With the camera equipment that had reached him from Ireland before Christmas, he and three other reporters spurred their horses towards the rising cloud of smoke. The wind that had blown the Boer rifle fire away from their ears turned and brought with it the deep sounds of exploding ammunition boxes. Then nothing. As they rode towards the Crocodile River, there was only the billowing smoke and silence.

Anything less like a British divisional headquarters was hard to be seen. Even if the officers had thought to ride after the Boers their saddles had been burnt in the fire, their horses scattered in the bush, and the one patrol that crossed the river led by a blue-blooded young subaltern looking for excitement came back with the story that the Boers had split off in seven different directions. They were still waiting for the recalled troops from the Bechuanaland border to pursue the Boers and the captives.

Billy, being an Irishman with a sneaking sympathy for the Boers, saw the funny side of it: the British were running around like chickens with their heads chopped off amid the sound of grunts and wallowing hippos from the pools. By the time the blood-red sun began to sink into the bush, splashing the flowing surface of the Crocodile River with red, some semblance of order had returned. The fires were out, and the men killed in the ambush had been buried with a brief service by the padre. Everyone, including Billy, was nervous of a second Boer attack under the cover of darkness, the power of Africa enveloping the men far away from the green and safe pastures of England where predators no longer existed. Out in the dark, hyena circled, having long smelt the blood of the dead, their eyes lit up with stark penetration by the one British searchlight that worked, probing the smouldering bush and hippo-grunting river for the enemy. By the time all the light had left the heavens, the screech of the cicadas and river frogs was deafening while far across the river a lion roared and was answered, the sound churning deep fear into Billy's bowels. The burnt-out camp was dark except for the intermittent probing of the searchlight.

At close to midnight a troop of mounted dragoons, their horses savaged by riding through the bush in the dark, rode into the camp attracted by the searchlight which identified them before shots could be fired. Then the light gave out and only a lacework of stars, layer after layer, showed Billy there was something else other than the primal dark. No one slept, everyone waiting for the dawn, and when the moon rose at three in the morning, it was only a thin crescent below the stars and threw no light on the darkness. Everywhere the night belonged to the animals. When a voice called from across the river even Billy wondered if it was the spirit of a dead sentry trying to find his way to heaven. Then everyone waited for the Boer attack that never came.

GENERAL GORE-BILHAM WAS NOT AMUSED. The blisters on his shoulders had burst and his bare feet were bleeding from toe to heel. His senior colonel had been half carried through the bush having been bitten by a black scorpion and was probably going to die. Only the general had stopped his officers blundering across the river in the night. Having told his officers to lie down and find cover, it was the general himself who announced their presence from behind the twisted trunk of an old acacia tree. Then he had stood up with the rest of his officers.

Billy, standing with his camera on the bank of the river, had a clear view of Major-General William Gore-Bilham on the opposite bank. The man was dressed in his one-piece underwear and did not seem to care who saw his predicament.

"Someone bring my cloak across, damn you," he bellowed.

Billy, sensing his chance of a lifetime and blind to the lurking crocodiles, waded into the water where there was a drift that would take him to within twenty yards of the opposite bank. Having gone across as far as he could with adrenaline pumping through his body and his mind as clear as crystal, Billy took his photographs of the general that were to syndicate around the world.

IN PRETORIA TWO WEEKS LATER, Colonel Hickman, Chief of British Intelligence in South Africa, received an order from Major-General Gore-Bilham to meet him at divisional headquarters at two-thirty in the afternoon.

James Brigandshaw, included in the order, remembered the general well, having been told that British soldiers did not run around the bush without a proper chain of command. On the general's desk were different newspapers but as they were turned around one by one for army intelligence to read, all of them showed Billy Clifford's photograph, only the captions changing. All the newspapers were South African except for the *Rhodesia Herald*, the English papers still on the water.

"Every paper in England and America will front-page this photograph! How did your censorship allow this out of the country?" Despite his well-peeled nose, the general looked no different to James. "Can you think what my club will say? Improperly dressed, my God. I want that Boer rebel now more than ever. I want him hunted down. I want him caught. I want him tried. I want him hanged by his neck. Brigandshaw! You mentioned a bushwhacking brother with a lot of dirty linen. You wanted commandos on horseback like the Boers. Trying to catch that damn man in a dragnet is like eating soup with a fork. Every time you get a bit on the fork it dribbles off before you can get it to your mouth. Hunt the man, if that's what it takes."

"How is Colonel Hall?" asked Hickman politely.

"Dead. Killed by a bloody scorpion. If it hadn't been for the smoke and the searchlight none of us would have come out alive. Look," he said and pulled his right foot out from under his desk. "No shoes, dammit. I'm padding around the officers' mess in a pair of socks with everyone looking at my photograph, of me, sir, in my underwear!"

"I believe General Oosthuizen left you water," said Colonel Hickman.

"Brigandshaw," shouted the general. "You have a problem, sir. Hunt the man, you hear me. Dismissed."

Outside in the corridor and very quickly, James asked a question. "Has anyone in the press found out the true identity of the Giant?"

"Yes, Martinus Oosthuizen. Why? You can leave for Rhodesia tomorrow. Can't have the Boers making fools of us, now can we? I liked the one headline: '*Stripped of more than his uniform, stripped of his dignity*'. You do see the problem don't you, Brigandshaw?"

"Do you mind, sir, if we find a place for a very private conversation? You see, Tinus Oosthuizen was my brother's mentor and partner. When I suggested asking my brother to hunt the rebel Boer, I had no idea of his true identity."

"Then don't tell your brother."

"Isn't that dishonest?"

"Oh, James, come and have a drink with me in the hotel across the street. We all talk about being officers and gentlemen. Most of us even think we are. You and I have a job to do. We have a duty. The filth of war comes in more than one set of clothing. Ask the general."

"I can't lie to Seb."

"What the eye doesn't see, the heart doesn't grieve about. Don't tell him. That's not telling a lie."

"And if he catches him or kills him?"

"Then it will be too late."

"He'll never speak to me again."

"I rather gather your family didn't speak to him either for a long time. Whatever you say about Tinus Oosthuizen, he's a rebel, a traitor. James, his mother was a McDonald. He lived in Rhodesia under the protection of the Crown. We can't have people going around biting off the hand that feeds them. He should have stayed at home with his English wife and children. Now, you go and get your brother into the army. And that's an order. Which is more important, your brother or your country? He also benefits from the

Crown's protection. Now it's his turn to do something in return. In a society, you can't have the benefits without a contribution."

"Do you think they'd hang Oosthuizen if they caught him?"

"Who knows? Maybe. Maybe not. Probably not if that helps you. This has gone on far longer than it should have done. Snuff out the Boer hopes and the suffering comes to an end. These camps are a disgrace but the only way to stop the disease is to let everyone out to roam the bush, and that's equally dangerous for women and children. The way to end their misery is to stop the war quickly. All this Oosthuizen is doing is prolonging the agony and some of the Boer fighters agree and have come across to the British. Only a few. But it's a start. The damn Boers should have given in when we took Pretoria."

"But they didn't," said James.

The next day, and not for the first time, James began the ride that would take him north, over the Limpopo River and through the mopane forest to his brother's farm on the banks of the Mazoe River.

THE LETTER from Harry from his school in Cape Town left Sebastian with a sinking feeling in his stomach. Emily had written to Alison telling her the boy was back at school and Harry had waited in vain for his invitation to the farm in Franschhoek. He could only imagine he had said something to offend Uncle Tinus on his last visit, it being difficult to remember Uncle Tinus was really a Boer. Harry had explained his dilemma to his mother in his earlier letters after the railway line south was open and he had been able to go back to school. There had been no word from Alison and both of them had thought the war was the reason: correctly, Alison was taking the side of her husband's family. The lack of communication was a product of the war which would go away when hostilities came to an end.

During the Christmas school holidays, Harry, unable to go home because of the dangers of travelling by rail with the trains still being ambushed by Boer commandos and, bored to tears, had persuaded an older schoolfriend to drive out to the farm, Kleinfontein, to at least apologise for what he might have said. Seb, reading the letter between the lines, saw his son was homesick; Alison had been his second mother. Seb even thought Harry's feelings were hurt, being cut off without a word. The friend's father had lent them a horse and trap and off they had gone early one morning, knowing that if they were not welcome, they would have to drive themselves back before dark. On a beautiful morning and at a spanking pace the two boys set off for the Franschhoek Valley to find Uncle Tinus gone to the war and Aunty Alison in a state that barely let her give them lunch let alone invite them to stay for a few days which had been their hope. To make it worse, nine-year-old Barend refused to speak English and never even asked after Harry's sister Madge. Tinka had seemed pleased enough to see him but she was only five years old. With Aunty Alison returning to her room straight after lunch the boys left to drive home, passing the heavily drawn curtains of the room Harry knew to be his aunt's. Harry said it was the most embarrassing day in his life, and his friend had not been amused having driven all that way just for lunch.

It was a week of surprises for Seb. His brother, Reverend Nathanial Brigandshaw and his family, paid an unannounced visit. Soon after, the new Mrs Francesca Shank brought her ten-month-old son for her first visit since going to live with Jeremiah Shank, becoming the mistress of Holland Park, the twenty-thousand-acre estate on the Hunyani River. Fran had been full of Lord Holland, Jeremiah's mentor, arriving for a visit. Politely, Seb had turned down the invitation to take his lordship on a hunting safari into the Zambezi Valley, telling Emily afterwards how strange it was that people popped up in life when they wanted something.

Three days later James rode through the palisade and Seb was on his guard.

"What do you want?" he asked his brother pleasantly but bluntly when he, James and Emily were seated in deck chairs under the shade of a msasa tree with the river nicely visible through the trees, the lawn in between cut perfectly, the flowers around the tree trunks blooming in a riot of colour, bougainvillea climbing up some of the trees splashing red, orange and mauve all the way to the top and the clear blue sky.

"We have a problem with the Boers who won't give up."

"It rather looks that way. Seems one of your generals was made to look a first-class fool."

"You read about that," said James uncomfortably.

"Yes. We do have a newspaper. Frankly, I thought it rather funny."

"One of the colonels died from a scorpion bite."

"Should have cut out the poison straight away. Probably a black scorpion."

"That's why we need your help, Seb."

"You see, Em, I was right. Whoever comes to see us wants something. Nat was here the other day. Had something on his mind but whatever it was he left without telling us. He didn't even lecture us on not going to church."

"Arthur's dead."

"Arthur!" said Emily, thinking with aversion of the man she had been told to marry after Seb had been sent out of England when he was seventeen years old and Emily pregnant with his child.

"He got so fat and debauched his heart gave out."

"Well, why didn't Nat say?"

"You'd better ask him. Arthur only had himself to blame. Too much money without any responsibility. And father's favourite. Poor mother. Poor, long-suffering mother. She's had a terrible life. All that effort with us children and none of us there to give her hope. She hates your ancestral home, Emily. Did you know that? If mother had her choice, she would go back north to the village where she was born. But now she's Lady Brigandshaw, the friends of her youth would have nothing to do with her. You can't go back, you know... Now, let me tell you how I think this war can be brought to a conclusion and how you can help. You're an Englishman, Seb. You have a responsibility. You can't run away from your responsibilities in life."

"I'm going for a walk with the dogs," said Emily. "I don't think I want to hear. When people start talking about other people's responsibilities, I don't want to hear. Mostly they are passing the buck, as I believe they say in America. We have a cousin in Canada, somewhere. Heir to Father's title. Now, why did I think of the lumberjack all of a sudden? Madge, come along. We're all going for a walk. Go and tell Grandfather and make sure he brings his forked stick for the snakes. Now, where are those dogs?"

THEY WAITED for Emily and her entourage to reach the path that ran along the bank of the Mazoe River made by the daily walks of the family. They could hear the fox terriers long after everyone was out of sight. Without saying a word, Seb got up and came back with a bottle of whisky and put it down with two crystal tumblers on the low table between their deckchairs. Shortly after, a servant put a crystal jug full of rainwater down next to the bottle with a plate of finely cut biltong.

"The whisky, yes," said James, "the dried meat I never wish to eat again."

"I forget. My father-in-law never touches the stuff after he came back from the Mashonaland Scouts."

"He looks well."

"Misses Greg. They were friends for a long time. Fran was over here the other day with her baby boy. Wanted me to take some aristocrat hunting. Did you know the boy's Greg's? Fran told Em they got together just before he went off to war. I rather like the idea of Jeremiah Shank bringing up someone else's child thinking it's his own. He thinks he's so smart it's painful. Some kind of poetic justice for pursuing me and Em. Man's rich, can't deny that. You wonder where the brains came from; family was dirt poor from the east of London. Must be a throwback somewhere, if you believe in breeding. Maybe Shank disproves this point. Rather nice if he did. Gives everyone a chance if they take it. Why have you never married, brother James?"

"You are changing the subject."

"There is nothing to change. I have told you more than once I will not kill my fellow man."

"If he's pointing a gun?"

"Plato had something to say about that only he was talking about knives not guns. He said no one is ever sure if the other man will kill so self-defence doesn't exonerate murder. Murder is murder whatever its form. The Bible says *though shalt not kill* but the Christians somehow have excluded a just war, if there ever is such a thing. Some people say if your cause is right you can kill as many people as you like; the good man can kill his bad man. No one ever tells the truth why they do things. Somehow they make the most horrible acts honourable. That old man on his stoep in Pretoria that went off to Switzerland with the Boer treasure once Pretoria fell, was a man overwrought with pride. So he took his people to war and once the killing began everyone had a pride, but it was now mixed with hatred. The British, knowing they could not control the wealth of the gold mines without controlling the country, found their high horse with the Uitlanders, foreigners to Kruger, people exploiting his country to whom he would not give the vote. He never said, 'I am a man of great pride and wish to remain President at any cost to my people'. We were unable to tell the world that if Kruger and his people did not give us their gold, we would kill them. The lives of all men are thick with hypocrisy. If you want to keep a friend, brother James, never tell him the truth, only tell him what he wants to hear. Now try to convince me to take up my guns and kill my fellow man."

"If you agree that war is bad then it is good to stop it quickly. And, just to remind you, if during the rebellion here in 1896 your fellow Englishmen had not taken up their guns, you and your family would have been killed. When the danger is far away, sweet words of righteousness are easier to say. Man, even in his most primitive stage, has always been in a state of war and peace, having either just fought a war or knowing one is coming; without power, there can never be a peace, which is why I became a soldier. Right and wrong are always interfered with by reality. The reality at the moment is a war between England and the Boers. The right and wrong of its cause are pleasant talk away from danger. Forget about the morality, old chap, you can't just run away from your responsibilities and leave them to the other members of your society. It is why we have societies, nations, tribes to protect each other from our natural enemies. And we all have enemies, however good we are. Any man who possesses something his neighbour covets has an enemy. And man by his nature is covetous."

"But the Boer is not my enemy."

"But he is the enemy of your country. England may say in the future when you Rhodesians need help that your enemy is not their enemy. But the Australians, Canadians, New Zealanders fighting with us against the Boer understand that any threat to the empire is a threat to themselves, and if we ever stop thinking that way, the parts of the empire will be picked off one by one and destroyed as we know them. You just can't have only the benefits of a society any more than you can agree with everything within that society. You can't just choose which part of the mutual protection you wish to perform, old chap. Life doesn't work that way."

"Why do you want me so badly, James?"

"Because you know the bush better than most Englishmen and if we are going to capture the Boer generals who say they will fight to the bitter end, we have to go into the bush and hunt them."

"I don't even wish to hunt animals anymore."

"As an Englishman, you have no choice."

"And which particular Boer general do you wish me to hunt?"

"The Giant," said James softly, watching his brother's eyes for recognition.

"I suppose you want to tell me all the bad things he has done."

"That will be a start."

"And who is he? What's his real name?"

James got up from his deck chair and walked with his glass of whisky towards the river before he was able to make up his mind.

"We don't know, old chap," he lied. "We don't know," said James looking his brother straight in the eye, "but he's the best of their guerrilla fighters. That prank with General Gore-Bilham has given the Boers a new lease of life."

"Tell me the way he operates. How, for instance, did he catch the general with his pants down?"

"It's no laughing matter, Seb."

"Probably not. Anyway, at least we know this Giant has a sense of humour. But why didn't the general die of thirst?"

"The man gave them three water bottles each."

"Then he's also a man of honour and he also respects the bush. Sounds like our man knew his captives would get back to camp. He was sending you a message of defiance… Why don't you try to negotiate an end to this war?"

"We are trying."

"And if I can capture this Giant, you think he will negotiate?"

"That is our hope."

"I don't mind capturing the man though I am not sure if I know how. I just don't wish to kill anyone. Would it help if I went into the bush to find the man and talk to him, persuade the man to negotiate?"

"You'll hunt him then?"

"But not as a soldier."

"You'll need soldiers for protection. This war, Seb, has to come to an end. There's another problem. Their women and children in these camps."

"Tell me about them. There's nothing about that in the papers."

With secret relief, James sat down in his deckchair. He had found the way to make his brother go to war. In vivid detail, he described the hell in what some were beginning to call the concentration camps.

"You see," he concluded, "now you know why we all have to do everything in our power to stop this war."

3

MAY 1901

*S*arie Mostert's only excitement was to wake each morning in the hut and find everyone alive. The quickly built hut had replaced the tent, but the ground area was the same and the four families lived diagonally across from each other with the cooking fire in the centre and a hole in the roof to let out the smoke. Typhoid had swept through the close confines of the camp killing six hundred and twelve people but in hut twenty-two, with Sarie in strict control of their habits, no one had fallen sick. By one of the many tricks Sarie had learnt in the slums of Pretoria as the dog lady, she had channelled the rainwater from the roof into closed containers that were jealously guarded inside the hut. The food was washed and cooked with the rainwater, and no one was allowed to drink anything else. The strange mix of containers had been filched from the British who threw them away; some had contained cooking oil, some paraffin for the lamps, and every meal or drink had a taste of something bad. When the rain fell, Sarie had the members of the hut, from children to the old woman Piers and Karel called Ma, out collecting water. Even when it was cold at night, the regime of changing the containers went on until every one was full. Some humid evenings. that changed to cold when the sun went down, precipitated dew, and not a drop of moisture was allowed down the improvised gutter pipes without ending up in the jumbled collection of containers. Water dished out by the British was used to wash their bodies and their clothes but was not allowed into their mouths.

Most of the day and night when she was not being told what to do by

Sarie, Helena Oosthuizen sat on the floor in her corner of the hut. She looked and behaved like an old woman of seventy and kept to herself, her mind blank. Having convinced herself that everyone was dead, there had been no point in thought. With her eyes closed, she made her mind a blank, only responding to orders from the girl who had once been her servant. Guarded by Sarie, she had been left on her own as the weeks and months trailed by with everyone, except Helena, wishing the war to be over.

Taking each day as it came, Sarie's triumph was waking with them all alive in the morning. To remain sane she neither thought forward nor back. To think of open space, her dogs or Billy would make her cry, and there was no place for the luxury of crying until they all went somewhere else they would hopefully call home.

Taking her daughters by the hand she went off once again to complain to the British about the food and to beg for extra blankets. At night in the middle of May it was bitterly cold on the highveld. She could have been talking to a brick wall, she told herself, as not one of the soldiers understood a word of Afrikaans. They just smiled at her and did nothing, making Sarie want to scream with frustration. Even the few words of English she had learnt from Billy were useless.

THE SWING HAD BEEN BUILT by Harry on his extended holiday from school. Hanging from the tallest tree on the bank of the Mazoe River it could take the rider out over the water and far back towards the homestead. The clean, tall branch that gave the swing its reach was as thick and strong as an elephant's trunk but only Harry in his frustration had taken the swing to its zenith.

Emily held the ropes at elbow height and pushed gently, her feet together in front of her. May was the best month in Rhodesia when the heat had gone and the trees were still green. It was early in the morning and the sun was yellow on the trees, the air soft and windless. There was not a sound from the houses behind and, being a Sunday, none of the servants came up from their compound. In front of Emily, the river flowed on its long journey to the Zambezi; it was quiet and gentle, a friendly river.

As so often happened when she was alone, her mind went back to England and she smiled ruefully to herself that all that had brought her here had begun on the soft moss beneath an English oak with the tall bracken guarding their sanctuary, the hum of summer insects sweet melody in their ears. And then came Arthur, dead Arthur, and she did not feel a thing for his passing. Swinging harder, she castigated herself... It was never good to think evil of the dead, however far away. Hers was not the first arranged marriage in the family and without even one of them, she would not be swinging from the trees in the middle of nowhere in the middle of Africa, a family of English surrounded by people she had never known to exist before her flight with Seb from England. The log floating by in midstream looked at her with large round eyes, turning the harmless wood into a live reptile, and when the swing came back she let go and dropped to her knees on the bank. The shiver of fear made her almost rattle.

SEB HAD WATCHED her ever since she had left their house and had come out to sit on the bench under the msasa tree while he plucked up his courage to tell her what he had to do. When she fell off onto her knees, he ran down the lawn to find her shivering from fright. Emily looked at him from the ground.

"There is a crocodile in the river. I thought it was a log and then it looked at me. Oh Seb, the eyes were the most malevolent eyes I have ever seen. It was as though he hated me. Can't we go back to England now that Arthur's dead?"

"What would I do? What would we live off?"

"We still own our shares in African Shipping. With the war, they must be worth a lot more than when Tinus sold his shares. Please, Seb. It was like someone walking over my grave. A premonition of evil. Please, Seb, I want to go home."

"This is our home."

"No, it isn't. We came here because we had to come here. We ran away with Harry. Now we can be married and even if some of the country people cut us dead, it's better than living here."

"Em. You forget the children. Harry's a bastard. So are Madge, George and little James. It isn't a problem here. They will marry other Rhodesians as the country thrives and grows. Your father can't go back. He gave up his money to annul your marriage. Outside of this farm, he doesn't have a penny. You mustn't let a crocodile floating out in the river frighten you."

"But it did, Seb. It frightened me almost to death."

"Come on up to the house and I'll make some tea."

Wearily Emily got to her feet.

"Are any of the children awake?" she asked.

"Not yet. And I'll take your father some tea in bed."

Arm in arm they walked back to the house through the gate in the stockade.

"Don't you think it's beautiful, Em?"

"Yes, it is."

"Look, I'll tell you what we'll do. The moment this war is over, we'll have ourselves married in church. Even Nat will consider you a widow. A sinner yes, but the Church always talks of repentance and forgiveness."

"What has the war got to do with it?"

"I'm going away, Em. There's something very important I have to do."

"Oh my God! Why now? Why you? It's James! Now do you believe in premonitions? You're going to die and leave me and the children in this wilderness. Please, Seb. Let's take our chances and go back to England."

As SEBASTIAN BRIGANDSHAW was riding south leading a second pack horse, some three hundred miles away to the southwest Tatenda was slowly riding north through the bush, two mules unwillingly following on a long leash. Zwide had died three days before and on his deathbed, he had confided to Tatenda the whereabouts of Lobengula's gold.

"You must take care of the people's gold and only use it for the Chimurenga that will free the black people from being the white man's servant," the old induna, general to Lobengula, the last King of the Matabele, had told Tatenda in the small, dark room at the back of Jack Slater's butcher shop, the iron bed on which Zwide was dying two bricks off the ground so the *tokoloshe*, the small people, could not look into his eyes. In the bush-timber roof rafters, three bats were hanging upside down in the semi-dark, with only the light of the sun filtering through cracks in the badly built shed.

"Make the gold safe and if in your lifetime the rising does not come, entrust the gold to a man like yourself. Only the gold can buy us enough guns to kill the white men when they have finished killing each other down south."

Slowly and with pain as the great cancer destroyed his body he made Tatenda repeat the praise song he had composed for Lobengula's funeral.

"The Shona and the Matabele are now brothers with the same desire to kill the white people. We are men of men who will not live forever like dogs in the white man's kennel."

When it was over Tatenda, no longer interested, had left the old man where he was for someone else to find and bury.

The mules being pulled behind the horse carried empty leather saddlebags that Tatenda had bought with one of the gold coins Zwide had given him. At twenty-five his aquiline features, a throwback to some itinerant Arab trader, were harder, the pointed ears sharper, the black eyes cold and full of hate. The passion of his conviction took him ever north towards the second cave where Zwide had taken the gold and ivory.

BACK IN BULAWAYO, the Jewish pedlar looked at the old Portuguese gold coin in the palm of his hand. "Lobengula gold," he said out loud. "Where else would a black get a coin like this? That man had no idea of its value. Maybe there are more." He talked loudly to himself as the fever of gold flooded his mind. "Now who can I trust to follow that black man?" Having trekked through the bush for ten years, Isaac Stein was sure he could find and follow the distinctive trail of a horse and two mules. "You are an old fool, Isaac," he said. "You can trust no man with gold." Quickly, he put the two horses into the shafts and without telling anyone, left Bulawayo in the same direction he had watched the black man leave with the mules and Isaac Stein's leather saddlebags. For the first time in a very long time, he was excited.

TEN MILES TO THE NORTH, Tatenda was making a vow to his dead parents and siblings, massacred by the impi of Matabele.

"First, we will kill the white men and then we will turn our guns against the Zulus who call themselves Matabele. The people of Monomotapa, the Shona, will rise again as the great power of central Africa. This, my dead parents, I swear to you and all my ancestors."

ON THE FIFTH day of his journey, Isaac caught sight of the mules for the first time having followed the trail through the mopane forest, the footprint of the two mules quite distinctive from the horse. Every night his quarry had stopped and made a fire, making his pursuit as simple as following a road. The bush, empty of people, had only twice made him deviate to find a way around for his small covered wagon where the horse and mules had been able to go straight ahead. At the end of the third day he had thought of giving up but each subsequent day he had said he would try another. Even as he looked at the mules and the lone rider Isaac was no wiser as to their destination. From where he stopped on the wooded hill he could look down and see the horse and the pack animals as they moved through the trees. The black man was maybe a mile ahead of him and through the binoculars, he could make out what he thought was a rifle in a holster next to the rider's right knee. To the left, about three miles away, rose a jagged outcrop of vast round rocks the size of small mountains. Isaac got down from the bench, letting the reins loose on the back of the horses. The two animals dropped their heads and began pulling at the brown, dry grass while Isaac watched his prey from the shade of a tree. In two hours the sun would go down and the man in front would make a fire while Isaac took refuge from the wild animals in his covered wagon. Looking at the barrier of the great rocks, Isaac estimated the line of mules and horse to be heading for the centre and not a detour that would take them around through the forest. To be sure the man in front was unaware of his presence, Isaac refrained from making a fire. When the light had gone from the sky completely he climbed into his wagon and for more than an hour, he prayed to his God for guidance. Then he slept through the night at peace in both his mind and body.

TATENDA HAD BEEN unaware of the eyes watching him through the glasses but had been certain he had found the right range of low mountains. Instead of memorising each word of the king's praise song, he had memorised each of Zwide's directions. He had travelled northwest by the sun during the day while checking his position each night by the cross in the sky made of four stars with two bright stars below the cross. When he had reached the Shangani River, where Zwide had won his greatest battle, he had not crossed but kept along its banks looking for the great rocks that pushed up from the mopane forest. When the sun had been sinking behind the great, round mountains he had waited to be shown the one shaped like a buffalo. Exactly as Zwide had said, as the ball of fire through the last flames of day brushed the sky behind the rocks blood red, Tatenda had seen the one he was looking for. That night, he had talked to God through his ancestors and when he finally slept by the fire he slept comfortably, not even remembering in the morning the times he had been awake to stack more wood on the fire.

All through that night, not even the lions made a sound.

LIKE ANY YOUNG man in love, Isaac was driven by his passion to provide a good home. He had met Deborah Landau ten long years before and, despite the miles, he had travelled from Johannesburg to supply the outlying farms with everything from buckets to the new-fangled binoculars, but had never made enough money to satisfy Deborah's father. Then the war had come along and driven him over the Limpopo in the hope that the new settlers in Rhodesia would make him rich. The problem with Isaac when it came to business was quite simple, people said... He was just too nice. Instead of paying less than he should when he bought his wares, he gave a fair price. When it came to the selling, the idea of cheating a man who most often had just given him dinner went against his way of life. To add to his problem, whenever he found a farmer really down and out on his luck he was oft inclined to lend the man money that he knew he would never see again.

Now, in his desperate need to satisfy old man Landau, he was going to rob a man of his gold. Isaac had slept so well through the night that the sun had warmed the canvas of his wagon before he woke. When he climbed out in excitement and trepidation, there was no sign of his quarry. Patiently he glassed the bush from his hilltop, concentrating on the path towards the great, bald hills. His hobbled horses had moved some distance from the wagon after finishing the water in the bucket he had put down for them before going to bed. After half an hour the sun was too hot for his jacket even under the shade of a tree. Showing thick braces holding up his baggy pants, Isaac put his coat in the wagon. The alarm call of the grey lourie was quite distinctive and sounded like a man saying 'goaway' all in one word, the one word repeated as the bird hopped through the branches of the trees to get away from the danger. Lifting his head from the wagon, and with the smile of hope on his face, Isaac went back to his vantage point where he waited. When the bird call came three more times, he was certain. The man on his horse and the mules were heading for a bald mountain that somehow looked like a buffalo.

The only thing Isaac Stein had not worked out since leaving Bulawayo was how to rob the man even if, after all, the man had anything to rob. Then Isaac remembered the rifle in the saddle holder and felt quite queasy.

TATENDA FOUND the entrance to the cave behind the twisted tree that had somehow forced sustenance from a crack in the rock. Once through the small entrance, the cave was wide. After waiting for his eyes to become accustomed to the semi-darkness he walked forward, hunching his shoulders to keep from hitting his head on the roof. Further on he could just stand up. The smell of old bat droppings made him hold his nose. With his eyes still unsure of the light, he rubbed his left leg on something hard and smooth sticking up out of the ground. Running his hand along the obstruction he moved around and slowly on into the cave, rubbing his fingers on the palm of the hand that had touched the smooth surface he thought was rock. Ten slow steps further in the dark the excitement hit. The smooth, curved rock that his hand had followed to the end was the thick smooth tusk of an elephant. Then his foot snagged on something lower down and when he bent to the ground, his hands found an iron box. After waiting ten minutes sitting on the box his eyes finally grew accustomed to the dark. He counted three boxes next to a pile of ivory, some of the tusks as thick as his thighs. When he picked up the boxes, they were small and heavy. One by one he humped them across to the light at the entrance to the cave.

By the time the sun had reached its zenith, the gold coins had passed from the iron boxes into the saddlebags that hung over the mules. Checking the ground around the mules and empty boxes, Tatenda began what he knew was the most important journey of his life, the journey that would one day free his people from bondage.

THREE HOURS LATER, having followed a devious path down the hill with the wagon, Isaac stood over the empty boxes, old, rusted and broken open. On the ground next to one of the boxes stood the clear impression of the President of the Transvaal Republic, Oom Paul Kruger, who had taken himself and his own gold millions off to Switzerland soon after Lord Roberts had marched into Pretoria at the head of an army. Checking the prints made by the mules on their journey away from the boxes, there was no doubt in Isaac's mind. The pack mules were carrying a new and heavy load that sunk their hooves that much further into the ground. It was also clear by the scuffles on the ground that the man he had followed for so many days had been forced to pull the mules to make them walk with the new load pressing heavily on their backs. Away from the scuffed footmarks showed where the boxes had been found and within a minute Isaac was bending behind the gnarled tree and hunching his shoulders to walk through the entrance to the cave. Overcoming his fear of the pitch-dark cavern and the terrible smell of the bat droppings, Isaac waited for his eyes to become accustomed so he could see what was hidden in the cave. One of the bats having had enough of the disturbances flew past the top of his head, the wind brushing his skull and making the hair on the back of his neck stand out straight. Only by thinking of Deborah could he stop himself bolting back into the light. Praying all the time to his God, Isaac moved deeper into the cave. Taking the box of red-tipped Swan Vesta matches from his pocket, he lit one of the long sticks and held it above his head. By the time the flame went out, Isaac knew the only problem in his life was over. For sixty years, from the time of Mzilikazi to the time of Lobengula, each white hunter had brought back to Gu-Bulawayo and the king's kraal the best pair of tusks from their hunt as a tribute. Lighting the second match, Isaac walked around the pile. He found the pit where the iron boxes had lain on the ground, with droppings clearly marking the squares.

"Well, there's no time like the present," he said loudly, and pulled the largest elephant tusk from the pile and stumbled with it back towards the light at the exit to the cave.

Taking the oil lamp from the roof of his wagon he began unloading the picks and shovels he had intended selling to the gold prospectors still scattered across the country, lost in their own search for wealth. In a large pile on the far side of the wagon from the entrance to the cave was a pile of ironmongery, all of it carrying the mark of *Made in Manchester*. By the time the sun turned blood-red behind the great bald mountain of a rock, the wagon was as full as it ever could be and Isaac was back on the box, the leather reins in his practised hands. With more creaks than ever before, he got the horses moving and drove them down his own trail on the long ride back to Johannesburg.

He turned back once. With the sun behind the rock, the shape of the buffalo was quite plain to see.

"Good luck, whoever you are," he called behind to where the mules and horse had gone east. "And thank you."

Shortly afterwards, when he could no longer see his own trail, he stopped for the night, making a grand fire. With the horses once more watered and hobbled, he knelt down next to his wagonload of ivory and prayed his thanks to the Lord.

Just before he dropped off to sleep beside his roaring fire he smiled to himself... He still had had no idea how he was going to rob the man of his gold. That night and for the first time since seeing the Portuguese gold coin, Isaac dreamed of Deborah Landau and all was well in their world of dreams.

FOUR HUNDRED MILES to the east, in the direction Tatenda was riding with the mules, the witch was preparing her revenge. Having spent all her life breeding fear out of superstition, everyone who lived in the sprawling cluster of snake- and insect-infested grass huts feared the old hag they had once, for a brief moment, called the Prophet. Others controlled their people with soldiers and the threat of physical harm; the witch controlled her people with the fear of the dark spirits, fear she had instilled in each of them, and it never went away.

The smelling out had been rumoured for months, small signs spread by the witch. Now, when she knew no one would challenge the fear that lived in each of them, she disappeared for a week into the heart of her cave. When she reappeared to the full moon, carrying the skull of the predecessor she had poisoned, covered in old and filthy skins with necklaces of bones, some animal, some human, draped around her neck and falling to her skinny, naked knees with the leopard at her side, everyone in the village, including the chief, shook with fear. All night long the cackles came from the tops of different trees and no one slept, cowering in their windowless huts consumed by fear of the spirits. Even the small babies cried all through the night. When the sun rose over the mountains that dropped down a great escarpment into the Zambezi Valley, the witch announced her smelling out to find the man or woman or child who had cast a spell over the chief to stop his seventh wife from falling pregnant after twelve new moons. With a flywhisk made from the tail hair of a long-dead buffalo, she went from hut to squalid hut, sometimes striking the door until the occupants came out into the light, trembling and petrified with fear, all the doors of the village shut in the hope of reprieve.

After two long hours of her slow, erratic searching, many villagers cowered under the big tree around which the dust-blown village sprawled, each one waiting with dread for the whisk to slash their face. The leopard, bored with her antics, had gone back into the cool comfort of the cave and gone to sleep. When the sun rose to its zenith, everyone but one in the village, including the chief, had been summoned under the big tree. The witch, at the height of her power, plunged a torch into the cooking fire that never went out and handed the flaming faggot to the chief.

"Burn down his hut," she commanded.

"He is my son."

"He has cast into you the evil spirit. Burn the hut with all his family or the whole village will die. I have spoken with the spirits. Do as I say or die, all of you." The cackles, as she projected her voice, came from tree after tree, darting back and forward while the torch flew round in circles flying sparks among the nearest huts.

"Kill him," she screamed. "Kill the chief and burn his son. *Kill him*."

In the dry heat of the new summer, the hut, torched by eager hands, exploded in flame. The door was wrenched open and a small boy ran from the flames to be picked up by the screaming mob and thrown back into the fire. Under the big tree, the boy's grandfather was being torn to pieces, cut and chopped with small-headed axes, the nearest of the mob screaming out their fear in the bloodlust and joy of not being killed.

When the frenzy died down with the flames, the witch had gone back to her cave. Stroking the leopard's sleeping head she smiled with satisfaction. Not for a long time would anyone else challenge her power.

TATENDA SAW the plume of smoke rising to the noonday sky and wondered what it was. The clouds, white-topped and grey below, were motionless in the blueness of the sky and the smoke rose straight up before bending with the wind. After watching the smoke and discounting a bushfire, the woodsmoke touched his nostrils.

Before riding into the Kalanga village that evening he slipped the heavy saddlebags from the mules and hid them deep in a thorn thicket, cutting his legs and arms on the thorns. Taking precise directions from trees and rocks, he rode on into the village he had left to fight the war of liberation four years earlier that had ended with him running away to Bulawayo. The ally, the one that would guard the treasure deep in the leopard cave, was the witch.

The hut of the chief's son was still burning slowly, sending small curls of smoke from the ruins. The smell of cooked meat came from the embers and charred black humps showed in the ashes where the family had burnt to death. No one even looked at the smouldering pile, and when he asked for the witch they ran away. Pieces of a bloody corpse lay in the dust, covered in thousands of buzzing flies, and no one took any notice. Some of his old friends gave him a half-smile, but no one looked him in the eyes, and Tatenda knew better than to ask what had happened in the village.

Leading his animals away from the squalid huts and smell of death, he walked them to where he had first found an entrance to the leopard cave where he made his camp and waited for the morning. The moon almost full was bright and the dotted clouds shone silver in the night sky. All night hyena prowled the village, smelling the blood of the fly-blown corpse under the tree, their cackling laughter echoing the cackles of the witch. For the first time since finding the gold of Lobengula, Tatenda slept fitfully, dreaming the fire was going out, and the hyenas were ripping his arms and legs from his body.

When he woke in the morning, the hut in the village was still smouldering. When he walked along to the village, the corpse had gone in the night, the only leftover being black clots of dried blood mingling with the dirt that not even the flies were interested in. All day and alone he waited for the witch, and then he went back to the cave entrance and spent a second tangled night.

On the third night when he woke, the fire had died down so low he had to blow on the embers to bring back the flame and comfort. Feeding the fire, he felt safe as the flames leapt and showed him the trees and surrounding rocks. Just before dawn he smelt the fetid smell of leopard and drew his coat closer around his chest. Only when the first dove called to him in the morning did he walk away from the fire. Gently he stroked the muzzle of his horse and then the long, donkey-like ears of the mules. When he went to the village, the blackened and charred humps still lay in the circle of the ruined hut, the putrid smell pervading everything in the village. Again all day, he waited for the witch in vain, and still the villagers were loath to speak to him, as if after arriving so soon after what he saw as a tragedy he was part of the omen, of their evil.

The fourth night and next to the biggest fire of his journey, Tatenda slept from physical and mental exhaustion and woke to find the only light in the sky given by the layers of the stars. The moon had been down for some time and the fire was low, the only light issuing from the red-hot coals. At first, he could only smell the old hag but when he moved up from the ground on one elbow, the witch cackled and stepped forward from the black darkness of a tree. As the coin spun towards him, the soft gold caught the glow of the red-hot embers before the metal hit him in the chest. Standing next to the witch, the yellow eyes of the leopard glowed from the fire. When it opened its mouth, he could smell the fetid breath from eating the rotten corpse of the chief.

"Why did you hide the gold?" she asked.

"To bring it safely to you. It is gold for the guns and the second Chimurenga."

"That is good. Go now in the night with your mules and bring me the rest of the gold."

"Who found the bags in the thorn thicket?"

"The ancestors told me in a dream."

The fear of the spirits stopped him thinking clearly and questioning how the spirits had brought the one gold coin that lay in the dust next to the fire. The mules and horse caught the smell of the leopard and tried to break their tether. While Tatenda was calming his animals the witch and leopard vanished. When the saddle was back on his horse and with the mules on the long rein, at the first touch of morning light he rode from his camp.

At the thorn thicket, he searched all morning, checking his rocks and tree markers time and again until he finally understood. Whoever had given the witch the one coin was not an ancestor.

Riding back as fast as possible he pushed behind the covering of bush and tree at the entrance to the cave, waited for his eyes to pierce the gloom, and walked deep into the cavern. With the sun in the wrong position, he could only see a pinprick of light high in the cavern of the roof where once a year a beam of light fell directly to the cavern floor. Again he smelt the leopard and called out to the witch. The sharp single click of her tongue on the roof of her mouth echoed in the cavern. As the witch's cackle ricocheted around the cave, the back legs of the leopard ripped open Tatenda's belly, spilling his entrails on the floor among the long-dead bones. Then the incisor teeth ripped out his throat, and the world was gone to him.

4

JUNE 1901

*B*illy Clifford could not make up his mind whether to write the book as fact or fiction. To further his career as a journalist he needed the prestige of a well-received book. A history of the conflict in Africa from a writer who had lived through the war would give him the stature among his peers that would last months and be forgotten when the next crisis sent the writers of the world scurrying somewhere else. Fact stayed where it was, a reference for future historians, Billy a footnote in someone else's book. Fiction, good fiction, lived forever.

For months, Billy had been secretly studying the people involved in the conflict so that when he sat down at his desk back in Ireland, the replay of the pictures from his mind would be as real as they had been in the flesh. Home in Dublin he would carve in stone the war that had raged around him for so long.

The long bar at the Criterion Hotel in Johannesburg's Jeppe Street was a lonely place for men away from home. The barman had retreated to a stool in his corner and the only other man on the same elbow of the bar was easy to study without making it obvious. The man looked like a defeated Boer with the old slouch hat on the bar unclipped to its side. Billy could see the sweat stains where the hat had touched the owner's head, the wide brim cleaner, a lighter brown.

Every time the man wanted a drink he lifted a finger. The man had neither spoken nor moved from his stool.

Mentally stealing the man's features, Billy put his age at nearer forty than thirty; the face had a tough, leathery texture from too many years in the African sun, the hair bleached white, the hands rough from manual work, the part of the eyes that Billy could see a pale blue; the man's shoulders were powerful. The trousers had leather patches home-sewn to protect the insides of the thighs; the leather waistcoat was mottled and coloured grey and unbuttoned, the skin soft and pliable; on the man's feet were high leather riding boots such as the Boers wore on commando.

The notes of conflict, the points that shared nothing with a defeated Boer, were the long, almost white ponytail that hung down the man's back and the fact he was cleanly shaven.

Lost in his reverie, Billy stared past the man's right ear.

"Didn't your mother tell you, old boy, that it's rude to stare?"

"You're not a Boer," said Billy in surprise. "What's that waistcoat made from?" he asked loudly.

"The skin of a baby elephant. At a time when I didn't know any better, I killed its mother and father for their tusks. You ever killed anything, Irishman?"

"No. I'm a journalist."

"Good."

"They have a good table I hear. Would you care to take supper with me? My name is William Clifford of Dublin. Everyone calls me Billy."

"Sebastian Brigandshaw, from Rhodesia. Most people call me Seb."

THE WALLS of the dining room were panelled with dark mahogany. The silver on the white, heavily starched tablecloths was heavy. Candelabra sat in the centre of their round table burning three candles. There were three other tables occupied in the room and soon after they sat down, a group of British officers took the table next to them. They all gave Seb's dress code a stare.

"I don't have formal clothing," he explained to Billy. "Em and I don't dress for dinner. Some of the newer farmers make a whole paraphernalia out of keeping up appearances. They think if they don't they will stop being British. Some of them dress up the blacks to make them look more like English servants. Keeping up the standards and all that rubbish. Look a prize bunch of fools if you ask me, stuck out there in the middle of the bush. More likely to have a wild animal knock on the door than another Englishman. What the hell does it matter what you look like if there's no one else to see? I have a mind to ban mirrors right across the world. Stop people staring at themselves. Vanity and pride, Billy Clifford, are terrible things. After the war, this management will throw me out dressed in the skin of an elephant. For the moment I hope we are safe."

At the long table next to them the six young officers got to their feet. A man with a drooping moustache, a bright red nose and red cheeks sat himself down at the head of the table. The colonel who sat down next to the grey-haired man surprised Billy by waving at their table.

"My brother James. We try not to greet each other in public. The man next to him, I suspect, is the head of British Intelligence. My new employers. They want me to run around in the bush, find the Boer generals who won't stop fighting and talk some sense into them. There's one in particular they call the Giant."

"How do they think you are going to do that?"

"I can follow a trail at the gallop. Nothing clever. After years, anything broken or turned in the bush sticks out like a beacon of light. The wind eventually discounts the normal and registers the change."

"Do you speak Afrikaans?"

"Yes."

"He speaks perfect English, the Giant. Gave him his name. Took the photograph of General Gore-Bilham in his underpants."

"Why do they go on fighting when they know they can't win?"

"There are many reasons and none of them the reasons they give out. They call them Bittereinders, and that's the only part that is true. They are bitter but mostly for all the wrong reasons. I understand them. We have bitter men in Ireland. The Boers think we Irish sympathise with them, two nations who have felt the yolk of the British Empire. Mostly they are men with grudges, men with nowhere to go, who for the first time in their lives have found a home in a cause, found themselves among like-minded friends. And they don't want to give it up. All the patriotism is an excuse for not wishing to face the reality of their lives. In wars, men who would have been failures become heroes. Most of the men out there in the bush don't want to lose the one time they mean something in life. Some of them may be patriots. Some of them may have political ambitions. Some of them just can't find an honourable way out. For most, it has become a way of life that they like. A young dead man doesn't have to face his responsibilities. Maybe some are just very brave men. You can take your pick when you talk to them if they'll talk to you. If you are a threat, they will kill you. Gore-Bilham wasn't a threat, so they took down his trousers and made him a fool... Why doesn't your brother come across and talk to us?"

"Not in public. Father pays him an allowance which, even though the cause of the problem is dead, James thinks he will lose his money if he talks to me and father gets to hear. Money is everything to people like my brother. Fact is, it's everything to most people. So I'm not going to jeopardise his inheritance by making a fuss.

"Now, seeing you talked me so easily into having supper I want you to tell me what has really happened in this war. I want to know about the concentration camps where women and children are dying by the thousands. Kitchener has burnt down most of the Boer farmsteads, I understand. The British wish to extend universal franchise from the Cape to the Transvaal and the Free State which would give the blacks and Uitlanders the vote and turn the Boers into a minority with no political influence. The British, I suspect, want one southern African country from the Zambezi to the Cape under British rule. Rhodes, I know, plans a British railway line from Cape Town to Cairo from which British power will enforce law and order, Christianity and trade... The man's father's a parson. You are the one with the knowledge, Mr Clifford. In return, I will be happy to relate a few bush anecdotes for your book. Now, when is your paper going to expose the horror of these camps to the public at home? That behaviour, if it is true, is quite unacceptable to Englishmen... Oh, and don't get me wrong. It's far nicer to have supper with someone else than eating on one's own. There are two things people should avoid doing in life: eating or drinking alone."

"Do you like farming?"

"Yes, I do. Isolation has the advantage of avoiding other people's poison, the poison that is in their heads turning everything to be looked at from their own perspective, their own point of view. A farmer's problems are the basis of life and the closeness to nature is similar, I think, to the closeness some people feel to God. I understand the Boer with his land and his Bible. Once I asked my brother the priest whether God was nature or nature, God. Within each of us is the nature that made us, the evolution of the species. The priests will tell us that God is in each one of us. In the bush, nature follows us and watches us, whether a butterfly or a lion. I am constantly reminded of great beauty even out of the rainy season when the bush crackles in the dry but nothing living moves in the heat of the day. I can sit on the banks of an African river and be full of joy watching the animals and the birds, just being part of nature. If nature is God, Mr Clifford, I am a very religious man."

"You are lucky to have found what you want. Very few of us do."

"Which is why this war must be brought to an end so the Boers can go back to being what they were in the first place, farmers."

"Do you think the white man should have brought to Africa his mission from God and his medicine?"

"No. He should have left it to natural evolution. Life becomes too complicated when you play around with the laws of nature. A short, sweet life is better than a long and ugly one. Never interfere with nature. I rather think it is tantamount to interfering with God."

"A lot of men think they are gods."

"And all of them are wrong."

THEY WERE the last to leave the restaurant and go to their rooms; James, Colonel Hickman and their party had left soon after eating their meal. Billy and Seb had shaken hands at the foot of the stairs, ships in the night never expecting to talk with each other again. When Billy came down to breakfast, he was told that Mr Sebastian Brigandshaw had left at dawn with the newly promoted Colonel Brigandshaw and six troopers of the Mashonaland Scouts. The tall, blond man had been dressed in civilian clothes, the rest in uniform. And no, Mr Sebastian Brigandshaw had not left a forwarding address. Disappointed in losing such a good source of information, he cabled his newspaper in Dublin and by late in the afternoon was reading their reply. His editor had also heard rumours of concentration camps and he was told to make a full investigation and take photographs.

With meticulous and devious care Billy Clifford went about finding out where the British Army was herding the Boer women and children before setting out on another of his long journeys alone into the veld. At night it was freezing cold but this time he was organised with the right equipment and slept under the layers of crystal clear and twinkling stars better than he had slept on the lumpy and curved mattress in the Criterion Hotel, the sleeping bag, thick with lamb's wool, pulled up to his nostrils, the hood down to his eyebrows. Each night by his fire he looked up at the great dome of heaven that was too vast for his mind to comprehend. Most nights he heard the bark and snort of wild animals but after a full day in the saddle, and with the fire bright as protection, not even the roar of an occasional lion could keep him awake.

AT THE FIRST CAMP, the rows of graves told a bitter story. Most of the mounds were short and small of width, some the size of a shoebox. The names were burnt onto wooden crosses. Billy counted seven Bothas, one large, the size of any grave in Dublin, the rest smaller and smaller down to the one the size of a shoebox.

Inside, the British let him look in at the huts, squalid and mostly dirty, but if there were any inmates able to speak English, none were willing to talk to the *Irish Times*, despite Billy's show of horrified sympathy. There were no military doctors or nurses. Even the guards were apathetic. Whatever they did was not enough to prevent the spread of disease among a people who for generations had lived in isolation on the veld.

Everyone blamed everything on the war. "There's a war on, mate, 'ain't you 'eard?" was the common refrain. "Two of my mates are also buried on the veld," said a private. "Soon as the buggers stop fightin' we can all go 'ome, can't we? Stands to reason. Far as I'm concerned this lot can go 'ome right now, but the sarge says they wouldn't last a week on their own. The blacks, the sarge says, them blacks'll take revenge for chasin' 'em off their land. Stands to reason. Go and tell Smuts and Botha to stop fightin'. Not my bleedin' fault they die of measles. What made the silly bugger come out 'ere in the first place? Sarge said they were running away from the Catholics, whoever they are."

"I'm a Catholic," said Billy.

"Then it's all your bleedin' fault, ain't it? Stands to reason. All I know it ain't my bleedin' fault. You sweat it out in the sun during the day and freeze your balls at night. And without the missus."

WHILE BILLY WAS VISITING his second camp with the same result, Seb cut the spoor of the Boer commando. After careful inspection of the trampled ground, he looked up at his still-mounted brother.

"Two hundred plus horses. No wagons. Crossed yesterday. The ants have burrowed up again and covered bits of the track. The flies have lost interest in the horse dung. No moisture. Thirty-six hours. You want to follow?"

"Of course. You want to talk to them, remember?"

The troop was sixty miles as the crow flies south of the small town of Vereeniging, six miles over the Vaal River. James's intelligence had been right. The Giant was making a foray into the Free State. The target had to be the railway line to Johannesburg.

THE BLACK STALLION Jeremiah Shank had called Diamond was a poor replica of the animal that had left the farm in Rhodesia. Constant movement and lack of winter grazing had left all the animals undernourished and half their normal weight. The dirty, ill-kept men in tattered clothing were also skeletons, the only thing clean being their Mauser rifles and the eyes of the Boers who were ready to shoot them. Any fat on Tinus Oosthuizen that left

Kleinfontein in the Cape had long been spent. Some of the men walked beside their horses to conserve the animals' strength. Magnus du Plessis walking next to Tinus had not spoken a word all morning, though he regularly checked their position by the position of the sun. Tired, exhausted men easily rode round in a wide circle finding their own tracks a day later. The exact position of the two hundred-horse commandos at a specified time was as essential to the campaign as the men and guns and Tinus used every skill he had learnt in his long years as a hunter to bring his men to the rendezvous with de Wet and Smuts. Then they would hit the British, replenish their food and guns and bombshell into small groups throughout the Free State bush. The full raid would amount to fifteen hundred men and the small British garrison could not withstand an attack of such magnitude.

ON THE WALL MAP, Colonel Hickman again moved the position of the Mashonaland Scouts. In the town of Kroonstad, a highly armoured train was ready to move north while a brigade of mounted infantry stood ready to ride three miles into the bush. Their first orders had been to ride into the Free State for the small town of Lindley where British Intelligence falsely rumoured that the will of the wisp, General de Wet, was resting his commando. Outside Parys, a small town on the Vaal River, two brigades of Scots Cavalry were ready to ride at a moment's notice. Between the Scots and the mounted infantry, Hickman controlled a brigade of Australians, whose job was to look as visible as possible. Behind James Brigandshaw, the Scots Cavalry and the mounted infantry ran a thin line of copper wire giving Hickman his control. The Australians patrolling the railway line were as much bait as protection. With Sebastian Brigandshaw following the Giant like a bloodhound and accurately assessing his speed and direction, the colonel was beginning to enjoy himself. Next to him in the control room, General Gore-Bilham sipped brandy from a large balloon glass with a look of satisfied retribution. This time he was the cat and Tinus Oosthuizen the mouse.

"Are you quite sure the commando ahead of Brigandshaw is the Giant?" he asked for the third time.

"We had a report he was in the area but it doesn't matter. They will all join forces to make an attack. Follow this one close enough and all of them will come together. When we kill or capture Oosthuizen, de Wet and Smuts, the war will be over. Botha and de la Rey will surrender."

. . .

"THEY'VE BACKTRACKED on their own spoor," said Sebastian. "The weight of the print is going the other way. Look, you can see that hoof mark is on top of the one more heavily indented. The horses are unshod. Then horsemen dismounted and went back again after the detour to muddle their direction. The destination has not changed but they are now no more than twelve miles up ahead. I will now go on alone. They will think me a messenger from de Wet or Smuts."

"Follow them with us until the morning. Then you can go alone. Far better we bring in the army and you can talk to their general when he is under armed guard."

"No, James, I will then be his enemy. We will make camp in those trees. Tomorrow, then."

"TOMORROW, THEN," said Magnus du Plessis. "It all comes together tomorrow. At noon, all three commandos attack the British garrison at Kroonstad and burn it to the ground. Tonight we sleep. I am both terribly tired and terribly excited."

JAMES HAD PLACED the guard next to the horses. Sebastian smiled to himself in the dark. The moon would be up in half an hour. Tomorrow was a full moon. They really did think him a fool. Even if Billy Clifford had not described his friend over dinner, a verbatim and professional journalist's report of an interviewed British soldier who had seen the Giant, Seb had known since Harry's letter from Cape Town. Tinus, away from Kleinfontein, had joined the war. Every move to cover their tracks of the horsemen up ahead had been explained to Sebastian time and again. The direction of the Boer commando was on a specific course of an intersection and only a man who had hunted the bush most of his life would know how to navigate day and night to make a rendezvous at an exact time. There was no doubt in Sebastian's mind the Boer leader up ahead was his partner, Tinus Oosthuizen.

Ten minutes before the moon came up, Seb made his move. The Scouts and James were asleep around the fire and the single guard next to the horses was relieving himself with his back to the fire. The man had been told to watch the horses by Colonel Brigandshaw but even if he had counted the sleeping bodies around the fire, he would still have made the number seven: Seb, before vanishing in the night, had filled his sleeping bag with handfuls of dry, springy grass.

Once the moon came up and he had taken his position from the stars, Sebastian began the mile-eating jog of the Zulus. Even in the moonlight he never lost the spoor of the horse commando. Many of the cuts in the ground made by the hooves of the horses were easier to see than in daylight, the moon-shadows throwing regular patterns that were as easy for Sebastian to follow as a railway line. Once he tripped and fell, rolling with his rifle and bruising his hip on his water bottle. With the big bush hat back on his head, Seb ran on into the African night.

HALF AN HOUR after the sun came up Colonel Hickman, back in the control room after a restful night's sleep, was handed the message from James Brigandshaw.

Our man has flown the coop. Suspect he knew all along. I will follow the spoor myself.

When General Gore-Bilham arrived after breakfast, Colonel Hickman kept the wire to himself.

"Can we let the decoy train go?" asked the general cheerfully. He had eaten a good breakfast and was feeling pleased with himself... The man, of course, would be hanged by the neck as a traitor.

"Worst crime in the world, turning on your own people," he said out loud. "Biting the hand that feeds them. Treason, Hickman. Worst crime in the world. Can't have our own people turning on us, now can we?"

Not wishing to probe the general's mind, Hickman agreed with him. 'Problem is,' he thought, 'he's one of them, not one of us.' Then he thought how true the words of Oliver Cromwell, Lord Protector of all England, had been: 'It's only treason if you lose.'

The second message from Colonel Brigandshaw was short and to the point.

Lost the spoor.

"We have a problem," he said to Gore-Bilham, who was pouring a cup of tea.

. . .

HAVING CHASED a phantom spoor that had more to do with a herd of buffalo than a horse commando, James Brigandshaw admitted to himself that not only had he lost contact with the Giant, he was lost and would have to ride back on his own copper wire. Making temporary camp in a clump of trees, he cursed underestimating his brother. For a moment he felt a twinge of jealousy. Sebastian's partner was more of a brother to him than his own family.

THE ARGUMENT HAD GONE on all night and through the day as Tinus and Seb walked side by side next to the black stallion, only the sick in the commando riding the best of the horses. Their time and position were perfect for the rendezvous.

Seb had waited for the moon to go down before penetrating the Boer camp. He had come upon the camp three hours after leaving his grass-stuffed sleeping bag.

When Tinus woke up from a restless sleep Seb was gently blowing on his ear.

"Good morning, Tinus," he said in English.

"We're not hunting tonight."

"No, but people are hunting us. Wake up slowly, my friend. This is not a dream and I'm not a ghost. Your men are very tired and easy to crawl past."

"Something wrong, general?" called the man next to them in Afrikaans.

"No problem," answered Seb in the same language.

THE BRITISH NET began to close just after General Gore-Bilham had eaten his lunch. He was enjoying a cigar with his after-lunch brandy. The Scots were in pursuit of de Wet, and the Mounted Infantry had found the tracks of Smuts. Only the Giant was lost to the British somewhere in the bush. By teatime, the Mounted Infantry and the Scots had lost the fresh spoor but Hickman had made up his mind.

"They're after the garrison at Kroonstad," said Colonel Hickman to General Gore-Bilham.

"Don't be ridiculous. That's no fortified British camp."

"I want the Mounted Infantry to fall back on Kroonstad."

"And leave a hole in the draw net? Don't be so bloody stupid."

"There are only three hundred men at Kroonstad."

"With machine guns and artillery. Hickman, you've lost your mind. You intelligence wallahs are always thinking of something. In India, we didn't have an intelligence department. Far better. No distractions."

Once again, Colonel Hickman kept his temper. 'And what happened in the mutiny?' he said to himself.

"MANY OF MY burghers are from the Cape," said Tinus Oosthuizen. "The British will try them for treason. Can you guarantee they won't, Seb? Of course you can't. The only thing we know how to do is go on as we are. The women and children are now a British responsibility. There's nothing we can do."

"Surrender. For God's sake surrender."

"Would you surrender if the whole British people were at stake? If the Boers lose political control, they lose their nation, their language, everything they have been for two hundred and fifty years in Africa. Give the Transvaal and Free State independence, Cape Boers immunity and we can all go back to living side by side with the British."

"I have come a long way to plead with you."

"Seb, too many people have killed each other. The goodwill of two white races together in Africa has gone. The Boers will hate the British for a hundred years. And don't come back to me about my mother and Alison. I am a Boer. For now, Sebastian, you are my prisoner. I cannot jeopardise my men by letting you go. Or better, my friend, will you fight with us?"

"You know I can't do that however much I understand."

"When we attack, you can make a run for your British lines."

"Tinus, please."

"There's no please. This is war."

"It's also a trap. De Wet and Smuts are being shadowed."

"How do you know about de Wet and Smuts?"

"The British aren't as stupid as you would sometimes like to think. They have their own intelligence sources. When I found your spoor I reported your direction."

"How?"

"They pulled a line of copper wire behind us. They have been tracking you like a wounded buffalo. Either surrender and get the war over or make a run. I know there are two brigades of Scots Cavalry. The Scots Guards, Tinus. Some of the best soldiers in the world. And they are fresh. And so are their horses. Get out before they pull the noose around your neck. Now. You made a fool of Gore-Bilham and he's the one after you."

"Then he'll hang me anyway."

"If you surrender with de Wet and Smuts there will be a peace agreement. Gore-Bilham is not the British government. Many people in England have had enough of this war. They have a respect for so few fighting the whole bloody empire. If you surrender, your women and children will stop dying in the camps and I don't think the British would hang a soldier who surrenders voluntarily. If that isn't enough for you personally, disperse your men and go north into the bush. What about Alison and your children?"

"What about my people? You think Barend would ever look at me if I ran away?"

Colonel James Brigandshaw had waited for the night sky to guide him home. Never again would he allow his compass to be carried by anyone but himself, let alone his brother. Within half an hour of telling Colonel Hickman Seb had flown the coop the wire had gone dead, and when they had tried to follow it back, they found one severed end but not the other. An animal had snared the copper wire, broken loose and run off with the other end caught in its foot. After three hours of fruitless search in the long elephant grass, they had made a second camp and waited for the night sky and the beacon of the Southern Cross.

Once they had found familiar ground they slackened pace, letting the horses take their own speed, jogging gently through the long, brown grass that came to their knees. The open plain gave way to foothills and a pass that would take them through the low range of hills. Once James struck the railway line on the other side of the hills, he would find the headquarters laager of Gore-Bilham and Hickman and be in time to take part in the encirclement of the three Boer commandos at the place he suggested they would rendezvous. The pass took them through a gap wide enough for a wagon and when they came out to look down on the small valley, they found it crowded with Boer horsemen. Signalling the Mashonaland Scouts to dismount and take their horses out of sight, James got down on his belly and in detail studied his prize through his glasses. After three minutes' search, he recognised General Jan Christian Smuts. He had lost Oosthuizen but found a far bigger prize, the man who had been President Kruger's attorney-general in the Transvaal Republic. Even Gore-Bilham would forget Sebastian's betrayal.

Smiling to himself, he had begun to crawl backwards away from his line of view into the valley when down below everyone began to round up their horses and jump into their saddles. By his estimates, there were a thousand men down below.

"They're going to the rendezvous," he said with satisfaction.

WILLIE VAN TONDER was a man of forty, the elected commander of his troop of twenty Boers and the leading farmer in his small community at home. A flash of the reflected sun had drawn his dark brown eyes to the lip of the valley like iron filings to a magnet. A stolen pair of British binoculars had gone to his eyes and been focused quickly enough to see James order his scouts out of sight. There were seven people on the hill when he counted, six wearing wide-brimmed hats while the one giving the orders looked to Willie like an officer in one of the fancy British regiments. The man had a plumed feather on the side of his hat. Willie watched the officer drop on his belly and caught a second glint of the sun's reflection from the lens of the glasses, the first having come from a polished button on the officer's uniform.

Quickly, and with fear gripping his stomach, he had walked across to General Smuts.

"It's a trap," he said to the general. "A British officer has his binoculars on us right now. They're waiting for us."

"Up-saddle and disperse!" came the immediate order.

To JAMES BRIGANDSHAW'S ASTONISHMENT, the men down below began to move out of the valley at the gallop in the opposite direction to the rendezvous, straight up the pass he had just followed. Thankful his horses had not been extended, he led the charge out of the pass away from the angry Boer commando, kicking up the dust down below.

CHRISTIAAN DE WET was a phantom to the British. Every time they tried to draw the cord tight around the neck of his commando he slipped through the noose. Half an hour before the two regiments of Scots Cavalry would have made contact with his six hundred men, outnumbering them more than two to one, a Boer scout, using the skills he had learnt through his life hunting buck, cantered into de Wet's camp.

"It's a trap. They're making a sweep with mounted men. Somehow they know the rendezvous."

"Up-saddle! Up-saddle!"

Within minutes de Wet's men were remounted and galloping south.

When James burst out of the pass that would barely take an ox-wagon he was confronted with a second Boer commando kicking dust so high only the front riders could be seen for what they were.

"De Wet," he said out loud before charging out onto the plain, veering away from the dust cloud to cut around the hills and back to the railway line. When his horse was almost blown he brought the animal down to a walk. When he looked back from the saddle, he watched Smuts and his commando veer south having cut through the pass. Quickly, the two dust clouds merged into one.

To the northwest and twenty miles from Kroonstad, Tinus and his commando reached the rendezvous on the Vals River where a Boer homestead had been burnt to the ground by the British. Sebastian had spent the rest of the day trying to convince Tinus the rendezvous was now a British trap.

Half an hour before the sun went down on the ridge that surrounded the abandoned farmhouse, horsemen began to appear on all sides.

"Now do you believe me?" said Sebastian.

"Up-saddle!"

Leading his men in one concentrated thrust Tinus galloped at the cavalry on the ridge who had dismounted to take better aim. The British bullet that hit Sebastian knocked him straight out of the saddle of the spare Boer pony he was riding, the pain greater from the smack on the ground than the bullet that had smashed through his shoulder.

Tinus broke through the line of kneeling soldiers with comparative ease... Shooting a galloping horseman was more luck than judgement. Having broken through, the Boers galloped in all directions to give the British as many ways to chase as there were Boer horsemen. Raising his rifle above his head he cheered. It would take a month to bring his commando together again but they were free of the British trap. Alone he brought the black stallion down to a canter from the full gallop and turned in the saddle to look back. The British were galloping all over the plain in pursuit of the Boers exactly as the Boers had intended. Coming towards him at a steady gallop was a small group of British cavalry. Tinus changed the direction of his horse, bringing the animal back to the gallop. When he looked back the tight group had also changed direction.

The sun was down behind the hills and throwing red shards of light at the wakening heavens. The only thing the British captain missed in the hunt was the hounds, the baying of the hounds. Slowly and with arrogant confidence, as if he were riding down an exhausted fox, the man led his men as they overtook their quarry.

"He knows he's being hunted. By the time the sun sets tomorrow, Gore-Bilham will have made me a major. Corporal McIntosh! Go ahead and around the fugitive. Cut him off and shoot his horse if he doesn't surrender."

BILLY CLIFFORD WATCHED the man he would now call Martinus Jacobus McDonald Oosthuizen in his lead story. Major-General Gore-Bilham sat outside his tent in a low canvas chair he intended taking on his hunting safari when the war was over. Next to Gore-Bilham, Colonel Hickman was looking at the skeleton of a man the newspapers had called the Giant. Billy had taken the required photograph of the bent figure the captain had walked from the rendezvous on the Vals River. McIntosh had shot dead the black stallion Jeremiah Shanks had once named Diamond. The full beard was mostly grey and a bald patch showed on top of the man's head, the once chestnut hair, lank down to his shoulders, the colour of pepper and salt.

TINUS LIMPED from the fall from his horse and his only satisfaction was most everyone else had broken through the cordon of British cavalry. If the general he had debagged, now sitting with his booted and gartered calves thrust out from where he sat in his chair, had feathers, he could not have looked more like a vulture first on the kill. The man next to him with the red nose and drooping moustache stood up.

"General Oosthuizen. I am Colonel Hickman. The general you have met. It is my sad duty to inform you of the charge of treason you will face in Cape Town. You will have been perfectly aware that British subjects fighting against the Crown will be tried for treason and should they be found guilty, hanged by the neck until they are dead."

"I am a Boer soldier. A Boer. My ancestors came to this country more than two hundred years ago."

"Let the courts decide, sir."

"I am a prisoner of war."

"You are, sir, a traitor," said Gore-Bilham from the comfort of his chair.

"I barely recognised you with your trousers on," said Tinus, smiling for the first time since his horse had been shot from under him.

· · ·

A BRITISH MEDICAL orderly had found Sebastian where he had fallen in the waist-high grass. The pain in his broken hip and shattered shoulder had reached the screaming stage where he wished to die. No other thought pumped through the agony of his brain. To Sebastian, the half-hour lying hidden in the grass had seemed an eternity.

"Come here, cock. We got one," the orderly had shouted to his companion, combing the scene of the battle for bodies. "Bloody Boer, by the look of 'im."

"I'm actually a bloody Englishman," said Sebastian through his teeth.

"Get a stretcher! The bugger's alive and speaks English. Look, cock, no offence but if you're an Englishman where's your uniform? You're dressed like a Boer even if you do talk highfalutin' English. Now, where's it hurt?"

"Everywhere. The bullet hit my left shoulder, and I broke something falling off my horse. My brother is Lieutenant-Colonel James Brigandshaw, second in command of British Intelligence. I was trying to talk to the Boer general."

"Well, you'd better shut up talkin' now. Fact is, whoever you are, you're a lucky sod. The bullet went clean through your shoulder and out to the other side. Mind you, 'nother hour and you'd 'ave bled to death... Chalky," he said standing up in the grass, "bring the stretcher," and then looking down at Seb, "What we do is plug the hole both ends and stop the blood oozing out... Come on, Chalky, the bugger's passed out."

BOOK 7 - REVENGE

1

JULY 1901

*B*illy Clifford interrupted his piece on the concentration camps to follow the trial of the Boer rebel, General Oosthuizen. Not only had the British proved his domicile in the Cape but before that, the man had lived in British Rhodesia. Oosthuizen was a British subject who had deliberately, on his own volition, taken up arms against the British Crown, causing the deaths of over five hundred British subjects in the murderous guerrilla campaign that he had unleashed in the Transvaal, the Free State and the Cape. The British were adamant... The man was a murderous traitor who should be spared the privilege of a firing squad and hanged like a common criminal.

All Billy's efforts to interview the prisoner in Cape Town central prison were denied under the emergency laws generated by a war that was dragging on with no end in sight. His article *The man's a Boer* was received with enthusiasm by readers in Dublin and quoted in English papers who were sick of the war and Kitchener's British methods. Billy had to smile... There were always newspapers looking for political points. He even travelled out to the farm Kleinfontein in Franschhoek Valley in an attempt to interview the prisoner's British wife.

To score points for the government, several English newspapers picked up his challenge saying the *Irish Times* was talking rubbish. Not only was the man a British subject, resident in a British colony, but his mother was also British, his wife British and, by the common process of descent, his three children were three-quarters British. What kind of man took up arms against his own children?

At the farm, the long barn-like house with a veranda running the length of one side was shuttered and the listless, even surly servants were unable or unwilling to answer Billy's questions in English. It was obvious he was not the first reporter trying to interview the prisoner's wife.

SEBASTIAN, flat on his back in the British military hospital in Cape Town, read the newspapers and there was nothing he could do. His right hip, fractured in three places, would make walking a painful experience for the rest of his life if he did not stay still and let the bones mend; the bullet wound in his shoulder was the least of his problems.

HARRY BRIGANDSHAW, who had turned thirteen in April, was told by the headmaster of Bishops School that his father had been badly wounded in action and was lying in a Cape Town hospital. On the same day, he read the newspaper and realised the rebel traitor, captured and about to be hanged, was the man he had called Uncle Tinus all his life. The pride in his father for at last going to war was doused by cold fear for Uncle Tinus. For the first time in his young life, he found himself on both sides of a deadly conflict. To call Uncle Tinus a traitor was like calling both of them cowards for not being willing to fight each other in a war. Uncle Tinus was an Afrikaner, so was Barend, Tinka and young Christo. In young Harry's mind, there was no doubt whatsoever. Suddenly the world of principle, of right and wrong, that had seemed so simple the day before, was thrown in his face, and what had been an uncomplicated life that lay straight ahead down a long sunny path was shattered. Everything that Harry had been taught, from religion to being an English gentleman, no longer made any sense. If the British High Command was going to hang his Uncle Tinus for doing his rightful duty, how could they call themselves gentlemen? And if they were not gentlemen, who were?

By the time he reached his father's bedside, he was a very confused young man.

SEBASTIAN, looking up at the strapping lad standing beside his bed, realised the boy was turning into a young man and for the first time in his life he wondered if he was growing old. Harry offered his hand to shake.

"Shoulder took a bullet," said Seb, shaking his head. "Do you know about Uncle Tinus?"

"Yes."

"I can't move. Hip's the problem, not the shoulder. Go to the offices of African Shipping and if he's not in Cape Town, wire Captain Doyle and tell him Uncle Tinus needs his help. He helped me when I was put in jail. Then wire your grandfather to come to Cape Town. The wire will stop in Salisbury but can be sent by hand to the farm. Your mother is to stay where she is. I am not the problem. Uncle James is avoiding all my messages, so find out where he is and go and see him. You think Madge and George can look after your mother?"

"Maybe she should take them into Salisbury and stay at Meikles Hotel?"

"Good. Put that in your wire. Then I want you to go and see Uncle Tinus and tell him not to worry."

"But Uncle Tinus is in jail."

"Make your Uncle James get you through the door. There's a reporter for the *Irish Times* who made a story out of Uncle Tinus. His byline says 'Clifford'. Find him and bring him here."

"Are you in pain, Father?"

"Not the kind you are thinking about. That man means more to me than any brother."

ALISON and the children had gone to stay with Elize du Plessis, the wife of Magnus du Plessis, on the other side of the Franschhoek Valley, all thought of her miscarriage drowned in the horror of what was happening. The worst part had been accepting the advice of the lawyer she had employed to stop the British from hanging her husband.

"Don't even try to see him," said Mr Gotlieb of Gotlieb and Stein. "We have to make it clear the man's a Boer fighting for his country. An English wife will question his motive. Get off your farm and keep away from the press. And may I warn you, this is not going to be an easy case to win."

"You think they will hang my husband?"

"Yes. As an example to the rest of the Cape Boers. The British want to stop any new fighters joining Smuts or Botha. Keep out of the way and I will do my job. But under no circumstances are you to visit the jail or appear at his trial."

"We had an argument before he left. I'd had a miscarriage and was feeling the world had come to an end. Tinus will think I've deserted him."

"I will explain. Write him a letter for me to give to him. Just don't let the newspapers take a photograph of General Oosthuizen being visited by his English wife."

"Who made him a general?"

"His own commando by a vote, confirmed by Smuts and Botha. He's a Boer general, don't you worry about that."

"Then how can they hang him?"

"Because he's also a British subject. Maybe more because the Boer army has defied the might of the British Empire for too long. Kitchener wants it over and doesn't care by what means he stops his men being killed by Boer guerrillas. And there's General Gore-Bilham. Your husband made a fool of him. Better he had shot the man dead."

"WHY IS the traitor lodged in a civil jail?" asked General Gore-Bilham. They were seated in the officers' mess at the Castle in Cape Town where Gore-Bilham's command was back in reserve from the front. Being the senior officer at the Castle, the rule of not talking shop in the mess did not apply to him. Having no wish to get into a discussion on the Boer general, the lower-ranking officers at the table used the rule to keep their mouths shut. The large majority of the men in the room were horrified by the thought of hanging an adversary captured in battle. Colonel Hickman, watching from the far side of the round table, wondered silently if the general would have preferred a bullet in his head rather than losing his trousers... Some men had the strangest of priorities.

"And what do you say about that, Hickman?... Someone tell the mess steward to put some more logs on the fire... Well, Hickman?"

"Sub judice, I'm afraid, sir."

"But the army should try the man."

No one looked at the general and James Brigandshaw, sitting next to Colonel Hickman, drummed his fingers on his knee under the table.

"Go and put some wood on the fire!" snapped Gore-Bilham to the mess steward who was standing behind James.

"There's someone to see Colonel Brigandshaw."

"Send him in, dammit, and put some wood on the fire. There's a black south-easter blowing outside."

"The man's more a boy, I would think, and asks his uncle to meet him in the office of the military police. He was trying to walk through when the MPs picked him up."

"Put some wood on the fire, dammit! Brigandshaw, do you even have a nephew in these parts?"

"Yes, sir. At school here."

"In the colonies?" replied Gore-Bilham, horrified.

"Yes, sir. My brother lives in Rhodesia. May I be excused, sir?"

"I don't care what anyone does, provided the steward puts wood on the fire."

"Right away, sir."

OUTSIDE IN THE QUADRANGLE, James could hear the banshee of the howling wind that cut Table Bay in half. The Castle, built by the Dutch, was sheltered by Table Mountain along with a slice of the bay. No ships had entered the port or gone to sea for three days. Halfway across the quadrangle, it began to rain. If the presence of his nephew had not been announced in public, he would have made an excuse. James knew perfectly well Sebastian was lying on his back in the military hospital. He also knew the British, prodded by Gore-Bilham, intended hanging his brother's partner very publicly and there was nothing he could do. If they had caught Smuts and de Wet the war would have been over and hanging men like Tinus Oosthuizen would no longer have been politically necessary. And he blamed Sebastian for running off in the night.

"Ah, young Harry, what a surprise," he said.

"I want permission to visit Uncle Tinus." The boy looked at him with loathing.

"Nobody looks at me like that, young man."

"Then get my real uncle out of jail."

TINUS READ the letter from his wife twice and gave it back to Gotlieb for burning. Then he smiled happily at the lawyer.

"I don't understand how you can smile," said the lawyer. "This is deadly serious and under martial law, you will face a military court even if for now they have you in a civil jail."

"I've done nothing wrong and my wife loves me again. So does my son. I could have died many times in my life by a lion, elephant, or buffalo. Once even a honey badger tried to chew off my balls. Any one of those flying bullets could have taken off my head. Bullets are hard and very final if they hit you in the right spot. I'm forty-four years old and have lived every moment of my life. They'll hang a man who's had a good life, whose wife loves him, his eldest son no longer despises him, and he's rich so his family will be all right when he dies."

BOOK 7 - REVENGE

"They won't be. If they find you guilty of treason all your property will be forfeit to the Crown."

SIR HENRY MANDERVILLE looked at the handwritten message on the telegraph form and understood. Together with his daughter and grandchildren, he left the farm on the banks of the Mazoe River. Maybe his title would have some weight in a world foolishly impressed with old titles, and even if it was just possible, he would give it a try. Hiding away in the Rhodesian bush could not get him far enough away from the problems of man. Or had he always been just running away from his responsibilities?

With the railway line at Fort Salisbury and the tracks traversing the former Boer republics through the arid veld of the British protectorate of Bechuanaland, it would take him just five days to reach Cape Town.

AFTER LISTENING to Sebastian for over an hour, Billy Clifford could find nothing in the story he could use to help the Giant. Having brought the focus of attention, Billy felt guilty for the man's predicament. If he had never made Oosthuizen a celebrity, no one would have made all the fuss.

"Why is it when you're needed most you can't do a thing?" asked Sebastian.

For a moment Billy was going to tell the man lying on his back in the hospital bed about his fruitless quest for Sarie Mostert. The dog-lady had vanished without a trace.

"We all have our problems," he said.

"How soon will they hang him?"

"In a couple of weeks."

Outside, the wind was rattling the hospital windows.

CAPTAIN DOYLE, seated at his office desk in London, wondered why bad news always came together like a flight of devils from a cloudless sky. He put the telegraph form on the table upside down and for a moment forgot the repulsive little man seated across his table.

"Not bad news?" said Jeremiah Shank in his half-cultivated accent. His pronunciation of the word news had a strange parallel with the rope that went around a condemned man's neck. When Shank repeated the sentence, Doyle felt the doom of the white hunter and shuddered. He had known it before but now he was certain... The man on the other side of the desk was evil. He began tapping his fingers on the table. The *Indian Queen II* was sailing on the tide not five hundred yards from where he was sitting in the London docks.

"I've got more shares in African Shipping than you, Doyle. Over forty per cent. I want to have my say, see. Board of Directors. Chairman, I thought. You can keep on runnin' the place but I want my say."

"The consortium controls over fifty per cent."

"So you've said more than once."

"I have to leave for Africa on the tide."

"I don't care whether you have a shit in your chair. I want to have my say. You see, cock, you've never paid a dividend and that ain't right with all my money invested."

"I bought new ships. The company's worth far more."

"Then sell it and give me my money or pay a proper dividend. My solicitor says..."

"I will give you an answer in a month."

"Thirty days, cock. No problem. 'Ave a nice trip. They're going to hang 'im. Bloody traitor. Just lucky I bought his share when he sold or they'd all be forfeit to the Crown. Better me as a director than the government. See you in a month, sonny boy. It's been nice sailing with you again. Lucky for you they didn't kill your fornicating partner or I'd 'ave bought his shares. All very well having lots of ships but in this world, you need cash to protect yourself... Ah, that one you didn't know, by the look of you. Tell you what, Doyle, I know more about your company than you do. Brigandshaw's in a hospital and you didn't know. Shot by the British. Makes you laugh really. All that hunting and he gets shot by his own side."

When the door to his office slammed shut, just hard enough to make the point, Captain Doyle got up and looked out of the window. It was a beautiful English summer afternoon and more than one ship would be ready to sail on the tide. In the old days, he could see the tall masts from where he stood. For the first time in his life, he would be sailing into the Cape of Storms as a passenger. It was winter in the Cape, he remembered.

THE TRAFFIC outside 37 Pudding Lane in Bermondsey had been a dray pulled by an old carthorse that was so old it was a miracle the flat wagon carrying the barrels of beer moved at all. Even in poverty, there were public houses doing good business and once a week Ethel Shank watched the same beer-cart trundle iron wheels over cobbled stones, the only sign of brief hope in the wilderness.

There had been rumours before, all verbal. When Fred the coalman drank his four pints of mild and bitter on a Friday in the Duke of Clarence, he reckoned it was the only day of the week when his throat was not choked with coal dust. Ethel had her one glass of port and lemon and Fred four pints, no more, no less. In the thirty-three years they had been married, the ritual in the Duke of Clarence had been the same, and the only time either of them did anything that wasn't work or sleep. They rarely spoke in the Duke of Clarence, to themselves or anyone else, though each of their neighbours received a warm smile of recognition. It was the way the community enjoyed their recreation, the luxury of sitting down doing nothing.

Vivian Clay was the only one in Pudding Lane who did not work with his hands. Most of the day he stood at a lectern in the City filling in the records of the company's claims in a leather-bound register that weighed twenty pounds. The beautiful copperplate writing of young Vivian Clay had landed him the job forty years ago and not a day had gone by without the same repetition. Apart from a small increase in his Christmas bonus, his pay had stayed the same. When he retired in ten years' time, eighty per cent of his wages would be paid for doing nothing, the great shining light at the end of a lifetime's toil.

The previous evening, Fred and Ethel had sat on the bench outside the Duke of Clarence, it being so warm; a long weathered table made from an old railway sleeper stood in front of them, though Fred never rested his pint for fear of it tipping in the cracks and spilling his only pleasure. Vivian, passing on his way to the bar, dropped the day's copy of the *Evening Standard* in front of them. The paper was folded into four so Vivian could read on the train. It was like opening a concertina... In the train, there was no room for moving his elbows. For thirty years, the manager of the insurance company read the morning and evening papers and when Vivian left to go home, he took both papers from the wastepaper basket where they had been thrown.

The paper in front of Ethel and Fred was folded to a picture, in grainy black and white, of a man in a silk top hat.

"You always said, Eth, there had to be two Jeremiah Shanks," said Vivian Clay. "But that's 'im, I tell you. Recognised that droopy eye anywhere and the twisted nose. Ascot, I tell you. In the royal enclosure with his new wife. The paper says he 'as a son. Congratulations, you're grandparents. Hobnobs with his mentor Lord Edward Holland. Your son's a millionaire."

Ethel had not worked all morning, sitting in the parlour with the window open staring out onto the street. The coincidence was far too great and if the truth came out and was known in Pudding Lane, it would ruin

Fred Shank for life. The good, solid man who had always provided for her and the kids would know she had married him on a lie, would know she had made him marry her knowing she was carrying another man's child.

"I've got a grandchild," she said out loud and then began to cry.

FRANCESCA SHANK, born Cotton, was in her element and thanked the day she had married Jeremiah Shank. Wealth, real wealth, overcame any impediment. The drooping eye, the twisted nose, the short stature, the look that made most men want to punch him in the face, were forgotten. The relatives in Godalming, her doting father, the red setters, all had been visited and even if some had sniggered when she left, she had seen their gleams of envy. Living in the country keeping up appearances with not enough money, paled against the house in Park Lane overlooking Hyde Park and the great estate in Africa where all the right people in London were clamouring for invitations to shoot big game. And best of all for Fran, her son would inherit the little man's money but not the little man's blood. Fran, above everything else in her new world of wealth, had become a snob. Knowing the best way to keep a man was to keep him on short rations, Fran made it as difficult as possible for Jeremiah Shank to have sex. Clothed and safe in public she flirted with him outrageously. In bed, she went as cold as a fish. Then, when she saw his interest waning, she gave him what he wanted in spades. Happily, in London, even though he probably knew she was playing a game, he could not give her a clout. There were rules in society even Jeremiah understood. The little man who had sailed before the mast as an ordinary seaman, who had taken elocution lessons, who was richer than most men with English country estates, wanted above all to be accepted by the men and women who ran high society.

Sitting at the piano on Thursday nights when open house was the order of the day, she played Bach and Chopin and smiled to herself. In the nursery her son was being tended by a nanny, the kitchen was run by the cook, the house by the butler and Fran was left to do what she had always wanted to do most, play the piano. It had taken her a big wide circle to come back home but here she was, she told herself, right in the heart of things. Only sometimes alone did she think of Gregory who had made it all possible and given her the son asleep upstairs.

LORD EDWARD HOLLAND, being a younger son, had never been forced to marry to protect the family title. Edward, Teddy to his friends, was now

fourteenth in line to the title of Marquis of Surrey, his brothers' sons having
produced their own sons... The title, so far as Teddy was concerned, was
quite safe. If he had married, they would have made him move from the
family estate but as a bachelor, he could stay where he was until he died.
Everyone liked Teddy Holland. He was good at a dinner party, drinking
enough to be part of the fun but never too much. Never, ever, in his life had
he told anyone what he really thought of them. Always and with
premeditated charm, he told everyone what they wanted to hear about
themselves. Even the generation of his nieces and nephews came to the
sympathetic shoulder of Uncle Teddy where anything that was said never
went one step further. Unbeknown to him, playing his own fiddle in life he
played a vital part in the harmony of the sprawling family.

   Teddy had reached the age when there was more to look back on than to
look forward to, a time to recognise his mortality when friends from the old
days at school were dying off, a time to ask himself what it was all about, to
think of God, to realise how little he really knew. Only then, in the black,
dark hours in his bedroom in the old family home, surrounded by the
product of twenty generations, when he could not sleep and blamed the
food and drink instead of age, he began to understand the greater
probability, that his only chance of immortality, his only purpose, was to
have children. He could then die, but the species of well-bred Englishmen
would live after him to the end of time. There was no point in guessing
anymore. He had to know. For the sake of his soul, he had to know once and
for all.

ETHEL SAW the toff step down the hansom cab and heard him tell the driver
to wait. The horse and dray had stopped outside the Duke of Clarence and
old Stan Conway was unloading barrels of beer with the help of young Ben,
the landlord's son. The smell of fresh horse manure was strong and
comfortingly pleasant. The toff was obviously lost and was looking for
directions. The man's beard was cut sharply to a point; the sideburns and the
beard were almost white.

   The noise of the door knocker banged through the house and Ethel left
her window and walked through the passage to open the front door.

   "Hello, Ethel. My name is Edward Holland. You probably don't
remember me but I received a postcard some many years back reading
Jeremiah Shank. Is he our son?"

   She stared at him, unable to reconcile the old man standing at her front door and the dashing young aristocrat in her memory who had seduced her in the gazebo at Bramley Park.

"Yes. Now, will you go away?"

For the first time in his life, a door was closed in his face. Stunned by the swift conclusion, Teddy stood looking at the knocker. From the other side, he could hear the woman crying.

"Ethel! Do you want some money?"

Slowly the door opened.

"Money. You people only think of money. Please don't tell 'im. Anyone. My Fred's a good man. It'll kill 'im. Just don't tell Jeremiah and 'ave 'im bustin' in 'ere and ruining the lives of all of us."

"He'd have less reason if he knew I was his father."

"That boy's evil. He'd use it to torment us. He'd enjoy making us all miserable. See what happens when you do something wrong. Evil, he is. I feel sorry for his wife."

"So you know about his son?"

"In the paper... What they call 'im?"

"Edward."

"So he knows?"

"No. I'm his mentor. Gave him a start in business. Ethel, you have my word as a gentleman. Only you and I will ever know. You see, all the way along I couldn't see what I could do for you without making it worse. I'll go now before the neighbours talk. I wanted to be certain. He's the only child I ever had."

When he had gone, instead of crying, Ethel burst out laughing.

"Gentleman, my arse. More man and less gentleman and you wouldn't 'ave seduced me in the first place. I'll take Fred the coalman any day." Then she thought for a moment, "Poor bugger don't 'ave no kids he can call his own. That'll teach 'im."

That evening when Fred came home from delivering sacks of coal she sat him down in the parlour with a cup of tea. The kids were out playing in the street and down the alleys. The window was open to their backyard. She could smell the stocks Fred had planted in the spring. It was better to face a problem straight on, she always told the kids.

"There's somethin' I've never told you, Fred. Should 'ave done, likely. I was young and frightened. But I owe you the truth before someone else whispers in your ear. Our Jeremiah is not your son."

"Eth. You think we could break the rule and go down the Duke of Clarence? Then I can celebrate. I'd hoped you'd tell me that ever since he opened his mouth. I knew, Eth. Even a coalman can count up to nine months. I'm goin' to 'ave five pints and get drunk first time in my life. Yous goin' to 'ave two port and lemon. He may still be your son but it's my house. So ever 'e comes round 'ere looking for trouble I'll throw the little squirt down the front stairs into the street. Your mother told me she thought you were up the pole from young Teddy Holland, up at the big 'ouse. But it didn't matter. We loved each other. Now, come on. In all them years you never saw Fred Shank drunk... Tonight's the night!"

SITTING next to his wife at the piano not four miles away as the crow flies, Jeremiah Shank gave a sudden shiver and Fran stopped playing the piano.

"What's the matter?"

"Someone walked over my grave."

The townhouse in Hyde Park with twelve bedrooms and a reception room larger than three houses in Pudding Lane might have been as far away as the moon from the Duke of Clarence.

"Better we go back to Africa," he said.

"Why? This house is such fun and Africa so boring. You frightened one of my admirers will seduce me?"

"Even you know which side your bread's buttered. There's one thing I have learnt in life. You can fool other people but you can't fool yourself."

"What are you talking about?"

"They're laughing at us, Fran."

"They may be laughing at you, Jeremiah Shank, but they are certainly not laughing at me. Anyway, who cares?"

"I do."

"Then you're a bigger fool than I thought you were."

"You married me for my money."

"And you married me for my class. Everyone trades, Jeremiah. It's what makes the world go round. If everyone had what they wanted, life would be boring... Anyway, they don't laugh at you. They envy you."

"You think so?"

"I'm sure." Then she went back to playing the piano, satisfied with the new look in his eyes... She had perfectly stroked the feathers of his vanity.

FURTHER SOUTH AT HASTINGS COURT, Lady Mathilda Brigandshaw watched a man in uniform ride up the driveway through the avenue of trees. She could only see him intermittently as the horse and rider passed between the oak trees that had been planted by Sir Henry Manderville's ancestors. She had first heard the clip of the horse's hooves and turned in her seat in the bower that overlooked the artificial lake, landscaped into the countryside by Sir Henry's great-grandfather. She was sixty-one and felt every year in the joints of her fingers, the joints of her knees and ankles. The warm evening sun reflected from the water; all around insects were busy in the drowsy summer's day. Annoyed at being disturbed in the one place she found peace, Mathilda placed the thick stick on the ground in front of the old wooden bench and hoisted herself up. After a moment the pain subsided in her knees and she began the slow walk back to the house.

The butler met her halfway up to the big house. She hated servants. Could see no reason why they were needed. She could make a bed and cook a meal. And they were always around, watching what you did. 'Gives me the creeps,' she told herself while racking her brain for the name of the new butler. There had been so many since The Captain had bought Hastings Court and tried to tie himself into the Manderville ancestry. She was no good with servants, she knew that and they knew she was no better than them... Her Cheshire accent as strong as when she had been a child. And The Captain bellowed at them, forgetting he was no longer at sea, the all-powerful captain of a ship.

The man in uniform had been shown into the high-ceilinged library; the French doors open to the wide veranda that overlooked the park her husband had extended by buying surrounding farms. Flowers grew in profusion, tumbling out of the giant pots that marched along the front of the veranda protecting the ten-foot drop to the gravel driveway. There were seven gardeners and not a weed showed among the flowerbeds or in the driveway.

The man in uniform had walked out from the library to look at the view. Hearing the old woman's stick on the wooden floor he composed his face and turned back to the library. The woman was carrying his calling card in her left hand, the right fully occupied with the stick.

"I am Lady Brigandshaw. To what do we owe the pleasure, Captain Tanner?"

"No pleasure, madam. I bring bad news from the war office. Your son..."

"*James* is dead?"

"James, madam?" Discreetly the officer looked at the piece of paper he had been handed at the army training camp three miles from Hastings Court. "It says here, your son's name is Sebastian. I am so sorry. There must be a mistake."

"Sebastian! But he's not in the army."

"So you do have a son by the name of Sebastian?"

"Of course I do. How would I know he was not in the army?"

"There's no rank, admittedly, but he's lying in our military hospital in Cape Town."

"What's he lying there for?"

"He's very badly wounded. I regret to inform you, the doctors fear for his life."

"Why didn't you inform his wife?" bellowed The Captain who had been taking his afternoon nap and had told the butler not to disturb him on pain of dismissal.

"He doesn't have a wife, according to army records, sir. You would be Sir Archibald Brigandshaw, I presume? Captain Tanner, Royal Artillery. You and Lady Brigandshaw are listed as his next of kin."

"What's the reprobate done now? Hasn't he caused enough trouble? Never married her, I suppose. All the children are bastards. Now, if you have something important to say..."

"Your son Sebastian is dying of wounds, sir. I would have thought..."

"I don't give a damn. That boy's name is never to be mentioned in this house even if he is dying. Good day, sir."

They both listened in silence, the butler having made his escape earlier. The library door banged behind him.

"There is something else, Lady Brigandshaw. The army will give you passage to Cape Town. With the new steamships, the journey can be made in eighteen days, weather permitting. The army thought the funeral..."

"He's not dead yet."

"I'm to inform you there's a ship sailing from Southampton the day after tomorrow."

"I think we have our own transport, thank you. My husband owns Colonial Shipping. Will you take a glass of sherry, Captain Tanner? Then you can tell me how Sebastian came to be lying in a military hospital. Has anyone in the army told poor Emily?"

"Who is Emily, madam?"

"The mother of his children. The woman who should have been his wife. And with Arthur dead and buried I'll have a word with him about that... What is your name?" she said to the butler who had appeared soon after eavesdropping the word 'sherry'.

2

AUGUST 1901

*I*n the middle of August, the *Indian Queen* (the second of the same name) steamed into Table Bay. For Captain Doyle standing alone on the foredeck, it was *déjà vu*, only last time the prisoner was Sebastian. What he was going to do to help a situation already out of control was beyond his thinking mind. Enough, he was looking at Table Mountain and hopefully Tinus Oosthuizen was still alive.

When the ship docked Captain Doyle was the first ashore. The sky was clear but the wind cold and he was glad the Cape Town manager of African Shipping had recognised the *Indian Queen* coming into the harbour. Inside the company carriage with the doors closed he ignored the rug meant for the passengers' knees.

Half an hour later, Sebastian saw the man who had been more loyal than a father, walk purposefully down the ward.

"Is Tinus still alive?" asked Doyle. "How are you?"

"Yes, he's still alive. The trial is two weeks from yesterday. A military trial. They moved him last week into military custody. Gore-Bilham has him in the Castle. And thank you, the hip's mending well but the pain is still there. The bullet through the shoulder was clean... Have you got any influence that can help Tinus?"

"No. I can give him moral support but no one can influence a British military court."

"Emily's father thinks the same. An Irish newsman has tried his best. All it did was make Milner hand Tinus to the military. The British High

Commissioner is a modern Pontius Pilate. Washed his hands of what he now says is a military problem. Alison has appointed a solicitor who has been able to do nothing. Can you go and see Milner? Gore-Bilham?"

"And say he was my partner? That his money came from an English partnership, an English shipping line? Better to go and see Smuts or de Wet and plead they stop the war to save Tinus's life. He's a hostage to make the Boers stop fighting. This is politics, not justice. Where in history have the English tried their prisoners? What would happen if everyone started hanging their prisoners-of-war?"

"Billy Clifford tried that angle and all he got back was traitors; people who are traitors to their own country are hanged."

"But Tinus is not British."

"Neither was Milner by birth. He's a German. He's a naturalised British subject and if he takes up arms against the Crown, they'll hang him just the same. Tinus lived most of his life in British colonies under British law. He's going to be made an example for any Cape Dutch who wants to join the Boers. I went to find Tinus in the bush to tell him to stop before it was too late. He even told me he knew the consequences. What he didn't know, the lawyer tells me, is the British will confiscate Kleinfontein. Why I asked you to help, old friend, is I thought I was going to die. Or rather the doctors thought I was going to die. I want you to know Alison receives half my shares in African Shipping but they can't be registered for fear of confiscation. Alison is proud. You must tell her the money was always his. She must never think it is charity. Which it isn't. Without Tinus, I would not have a penny, more than likely. And you would be a retired captain of one of my father's ships and eking out a living in some boarding house in Liverpool."

"Will she sell the shares?"

"Probably. To buy back Kleinfontein. Half of my shares are worth more than all of his when he sold out."

"Jeremiah Shank owns forty-one per cent of African Shipping, the public a mere six per cent. Every time a share came onto the market after the public listing, Shank was the buyer."

"But we only floated thirty per cent."

"Barings sold him the Tinus share and their sponsoring broker allocation. Quite legal. The man could have used a nominee to own the shares. When you go public, you always take the risk of losing control of your company."

"Then why don't we both sell our shares on the open market?"

"*Original* partners dump shares? The shares won't be worth ten per cent when the press finds out."

"Then sell the company to Shank."

"And let him win again? Don't you remember he put a noose around your neck?"

"Sometimes you have to lose a little to get what you want."

"And what do I do? I'm only sixty. Look older, yes, from all the years at sea. I'd be dead from boredom six months into retirement. I never had a wife. No children. I married ships and the sea. My ships are my children."

"Then we will find another way for Alison."

"Even military courts don't hang prisoners with extenuating circumstances."

"Not unless the general choosing the judges is biased. There won't be a jury. Five army officers and I'll bet Gore-Bilham himself will be the senior officer. In the army, if a senior officer gives you an order, you do what you're told."

"He won't give them an order to find a man guilty before he's tried."

"He won't have to. They all saw the news picture of Gore-Bilham without his trousers. He'll pick four ambitious men. A man rises in a government, a corporation and certainly the army by doing what is rudely called 'arse-creeping'. Those four men will be fighting for the privilege. Make a fool of a man and he will always be your enemy. Why I like living in the bush, far away from people. I have come to understand and respect the animals. I have never understood man."

"Can't we break him out of jail?"

"I've been thinking of that."

"DON'T BE BLOODY STUPID," said Henry Manderville. "And keep your voice down, Sebastian. The word sedition springs to mind followed quickly by treason. Anyway, he's in a prison surrounded by a British garrison. I went to the Castle and did more harm than good. The man was polite. Offered me a glass of sherry. Listened carefully to every word I'd had to say, smiled with satisfaction and ordered himself another sherry. Told me what I had said confirmed what he already knew, that Tinus is a British subject. I tried the years north of the Limpopo before Rhodes hoisted the Union Jack. I pointed out Tinus had done nothing to become a British subject, that in those circumstances he was equally a subject of King Lobengula, that all the Englishmen hunting before the occupation were subjects of Lobengula and not Queen Victoria. The man went purple for a moment and then smiled. He explained the white hunters were visitors, not permanent residents, that when Tinus joined us, owning part of the farm, he automatically became a

British subject as the farm was his permanent residence. The man had the cheek to thank me for being so helpful. And if you want to fight your way in and out of the Castle, you need an army. Forget the fact you can barely walk on crutches. You can't get away from their rules and regulations, however far you run away. Just ask the Boers."

"What are we going to do?" asked Sebastian.

"Pray to God. Just pray to God."

THEY HAD GIVEN him a writing table and chair and an oil lamp that spread the light over the pages. He was writing to his children. The journal was in Afrikaans, the new language that over two hundred years had grown out of Dutch. The rest of the room was comfortable and Tinus suspected the previous occupant had been a British officer. It was a room furnished for a male and everything was practical, nothing frivolous. The food was good and the mess steward apologetic when it was cold as the officers' mess kitchen stood on the other side of the Castle. According to the steward, it would have been better in summer.

They had all come to see him including young Harry Brigandshaw, who he had carried so often on his shoulders through the bush. Captain Doyle had just visited and hinted Alison and the children would never be short of money, which was nice. The old English aristocrat, Sir Henry Manderville, had made his visit two days after seeing Gore-Bilham, and the children were right, the man was quite potty, delightfully potty, talking, very quietly, of digging a tunnel under the Castle wall. Alison had got over the loss of the baby and was back in control of her life. Mostly they had talked about the early days on the banks of the Zambezi River. She had refused to bring the children. Both of them knew he was going to hang which was why they talked about the old times. Life was indeed a mosaic and hanging by the neck from a rope was part of the pattern. He was forty-four and had had a good life and no one knew if the rest was going to be better than the past. Without the British rope who knew how long he was going to live? It had to end somewhere. The lawyer was a fool which somehow made it better.

Alone, day after day, he faced his own mortality and tried to think of God. If he was honest with himself, he could find nothing in a faith that would prove itself when he was dead. If there was a God, he was ready to face the jury inspecting his life. If there was no God, it would not matter. Religion, he rather thought, was for the living, not the dead. And so he had come to the journal.

The only thing Martinus Oosthuizen knew he would leave behind from his mortal life was his children. Maybe they were his only immortality and if so he wanted them to know as much about the people that had made them as possible: the seven generations of Oosthuizens in Africa which by some quirk of politics had turned him into an Englishman; the childhood he had spent in Graaff-Reinet helping to build the system of flood channels where water gurgled down the sides of the streets so that each garden could open a small floodgate to make the gardens green and beautiful. He could see them still as clear as thirty years ago. The years hunting alone in the bush. His regret at never seeing the Great Elephant, only the great pads in the dry dust. All he knew and understood he wrote down in the journal and the days went quickly towards his trial. Inside the locked and guarded room was the world he had seen.

"What a wonderful life," he said out loud so many times. "How many people can be so lucky? If there isn't something more after this mortal life, what was the point? There has to be a point."

For hours, staring into nothing, he racked his brains, the trial far distant in his mind. If there was not a God, and all God promised, just what had been the point? Why had his life been so beautiful?

Then, lying back on the bed, he transported his mind back into the bush and ran again with the animals.

THE CAPTAIN, Sir Archibald Brigandshaw, Baronet, sat alone at the end of the mahogany table in the dining room of Hastings Court. The polished surface shone from the energy of the servants. One place had been set on a table that seated thirty, the empty chairs and empty polished wood testimony to the greater potential. Sir Archibald, as befitted the first in what would become a line of hereditary knights of the realm, had dressed for dinner, the white starched front of his shirt studded with diamonds, glittering each on its own from the light of the chandeliers that hung over the table on chains thirty feet long, disappearing up into the dark of the vaulted ceiling. Up there, lost in the gloom, cherubs played the trumpets to the heavens, dulled by age and woodsmoke, and last seen with certainty by the human eye in the reign of Charles the First.

Long before, the dining room had been the Great Hall of the first Mandervilles. Still, and also long forgotten from lack of use, the small minstrel gallery looked down on the old man eating his supper alone, the only sound the clatter of silver on fine china. Somewhere in the vaulted wood of the ceiling were the lost notes of the minstrel lutes. Lower down, the walls draped with heavy tapestries to hide the moulds of age, the eyes of ancient Mandervilles looked with the fixed stares they had shown the long-dead painters. Some, the women mostly, faintly smiling, most staring at the certainty of their deaths. All but the very new had lost their names. One so high and dark had crashed to the old flagstones three nights before, sounding a long echo from the past and making The Captain jump from his chair with fright.

The soup went, followed by the fish, replaced by a small, plump fowl sitting at the centre of the plate. The Captain chewed portions of the bird, masticating the dry breast, his mouth as dry as the chicken's bones. The swallowed food caught in his gullet and was followed by a gush of red wine from a crystal goblet, the Venetian blue of the glass delicate and beautiful in contrast to the gnarled hand of the old seaman missing its pinkie finger, frozen, lost long, long ago, turning the Horn.

After he had his knife and fork together, the fowl was taken away, the Venetian goblet was filled by the second servant, the first waiting for The Captain to stand, turn to the long sideboard and carve the sirloin of beef. No one spoke a word, and The Captain kept his seat, stroking what was left of the pinkie finger of his left hand. The servants waited, the only sound the soft purr of the methylated spirit lamp under the silver dish, covered by a silver dome, in which the beef awaited the carving-knife. Again the goblet was filled and still The Captain kept his seat. He was thinking. Suddenly and horribly, into the empty hall, he gave a laugh. The wine servant behind his chair took a pace back.

The Captain, deep in his memory, was running with full canvas towards the American port of Mobile, the coxswain holding the spokes of the ship's wheel rock solid to catch the wind. They were both smiling, the hold full of English guns made in Sheffield, the Yankee navy nowhere to be seen, the cotton waiting on the wharf, the blood of youth pumping through their veins. He could still see Eddie Doyle grinning with excitement, all the crew willing the ship faster for port and safety and the bonus of their lives.

Again he laughed, remembering.

Slowly, far away in his mind, he rose to carve the roast beef. At sixty-five he should not have tottered. The servants, afraid of the old man's backhander, had turned away. With a look of bewildered surprise, The Captain fell down on the stone floor and died as the methylated spirit gave out and the faint sound of hissing stopped.

In the end, the butler had to bury him.

THE PAIN HAD GONE from the hip to the right shoulder where the bullet had torn through the ligaments and the laudanum, given to Sebastian by the male nurse, had just begun to float his mind out of his body. Somewhere in the picture he saw his mother and smiled, the primal instinct from birth sending the feeling of safety. When his mother spoke he knew he was hallucinating on the opium.

"You look absolutely awful," said Tilda Brigandshaw, looking down on her son. "They don't look after you. Anyway, it's good you're alive as it would have been a lot of bother coming all this way and finding you dead. People always exaggerate. Even when people are meant to be dying. How many times have I heard in my life someone say, 'look at him, 'e's half dead.' Now, sit up, talk to your mother and stop grinning like a Cheshire cat. Daft, I say. Never saw a cat in Cheshire grin once in my life and I grew up in Cheshire. Same as your father and now 'e's dead so they say but I'll believe that proper when I get back home. The office here says he died of a heart attack while he was having 'is supper. Anyway, you're alive which is something. And where's Emily? And all these children I've heard rumours about when I've only seen Harry?"

"He's sedated," said the male nurse who had walked into the ward to stop the woman talking so loud. "The opium makes them conscious of their surroundings but a strong dose makes it difficult for them to join in, Lady Brigandshaw."

"Is he dying?"

"Without any new infection, there will just be a lot of pain while the wounds heal. The shoulder where the bullet shattered the ligaments is the problem. My job is to keep the wound clean and even if I have to say so myself, I'm good at my job. Your son will recover fully. A famous white hunter, I'm sure he's had far worse than this in his life many times."

"No," said Sebastian, trying to bring his mind back into the body. "Is that really you, Mother?"

"You'll be quite all right now your mother's here."

"I'm glad." Without being able to control them, his eyelids closed and Sebastian went to sleep.

"You can sit with him as long as you like. Mothers have a healing power with their children even when they are grown men with children of their own. Talk gently. There are other patients in the ward. He'll wake in an hour or so and be able to talk."

EDDIE DOYLE HAD GONE to the Tulbagh Tavern more out of boredom than a need to get drunk. After a week he was certain there was nothing more he could do to save Tinus but, he did not want to go back to England until after the trial that was scheduled for the following Wednesday. It would be all over by the end of next week, and time hung heavy on a man alone with no work to do to cover over his loneliness.

The Tulbagh Tavern was inside an old stone building with a clock tower on top; the windows were small to keep out the storms that raged around the Cape in the winter; in the summer, they sat outside on wooden benches and watched the seals playing in the water between the ships. The winter fire at the base of the big chimney was cheerful and Eddie Doyle drank his beer for something better to do. The tavern was full and the smoke from many pipes blued the air. He had found a small table at the back and sat alone, the barmaid vigilant enough to bring him a second beer when he had slowly finished the first. No one had taken any notice of the old seaman from the time he had come into the bar. His ship that had brought him as a passenger from London had unloaded and gone on up the east coast to pick up a cargo of cloves at Zanzibar.

The second and third drink came as he enjoyed the fire and his memories. Only intermittently did the thought of Tinus Oosthuizen hanging by his broken neck bring him back to the present. People, mostly from the ships in the harbour, came and went. Mingling with the seamen were whores of every age, shape and colour but they left the old man alone in the corner.

When he was thinking of the past, the table next to him could shout but he did not hear. Then suddenly he was jerked back to reality becoming aware that two men were familiar and one of them was getting up and coming to his table.

"Captain Tucker of the *Mathilda*, Captain Doyle. A long time. Mind if I sit down? Just 'cause Colonial Shipping fight tooth and nail for cargo with African Shipping, don't mean the captains can't talk. Fact is, there's somethin' you should know."

"Please. Sit down. I am here on non-shipping business."

"Fact is, Captain Doyle, The Captain's dead. You two built the company, so to speak. Thought you might like to know. I won't sit down. Just thought you ought to know like I said. Many times I 'eard about that trip round the Horn and never once did he not mention your name."

"Dead, you say?"

"Yes, he's dead. Company office 'ad a wire. Heart attack."

When Captain Tucker turned his back small tears began to flow freely down the old, weathered face.

.   .   .

SHORTLY AFTER THE TWINS, Klara and Griet turned seven, a new strain of flu rampaged through their concentration camp killing a quarter of the young children and old people. For the first time, they recognised fear in the eyes of their mother. The old woman in the corner of hut twenty-two had withdrawn so far into herself she might have been dead and would have died without being spoon-fed by Sarie Mostert. Sarie, never afraid for herself, worried about everyone else. When the flu struck with terrible repetition, she forbade anyone in hut twenty-two to leave the small shack and stopped the British coming through the door. All the food and water she collected herself. Every time the night-bucket was used she took it out and brought it back washed clean, day and night. The fight to make everyone in hut twenty-two survive had become personal. From her experience in the slums of Pretoria, the dog-lady knew quite well that once a disease crept into the sanctuary of their hut, all the weak and all the children would probably die.

Only when the situation was out of control did the British face the problem, and with the doctors and nurses came the press followed by an international howl of disgust.

THE HIGHVELD CAMP was one of the smallest. The first to get sick had been a British soldier who caught a bad cold on the boat out from England. He had gone about his duties coughing. The germ he had picked up in England was common enough in the back streets of Manchester but had never before been seen in Africa. What was a nuisance for Private Higgenbottom was deadly for the Boers.

By the time Billy Clifford arrived to continue his series on the concentration camps, eighty-three children and seven grown-ups had been buried in the earth next to the camp. Billy wrote back for the *Irish Times*, that 'the problem of life was life itself. That man in war, in his quest for dominance, created misery for everyone, including children.' Later, Billy's article went on: 'From the first recorded history man has fought wars and what we so blithely call our civilisation is a sham. The fault lies in the very nature of man, the meaning of his survival, the evolution of the strong over the weak. It is to ourselves, each one of us, we must turn to give the blame, as in each of us, through our ancestry, given the right call, the right reward, women pushing forward men, men singing with excitement, is the seed of war. To blame others is only the second nature of man.'

More out of wild hope than expectation (it had been Billy Clifford's habit to check the list of Boers in the camps for one Sarie Mostert) he asked for the list of prisoners. When the name sprang from the page in the British guardroom, his blood went cold and his hands began to shake.

"Is this person still alive?" He pointed at the name.

"She'll be alive," said the duty corporal. "She's the dog-lady. Shuts everyone in the hut. Only clean hut, I reckon. Lots of the others kind of give up, you see. Not nice being locked up. That Sarie made us teach her English. Before the flu, we were teaching her twins English. She told us back 'ome in the slums of Pretoria they called her the dog-lady. Lots of dogs... You think this war'll be over soon? Can't stand the flies. And I don't like this place neither. Poor buggers all dying like that. Not right is it?... What you want with Sarie?"

"We were separated. Seven, nearly eight years ago."

"Come on, mate! You speak this Afrikaans then?"

"Not really."

"How did you talk?"

"We were in love. It didn't matter. How old are the twins?"

"That's easy. It was their seventh birthday just before the flu."

"If I marry her, can I take her out of the camp?"

"Ask the colonel. You being British don't seem a problem. What about her kids?"

"I rather think they are mine."

THE DOOR OPENED and the voice he recognised so well spoke through the crack between the jamb and the door. He could just see the tip of a pink nose.

"You no come in," she said in English. "I come out, see."

She came out backwards to close the door and Billy caught a glance of two small people catching a glimpse of the outside world. One of the children stuck her tongue out before the door slammed shut and Sarie turned round. First, she saw the corporal from the guardroom and was about to say something when she took in the man standing next to the soldier, squeaked and jumped clean off the ground into his arms, knocking Billy flat on his back where they lay hugging each other, tears mingling with tears.

When they disentangled to look at each other, the corporal had left them and gone back to the guardroom.

Five minutes later, Billy Clifford was introduced to his children.

Nothing, as Billy was to find in the coming weeks and months was as simple as it seemed. The colonel, a dried-up bachelor of sixty, had not a romantic bone in his body. But even had he agreed, Billy knew it would have made no difference. Not until the war was over, and the Boer women and children were allowed to go back to what was left of their homes, would Sarie Mostert leave the old woman who sat in the corner of the hut with her eyes permanently shut.

"If I don't spoonfeed her she dies. Not good way to start happy, see. She, like children, my responsible. I stay for war. Then go Ireland. Long time I look after that old lady, I want her go home to her sons. I go now, it bad rest of time for us. When old lady back at Majuba farm we make family... How you like my English? Not bad, hey?"

"I love everything about you, Sarie Mostert."

"If you love so much, maybe all stay Africa and you become big, big writer. What you want, hey? I remember. Everything."

THE BRITISH WERE to be his judge and executioner. The two brigadiers had made no eye contact with Tinus standing in front of his chair looking at his persecutors. The soldiers standing guard at the doors to the room in the Castle looked puny in comparison to the giant of a man mocking the three officers seated at the judgement table. He wore a waistcoat made from the skin of an elephant to remind him of the years of freedom hunting alone in the bush. They had made him take off the leather hat made from the skin of the same bull elephant. It sat alone on the single chair that was all that was left to him in a world once teeming in game. For long seconds before the trial began, the trial that he knew would find him guilty, Tinus stared into the cold, smug eyes of General Gore-Bilham seated between the brigadiers. Both of them were remembering the debagging of the general. Tinus smiled and tipped his head. Had the hat been where it should have been he would have raised it to his judge and executioner.

The lawyer Alison had found began to ingratiate himself to the military court and Tinus sat himself down. Comfortably, he crossed his legs and let his mind wander. He had found many times in his life when there was nothing he could do to save a situation it was best to do nothing and allow the inevitable to take its course. If the new King of England or his representative chose to stay his execution, so be it. He was what he was. Had done what he did.

It was all very efficient and very quick. He was a rebel. He had committed treason. He was to hang by his neck in the morning and there was the end of it. They had all come, his friends, the people who had made up his life, for better or for worse, some happy, some sad, some parts remembered with joy and mostly the bad parts lost with the passage of time. It was the mosaic of his life. Alison would forget the pain in the end. Barend would forget the pain and remember his pride. Tinka would marry and have her own children and tell them the story of their grandfather. Christo would never know his father and live his life with an empty hole that would always echo in his mind.

They had brought Sebastian on a stretcher and the two had silently shaken hands before all the words began to spill. Neither could speak so the silence had been better for both of them. The young lad he had shown the bush would recover and live to go home to where they had all been happy. The animals would still be there. The fish eagles would still call from the sides of the river. The rain would come. Crops, new crops, would grow. Life would be the same without him. He was mostly significant to himself; he the centre of the universe.

Captain Doyle had come, the first man to buy his ivory, the man who had given him the money to buy Kleinfontein that was forfeit to the Crown.

The old, bumbling aristocrat, Sir Henry Manderville had come and tried his best. The kids had been right. Potty. Pleasantly potty. But in all of it, he suspected the flush toilet still worked on Elephant Walk. He smiled at the memory.

And silently, throughout the court, the Afrikaners had come, the Boers who had stayed in the Cape, the wives of the Boers who were still fighting with Smuts and de Wet. And when he turned right at the end and waved at them, many were crying.

THEY LET him see his wife as was his due; they gave him a good meal as was his due. But in the morning at the first light of the new day, they dropped the trapdoor from beneath his feet and hanged him by the neck.

Outside the main gate of the Castle, where Sebastian had stayed all night, they heard the bell of death toll three times.

"I think it is time for all of us to go home to Rhodesia," said Sebastian. Inside the hired coach, they had covered him in blankets to keep out the Cape winter. Only the wound in his shoulder ached. There had been no rain all night. Harry, who had not been at the trial, had stayed with his father. The rules had been made by Tinus. None of the children at the trial. No one to see him die.

"Will Aunty Alison come back?" asked Harry.

"Not now. They will in the end. We are their only family. There's no one else."

"Will they have any money?"

"Yes, Captain Doyle has decided to sell African Shipping to Jeremiah Shank. Half our share will go to Alison. He's coming to visit Elephant Walk. Even stay. Strange thing of it all, he's taken my father's death badly. When men make friends, it's a strange thing. I hope you'll be lucky yourself, Harry. Now, help this cripple to sit up a little and you can drive us home. But first, take the nosebags from the horses. There's nothing more any of us can do for Tinus except keep his memory tight in our minds. This will not go down as one of the great days of the British Empire. I hope, son, you never have to fight a war. Oh, and your grandmother is coming with us. She always hated Hastings Court."

"You haven't cried."

"Oh, I will, Harry. I will. I am just too annoyed with my own people to cry just now. He was my friend. Yes, he was my friend. Silly, isn't it, how the tribes of Africa always want to fight with each other, even the white tribes."

"But they will stop fighting when Africa's civilised."

"What's civilised? You think what we British have just done to a brave man is civilised? I don't think so. I'll give you an article to read written by Billy Clifford. He says war is part of our nature. That it will never stop. Sadly, I rather think he is right... Drive first to the hospital where I am going to discharge myself. Then to your grandmother's hotel. There's nothing more for me to do in this war. My friend's dead, Harry. My friend's dead! The bloody bastards hanged him! Not even a firing squad. It's a horrible world. I wanted your mother, Harry. And they even tried to take her away from me those long years ago."

Harry Brigandshaw got out of the coach to attend to the horses. Never once before in his life had he seen his father cry.

3

SEPTEMBER 1901

The Boer ponies were in good condition for the first time in more than a year. Good spring rains had turned the highveld a lush green. Kei, sitting on a high rock in the middle of an open, green plain, gently stroked Blackdog's head. The bitch lying in the long grass at the foot of the rock was pregnant again and would soon have to be carried on his saddle. Piers had made him drown the last litter and both of them had been sad for days as the pups had not even opened their eyes. The four dogs and the bitch were panting, their tongues hanging out as far as they would go, dripping with sweat. There was no shade for miles around. Ahead, the remnants of Tinus Oosthuizen's commando moved slowly through the new grass. Even to Kei, it looked as if they had no known place to go or come from.

Kei was the scout left on the high rock to warn of danger and give the Boers time to gallop from the British. He had an off-white shirt in his saddlebag that he would put on at the first sign of danger. It was Piers's job to turn in his saddle regularly and look for the white shirt.

The hobbled horse grazing the new grass near the bald rock was a Basuto pony with rope for reins, a blanket for a saddle and no stirrups. Twice a British patrol had caught up to Kei on his various vantage points as the war simmered and flared across the veld. As expected of him he looked dumb when approached by the soldiers. He was a black man who had strayed into a white man's war and each time they left him alone.

Blackdog was the first to pick up the lone horseman riding hard towards the Boer commando and Kei focused his stolen British Army binoculars on the rider. The man was dressed in rags like the rest of them. His beard was thick and black and even at three miles' distance, Kei was sure the man was a Boer. As the sun began to make its drop over the horizon, Kei watched the lone rider close with the commando. As the sun tinged the clouds pink, Kei slipped down from his rock followed by Blackdog. Untying the hobble, Kei mounted his pony and with the dogs running behind, galloped for the horse before they were lost in the dark. They had not lit a fire for a year.

When he reached Piers talking to Karel, his pony was foaming at the mouth and he gave the animal a pint of his own drinking water. The dogs would have to wait until they found a stream. Most of the men left him alone. Only Karel and Piers talked to him and sometimes Magnus du Plessis the new commander, but that was when he wanted to give Kei an order. If he could have thought of something better to do with his life, he would have gone off with the dogs. He kept with the commando more from the force of habit. Majuba farm didn't exist. The gold of Lobengula didn't exist.

Piers put a billycan of water down for the panting dogs that Blackdog drank after a brief snapping argument. The three dogs and the bitch sat back on their haunches and watched with resignation. Piers sat down next to the dogs and looked at Kei in the torchlight.

"The British have hanged General Oosthuizen," he said in Afrikaans. "General du Plessis and the rest of us want our revenge. There is a *dorp* ahead with a British garrison. We want you to go into the *dorp* tomorrow. We will reach a stream in an hour. The land here belongs to Shalk Pretorious. Even without the moon, we will find the water. The dogs will be all right. Will you scout the *dorp* for us, Kei? The day after tomorrow we want to attack before first light so we must know where to look for them."

"Why did they hang the general? He was a prisoner."

"You see, if the British conquer this land they will murder us at will. Boer or black man."

THREE WEEKS after Magnus du Plessis swore on the Bible his oath of revenge, the first report came into army intelligence at the Castle. The *dorp* next to Shalk Pretorious's farm had been annihilated.

The small garrison of twelve men had been forgotten, and no instruction given to the sergeant to report his condition and that of his men. Everyone in the *dorp* knew Shalk Pretorious and all of them were frightened of retribution. Twenty days after Kei had scouted the exact location of each British soldier and the Boer attack had gone ahead, a

British patrol called in on its way to relieve a blockhouse in the chain set down by Kitchener to flush out the last of the Boers, the Bittereinders, who refused to lay down their arms. The townsfolk had left the bodies where their throats had been cut and the sergeant where Magnus du Plessis had shot him in the middle of the small square. In fear of their lives, everyone except the blacks had evacuated the village and left it to the scavengers. The sergeant's bones had been picked clean by the vultures and crows. The blacks gave the British soldiers blank looks and were unable to speak any language the British lieutenant could understand. When he reached Kitchener's fence and blockhouse, he handed a full report to the retiring lieutenant who was taking his men to Cape Town on leave.

The bodies of two British patrols were next reported. A blockhouse in the long line of blockhouses across the highveld was attacked and everyone killed. The pattern coming into James Brigandshaw's command centre was exactly the same... No one had seen anything... Every one of the British had been killed.

"Are you thinking the same thing, James?" asked Colonel Hickman.

"Exactly the same. This is revenge. An eye for an eye. Most likely General Oosthuizen's commando with someone else in charge. Throughout the entire war, there have been wounded after a skirmish. Every one of these soldiers has either died in a firefight, had his throat cut, or been executed. The Boers don't seem to care anymore. They are killing British soldiers right under our nose. It's almost as if they want to get themselves killed."

"No man wants to die."

"They do if they feel sufficiently guilty. Tinus Oosthuizen only went to war long after we marched into Pretoria. The pressure must have been enormous. Every farmer in Franschhoek is a Cape Boer. Someone pushed him. It must have been terrible. His mother a Scot, the mother of his children English. The man had even given up hunting for ivory as he didn't want to kill the animals. Our esteemed General Gore-Bilham in his private hate has killed over one hundred British soldiers. Unless we do something swiftly, there are going to be a lot more dead. Hate, guilt and no way out make a powder keg. This is a private war. We must kill or capture this Boer commando. I'll plot each of the attacks and see if there is a pattern. They must have a lair."

MAGNUS DU PLESSIS prayed to his God on his knees. Every British death was part of his holy war. Hatred and righteousness mixed in his mind to create a fanatic. The obsession to kill British soldiers seethed in his belly and every time he prayed he finished screaming at the heavens.

"I will revenge you, Tinus," he shouted. "I will send you a great host of dead Englishmen. You will see!"

Karel watched the man whose mind had snapped soon after the lone rider brought the news. He looked at Piers and Piers looked away. Both of them were sick to their stomachs of the executions. Kei had stopped talking to anyone and watched the new general screaming on his knees with a mix of fear and, Karel thought, even understanding. Of course, they were all going to be killed now as every British unit would be looking for the scourge that took no prisoners.

Karel unwillingly played through his mind the first attack and the sergeant, unarmed and with his hands up, walking across the small dusty square with a timid smile on his face.

"I surrender," the sergeant said in English and then, just to make sure, he repeated the words in Afrikaans.

"So did my friend," the new general had said quietly in English so again there was no mistake. "You people murdered my friend," he then screamed at the top of his voice and shot the sergeant through the right eye. Three more times the commando watched Magnus du Plessis shoot the dead sergeant on the ground, finally kicking the body.

"How do people hate so much?" Karel said loudly.

"I'm just tired," said Piers. "We can't win but we go on. I want to find a quiet spot away from war and people and find out in my heart if there really is a God. At the moment I am not so sure when I look at Magnus du Plessis."

"He made Uncle Tinus go out for the Boers. I think he has found out it was wrong to force another man to go to war. He wants to wallow in the misery. Drown himself in the blood of his enemy. He can't even see that God forsook him the moment he shot the sergeant in the square. I rather hope for Magnus du Plessis there isn't a heaven or a hell. That God does not exist. My brother, it is time for you and me to ride away. There is evil over there. We will all go tonight with the dogs. Enough good men have died for no good purpose. Soon, the war will be over. We'll each find a wife and have big families and forget what we have done these last few weeks. Uncle Tinus would not have wished this to happen. Revenge and retribution have to stop."

"It never will," said Kei who had been standing behind them for the past few minutes. "But it is good we go from here. Maybe the farm has not been totally destroyed. The land will have been fallow for two seasons. The crops will grow."

"The British won't let us go home," said Piers.

"Then we will go north," said Karel. "Stay deep in the bush until this war comes to an end. I don't want to kill anymore. Our new general is mad."

FOR MAGNUS DU PLESSIS everything had gone. His friend, murdered. His people scattered in the wilderness. His farm in Franschhoek forfeit if he returned. His family alone. And now they were deserting him. The blood of Tinus Oosthuizen had deserted him and soon, even the power of revenge would be lost to him.

"God," he called in his agony, "why have you forsaken me? Why have you forsaken your chosen people? We left the land of Europe to follow your word in purity, the purity given to us by John Calvin. In the wilderness, generation following generation, we followed the purity of your word. Why have you forsaken us to the British? Why do they want our wilderness where we pray to you and live by your book? Why did you let them come here? We, dear God, are your chosen people. What have we done for you to forsake us? Oh God, can you hear me? If you do not help us, we will perish. God, they killed my friend. I made him come to war. I made him, God. Made him leave his family. God, I killed my friend, and you have forsaken me. There was the word and now there is nothing. Without you there is nothing. No meaning. No before or after. Everything that is life has no meaning. We are as the cattle. Animals. To eat and to be eaten. There is no soul without you and you have forsaken me. Why did you give me life to forsake me? If you be there God, up there, the God my heart so aches for, strike down a bolt of lightning. Kill me and I will be happy. Kill my mortal life and bring me to you, God. Please bring me. If there is a God in heaven strike out my misery. Everything has gone but you God. Prove to me you exist. Strike me down. Dear God, I want to die."

He stood on the rock, his arms to heaven, waiting. Behind, the few Bittereinders watched and heard his agony. And nothing happened. The blue heaven stayed its perfect blue, dotted with perfect clouds. No sound of thunder. No rent in the sky. Nothing.

Most of the men, dressed in rags and hungry, turned away in embarrassment; some even hoped the sky would rend asunder and take them all. They knew the war was finished, like themselves. They had fought and lost. It was the will of God and God punished his people for their sins and the sins of their fathers.

"Khaki!" The shout rang in the clear highveld air. "Up-saddle!"

And from his small mountain, Magnus du Plessis came down from trying to talk to God and ran for his pony. Even without Kei and his white shirt, they outrode the British, the power of self-preservation as strong as their belief in God. There were twenty-nine Boers left, galloping through the new grass already up to their knees.

"We will fight another day," shouted Magnus du Plessis who had taken the lead. He had forgotten the lack of God's thunderbolt.

THE BRITISH PATROL watched the Boer dust disappear ahead into the hills. Within half an hour the position of the Boer remnant had been reported by wire to James Brigandshaw in the Castle at Cape Town.

THAT NIGHT, Karel, Piers, Kei and the dogs broke through the fence between two British blockhouses, cutting the wire in the moonless dark, the hooves muffled, the dogs silent. Through the rest of the night, they rode slowly north, checking their position from the Southern Cross. In the morning, when the sun paled the sky, the two brothers rode on either side of Kei. In front trotted Blackdog. Behind, like scouts protecting the flanks, coursed the three dogs and the pregnant bitch that belonged to Sarie Mostert.

"We'll ride over the Limpopo River," said Kei. "There's something I have to tell you. Something you can help. And something to show you."

From deep within his right saddlebag, Kei pulled out Zwide's head-ring. And as they rode north in the sweet clean air of a day free from war, he told them the story of Lobengula's gold, spreading the legend.

"You want us to look for the old king's gold?" asked Piers.

"It exists," said Kei. "The trouble is nobody knows where. No, that gold gave me enough trouble."

"Why does everyone want to be rich?" asked Karel.

"It is in all men," said Kei. "What wouldn't I have done with all that gold."

"What would you have done?" asked Piers.

"I would have found a place and made myself a king. With all that gold I would have bought enough guns to fight off the British."

"And who would have used the guns?" asked Karel.

"There are always people if you promise them enough. Fight for me and I will make you rich. Give you land. Give you women. Never fails. Most people don't have a chance. Any chance is better than none. Sitting, waiting to be robbed of the little you have has never been attractive. You Boers taught that much to us blacks. Promise anyone a better life and give him a gun and he will fight."

"So you are going to look for the gold?" said Piers.

"Maybe."

"And where do you get the guns?"

"Someone will always sell me guns for gold."

"What's the matter, Karel?" asked Piers.

"Someone just walked over my grave."

THE MAP SHOWED the line of blockhouses across the veld that was meant to box in the remnants of the Boer commandos that still refused to surrender. James even knew the name of the man leading the commando that interested him most. For a price, there was always a spy in every community.

"Another Cape rebel and Tinus Oosthuizen's neighbour. Through General Oosthuizen, we should have offered the other Cape rebels amnesty. Not hanged him. Well, whatever, this du Plessis is trapped between the fence and our new sweep. With your permission, Colonel Hickman, I wish to go north and make sure he is caught but I want General Gore-Bilham's assurance the man will not hang for treason."

"Really, James, you can be ridiculous. The man's a murderer. He kills prisoners."

"But didn't we?"

"The war will be over any day soon and then it will be different."

"Good. Because here is my letter resigning my commission after this last journey north. My father had a warped sense of humour. When Arthur died, I became my father's heir. But there are strings attached. Not to the baronetcy that is the right of the senior surviving son or grandson. Father entailed Hastings Court, that was no problem, but it means it can never be sold or mortgaged. I am sole heir to the rest of his estate after legacies to Mother and Nathanial. My youngest brother gets not a penny. Fortunately, Sebastian has made his own money. Colonial Shipping and its subsidiaries are subject to a separate trust which requires me to run the company in exchange for all the profits of the company. I am not allowed to sell one share and if I do, the conditions of the will may be offered to Nathanial and if he fails to respond, the company shall be sold and the entire proceeds are given to the Mission to Seamen. Nat and I lose our allowances.

"As you well know, I could never stay in the regiment without a private income. The higher the rank, the more one needs. Running a shipping company will be like joining the navy. Terrible thought and God forbid but the principles of command are just the same. It would not be fair on Nat to make him choose between his work among the heathen and the business of making money. His wife would disagree but that's another story. So you see, sir, I have to go home. The war as it stands is an irritant. The Boers have lost the conventional war and largely the guerrilla war."

"When are you going north?" asked Colonel Hickman, pocketing the letter of resignation.

"Tomorrow on the four o'clock afternoon train."

"I'll miss you, James. So will the army."

"Thank you, sir."

AS LUCK WOULD HAVE IT, the last evening was a Monday, dining-in night, and every officer in Gore-Bilham's command was required to dine in the mess that night. No one ever looked for an excuse unless he wished to stay the same rank for the rest of his army career. With his resignation letter in Colonel Hickman's pocket, James was tempted. The very look of General Gore-Bilham made him sick. But after so many years in the army and with many of his fellow officers his personal friends, James dressed up in his number one uniform, took himself across the cobbled courtyard to the mess, took the required glass of dry sherry from the mess steward and walked across to the senior officer in the room to show his respect as required by army protocol.

General Gore-Bilham was trussed into a red monkey jacket and below the short jacket that only came to his waist, he wore dark blue trousers that accentuated his large behind. The thought of the man in his white long johns after being stripped by Tinus Oosthuizen brought a smile to James's face as he waited his turn to wish the general good evening.

Interpreting the smile as a sign of pleasure at being in the presence of his general, Gore-Bilham broke off the stilted conversation of a junior officer trying to ingratiate himself and turned to the young colonel who was now a baronet, the title inherited from his father.

"Ah, Sir James," began Gore-Bilham forcing James to control a wince. "Colonel Hickman tells me you have to return to England and run the family estate. With privilege comes responsibility. Can't get away from it. Those of us who came from old families have to shoulder the yoke, so to speak. One day I must return to civilian life like yourself, Sir James. I should be grateful if you would take the chair on my right at dinner tonight. The war is going well. Smuts has sent another message enquiring our terms if he surrenders. Unconditional of course. Silly man. What else would he expect from the British?"

Before James could mentally vomit, Hickman took him away by the elbow.

"He's a pompous, patronising ass," said James quietly. "Never took much notice of me before the title. Doesn't he know my father bought his title and could barely speak the King's English? Father was a bloody pirate who made money, gave money to the Tory Party in exchange for a hereditary title. My father was obsessed with creating a dynasty, as was our general's grandfather. Both our families are as common as dirt. I admired my father when he was a sailor, a damn good sailor, but all this business of trying to make us Brigandshaw's old family is a lot of cock and bull. Why are people so impressed with a title or a lot of money?"

"Because they don't have it themselves. They either despise or fawn. Our general fawns. Hope you enjoy your food. He'll tell you all about his own estate in detail while you try to eat. The fact the money to pay for it was made by working the poor twelve hours a day, six days a week doesn't bother him. Just don't remind him his grandfather was in trade and that you, by the sound of your father's will, are going to be in trade yourself very soon."

"He's a snob."

"Funnily enough, we all are snobs in one way or the other. The poor who wallow in their poverty and hate the rich, taking great pride in what they are, are also snobs. That one's called inverted snobbery."

"Tell that to the poor. My mother knew what it was like to be poor. Hungry and cold and worked to a standstill. It's not very nice, she assures me."

"Man in all his manifestations. And you are right, James. I have never been poor."

"Why do people have to be poor?"

"That is the question sensible people have been asking since man was settled down in mutual groups of protection, giving up the precarious life of hunting and gathering thirty-odd thousand years ago according to Darwin. You see, in a group there has to be a leader, and leaders exact their price once they are in power however small their little band of men. One of the laws of nature. The strong or the rich eat first at the table.

"Many of the weaker tribes in Africa have asked for British protection so they can grow crops and get to eat them before the stronger tribes kill them for the food. In the end, they must pay for that protection and stability. Someone has to pay the army. The British are not a charitable organisation. Frankly, I think Africa will cost us far more than we get out of it. Look at the cost of this war in life and treasure balanced against the diamonds and gold. Rhodes led us in by the nose. Taking on responsibility for other people can often be more trouble than it's worth.

"I hope you don't find that yourself, James. Being chairman of a major shipping company will have its problems. And when you are at the top of the chain, you can't pass along the problem as so many of us are so fond of doing in the army. Huge responsibility can be as big a problem as being poor, but only those who have had huge responsibility know what I'm talking about. I wonder if our general sleeps so well at night having hanged General Oosthuizen? You see, under all that pomposity the man just might be human.

"Come on. It's seven-thirty. Everyone is going into the dining room. You are lucky tonight, James. You won't have to search for your name-place... Enjoy your dinner, Sir James Brigandshaw, Bart."

LIKE A BUCK CAUGHT IN A BUSHFIRE, Magnus du Plessis rushed the fence twice and each time recoiled from the intense heat of British retaliation. He was down to twenty-three men and the noose was tightening around his neck. With the fence and blockhouses, the space that had been the Boers' best friend had gone. Instead of breaking through the British lines into relative safety, they found the British circling round their back again while filling in the space in front. Turning and twisting, the remnants of Tinus Oosthuizen's commando fought for their lives like rats in a tight corner. With the constant movement forced on them by the British, the ponies were losing condition. The dried meat in their saddlebags was dwindling and there was never enough time to shoot and dry a fresh supply of game. There wasn't even time to pray or think of their wives and families. After two years for some of them, less for Magnus du Plessis, they had come to the end of their tether. There was nowhere to go and nowhere to hide.

"They'll shoot us down like dogs," he told them. "We must die like men for God and country."

"What country?" asked one of the men. "Die yes, but not for our country. Maybe we Boer never had a country. Maybe we never will."

"Let us pray," said Magnus du Plessis, stopping his pony.

Still in the saddle, everyone removed their hats and bent their heads and prayed to God for their salvation.

"WHAT ARE THEY DOING?" asked Lieutenant Green.

"I rather think they are praying," said James.

"Do we fire?"

"Not when a man has his hat in hand and is praying to his God. Dismount and find cover. Those men are very dangerous, Mr Green. Ah, there is Philby's signal. We have them neatly bottled up in this nice little valley... Mr du Plessis," shouted James. "I know you speak English.

"My name is James Brigandshaw. My brother is Sebastian, partner of the late Tinus Oosthuizen, for which I personally apologise as an officer and a gentleman. Your war is over. Fact is, the whole war is over. General Smuts has again enquired about terms for cessation of war. Please drop your rifles to the ground and put your hats back on your heads. You will be treated as prisoners of war."

"And hanged as a traitor?" shouted back Magnus du Plessis. Then he charged.

"He's coming, sir."

"I rather think you are right. Mr Green, please shoot that man's horse. Not the man, the horse."

"I would rather shoot the man."

"I would rather not shoot either of them. Amazing how fast these ponies can gallop. Shoot the horse, Mr Green!"

"Yes, sir. The rest of the commando has thrown down their guns."

The stumble of the dead horse threw Magnus du Plessis over the animal's head into the loose rock that covered the valley floor. By the time James got down from his horse and knelt next to the man, he was quite dead. In one hand he clutched a Mauser rifle and in the other a small book of prayer.

'The things men do to men,' James said to himself. 'And in the end, it does not make the slightest bit of difference. What is so important today is tomorrow's history.' He was shaking his head.

"Have a detail dig a grave for this man. There we will bury him with honour. In different circumstances, I rather think we would have been friends. Seb and I, Seb and Magnus du Plessis. Myself and Tinus Oosthuizen. What a waste of life."

"What do we do with the men who have surrendered?"

"Give them a good meal, by the look of them. After the burial, I shall be leaving, Mr Green."

"Where are you going, sir?"

"To England. Back to England. Let some other poor sods sort out the mess. We've made an unnecessary feud with these people that will last a hundred years."

EPILOGUE

PEACE

~

The eight-year-old twins, Klara and Griet, stared at the man on the other side of the railway carriage as it clattered through the dry bushveld of Bechuanaland. First, Klara thought, there had been Uncle Frikkie, but he had gone to the war and never come back. Then after the prison camp, they had gone home with the old lady to Majuba when Karel and Piers had come home with the dogs. The old lady had gone back to treating their mother as a servant, but they had the one-roomed hut that had not been burnt down by the British, all to themselves, and now that their lives were back to normal it was marvellous.

They had run with the dogs up to the mountains, a slow loping run taught them by Elijah who had come back with the remnants of his family from somewhere called the Transkei where there was so much water no one could see the end. There was still no sign of Kei or Blackdog and Piers had said he wasn't coming home. She had shot a small buck with the rifle lent to her by Uncle Karel and Griet had thrown a tantrum as she had wanted to be the first. Even the new house everyone was building for the old lady would be finished before the rains. With something called 'reparations from the British', Uncle Piers had gone off and come back with a herd of cows. Now she could drink as much milk as she could ever want. Life for Klara was perfectly wonderful, and then the man she was staring at had come into her life for the second time.

They hated him. Both of them. Shoes were put on their feet for the first time and made them sore. They were constantly dumped into tubs of hot water and scrubbed so the nice dirt-brown of their skins turned red and burnt in the sun. The dogs were kicked out of the hut. Their mother appeared in clothes Klara had never seen before. Next to the wooden bench under the mango tree, Piers built the man a table where he sat all day doing something they were told was writing. And to add insult to injury the man could only speak the language of the hated English, something he was now teaching to their mother who had lost all interest in her and Griet. Even now in the railway carriage as it ground to a halt, Klara watched her mother smiling at the man with eyes so soft they were melting.

Outside, black men were running up and down the carriages offering the passengers carved wooden animals. The window being down in the cool of the morning, a black hand came into the carriage with a wooden tortoise on the pink palm. She could not see the black man's face, only the hand and the carving on the pink palm.

"Tiny tortoise," said the man, first in Afrikaans and then in what Klara now understood to be English.

The man their mother had said was their father, which she knew to be a lot of nonsense, took the tiny carving from the pink palm and left in its stead a silver sixpence. The black hand closed over the coin quickly as the three dogs and the bitch, asleep on the carriage floor, woke up to the possibilities. When the twins stood up to look down through the open window, the black man was disappearing into the bush with his prize. The bitch was all for following when the man grabbed it by its collar and pushed up the window. Then once again he forgot everything except their mother.

"This tiny tortoise," said Billy Clifford in the English Klara could not understand, "will be a keepsake for the rest of our lives." Then he kissed Sarie softly on the lips.

For Klara that was the last straw, so she dug Griet hard in the ribs which started a fight. The dogs and the bitch jumped up on the seat which was right against the new rules. Two of the dogs, joining in the fun, began fighting with each other. The train lurched forward and threw the dogs back on the floor between the seats. Then it stopped again with a terrible clang and threw Klara back against the seat so Griet was able to get in a punch. The man they hated was shouting, which spurred them on. When the train lurched forward again, the man was thrown onto the floor on top of the dogs. Klara's mother began to laugh which made the twins get the giggles.

"This is going to be quite some family," said Billy, picking himself up.

"I rather think it is," said Sarie in Afrikaans. She found it easier to get the gist of the English rather than speaking it.

THE TRAIN that had left Cape Town four and half days earlier clanked into the railway station at Fort Salisbury that people were now calling Salisbury, the military origin having been swamped by private enterprise and the bustle of commerce. With the war down south over, the boom was just beginning in the new colony. British immigrants, many soldiers who had fought against the Boers, stepped off the train as soon as it stopped. The two railway engines, one at the back and one at the front, were letting off clouds of steam and noise. Black porters grabbed at the luggage of the bewildered passengers. Women in long dresses picked up the hems of their skirts above the loose gravel and dust. No one even saw the incongruity of hatboxes and leather trunks, men and women dressed in fashion right into the middle of nowhere.

Sebastian Brigandshaw, no longer even using a stick, but with a wry smile that understood the madness, searched the faces of the passengers. He was not quite sure if he would recognise the Irish journalist who had tried so hard to help Tinus Oosthuizen but the wedding invitation had gone out just the same, more as a gesture of thanks than an expectation of the man's arrival, let alone his newly found family that had somehow survived the concentration camp. The man had written by what could only have been return of post saying how much he was looking forward to the wedding, and could he bring the mother of his children.

Emily, who understood better than most the delicate way the man had referred to the woman, was sure that if the woman arrived, so would her children. With Alison, Barend, Tinka and Christo back at the farm, there were so many children a few more would make no difference. The man had gone on to write that he had taken a year's sabbatical from the *Irish Times* to write a book on the war that had, at last, come to an end, and which he had been following from the beginning. Just the place to write would be on a farm miles from anywhere and with no distractions where he could walk for long periods and let the plot run freely through his mind. So while they were attending the wedding they would be looking for a small cottage to live in, and if anyone could find him such accommodation he, and hopefully the reading public, would be eternally grateful as not only had he found a title for his story, all of which was based on fact, he had found a publisher who had given him enough money to finance the writing of the book. And since he was writing he asked Sebastian what he thought of the title *Seeds of*

Hatred, as the war had not only set English against Dutch but with Milner looking ahead to a new British dominion made up of the two Boer republics and the British colonies at the Cape and Natal, he rather thought the blacks would be left out of the political picture, creating the far worse spectre of a black-white hatred.

Sir Henry Manderville had read the letter and made the decision.

"Build him a house, Seb. A man of letters. Should be fun. I liked him. I can even put in one of Mr Crapper's inventions so he won't go bush happy. He will want to check with you about the animals from a hunter's point of view. We can all help. Something to do. One of the problems I find out here is having too much time on my hands. Send him a wire inviting him to the farm for a year. How old are the children?"

"I have not the first idea."

"The other children will enjoy the company."

Down the end of the train a carriage door opened and four mongrel dogs leapt out onto the gravel, the dogs cocking their legs against the train and the bitch dropping her bottom to the gravel and dirt. A young girl got onto the second step down when another gave her a push from behind. Nimbly, both of them jumped down on the mix of dirt and gravel. Both of them took off their shoes and called the dogs. The dogs ran back and sat down on their rumps next to the girls. Some of the ex-soldiers were looking at the girls in their bare feet. Behind the girls stepped down a young woman in a blue dress with a large blue bonnet who seemed among the noise to be telling the identical girls to put their shoes back on their feet. Even from fifty yards, Seb caught some of the words which were not in English. Then he saw Billy follow down the steps.

"As you know, she's Afrikaans," he said to Henry Manderville.

"Well, there's the mother of the children. And the children. And the dogs. Bet you a guinea, Seb, those children can't speak English. Now that will please young Barend. You know that boy really hates the English."

"After what we did to his father, I'm not surprised. I wonder what the ridgebacks and the fox terriers are going to say to those dogs? I'm beginning to wonder if my mother's idea of a big wedding was such a good idea after all. Pity about James. I was rather beginning to like my brother James towards the end of his stay in Africa."

"You think he'll be able to run Colonial Shipping?"

"Of course. He's taken on Eddie Doyle as general manager."

"And whose idea was that?"

"Mine... She's very pretty."

"Yes, she is. And so is Alison."

"And what is that meant to mean?"

"I may be the grandfather of your children but I have only just turned fifty. Even at fifty, you recognise a handsome woman... Mr Clifford!" he shouted. "We're over here. Do you have any luggage in the luggage van?"

"Hello! Afraid so. Three trunks. Hope you don't mind the dogs."

"Not at all," said Seb as they shook hands.

"This is Sarie Mostert and these are my twin daughters. Klara and Griet. It's rather a long story."

"Hope you'll put it in the book," said Henry, shaking his hand.

"Rather think I will."

Down on his knees, Seb was talking to the girls in Afrikaans.

"That's a relief," said Billy. "They can't speak any English. Where did he learn Afrikaans?"

"From his partner, Tinus Oosthuizen."

"Yes, of course. The man who links us all together."

BEING TREATED like a lady was a new experience for Sarie Mostert. The man with the blue eyes and yellow-white hair bleached by years in the sun had removed his wide-brimmed hat when introduced.

"Are you an Afrikaner?" she asked.

"No," laughed Seb, answering her in Afrikaans. "My partner was Tinus Oosthuizen. General Oosthuizen. We hunted together for years and to pass the long nights around the fire he taught me the language of his father... I miss him very much... You don't make many friends in life... I hope you'll be happy with us while Billy writes his book. I'm sure it will be very good. Alison, Tinus's widow, speaks Afrikaans. So does Emily, a little. All the children are bilingual and Harry also speaks Shona. That's my eldest son. When he was growing up he had a black friend. We never did find out what happened to Tatenda... Your children don't like wearing shoes."

"No."

"Neither do mine. Emily calls them little savages."

"Which animal gave you your hat?" she asked.

"An elephant. I hunted elephant for their ivory when I was young and foolish. I keep the hat to remind me never to do it again... With all these dogs I rather think you also like animals, Miss Mostert. What happened to her pups?"

"Kei took them. The father was Blackdog."

"Now that sounds interesting. Tell me on the way to the farm. The children can go with Billy and my father-in-law in the farm cart. You come with me in the trap and we'll lead the way. My father-in-law is rather starved for intellectual conversation and has been looking forward to Billy. Do the dogs ride or run?"

"They've been running all their lives."

"Haven't we all?"

AFTER AN HOUR it was clear both of them were trying to have different conversations.

"We seem to be at cross-purposes," said Henry Manderville. "When you live in isolation, you will understand. Seb, Emily, Alison, even Tinus when he was alive and living with us. We had all talked out everything that was in our minds. You want to know my everyday reality and I want to find out what is happening in England. Enough to ask, did you bring any books?"

"A trunkful."

"Then I am at your service. My impatience can wait. Now, what do you want to know?"

"Where are the indigenous people? I see herd after herd of animals but where are the people?"

"We rather take it for granted, but I have talked about it with Seb and Seb's brother, Nat. He's the missionary who is going to marry them after all these years. Says there is so much to do for the natives after they've heard the word of Christ. You'll see his new church. I think it rather incongruous, a great big red brick building in the middle of the bush. But Nat says it's just the start. The emblem of what Christ will do for them. The cross from the top of the church throws a long shadow when the sun goes down... At the beginning of the last century, a renegade general of Shaka Zulu went north to escape the wrath of his king. After many stops and starts, he conquered Matabeleland. With him from Zululand went some of the best soldiers in the world. What they wanted they took. What they didn't want they killed. The Shona, a loose affiliation of tribes speaking the same language, had no answer to the Zulu stabbing spear. In many ways, it was similar to the Roman short sword and just as effective. Mzilikazi, the first king of the Matabele, was succeeded by his son Lobengula.

"For decade after decade, they sent impis killing and stealing every year until Rhodes put a stop to it. In Africa, if you are strong, it's easier to live by rape and pillage than hard work. The Shona were decimated. We estimate a population of a quarter of a million in Rhodesia, an area the size of England and Wales. Nat says they need modern medicine. The infant mortality rate is appalling. There is very little order or government beyond the village level and the local chief. To get away from the Zulu assegais the Shona have lived for generations in the hills like rock rabbits trying to survive. Once, so they tell us, the Shona were the royal tribe of central Africa. There are strange ruins all over the place. What we British have to do is put in law and order so they can get on with their lives. There's an awful lot of work and their witch doctors don't like our interference. They won't want to lose their power over the people. We had a rebellion, but that's over and with all the new immigrants coming in we'll soon have the place humming. It's a very beautiful country, Mr Clifford. With God's blessing, we will make it flourish."

"The only snag is people don't like to be ruled by foreigners."

"We all have to be ruled by someone, someone we usually never know. Provided the ruler is fair and just I don't think it matters where he comes from."

"You should tell that to the Irish."

"Yes, I suppose I should. So you think the people of Ireland would be better off free of the empire?"

"Probably not. But their hearts think otherwise. Pride is a strong part of people. A proud people don't like to be told what to do by foreigners. The history of mankind is littered with wars of liberation. Liberation from class oppression. Liberation from poverty. Liberation from being told what to do by a foreigner."

"And the liberator stirring up the trouble is always after power. History is also littered with people trying to free themselves from their liberators. It's one thing to say what you are going to do for the people and another to do it. Most of your hopeful liberators are great orators or successful generals. The generals fare better. They parcel out the spoils to their cronies and kill anyone who wants a new liberation."

"Doesn't that sound like the English? Sort out Lobengula, restore law and order and give the land to the English pioneers who conquered the country."

"You know more about Rhodesia than I thought. Isn't British rule better for the Shona?"

"Maybe you should have asked them."

"Their leaders will say no. They want power like the witch doctors. With Lobengula dead they no longer have to fear the Matabele."

"Instead they have to fear the British."

"Does the cycle ever end?"

"Not until we destroy the planet."

"You don't believe in British justice? The rule of law?"

"Most often in life we have to choose between the best of many evils. The

Greek and Roman Empires are examples of periods of man's progress. I rather think the British Empire is another. But don't tell that to my Irish editor or my Irish heart."

"What I see is right, others see as wrong."

"Maybe all of us are using excuses to benefit ourselves. Only a fool cuts off his nose to spite his face."

"Maybe you should tell that to your Irish Republicans."

"Touché."

"The trick is to see the right from the wrong, the wood from the trees."

"I like your use of the word trick."

"You think we should have stayed out of Africa?"

"I think it will give you a lot more trouble than it is worth."

BILLY CLIFFORD STOOD up on the footstep in front of the farm wagon for a better view down into the Mazoe Valley. As far as his eyes could see, elephants were moving in a dust-covered line northwest, mile after mile of moving giants and, in between, the young herded by the old.

"What is it?" he said in awe.

"The great elephant walk," said Henry Manderville next to him. "I've heard of it. Never thought to see the migration. Why Seb named the farm Elephant Walk. Tinus knew. Every fifteen, twenty years the elephants move north or south. No one knows why. Primal instinct. Going on long before man. They swim the rivers, the little ones holding their mothers' tails by their trunks. Seb's lucky. The line is northwest of the farm."

"How long will it last?"

"Tinus saw it once. When they were crossing the Zambezi River. Riverbank to island. Island to river bank. Went on for days, flanked by predator prides of lion keeping their distance. Have a look through the field glasses. I can make out fifteen, maybe twenty lions sitting off the moving line in the long grass waiting for the weak. Away from the lion will be the hyena and jackal, scavengers waiting for the lions to kill. In the msasa trees will be vultures and crows, though it's too far to see even with the glasses. The crows are the last in line to pick the carcass. Nature at its most powerful, even horrible. Some die for others to live as life evolves down the thousands of centuries. That, Billy Clifford, is a sight you and your children will never forget."

"For the first time since boarding the train the twins have been quiet when awake." Billy turned to smile at them in the back of the cart.

"Come on," said Henry Manderville, "Their mother's waving. Seb's moving again. It's safe to go down into the valley if we keep to the east. Emily on Elephant Walk will hear the rumbling of the moving herds and wonder what it is. Even after years in the bush, my daughter can be frightened."

"The power of nature," said Billy as he sat back on the board that made a driving seat.

"The power of God."

"Will we ever understand?"

"However much we try, never. I don't think we are even meant to understand. I have tried all my life without success. Now there goes Seb in a hurry back to the farm! They've been in love since they were children and that's what makes it all worth the while."

Slowly, Henry Manderville let the horses take the farm cart down the pass into the valley. Ahead, the trap was picking up a nice speed towards Elephant Walk. Henry turned once more to smile at the twins seated on the trunks, quite happy to let life take them wherever it was going.

～

ELEPHANT WALK (BOOK TWO)

CONTINUE YOUR JOURNEY WITH THE BRIGANDSHAWS

The Boer War is over and for a time peace returns to Elephant Walk… but for how long?

Spending an idyllic summer in the heart of the Dorset countryside, young Harry Brigandshaw receives word. The unimaginable has happened. Returning to Rhodesia in haste, Harry and his family are shaken to the core, yet more is to come…

By1914, England is at war with those closest to Harry enlisting. With death visiting the Brigandshaws, a vengeful Harry heads for Europe. And as he moves up the ranks, a past university acquaintance is also making a name for himself – the invincible killing machine, Fishy Braithwaite.

Fishy and Harry's private lives entangle and hatred begins to simmer. Friends become enemies and the Brigandshaws' destiny is in jeopardy…

If the savage destruction of war wasn't enough, the Brigandshaws face even more human depravity in this gripping historical fiction series brought to life in Peter Rimmer's *Elephant Walk*.

DEAR READER

~

Reviews are the most powerful tools in our kitty when it comes to getting attention for Peter's books. This is where you can come in, as by providing an honest review you will help bring them to the attention of other readers.

If you enjoyed reading *Echoes from the Past*, and have five minutes to spare, we would really appreciate a review (it can be as short as you like). Your help in spreading the word and keeping Peter's work alive is gratefully received. Please post your review on the retailer site where you purchased this book.

Thank you so much.
Heather Stretch (Peter's daughter)

PRINCIPAL CHARACTERS

~

Alison Ford — A nursemaid
Arthur Brigandshaw — Sebastian's eldest and debauched brother
Barend, Tinka, Christo — Tinus's children
Billy Clifford — A newspaper reporter
Bess Brigandshaw — Nathanial's wife
Captain Eddie Doyle — Captain of the Indian Queen
Emily Manderville — Sebastian's childhood sweetheart
Elijah — Head foreman on Majuba farm
Ezekiel Oosthuizen — Father of Frikkie, Karel and Piers and brother of Tinus
Fran Shaw — Gregory Shaw's wife
Frikkie Oosthuizen — Nephew of Tinus
Gregory Shaw — Friend of Sir Henry Manderville
Harry, Madge, George, James — Sebastian's children
Helena (Crouse) Oosthuizen — Mother of Frikkie, Karel and Piers
Jack Slater — A company man and acting administrator of Rhodesia
James Brigandshaw — Sebastian's second eldest brother
Jeremiah Shank — A discharged and blacklisted seaman from the Merchant Navy
Karel Oosthuizen — Nephew of Tinus
Kei — A Majuba farm boy and son of Elijah
Lord Edward Holland — Jeremiah Shank's mentor

Martinus Jacobus McDonald Oosthuizen (Tinus) — Friend and business partner of Sebastian

Mathilda Brigandshaw — Sebastian's mother

Nathanial Brigandshaw — Sebastian's third eldest brother

Piers Oosthuizen — Nephew of Tinus

Sarie Mostert — A poor girl from the slums of Pretoria

Sebastian Brigandshaw — Central character of *Echoes from the Past*

Sir Henry Manderville — Emily's father

Tatenda — A native boy who loses his family and home after a massacre by the Matabele

The Captain, Archibald Brigandshaw — Sebastian's father

Zwide — King Lobengula's Induna

GLOSSARY

~

Baas — A supervisor or employer, especially a white man in charge of coloured or black people

Bittereinder — A faction of Boer guerrilla fighters resisting the forces of the British Empire in the later stages of the Second Boer War

Burgher — An Afrikaans citizen of the Boer Republic

Charles Rudd — A business associate of Cecil John Rhodes

Clive — Clive of India - A British officer who established the military and political supremacy of the East India Company in Bengal

Consols — A name given to certain British government bonds (gilts) first used in 1751 (originally short for consolidated annuities)

Dorp — Afrikaans for a small village or town

Induna — Tribal leader as well as a group of elite soldiers

Kerel — Afrikaans for a boy

Kloof — Afrikaans for a deep glen or ravine

Klop — Give someone a smack

Kopje — Afrikaans for a small hill in a generally flat area

LRAM — Professional Diploma for Licentiate of the Royal Academy of Music

Major Frank Johnson — Headed a pioneer expedition into Mashonaland and established Fort Salisbury near the Makabusi River

Mampoer — A South African moonshine made from fruit (mostly peaches or marulas) containing a high level of alcohol and drunk neat

Oom — Afrikaans word used in a respectful and affectionate form of address to an older man

Ouma — Afrikaans word used in a respectful or affectionate form of address for a grandmother or elderly woman

Rinderpest — An infectious viral disease of cattle and domestic buffalo

Rondavel — A westernised version of the African-style hut

Sub judice — Latin for "under judgement" meaning that a particular case or matter is under trial or being considered by a judge or court

Taal — The language of the Boers which would become known as Afrikaans

Tatenda — Shona for thank you

Topi — A pith helmet of Indian origin

Veld — Afrikaans word for open, uncultivated country or grassland in southern Africa

Vlei — Afrikaans word for low-lying, marshy ground, covered with water during the rainy season

Wallah — A native or inhabitant of Indian origin